SO-BDP-475

As Planned

AS PLANNED

Mead Lafond

Cabarrus County Public Library
www.cabarruscounty.us/library

Copyright © 2015, by Mead Lafond

All rights reserved. No part of this publication may be reproduced, distributed, or transmitted in any form or by any means, including photocopying, recording, or other electronic or mechanical methods, without the prior written permission of the author, except in the case of brief quotations embodied in critical reviews and certain other noncommercial uses permitted by copyright law. For permission requests, or to inquire about special discounts for quantity sales, signings, or other engagements, write to the author at the address below.

Mead Lafond
P.O. Box 1551
Harrisburg, NC 28075
Email: contact@mead-lafond.com

This is a work of fiction. All names, places, and situations are the work of the author's imagination and used fictitiously, and any similarities of events or resemblances of persons are unintentional and coincidental.

ISBN 978-1-943214-00-6
First printing, August, 2015

Printed in the U.S.A. by Gorham Printing, 3718 Mahoney Drive, Centralia, WA 98531.

PART ONE
FIGHT NIGHT

1

"I need more than this."

It could have been a metaphor in the making for the story of her life, the desire for something better than her existence as a food servant enduring the suggestive comments, groping hands, and invasive eyes. *I need more than this.* The words lingered and rang in her head, irritating her even more considering everything else that was on her mind that night. But mainly it was because Madison Davis was once again, in her eyes, shortchanged on a Cobb salad.

Donny Russ knew what was coming when she saw and inspected it with that disapproving look on her face. She pushed the salad back to him and he exchanged looks with his trademark contraction to the left side of his face, giving silent disapproval of the task of inserting more work into an already busy night. But recollections of his worst nights at work were the result of a few of these servers not getting their way, Madison being a repeat instigator. He grabbed the plate and fulfilled her wishes, too busy and a little too hesitant that night to protest.

At five feet nine inches tall, Madison currently stood as the tallest server at Lovelee's restaurant of Charlotte, North Carolina, ever since Ashley Starnes was fired two weeks ago. Ashley was a full inch taller than everybody else, and Madison was sorry to see Ashley go. *Ashley was fun. She was a firecracker and had a mouth on her. Too bad that's what got her fired... I could have used her tonight.*

As a member of the original crew of individuals who marched their beats with independent styles and personalities, Madison viewed the current troupe of gyrating breasts substituting for facility with abating disillusionment. *So many of these girls trying to be someone else and they all end up looking and acting the same. Try to stand out a little.* Madison made an effort to do just that, taking the tanning of her pasty white skin and highlighting of her naturally dirty blonde hair in moderation, obtaining just a hint of gold in both while keeping a safe distance from the staff's vanity baseline. And she was also capable of carrying her weight in a meaningful conversation if her table's occupants were worth the time and effort, which was a plus in acquiring the place's regulars who were not incredibly repellant.

It was once again MMA Saturday Fight Night, one of Madison's most hectic and dreadful days to work, along with a great many of the others'; it was a night complete with an increase of work exertion, double the conflicts with the kitchen, more 'wrong orders' one server could possibly imagine, even though it is certain the server got them right – the most likely culprit being a customer who was so wasted they forgot what they ordered twenty minutes prior - and a certain higher probability of conversations converted to near-legal molestations. The adventure of Saturday Fight Night is the sad guarantee of more of the headache and less of the tip money at the end of the night.

And she had two women to thank for all this fun: Robin Love and Jessie Lee. And a guy named Burton Black.

Robin Love and Jessie Lee were two college girls, Robin a business major and Jessie a marketing major at the University of Florida in 2003, and friends to a handful of female friends who worked at various vixen-themed restaurants in the area, from the better-known franchises to the copycat variants. Robin and Jessie heard the stories of harassment and bullying, and occasionally witnessed the misery on the nights they took a break from studying and paid visits to their friends.

The girls spent those years in college and those days off soaking up the environment of their girlfriends' jobs developing the idea for their own restaurant chain that would sell provocativeness to their male customers as a theme, but also provide a more pleasant work environment to the servers. It started as projects for their college courses, first for Jessie for a marketing project, and then they worked together when Robin had a major project due for her business final. Upon their graduation in 2004 and the coaxing of funds from a loan officer willing to sign off on a couple of girls with diplomas and big ideas, they brought their projects to life and opened their first Lovelee's restaurant in Orlando, Florida. By the time the first annual assessment was compiled they knew they were on to something successful, and the chain began to emerge in Florida: the next restaurant in Tampa, followed by Gainesville, Miami, Jacksonville, and Tallahassee. They became big enough for a corporate office, and chose Lakeland, between Orlando and Tampa.

The girls made their rounds and met the guys coming in, and discovered that Lovelee's was getting more frequent visitors from all over the southeast, with some wondering about franchise opportunities in their hometowns. Robin and Jessie crunched the numbers and realized the ground was still shaky to stretch out to other states on their own, so the girls opted for starting the franchise program and the locations grew outside of Florida: Charleston and Columbia in South Carolina; Atlanta and Athens in Georgia; Knoxville, Tennessee; New Orleans and Baton Rouge in Louisiana; Raleigh and Charlotte in North Carolina.

Burton Black's Charlotte franchise was one of the latest to open, about five years ago, and Madison Davis was a member of the opening crew. Lovelee's operated with flexibility in regards to the theme each location adopted reflective of the city's and surrounding area's character. While maintaining the structure of the uniform being a red spandex short shorts over a miniskirt and performance top that wrapped so tightly around the chest the girls felt as exposed as they did claustrophobic and on the verge of a panic attack, the uniform would on occasion differ in a theme specific to the locale, and the décor of the restaurant was fair game to, in Corporate theory, a degree of taste.

However, when the first lineup of managers finished mutating the adopted theme of the Charlotte Lovelee's, the thematic concept turned into a schizophrenic outburst of NASCAR, country music, motorcycles, local sports teams of varying flavors, and an occasional ring girl masquerade for the agonizing feature of the MMA Fight Nights, where their uniform issue for the event was black and white striped, shrunken referee versions of the original, the same mandatory uniforms for football games in the fall. For the next few years each new wave of managers manipulated their freedom of shifting the theme slightly to make the atmosphere an even more incoherent mess with the addition of chrome 1950's style diner panel and trim for some reason. And predictably the standard uniform began to lose fabric past the point of good taste to the ones who had to wear it until anonymous complaints by some of the girls to Corporate motivated Robin and Jessie to have a meeting with Burton and retighten the reins of taste, with a slightly looser top and a change in the shorts, not completely back to normal but close enough for compromise, back to something which resembled short shorts under a miniskirt. When Corporate became distracted with other locations and affairs, the older, worn-out uniforms were replaced with the lineup of new server issues, which looked to be designed with a loss of fabric along the production process.

It did not take too long before Ms. Love's and Lee's vision of a safe and creative work atmosphere to became just one of a growing number of brestaurants around the country manned by scantily clad women playing host to horny men with appetites for wings, alcohol, and scantily clad women who make passes as the women take it. Only a few of the original servers and kitchen staff remained there as Madison saw quite a bit of a server turnover rate as much as the other meat market eateries in the area. She could see how that could be possible even though, despite the vision of a more pleasant work environment, Lovelee's expeditiously fell into line with the other venues where the girls were ripe for the inspection and prodding. Still, most of the shifts at this place were pretty bearable in Madison's opinion. She did see her fair share of the packs of the local douche bags, as expected in a place such as this. There were the other usual customers: the regulars, the frequent creepers, the friends of servers who came in to take up space and help retain their friend's sanity on hectic nights.

And then there were nights such as this, the cologne-laced testosterone induced grunt fest that invaded their territory when the latest MMA fight was playing on pay-per-view.

The heat from the grill and fryers hit the servers' faces from their side of the food line, matching the heat from the pressure cookers of their feigned smiles they could afford to drop for the few moments they took to prepare to run their food, the heat being almost as intense as the anxiety and frustration of enduring the next few hours and the awaiting deliverance of greeting the end of the shift, hoping the money that remained in their grip when they walked out the door got them as close as possible to paying the rest of the bills that lurked on the kitchen table every night they got home from work.

It was all standard protocol for Madison, who saw her irritating wait for the corrected Cobb salad come to a close. It wasn't even for one of her tables; she was running the food for another server either too busy or derelict in her duties. She inspected the salad and figured it was as good as it was going to get that night and could not wait any longer. Besides, Donny quickly retreated to the fryers and would just pretend to not hear her. She dropped off the salad and did her best Donny Russ imitation while one of the customers at the table called out for her to refill their iced teas.

The route Madison took to drop off the Cobb salad strayed from the path of her intended duties in her own section, and as she found herself directly in the trenches of the war between the scents of hot sauce and cheap, rancid cologne, she quickly regretted her actions and made a hasty retreat to take care of her own people. Her station that night spanned the row of big circular tables that ran parallel with the bar, and the small two-top table adjacent to the row. The typical cast of characters was present in her jurisdiction.

Michael Seitz sat at the two-top. He was a quiet recluse, dark hair and dark eyes, the kind of nerves that caused all his movements to be slightly twitchy. He always sat in Madison's section, even if he had to wait for an open table. He was acting normal that night, keeping to himself except for the moments at the other servers' passing by his table to sneak in a quick glance somewhere below breast level. Michael was a relatively safe guy but predictably a nuisance when he whipped up the courage to hint at how fun a date would be. Madison was grateful that at least he tipped well, so she made certain to always let him down gently.

Michael was even quieter than his usual quiescent self as the round top next to him was occupied by the more normal regulars who did not make the servers completely uneasy. Steven Jenkins, a mechanic with Reid Motorsports, Jimmy Goforth, a dockworker at Coleman Freight Consolidated, and Waylon Barbee, an unemployed jack of all trades – Madison still had not known what he actually did for work no matter what amount of investigating she did - made plans to descend on the madness individually and merged into one of Madison's tables with room for a couple more guys should they happen to show up. These guys frequented the establishment so often Madison wondered if there was some possible way they could muster an hourly wage from the place.

"Is this going to be everybody for tonight? Where are your partners in annoyance?" she jested.

Steven broke away from his Blue Moon to be the spokesperson. "Darrell's working at the prison tonight and Kyle got a call from some lady in his neighborhood for some electrical work, the old lady who still has the wires from the silent movie days in her house. So you're stuck with us tonight."

"Are you ready for a cold beer for your hands there, Waylon?" she asked Waylon and his warming quarter-full glass of beer.

He hugged the glass closer. "Not yet, baby. Still working here."

"What is it you do again? When you're not squatting in here?" she joked as she tugged at his backwash in a glass.

"I haven't figured it out yet. I aspire to be an ambidextrous master debater. Do they teach that at the community college?"

Waylon knew how to draw the guffaws from her table of favorites. She rolled her eyes as she moved away from the table. "Finish your medicine."

The other two tables were occupied by different companies of the same types of apes, shaved and otherwise, obnoxious warriors battling in their own competition independent of the main event of the night: the war for alpha male domination of Charlotte, however diluted and obnoxious they might have sounded to the sober members of society, half of whom were attempting to convince Madison they were the perfect man to take back to her place that night. The only distinct difference was the dialect; while one group shouted in debate on the best octagon cage fighter, the other group shouted in similar fashion on who they believed would take home the Sprint Cup in NASCAR. The blend of perversion and machismo composed a hectic and potentially nauseating concoction of testosterone, but Madison travelled the congested circuit separating the tables like a veteran, shuffling around other frantic servers who were not as seasoned for the environment.

A few of the girls who were allegedly and technically working that night only by the fact that their names were on the work schedule, were virgins to the pain in the ass that was MMA Fight Night. But at least Megan DeWitt was getting her food orders to her tables. She had only been working there for a week and just turned eighteen but was doing much better than a couple of others who had been at Lovelee's for at least a couple of months; Tina's plates collected in the server window while she hid outside behind the dumpster for a prolonged smoke break and Molly had not been seen for the past hour, leaving the assumption in the minds of the managers that she went home and no longer worked there, and took the liberty of divvying up her section's tables to the other servers who wanted to make the extra money. Tina's patent absence left those willing to help out, or just looking to eventually get to their food waiting in the rear, to run her food out before the complaints bounced them back to the kitchen.

Madison took three plates destined to a table in Tina's section in the back of the dining area, through the diner chrome, around the Harley-Davidson previously owned by Alan Jackson and currently displayed at the Charlotte Lovelee's restaurant to gather dust. The table was just past the display of that god awful suit of some old-time country singer whose name she could never remember, some red and blue sparkly sequined suit in a classic rancher style from the forties or fifties. It made Madison feel she was staring at an outfit belonging to a mythical character from some alternate Midwest prairieland that criss-crossed the line between Will Rogers and Liberace. It also reminded her of the equally horrid sequined cowgirl bikini tops and micro-mini skirts attempted one year for the evening shift the night of the ACM country music awards, whose ensembles were unfortunately completed with gun belts. The prop costume must have been the misguided inspiration.

She arrived at the table right after she passed the nightmare of a suit. *Bucky Daniels...that's it.* She delivered the food with a smile to the three drunken stooges.

"Damn, now this is some good service. I bet you get a good workout here running all this food around. We need another pitcher and round of Jaeger shots, honey," said Stooge Left to Madison's pelvic region when his face contorted into a look of disgust. "Holy shit. What the hell is that?" Everyone shared a similar sour face, including Madison, with the exception of the stooge in the middle, who shouted a hearty laugh from his flushed face. "Jesus, Frank. Fire a warning shot or take it to the bathroom!"

Missing the rest of the conversation, Madison turned and smartly ignored the request for another beer pitcher and Jaeger shots. *Tina's on her own. She can deal with the gas attack. I have my own work to take care of.*

She stopped at the table of NASCAR debate shouters at the near end of her section where her work continued. "How are you guys doing on that Miller Light pitcher?" she asked to a table of five guys, three of which were shouting at each others' heads without waiting in turn, and the other two of which were gazing at her cleavage. She focused on one of the breast gazers, hoping to get a quicker response. "You want me to bring another pitcher to the table, hon?"

He finished the gulp of beer in his mouth and creeped his eyes down to her hips and started to squeeze the two of them together in a hip-to-gut connection. "Sure thing, sweetie. Put this next one on my tab."

She pivoted as smoothly as possible counter-clockwise to the other side of him to avoid getting further molested, topped off his glass with the remainder of the pitcher's contents, and gave her best showgirl smile as she glided away from the table still feeling a light stench on her hip. "Tell your boys I'll be right back."

His face was the first thing she saw when she turned to walk to the bar. Her eyes locked for a brief moment into the eyes of the new addition to the round top of her regulars, who was on his way back to the table with a shot of whiskey in his hand. After a pause which transpired much quicker in the world than in her head, Madison shook off her anxiety and reclaimed her showgirl casing, and continued to the destination of the server end of the bar to get her customers' drink orders, struggling to brush off the cold front to her body brought on by Ronnie Stover's entrance.

2

Ronnie Stover started his night with two Jim Beam shots at the bar before taking a third to her round top of regulars while Madison dealt with the apes. Anyone who knew Ronnie well enough knew this was his standard onset for the evening. Anyone who knew Ronnie well was a rarity in itself. He returned his eyes to his now empty shot glass. If not for the slight traces of silver making a halfhearted attempt to hide in his otherwise dark brown head of hair, the marks of experience as a rolling stone in the middle of a lifelong joy ride in the form of a few proud creases on his face, he would probably have looked on point with his twenty-seven years of age. The striking twin blazes of blue in his eyes are what made the difference, completing the ensemble of handsomeness, the kind of looks that could make most women risk a broken heart. He was a loner of medium build, definitely not the biggest guy in the place that night, but could hold his own in a fight if he absolutely had to. He had been gone for two years and was new in town to practically everyone in the dining area, except to the hardcore fixtures. It was the perfect night to be on the reflective side, with the regulars so drunk and happy they took little notice as they uttered their half-witty remarks at his head, not demanding a concurrence.

The bar was just as hectic as the floor, so the servers had to wait a few minutes for their drinks, and that was just fine with Madison; the steely alcove provided a makeshift sanctuary for her to stand idle and regroup by the bar area. Ronnie moved his gaze back to Madison momentarily as she finished her journey to the bar, raising his empty shot glass, either as a toast or a request for yet another. Madison quickly moved her eyes away to Karla.

Karla Nuñez was working the bar that night and doing a good job at communicating with the natives, as she always does, which was why she got scheduled every MMA Fight Night. Karla was a short, curvy brunette belle, and a couple of years younger than the mean average of the bartending staff. She was terrific at what she did, so she got the coveted bar position and the envy and jealousy of most of the other servers along with it, but she took the job nonetheless with no worries. Her genetic mosaic included being half Hispanic on her mother's side, the other half the product of a horny, irresponsible roughneck named Tyler down in Austin, Texas, Karla's hometown before being transported to Cannon as a young girl. She and her mother have lived in the same house since, with an addition, Karla's son Tyler; Karla named her child after the father as motivation to raise him properly, to bring up a boy to become a caring, respectful man toward women, to leave this world a Tyler to offset the piece of crap they left down in Texas. Her venting of her frustration through her son's name was further fueled as a result of falling victim to the same wayward type of seed-carrying man as her mother. As she talked up close and yelled across the bar to the customers and workers, one could see in her and hear in her voice the nurturing mother and the bartender an unruly bar patron need not mess with whether or not the manager on duty lacked the guts; she was just as sweet and personable to the cordial paying customers as she was feisty and bitter on occasions where she did not intend to take someone's harassment and a true bête noire in rare instances. Madison had known Karla longer than any of the other girls and still held her in a higher admiration than she did for any of the other girls with which she worked. She was a proud single mother left to care for her son Tyler after his father, unknown to the rest of the girls, decided against the responsibility after providing his services as the sperm donor, but she made no excuses regarding the situation. In fact, Madison recalled Karla having no regrets when telling the story:

I refuse to think of it as paying a price for getting too drunk and letting my guard down. Tyler has been worth all the effort. And if his dad stays the hell out of his life, that would be a nice dividend, too. He'd better not come back. I told him I was keeping my child, and as long as he stayed out of our lives he didn't have to worry about me or the courts going after him for child support, and that's fine with me.

Karla found her window to break away from the bar and took the pitcher from Madison. "Sometimes I feel like I'm getting a little too old for this crap."

You're younger than me," Madison replied. "Just focus on the alcohol and you won't smell the anymore I a couple years, maybe." Karla was merely a year younger and had been there just as long as Madison, but the quip sounded good at the time.

"My mama's watching Tyler tonight," Karla continued. "I'm ready to get this night over with. How are you doing, girl?"

Madison's suffering through her testosterone-drenched version of hell could be translated less in words than an exhale and a grunt, and that familiar look in her eyes.. "I'm just trying to stay busy enough to keep from thinking. He's here now." Madison's look turned to one of trepidation as she motioned to him. Karla's look turned to one of sardonicism as she already knew.

"I know. I served that asshole three shots already."

"I'm just trying to stay busy enough to keep from thinking." Madison smirked and referenced her empty beer pitcher. "These assholes want more Miller Light in this pitcher, Karla. I'll be back in a sec." Madison readied herself for the walk to the table full of regulars where Ronnie was sitting.

Jimmy Goforth was complaining about work as usual when she arrived. "So Rob quit because he got tired of their shit. This was after two years of bitchin' and cryin' and threatenin' to quit. Well, now we got this new guy Ryan. He's a dumb bastard. Actually, he would have to upgrade to 'dumb bastard,' so there's hope for the future for the rest of us." He broke from his sermon when he noticed Madison's presence and gave her hand a friendly squeeze. "Hey, darlin'."

She let out a small sigh of frustration with a smile struggling to cling to her face. "I'm sorry. I'm slammed tonight. They're running me ragged! I hate these fight nights." She said the last part like she was letting them in on the worst kept secret in the world.

Waylon laughed like always at The Server's Plight. "I know what you mean. I don't like these fight nights, either. I just like the drinking. I can't get into this stuff. It looks like they're all trying to make love to each other. The last fight that was on, I swear one of the guys stuck his thumb in the other guy's ass. I swear to God! Hey, you knew it was going to be like this tonight, girlie."

She made a face, weary but with a smile still attached, as the table roared with laughter. "That's sick, Waylon. Behave yourself." She pointed in the direction of the warming, partially full glass of beer Waylon was nursing for some time. "You need another beer?"

He hugged his glass closer. "I'm good for now," he said with his words now weighted with a playful rebuke.

Madison needed more sales and it looked like Waylon had not put his lips to the glass once since her last trip to the table, so she applied the peer pressure. "Well, stop nursing it. It's going to get warm on you, if it's not room temperature already. Less sick jokes and more drinking, sir."

She moved her salesmanship to the right to Steven Jenkins, who spoke up and made the stop to the table worthwhile. "I'll take another one when you get a chance, honey. I'll take a Newcastle this time around, and get my buddy Waylon another Miller Light on my tab." Waylon smiled and waved a 'thank you' gesture, and Steven continued. "Ronnie, you want another shot? It's on me for a limited time, so you'd better act now. Ronnie was telling us about his time in Florida. He hasn't been around this area in years."

"That's right," Ronnie proclaimed in a slightly fuddled manner to his empty shot glass. "Florida is nice, buddy. You guys should check it out. You'll wonder why you didn't think of it earlier. Makes me wonder what I'm doing back here, really. Don't expect me to be here for much longer."

"I remember him," she said in Steven's direction while facing Ronnie, the irked tone in her voice under the surface but showing a bit of evidence. His eyes raised a few inches higher than the shot glass but had still not made contact with hers. The tension cloud became overcast between them. Even the others in their inebriated blitheness could see it and Jimmy spoke up.

"Ronnie, you might have to sit at the bar tonight. Madison has this pit bull look in her eyes. With you, anyway," he said half jokingly, half reflective of his work bearing.

"That's a worse spot for him. Trust me on this one, Jimmy." Her response provided a level of ease to the group. "You need another one of those Beams, Ronnie? Or do you need to slow down for a little while?"

Waylon interceded. "She may be right, Ronnie. You already had three of those and you've only been here three minutes. You might want to hold off for a little while, but don't let me fill in for your conscience tonight." The table had a good laugh, which helped to dissolve some of the tension that had brewed between Madison and Ronnie. He looked up at her and extended a partial smile. "Go ahead and bring me another one, sweetie. It won't go bad on me if it sits for a while. I'll hold onto it until I'm ready."

Jimmy Goforth downed the rest of his beer during the conversation. "Hey, Madison..."

She answered as he held up his empty glass. "Another New Moon?"

He smiled and handed her the glass. "Am I that predictable? I need to change things up."

"Don't you dare! I like predictable," she said with a wink as she left. It was as true with her work life as it was with her personal life: she liked predictability. She enjoyed a shift she would set her watch to. *Jimmy Goforth, New Moon. Michael Seitz, chicken sandwich and a water with lemon. Waylon Barbee, the cheapest beer on tap unless someone else is paying for it. Then he'll have whatever he can get.* What she did not like were the tables such as the others in her section, those who wouldn't pay attention to her when she asked a question, those who studied and worked to memorize the menu, like they were about to make one of the biggest decisions in their life. Not to mention those who proclaimed their accomplishments or complained about their sore muscles from CrossFit sessions and MMA classes, especially on professional MMA fight nights.

There were too many servers waiting at the bar, either for their drink orders or simply because it was cooler than waiting at the server's area by the kitchen, so Madison opted instead to run an order of cheese sticks to one of Randi's tables and get to her drinks afterward.

Randi McIntosh was a wiry nineteen year old mess, a jittery and bubbly girl on her best days, and a tense, anxious tangle of emotions springing eternal at her worst, fair skinned sporadically tinted pink and sandy red hair, with aspirations to be an actress and model because every restaurant seemed to need at least one of these naïve but ambitious dreamers with eyes focused on Hollywood. So far, the extent of her exposure has come from photo shoots from the usual clan of regulars who have equipped themselves with a medium caliber camera and a photo editing software suite. The exposure from these big breaks has not extended much further than various social networking websites.

Madison neared one of her tables as Randi took center stage with her best attempt to entertain the guys who were squatted there when all they were really interested in was getting drunk, watching the fight, and getting a view of the contour of her breasts underneath her shirt when given the chance. Madison entertained herself as she approached the table by predicting the conversation before she got there: Randi would be telling the guys about bills and money troubles in an attempt to play to their sympathies. She arrived at the table behind Randi.

"...and the guy in the garage already changed the alternator out while I went to eat lunch. He says it's going out, and I don't want to get stuck on the side of the road. So it cost me another three hundred bucks, and I thought 'Whatever,' but I don't know how I'm going to make rent."

Her alternator didn't get replaced. Her car wasn't even in the shop. Madison taught her well: get the guys drunk, be the damsel in distress, and let the guys be knights in tin foil until they pay the tab with a nice tip.

Madison should have known better than to come up from behind, but she was in a hurry. "Here's your food..."

The entrance scared the hell out of Randi. "Oh my god, Madison, you scared the crap out of me. Here are your cheese sticks, guys. Thank you so much. I got a little carried away telling the guys about my car."

Madison handed off the cheese sticks and assessed Randi's mental state on such a hectic night, where she was on her spectrum of emotional stability. Madison's estimation put Randi's state close to the middle. *Could be worse.* "No problem, superstar. Just remember if you have food coming up. I'll be at the bar if you need me. Keep your head in the game."

After a moment for the kick-starting of the noggin and darting her eyes from Madison to the food station to Madison, Randi's eyes blinked into action and she gave Madison an acknowledgement. "Gotcha."

Madison got her drinks from the bar and returned to Ronnie's table to drop them off. "You are an angel. Come over here with my prescription, angel," Steven said in thanking her as she dropped off the beers in front of him and Kyle.

The wave of friction between her and Ronnie temporarily dissipated while Michael made a quick exit in front of Madison. "Bye, Madison. See you next time." He stopped momentarily in front of her on his way to the side exit door to give her a quick hug before he resumed his hasty exit.

She flashed her customer service smile held together with a tightened jaw. "Have a good night, honey."

Steven mumbled under his beer glass. "Bye, Michael. Stalk you later."

The others chuckled in amusement and Madison rolled her eyes, negotiated the emotional bargaining point in the circumcenter of shaking off the remnants of Michael's hug, joining in the other guys' amusement, and hoping Michael did not hear them because she didn't want to lose out on a good stream of tip money. "Knock it off, smartass." The tension picked up where it left off as she placed the shot of Beam in front of Ronnie. "Whenever you're ready." Their eyes met as she walked away.

The next stop was by the table of MMA fight ultrafans in possession of an empty beer pitcher and a protest from one of the apes occupying the table. "About time we get another pitcher here. We're dying of thirst," he scoffed in a way which caused Madison to believe he was making an attempt at humor. Madison recalled his first name beginning with a T, and his last name almost rhyming with douche, although the last name comparison was most likely imagined. In about forty-five minutes, it would not matter anyway.

Madison brushed it off with one of her motivational mantras to get her through instances such as this. *Let it go because the guy is an asshole and he doesn't matter in the big picture*, she dictated to her character in stenographic fashion while making the effort to not let it show on her face, masking it with plastic sympathy. "I'm sorry, guys. I'll be right back with a new one." She waved the pitcher around playfully. "Who wants to pick this one up?" she asked because everyone at the table was on separate checks.

Frank, the lightweight drinker and featherweight Casanova, who had told her at least three times how much she reminded him of Brooklyn Decker, even though she could not see a direct resemblance and chalked it up to his liquored up lenses, spoke up as he pulled her closer to him. "I'll pick that one up. Let me pick you up tonight, too. You know that girl in the swimsuit issues, Brooklyn Decker? You remind me so much of her, in the body."

Madison smiled and shifted away toward the bar rolling her eyes. "I've heard that a few times. I'll be back." She heard the other guys have a good laugh at Frank's expense on her way back to the bar.

Sometimes this can be good money, but I really need to use my degree and get out of this place ... one of these days. Just keep smiling and keep interviewing.

Tanya Beaver made room for Madison at the bar area so they could both wait for Karla to finish taking care of her own customers. Tanya's glum expression told her chapter of the same story they all were riding out that night. "I can't stand these nights. When is the next MMA fight? I think I'm going to be sick that day."

The tune was so familiar Madison could hum it every time she stood next to a fellow server on these nights, especially Tanya, one of the shortest, curviest girls who worked at Lovelee's. Madison smiled at the concentrated vexation emanating from such a small entity. "Take deep breaths and get through a couple more hours, Tanya. You could always pull a disappearing act like the new girl..."

Madison and Tanya answered in unison; Madison answered "Tina," while Tanya answered "Molly," and they both laughed. "Yeah, both of them, actually," Madison declared, shaking her head. "I think Molly decided to go home."

"One of these creepers probably abducted her," Tanya sneered.

The comment made Madison think of her friend Leanna, who had to experience that horror personally. Her body was never discovered, but the bastard who did it was; Madison mourned the certainty she would never be able to give the gift of sharing her experience. She shook off the flash of sadness by motioning her head toward the plates yet to be delivered, knowing a couple of them had to be destined for Tina's section.

"You could always help Tina get her food out."

"Fuck her. She can show her face and run her own food." Tanya's channeled inner bitch, in full force that night, made her periodic round. Just as well, Tina would not want Tanya to have to do her work for her; Tanya had been known to run other servers' plates for them if she was pushed into it by the floor manager, but would switch side items around before she left so the server would have to rectify problems as soon as they reappeared at the table.

Tanya motioned to the front corner of the dining area, to a thin, leathery-faced man in his mid-fifties, who was scanning her body from his seat about fifty feet away. "I've got that creepy bastard again. Every night he comes in, he looks the place over while he pretends to text someone on the phone, scanning the place for my section."

"He doesn't fondle you too much, does he? You should make him your sugar daddy," Madison said, not passing up the temptation to rile up Tanya.

Tanya displayed her disdain to Madison in the riled-up reaction. "You're one sick bitch."

"I've seen worse pairings," Madison replied. Her subsequent giggle was infectious; Tanya needed the humor at that point in her work shift.

"He's a total fucking perv," she moaned more to herself than to Madison.

"It's cheaper than a titty bar, Tanya. And they get to put their hands on you without getting their ass kicked by a bouncer."

"And I could make a lot more money. Maybe I should get a job there."

This gave both of them smiles and a temporary shield to pass the time. Madison briefly thought of herself engaged in the world of exotic dancing and gave herself the chills with the notion of having to check even more of her dignity at the door than she had to at this place some nights. *Maybe I should just do that and show my tits off while I look for the marketing gig. It would be more money and less hot sauce. Oh god, don't take yourself seriously on that one. You're just babbling.*

Tanya shook her head and took her drinks. "Thanks for the wisdom or the distraction, whichever one it was. Here we go again," she said as she trudged toward her station.

Karla entered the same way Tanya left. "When does this damn fight get over with? I feel like I've been knocked out, or tapped out, or whatever the hell happens to these guys who lose."

Madison gave Karla's terminology dilemma a quick thought. "I believe the technical term would be 'Take a smoke break by the dumpster for the next three hours.' Where has Eve been at? I haven't seen her in a while." Madison asked during the filled beer pitcher handoff, at that moment noticing that Tina had finally shown her presence, but appeared to not have noticed the derision referencing her work ethic, or just pretending not to notice it to avoid conflict.

Karla answered without scanning the dining area, showing her confidence in her instinct. "She's probably in the back, like always. You know how she is."

The wall that partitioned the kitchen and food prep areas from the bar and dining area provided the server area at the end of the bar with a small restricted view of the back leading to the dishwasher's station through the scope of a square cut in the wall. Madison glanced through the hole from where she was standing at and noticed a fragment of the emerald green tinted ring girl uniform bottom the servers were wearing that night on top of the giant steel sink at the hand washing station. She could see the rest of the landscape despite the view-blocking obstruction, but got a better look anyway just to prove herself right. She stood at a better angle closer to the opening and saw Eve Kennedy, a short, curvaceous brunette with a tanned shade of skin color that mingled between olive and cocoa, who was supposed to be taking care of the customers' orders, sitting to have a chat with Philip Martinez, one of the cooks who was supposed to be taking care of the customers' orders.

No wonder everybody's pissed off out there...besides being assholes by nature. How is she supposed to know what's going on when she's hanging out back there...

"Maybe you can have better luck getting Philip to do some work around here," Donny futilely suggested to her as he dumped a basketful of chicken wings onto two plates.

Madison showed him the pitcher. "I've got enough to do tonight. I'm sure you'll think of something."

"You could get the little cokehead away from him. That would help me out." Donny made the mistake of trying to dump them while observing the reason he was having to pull extra weight in the kitchen and partially missed the plate. "Son of a bitch. Hey, Philip, we're slammed!" He got no response. "I could grow some tits. Maybe he would pay more attention to me then."

While Madison dropped off the pitcher of beer and returned to the bar using the best route possible to avoid any requests and comments from the people in her section and succeeded, Donny's grievances pushed against Madison's memory, and before she knew it she was thinking back to this morning, to her job interview at L.D. Marketing, while she waited.

Come on, what's taking so long? If it was up to me, I would just wait here until we closed for the night. All of my tables could just walk away and the managers can pick up the walk-outs.

She finally finished her degree in marketing in the past spring and was now making her best effort to break free from this place, but the hiring prospects in the current economy were proving difficult for her, according to her expectations at least. Or maybe she was just being impatient because it was something she wanted. She wanted everything the world had to toss to her so long as she did not have to leave the frontier of the greater Charlotte area to catch it.

She fought the traffic into downtown Charlotte that morning, successfully skimmed all available magazines in the waiting room while she waited nearly an hour for her interview, and spent the next twenty minutes attempting to convince the managers how valuable of an asset she would be to their company while the three perverts in charge of hiring spent the entire time trying their best to be interested while catching glimpses of her cleavage and the linings of her torso, probably imagining what she looked like naked. She finished her sales pitch like a champion while cutting off their penises in her imagination.

She was not going to hold her breath for a second interview, although she might get one in order for the supervisors to get another look. *They might even bring the vice-president in for the next one*, Madison thought. She reserved the next span of moments for debate. *Should I give them more of a show to let them know what they are going to miss out on? How about I show up for the next interview with my blouse buttoned all the way to her neck for the next interview just to screw with them? Or I could just tell them to fuck off over the phone and save myself the gas.*

The table at the far end of her section was on her mind as she zoned out elsewhere. When she saw movement she brought her focus back to the present with the aid of a chill that spanned from her lower spine to her temples that stunned her legs and caused a suffocating swelling in her throat. Ronnie Stover was on his feet, albeit not with the stance of surety that comes with sobriety, but strong enough to make the journey toward her. Her breathing began to quicken, and a rush of pink swarmed her face. She could imagine a thin layer of perspiration lining her body as she exchanged a look with Karla at the beer taps. Karla saw the look on Madison's face and remained close by. Ronnie stopped by her side and stood facing her on firmer ground than she anticipated considering his labored trek toward her impeded by an alcoholic haze. *He only had four shots. He must've been drinking before he got here.* He took a good look at her from upper half to lower half and back up again to her eyes, which diverted during the standoff and fixated on the thin chain around his neck with the attached yin yang pendant. "Hey, Madison, there's something I need, but it's not on the menu. Why don't you just clock out and come on home with me?"

"Leave me alone, Ronnie. I'm busy. Sit back down and behave."

"We're not busy yet."

"And you're drunk. You go home by yourself and sober up." A pause for a slow, controlled deep breath helped Madison calm herself down. When she felt she was composed enough to speak clearly, she said "Why don't you take a walk, Ronnie? After you pay your tab, of course."

In the moments following her comment she felt relief from the tension, the complaints, the gaudy sequined country music memorabilia from yesteryear, and all the other miscellaneous bullshit conjoined in various ways somehow with Lovelee's. But her axons and dendrites could not long be fooled; the two were in standoff, and she soon felt the unsettled warning this state of serenity could not and would not last that night in the server area. Some of her customers in the nearer tables in her section noticed and she and Ronnie had their attention. They were joined by some others at surrounding tables and Madison felt the electrodes of anxiety prickle her face which encompassed her concentration until it was broken by the intersecting sensation of the sting brought on by Ronnie's smack on her ass.

"Cunt."

The inertia of suspense and awestruck rippled from the center of Ronnie Stover's derogatory comment out to the edges of the captivated audience at Lovelee's, which had spread to nearly the entire capacity of the restaurant, and the televised corporate product-sponsored event hyped across the country by promoters and publicly viewed and enjoyed by executives and celebrities was forgotten.

Madison broke from her locked gaze with Ronnie to dart her eyes over her audience. Her regulars at the far table took notice and were standing from their seats. In the immediate area, she saw was one of the guys in her section who had been groping her in intervals all night, and he had started strutting toward Ronnie like he was ready to step in and be her dickhead in shining armor.

Madison snapped back into the moment and drew back her right hand, and landed it in a strike to Ronnie in the side of his neck with an intensity and accuracy which surprised even herself. The area of the neck at which she connected with Ronnie was the brachial plexus origin and, if struck right, was enough to stun a man and drop him momentarily to the ground, which is where Ronnie ended up in a thud.

The adrenaline produced by Madison's actions shuttered the tension from the gawking crowd's silence who remained speechless long enough for Madison to break it.

"You asshole!"

All the witnesses dropped their astonishment singly and in small clusters in succession, and began to cheer the fight much more exhilarating, the local Battle of the Sexes live in front of their eyes. Karla Nuñez jumped across the bar to Madison's side and began kicking, Madison in the back of the head, Karla in the small of the back. They were witnessed by Randi McIntosh, who joined from across the dining area, contributing to the chaos with kicks to Ronnie's midsection. Eve Kennedy finally found a reason to come out from the hand washing station, and by the time she joined the others by falling into cadence to Randi's left, the electricity of the melee was full blown and had energized the surroundings.

Some whipped out their cell phones to record the moment on video. Philip Martinez was doing the same from behind the cook's station when he jerked his glance to the restaurant's security camera and adjusted it to point to the event while doing his best to keep his phone hand steady. Few witnesses remained in shock, greatly outnumbered by the opposition, customers and servers alike who cheered on the four girls kicking this poor son of a bitch in the back and in the front, the showcase production of battles between professional fighters televised via satellite from Las Vegas losing precedence to the circus of reality.

3

The unknowns of the night's aftermath and the consequences which awaited them were what really got to Madison under her skin, but she succeeded in keeping them suppressed. She knew there would be an arrest, a detention, an incarceration, and a release. The arrest was banal and uneventful. The detention process was tedious. And just finishing up; "Get up and follow me, ladies," some tough looking deputy said to them and they followed. Now Madison sparred with the bout of anticipatory anxiety awaiting the incarceration but dreaded the release even more. She was more ready for what was inside that cell than what would be waiting for her outside the jail. The realization hit her on the way. *I'm going to have a criminal record now. Great.*

The experience as a whole would have been completely bearable had it not been for Randi's tendency to be Randi in a stressful situation. She whimpered and began to hyperventilate while being handcuffed. She then cried while being escorted into the cruiser. Madison and Randi were seated in one cruiser, while Eve and Karla were seated in another. Getting Randi away from the chaotic scene and into the darkened capsule of the back seat of the cruiser provided the chance for Madison to make the situation more manageable by calming her down during the journey to their destination for the night.

"How long," Randi sobbed. "How long do you think," Randi sobbed. "Do you think they will keep us in jail for?" Randi struggled through gasps and stifled whimpers.

Madison anticipated what Randi would probably want to know, and she herself wanted to know what to expect, so she took the initiative from the beginning to ask one of the officers what was coming their way for the rest of the night. "They're going to keep us overnight until our parents come down and sign for our release and we sign a promise to appear in court." Increased anxiousness from Randi followed in the form of suppressed crying. Madison attempted to override it with more reassurance. "Don't worry, superstar, you'll be fine. We're all going to be together tonight. Just stay calm, and tonight will be over before you know it."

"I'll try."

The pep talk helped out, for the entire ride to the station. But when the girls arrived to the station and entered the building for processing, Madison resigned to the fact that Randi would just have to be counseled that night one phase at a time.

Madison was relieved that the experience did not live up to the hype, the worst part being the big cell block door, the sound of its electronic lock and the thud of its weight against the frame as it closed sending a ripple of shock and static through Madison's body. The holding cell at the county detention center was cleaner than Madison had imagined it would be. The blocks were concrete blocks painted a lighter shade of grey, and not an institutional green like she worked herself up to dread, or a sharp, bright white that would strain her eyes. Most of the agitation and nervousness she felt had to do with the cesspool she imagined getting thrown into that night, but the holding cell in reality triumphed over the stereotype. When she entered the cell and experienced the real picture of institutional smell and orderliness, as opposed to the cognitively painted one, she felt the assurance that she could make it through the night.

The holding cell housed some of the usual suspects that evening: a few prostitutes brought in on solicitation charges, a couple of girls brought in on separate assaults, and several simple drug possession and driving while impaired cases. The girls were processed in and brought into the cell in their uniforms, and greeted by plenty of catcalls from the male holding cell from those who got a chance to witness their entrance. The girls stood out both in the lobby for the male audience and in the holding cell with the females and their incredulous reaction. Upon their entrance, the girls were given the routine greetings given to intimidate the newcomers from various members that were currently occupying the space.

"Look what we got here. Did somebody order some wings in this motherfucker?"

"Damn, you girls came in here and didn't even bring some wings in here?"

"What the hell did y'all do? Did they start arresting you girls for bad service now?"

There was a reflexive instinct of the other three to inspect Randi's emotional output with a change in the atmosphere. The silent consensus was she behaved predictably, and started showing signs of a relapse. "I don't think I can do this," she gasped with a flushed face.

Eve pulled her onto her lap. "Shut up, bitch. You're gonna have to," she dictated to Randi with a smirk, and Randi did as she was told. She had no choice given the circumstances, but with Eve in the cell providing support, the end of the tunnel without the nervous breakdown was an attainable picture.

Randi McIntosh and Eve Kennedy found themselves classified as on-again, off-again, very close friends who were shrouded for a while in ambiguity and controversy at the intervals where their wanting intersected at needed moments. Eve was bisexual, enjoying the company of women when she needed spiritual or emotional sustenance, while her enjoyment for the company of men, in addition to the motive of lust, pertained to all things material. However, Randi was not as direct as to which direction her passions headed, and mostly just acted as if she was confused and unsure with her inner desires. Her origin into her relationship with Eve had been chalked up in scuttlebutt talk at work to experimentation and exploring her range as an actress, but Randi had not made any effort to confirm or deny those claims.

They hooked up for the first time one night around seven months ago, after some of the girls met up for drinks after work. Randi was terrified at anyone finding out about her crossing that forbidden line at first, so Eve humored her by tiptoeing around with her for the three weeks of discreet meetings. Randi soon found out, with the busybody ways and loose lips surrounding the restaurant, those three weeks were filled with secret missions that everyone knew about. Randi reacted in usual fashion and distanced herself for a while, not even speaking to Eve for days, but she eventually softened, and before long when she was lonely and bothered by life she trod across the line, and had since intermittently sought Eve's embrace when she was in need of companionship. As the months went by,

Randi stripped herself of her inhibitions and now rushed for Eve's arms whenever she needed affection, which was often given her emotional threshold, and she didn't care much anymore who knew it. Tonight was definitely going be labeled for the record as one of those moments.

The girls were now faced with the next chapter in the night's drama, which was on the verge of rolling into the earliest hours of the next morning; they were going to have to take turns calling home to let their families know where they were at.

"I can't call them now. I'm too scared," Randi immediately blurted out to begin the session.

Eve was next. "If Brenda answers, I'm probably going to flip. I need to wait a little while. Hopefully she'll be asleep by then."

"I'll go. I hope I can get Mom before she goes to bed," Karla said, stepping forward. Madison was relieved Karla stepped up and took initiative, because she was not ready either and wanted to wait a little longer before having to confront her mother.

"Karla Nuñez... Aunt Jenny, I'm glad you're at the house this week. It's me, Karla. Can you put Mom on the phone?... Hey, Mom. I've got some bad news. I'm in jail... I'm sorry, Mom. Tell Tyler everything is alright. Can you have Aunt Jenny look after him until you come get me out of here? I'll explain everything to you when you get here..."

Madison saw Randi's despondency and Eve's comforting and decided to get her call home over with while the damage control continued. She picked up the phone and turned to Randy Williams, one of the deputies on duty. "How does this work?"

He answered her without looking up from his stack of paperwork. "Follow the instructions. They are printed above the phone in front of you."

Asshole. Madison dialed and listened for the prompt to say her name. "... Madison Davis... Mom? It's me... I'm OK, I'm in jail. I need you to come down to talk to the magistrate... Please, I'm tired. I can't argue right now. It's going to have to wait until morning." She returned to the remaining two, but looked at Eve, because she knew Randi was going to be last.

"... Eve Kennedy... God dammit, somebody pick up... Brenda, I'm at the jail downtown... uptown, whatever. Tell my dad to come down here. I'll explain everything to him when he comes to get me out... God dammit Brenda, stop yelling! Please don't come down here with my father. I'm really not in the mood for you."

The last one left was as ready as she would ever be for the call. "... Hello? Oh, Randi McIntosh... Hello? Daddy? Oh my god, Daddy. I'm in... I'm in jail. I need, need... I can't breathe. I need you to come down as... fast... as fast as you can..."

As the night continued, while some girls processed out and were replaced by new offenders, and the more permanent fixtures got to know them, the other ladies in the holding cell began to warm up to the crew of the infamous event at Lovelee's, which some of the girls had already heard about from some of their friends. Karla mainly kept to herself and didn't bother anybody. Randi clung to Eve, as she sat on her lap for the rest of their stay, and the two kept themselves company. Madison took up the task of being the self-designated spokesperson charged with relaying the story of events which led to their overnight stay in holding.

"So then he smacks me on the ass," Madison told the audience while a couple howled and got wound up at the idea.

"Did you know who this dude was?" one of them asked.

"Yes, we do. I know him, anyway. Karla does also. We haven't seen him around here in a long time," Madison answered as she tried to remain focused on the story.

One of the other inmates finished the Cliff's Notes version of the story. "And that was when you girls laid that motherfucker out, right?" A bunch of the others cheered while Madison smiled. The movement even extracted a smile out of Eve.

The clamor caught the attention of one of the other deputies and he attempted order in the holding cell. "Settle down in there." From the remarks in the background, Madison determined his name was Fields – *lay down the law, Fields* – and he was one of the new guards – *get 'em, rookie.*

Among the catcalls and grumbles in the cell arose Eve's voice. "You settle down out there."

The other girls laughed, which bent Deputy Fields out of shape. "That is a direct order, ma'am. Tone your voice down and keep quiet!"

His agitation was her fuel; she made herself at home for the night. "You're the one getting all excited. Maybe you should go to the bathroom and rub one out. Relax yourself for a while."

Deputy Fields felt his temper ignited and suppressed by his embarrassment as Eve's quip was supported by laughs and cheers of many of her supporting cellmates. Deputy Harris, a thick black female guard who was three years his senior and more seasoned in handling smart mouths on the other side of the bars, came to his rescue. "Tighten up, baby doll. That includes those fat lips of yours, because I am NOT in the mood for what I'm hearing right now, this time of the month. You feel what I'm trying to tell you?" Her comment was met with a different reaction of chuckles from the repeat players in holding: they were entertained but not willing to get carried away and take their chances with Ms. Harris if they knew what was good for them.

Eve stood her ground with a grimace but did not answer until Randi tugged at her elbow. "Don't," Randi implored, then giggled in reaction when Eve lunged her face toward Randi's neck with biting kisses.

As the night progressed, the girls became the cult hit of the night, with the ladies as well as some of the deputies on duty.

Deputy Overcash was eager to see if any documentary evidence of the brush that had become the trademark of their featured guests had yet surfaced online, but had to wait until his supervisor left. The standard operating procedure for the sheriff's department prohibited the deputies from using the computers at the detention center for personal use. But, with government buildings in North Carolina joined in the movement of becoming smoke-free facilities, it also stated that smoking at the station was prohibited. So the subordinates had to wait until

Lieutenant Morton left in his squad car to 'make his rounds of the surrounding area,' which was his official excuse to leave in his squad car to find a spot for an unofficial cigarette break before Overcash could browse YouTube. He thought, given the time, he was going to run into trouble finding any videos and would probably not see anything online until at least after the bars closed and everyone got home, depending on the inebriation level of the public that night. He was proven wrong when he found several grainy low resolution videos already uploaded, along with a couple that were high enough quality for viewing.

"Hey ladies, I haven't been down to Lovelee's in a long time. Where is the security camera located at in that place?"

Karla thought he looked vaguely familiar, and now assumed that was how she knew him. She was the one who answered him, with the first words she had spoken in nearly two hours. "It's located at the end of the cook's station, overlooking the bar."

"That's interesting. This video looks like it could be the camera footage from the restaurant. If it is, it's already been leaked online. Let me browse around and see what else is showing up." One of the local news stations had an article on their website of the incident, which Overcash had anticipated. He backed up and explored further.

"Holy crap. Check this out."

What surprised him was finding a link on the Drudge Report. He clicked the link, and it took him to a national story on the website for the local affiliate for ABC. "It looks like someone at ABC has been working the graveyard shift, too. You ladies went national. Congratulations." A visit to YouTube revealed that members had posted not less than half a dozen different angled videos of the incident shot by amateurs with their cell phones in addition to the high quality video Overcash had viewed that may or may not have been the restaurant's security camera. After those videos were shared by other members on their accounts, the total reached to almost fifty video entries already. "This happened a few hours ago?" asked Overcash from the center of a gathering of curious deputies. "That's pretty impressive." Some of the videos had already scored up to nearly 200 hits. "Pretty impressive," he uttered to himself as he continued his surf.

Overcash clicked on the button to share the video on his Facebook page, which produced the nightly occurrence of stirring up Deputy Williams's emotions and causing him to drop his usually professional bearing. "Jesus, Overcash! Lieutenant Morton better not catch you doing that shit!"

Overcash chuckled while he clicked to post it. "Don't erupt on me, Mount Williams. If he does, my story is that you didn't see me do it. Besides, Lieutenant's not a friend of mine on here."

Sergeant Lomax, who seldom left the sanctuary of his office, unless an emergency erupted in one of the cells or his coffee cup emptied, yelled out from within, "You guys better not be doing stuff you're not supposed to be doing on that computer!" Overcash lead the mumbling chorus assuring the sergeant with a lie. "Is there any coffee made?"

"Shit," Overcash mumbled. "No, we're dry. I'll make some. It'll be ready in a few minutes!" Then he said low enough so the sergeant wouldn't hear him, "Don't come out," and started closing out the unauthorized evidence from the computer.

Madison smiled at the reassembly of order in the lobby. She turned around to her lady friends. "Pretty impressive, huh?"

The festive mood became drabber when Randi's parents arrived and finished the paperwork to get her out. Karla was next, about forty-five minutes later. Madison and Eve were not good friends and did not talk much at all in the final stretch, and those conditions remained normal on that exceptional night's event; Eve talked much more to the girls locked up for drug possession than she did to Madison, and the limited conversation fell solely along the lines of the previous night's tip money totals and their upcoming schedules.

The somber point of the early morning arrived when one of the female guards stepped up to the cell door. "Davis! Come on." It was Madison's turn to be let out of detention. Eve was still waiting for her dad and stepmother, but Madison would have opted to trade places with her and stay in holding by herself for a while longer before facing her mother for the ride back to her car at Lovelee's, a thirty minute drive of eternity.

Only in Madison's infancy years did she and her mother truly mesh in life. She knew her mother meant well but sometimes it was really trying to deal with the issue of her mother never quite seeming to be able to come to terms with the fact that she always came in second in her daughter's life after her daddy, even in the succeeding years after he took off and abandoned them. From her very early years, back in the days of the Tate last name, Madison still had fond memories of her daddy and the old, worn imitation leather couch and Sunday afternoon football games at their old house in Cannon, North Carolina, the sight of which never ceased to irritate her mother when she came home from church service with a car full of groceries and a confrontation to start. Sarah figured when Leon Tate walked out on the two of them she would be elevated the most important person in her life. And with Madison in a vulnerable situation and needing the support of a shoulder, Sarah Tate was within reach of getting her wish. But as her mother tried to direct her to a more proper churchgoing Sunday, Madison's young soul ingrained a resistance to the involvement in her life. She had to go with her mom to church on Sundays after her dad left, but in her heart her sermons were still preached to her on the couch afterward by Pat Summerall and John Madden, not to mention the Monday Night Gospel from the trio of Michaels, Gifford, and Dierdorf. The same results rang true for the other five days of the week between the two, and the relationship slowly spiraled downward from there through the years.

Madison faced the passenger side window and looked through it to the Charlotte landscape, and longed for the second leg of the journey back to her apartment without her mother behind the steering wheel navigating her Nervous System. She wished for a silent trip back to her car even if it would surely be tense regardless. From the beginning of the ride she had no such luck.

"I can't believe I had to spend all night waiting and filling out paperwork with the magistrate," Sarah Davis chided in a frustrated and disheartened state as she adjusted the temperature on the air conditioning, while Madison did the same with the radio, smiling – finding amusement was her way of dealing with these situations - and rolling her eyes as her face was pointed toward the free world outside the passenger side of the car.

"I hope you don't have anything planned early for tomorrow, besides church. You could've left me there until tomorrow."

Sarah jousted the radio with her finger and made the music disappear. "That is NOT happening. I wouldn't think of it."

"I would've survived a Sunday morning in there. Who knows, they might've had a church service in there," Madison egged on, which caused Sarah to look at her daughter in the car for the first time, temper flaring, which subsequently caused Madison to evaporate the smile on the exterior, leaving only the twinkle of a smile in her eyes.

"Actually, it's Sunday now, and I am going to church this morning, as usual. Maybe you need to start going to church again, instead of beating up on people at work. Do you even still have a job after what happened tonight?"

"Last night," Madison mocked carelessly and needlessly in habit. "I don't know. I'm supposed to work tonight. I guess I'll go in, and we'll see what happens."

Sarah appeared to hit an emotional limit. "You know, I try so hard, but...Never mind," she says in a gesture of giving up for the night. Madison felt she was getting her wish for the rest of the ride home but had an urge to hear the rest of what her mother had to say. She found that instance to be an ideal one to not fan the flames and just enjoy the rest of the ride back to Lovelee's. She did not seek to feed her mother's temper by being a smart ass in stressful situations; she just lacked the mindfulness. So the plan was to enjoy the rest of the ride in a slight tension, just as soon as she moved the center dashboard vent to give herself more air. Madison leaned her head on her mother's shoulder and played with the volume knob on the deadened radio.

Sarah softened as she eyed the action. "Go ahead." Madison pushed the power button and the sound blasted them both; Madison inadvertently moved the volume knob too much to the clockwise. They both jumped in their seats. "Madison!"

Sarah exclaimed to her daughter, trying to keep a stern demeanor, but the smile cracked through. Madison saw it and burst out laughing.

4

Madison shifted her head from the warm spot on the pillow to look at the clock.

10:44.

She did not get in until late, much later than when her mother dropped her off at her car in the Lovelee's parking lot. Madison felt little for going to bed last night and decided a drive through her hometown of Cannon was in order. The town in which she was born and raised looked like the wonderful dull and normal patch of home she remembered from her youth in the dark of night, just the way she wanted it while she tuned everything else out. She wasn't much for change, which made Cannon a bittersweet township for her to spend her life hanging her hat. For generations since just before the Industrial Revolution, the town barely strayed from its vast landscape of forests, pines and oaks in partnership, opening to swatches of open lands of functioning but slowly decaying farmhouses, well kept Victorian houses and other fawn-inspiring protected buildings, the never-ending churns and smoke from its two mills, tobacco in the north, textile in the south, and the sound of long standing high school football rivalry heard in the distance on autumn Friday evenings.

Now Madison spent the night digging her nails into the change. The tobacco moved north to the Dakotas and the textiles moved south to Mexico, and all the jobs with them. The local independent phone and cable companies were now part of multistate corporations, with the corporate jobs located in other states. And now the county jail, her hangout of the night before, just finished with yet another expansion and renovation, taking up more of the historic downtown landscape. The rest of the landscape was altered in ways that was good for business; the forests divided and the Wal-Mart's multiplied and cars were hitting fleeing deer in record numbers. Now the locals spent autumn Friday nights spread across five high school football fields as opposed to two and gathered to remember old high school memories of their youth and forget memories of real-life stalemates, for those fortunate enough to avoid unemployment line war stories of the past week.

It was all either crumbling or changing before her eyes, or both, but it was all visited in the early morning hours in her old reliable Honda Accord with all the windows down. It was much better than squatting in that confined jail cell. She didn't point the car toward her apartment until the first hint of the blue of dawn materialized on the horizon.

Now, with the sun in full view of a clear morning sky, she was in her usual spot on Sunday morning, lying in bed. She was normally asleep before eleven o'clock, but considering what happened the night before she was awake in bed and spent her waking period in that position staring at the wall.

The walls in Madison's bedroom were a light, pale tint of green, close to the shade of an avocado's insides. It was the same color of her bedroom walls when she lived at her mother's house. But when the house sold about four years ago and her mother moved to Huntersville, Madison stayed in Cannon, moved into an apartment, and kept the color. She also kept much of the rest of her old bedroom: the dark green curtains, the birch veneered clothing dresser, complete with all the battle wounds of childhood and moving, and the old beige painted full-sized bed frame she had had since the dawn of adolescence, although she ventured out of her comfort zone and purchased a new mattress to lay on the old box spring; the atmosphere surrounding her was all in need of updating, but it was what she was familiar with, so no renovations were on the immediate agenda.

That morning she stared at no point in particular on one of her avocado colored walls as flashes of memory of the events of the night before and early that morning flickered in her head. She looked at the clock on her dresser, which stared back at her with a face that read 10:48; she didn't make it to church to meet her mother, but both parties figured as much considering Madison had not been to church in years. That's why she let the phone ring at 7:45, because she knew it was her mother trying once more in vain to coax her into making an appearance at eight o'clock mass.

What Madison was not expecting was a phone call at just after nine that morning. She darted to look at the display anticipating seeing her mom's phone number. The caller ID told her the call was from work. She rolled toward the phone in order to both answer the phone call and have her questions regarding her employment status answered, even though she contemplated earlier that morning in jail that if Lovelee's decided to fire her over this incident she would most likely take it as a sign that the time had come to move on and take the leap of faith toward finding a better way to make her paycheck. So as she reached for the phone, she was prepared to take the news awaiting the other end of the phone regardless of her fate.

It was Bob Baucom, the manager working the lunch shift, calling to let her know that she, along with the other three girls, were replaced on the schedule for the week by Kerry Blanchard, the general manager, who had decided to suspend to girls as he mulled over terminating them.

Madison figured she would hear as much from them. She still felt the stinging butterflies but felt a sense of resolve in hearing the directive for certain. She felt worse for Karla and Randi than for her own fate.

Remember your worth. You have to move on sometime. Whatever; I have the day off now. She did have fun working there most days and made pretty good money so she felt no urgent need to change her routine. She would rather have known if she still had a job for certain, but if she was going to have some time off she might as well enjoy it.

She relaxed her head on her pillow and stared at the ceiling as she tried not to recall the flashback of bantering with her mother last night as she drove Madison back to the restaurant to her car. She remembered her mother chiding as if she was still next to her. *You just had to cause a scene before the eleven o'clock news, didn't you? It was on TV last night... I know I'll have to hear about it tomorrow after mass.* She figured her mother would have gotten the hint by now she had an independent spirit, and it pained her when they had these confrontations. Even though she lead the way she lived her own life, she hated the feeling that came with feeling she had let her mother down yet one more time.

The phone number. Where's my purse? It was in the moments Madison was wondering how many stations reported the story on the news last night when she remembered the phone number in her purse, an important number that she needed to call today. She lunged herself out of bed to her purse and fished for the textured heavy stock business card that contained the number for Ali Weinberg from Pink Front United, a feminist group located in the Charlotte area.

Ali sounded upbeat on the phone. "Hello, Madison. I saw the news online about what happened to you ladies. I'm glad you got in touch with me because I was looking to get in touch with you as well. So what happened last night?"

Madison gave Ali the rundown about what happened on Saturday, from the moment Ronnie confronted her at the bar to the moment the police put her in the cruiser to the phone call from Lovelee's that morning. "What do you think? Can your group help us out?"

Ali let Madison know she sympathized with her and the others and they did nothing wrong, and that son of a bitch otherwise known as Ronnie Stover had every punch and kick coming to him as far as she was concerned. "They can't fire you for this. I know some other groups in the Charlotte area. I'm going to see if I can get in touch with them today, and we'll see what we can do about this."

Madison felt better after talking to Ali or anyone who did not treat her like a criminal. She felt the motivation in her to get out of bed and check the computer to see how many news websites were talking about them a day later.

A bowl of milk poured ten minutes before was saturating the generic brand corn flakes into a soggy mess and a misshapen blueberry muffin on the table cooled beside it while Madison stared at the computer screen to the background of the local news on a flat television screen that was larger than necessary for the distance from the couch. Her concentration was diverted to the computer on her living area desk to the side of the rest of the landscape. It was all filtered through the lens of a Monday morning haze as Madison Davis looked to get energized after doing absolutely nothing the day before besides giving the call to Ali and receiving the call from her mother later that afternoon with her usual weekend pep talk about getting her life on track. She took the time before breakfast for the urge which burned in her once about every three or four months, not precise enough to be deemed ritual, but gets closer to it through the years. Her computer connected to the internet, the search engine brought up, the name Leon Tate in the bar. She hits Enter and gazes at the results without focusing, not brave enough to focus on the links to the text, the links to her answers.

On that morning, she was still not brave enough, and closed out the window.

As the local news wrapped up she returned drowsily and languidly to her impatient breakfast of drowning cereal and hardening muffin. In the transition from the closing of the local news to the introduction of the national morning news show she snapped to an awakened state when the preview of upcoming stories for the next hour included her and her co-conspirators in a familiar scene. She waited in anticipation as she ate her breakfast until the story began and the program broadcasted the camera footage of Saturday night's moment from the restaurant. Madison viewed herself in black and white as she kicked Ronnie Stover with the other girls in video that was most likely the security camera from the restaurant. *That must've been the video the guard saw on the internet at the jail. How the hell did it get out so fast?*

Leslie Fitzgerald's voice asked her guests during the video of the beating "What was going through your head? What were you thinking at this moment? What are you feeling today while you're watching the footage, while the nation is watching this footage with you?"

Then Madison heard Ronnie's voice narrated over the continuation of the footage which blended into the beginning of a loop. "I feel humiliated. I still hurt on a lot of places on my body. I'm sorry for what I did, but I really didn't deserve to get treated like I did that night."

The show then faded to the camera filming Ronnie, slightly bandaged and looking truly pathetic, almost on the verge of being too pathetic to be believed, sitting beside Wayne Irvin, the attorney he had chosen to represent him in his pursuit of happiness.

"What is the next step? What are you looking to get from this ordeal?" the announcer asked with a veneer of sympathy stressing from a core of cynicism fighting to break free.

When asked about details regarding specified damages, Ronnie took his cue to shift to the rear of the stage while Mr. Irvin took over with a prepared routine. "My client has endured considerable suffering and, as he has already stated, while he is truly sorry for any conduct toward any of these ladies, these actions were uncalled for and he is humiliated beyond measure. We will consider what reward would be sufficient for the suffering of my client, and if the courts would deem it to be fair."

As the segment came to a close and Leslie Fitzgerald thanked her guests for their time, Madison rolled her eyes and made the commitment to push ahead with the day with a smirk and a scoop of corn flakes.

Her iPod was playing one of the NOW albums, a song in the middle of the album that she couldn't remember the title of off hand, but the catchy beat was enough to satisfy the drive, even though the male lead singer sounded a little too girly for her taste. Besides, her mind was engaged on other matters. It was close to eleven o'clock, right at opening time at the restaurant, when an agitated Kerry Blanchard called her. He was calling the four of them in for an impromptu meeting but did not get into specifics.

With the humidity of the Monday still lingering in her head, Madison's phone conversation with Ali from Pink Front United ended up in the back of her mental file cabinet along with everything else that had nothing to do with the beat on her iPod and North Carolina traffic laws, but it was ushered front and center as she approached the parking lot. The view to the restaurant and parking lot from the street was obstructed by an energetic wall of women making their presence and agitation known with chants and signs.

HE DESERVED IT!

IT'S NOT RIGHT!

LET THEM WORK!

The section of the crowd surrounding the driveway in a barricade contracted to the car's turn toward it until the recognition of Madison in the driver's seat caused some of the participants in front to relay the information to the rest of the mass, and the emotional drawbridge separated to let her approach.

Madison was exposed just as quickly to the mob's perimeter as she was to a microphone in her face while stopped briefly as a news reporter asked for a comment. She did not comprehend every word given by the reporter, accompanied by the background of women yelling passages of encouragement, but she heard enough of the key words and assumed the nature of the question directed to her. She gave her comment at mic-point, fumbling through an assurance that they will keep positive, and hope they get to keep their jobs, all the while thinking *Wow! It's Diane Ferguson from Channel Nine News*.

She proceeded while acknowledging some of the supporters with a smile and a wave as she looked for a parking space. There were quite a few cars in the lot, probably filled up by the protestors, Madison thought to herself. She spotted a space just past the side door which was ideal considering she would not have to confront the crowd again should it become out of control.

Madison was surprised to see upon opening the door that many of the cars in the parking lot most likely belonged to customers; the early lunch crowd appeared larger than usual. She saw new faces mixed in with the old ones, along with a small handful in a category of their own: Steven Jenkins, Waylon Barbee, and Darrell Sloop at one of the round tops in the middle of the main dining area. *Do these guys even leave when the place closes? They might as well bring sleeping bags.* Actually, Darrell only made an appearance half as often as the other guys due to his work schedule as a correctional officer at the state prison across the county line. With a stance of average height, stocky shoulders, and above average thickness in the midsection, he possessed the typical profile for his line of work. Madison recalled one of her first conversations with him telling her of his hometown in Alabama, somewhere near Mobile. *Loxley, I think...* She was reminded of this every time he spoke to her.

"How you doing, baby girl? Rough weekend?" he joked as he greeted.

His thick accent made her smile. "Good morning to you too, Boss Man. Don't worry about it, nothing I can't handle."

"Too bad I was working this weekend. I wish I could've been here to put the whoop ass on that motherfucker. I'll be here this weekend getting my drink on, though." He was on a set schedule, worked five days and all weekend one week, and the next week he worked two days and spent all weekend drinking his stress away at Lovelee's. "Hey," he continued, "We're keeping that guy at the prison who killed your friend. He got a job in the kitchen and wants to stay. I'll make sure his stay in the hotel sucks."

Madison felt a wave of sadness for her old friend. "Make life suck worse than that for him." She was distracted by Kerry Blanchard's wave at the round top closest to the server station, who was already accompanied by Karla. "There's my meeting. Wish me luck. I'll see you boys around."

As usual, everyone was waiting for Randi and Eve, as they always seemed to show up last for important meetings. Madison made herself a sweet tea and sat next to Karla.

"I'm not going to wait for Eve and Randi. Let's just get started with you guys, and then talk to them when they decide to show up," an exasperated Kerry Blanchard said to half the gang. Karla had the gift of receiving the news of the meeting early by being first to the scene. The jubilant look on Karla's face led Madison to believe she had early insider knowledge of the meeting's purpose, and that the news was a spirit lifter.

Kerry continued. "I have had a talk with a couple of heads of women's groups in the area, and a woman news reporter. I didn't get a chance to say much. And now I had a shout with about 200 women. It was a one-sided shout at me while I came into work this morning. Considering the circumstances, I'm going to go ahead and put you guys back on the schedule. I've talked to corporate, and they think it would be good for business."

"And here I thought you were doing a good deed for us," crooned a voice from behind Kerry. The other half of the group had arrived, with Eve jumping at the chance to get on Kerry's nerves.

"Well, it's nice that everyone finally showed up," Kerry grunted. "How much did you ladies hear so I don't have to repeat myself?"

Eve's face brightened with artificial illumination. "None of it, sweetie. You'll have to start at the beginning."

Madison could almost hear Kerry's teeth grinding. As he repeated himself and discussed other miscellaneous informalities to make small talk, Madison's mind picked at the corporate spin in what her general manager said and matched sentiments with Eve. She was pretty sure the corporate office saw their suspensions to be bad publicity, and Kerry normally would not have given a shit if they kept their jobs or not. He discovered by that morning's crowd and the news cameras that this incident temporarily made the location semi-famous and that keeping the girls working there might turn out to be good for their sales reports. She was not buying his bullshit but was pleased with the outcome, more for Karla than herself or the others because she knew how Karla worried about the prospect of not working there anymore and about how she was going to provide for Tyler if this did not work out for them. Madison heard enough of what she needed to hear and could check this off on her day's agenda. She stood up to excuse herself. "I have to get out of here, Kerry. Call me if you need me. When's my next day in this place?"

"You can't wait a few minutes for me to finish?"

"It's not going to be necessary. When do I work next?"

Kerry was agitated with her wanting to leave so quickly, the flames fanned by Eve and Randi showing up on their own time, and was talking in his 'laying down the law' tone. The girls thought it was cute that he thought he was in charge. He fumbled through the stack of papers in front of him with a look of defeated embarrassment on his face. "Your next day is Wednesday, then all weekend," he mumbled.

"Oh, Madison," Randi projected I a vernacular stumble. "I have something to tell you."

"I have to go, superstar. Call me later," Madison said as she turned to go. She offered a high-five to Karla, who received with it with less fervor than the transmitter, relieved with the outcome of events but still not feeling particularly festive. Madison tried to push the motivation to a higher level in her by blowing her a kiss. "See you on Wednesday, buddy." Karla flashed a moderate smile to her exiting co-worker and friend.

Madison's big block of a smart phone started ringing as she was making her way to the car with the furor of the protest wall in the background, and she figured to wait until she was inside the vacuum of her car so she could hear the call through the clamor in the parking lot. She hurried to get into her car to attempt to answer it before being redirected to her voice mail. She caught it in time and answered. "Hello?"

"How did it go this morning?" her mother asked.

"It went fine. We all still have jobs," Madison told her as she concentrated on exiting the crowded parking lot edge without committing vehicular manslaughter.

It took mere moments for her mother to begin preaching one of her sermons. "You know Madison, you shouldn't be in a situation where you were this close to not having a job to make your rent. You need to keep that job until you get a chance to use your degree."

The sound of salvation to Madison's ears came in the form of a ringing coming from her purse, the ring from another cell phone. She dug out the small prepaid cell phone and flipped it open and scanned the screen.

INCOMING CALL: RED.

"Mom, I have to go."

The exasperation in her mother's voice was apparent. "Madison, drop by my house sometime this week. We need to have a talk."

The exasperation in Madison's voice was apparent. "I will, Mom. I'm all over the road, so I have to go. Good bye." She answered the second phone as quickly as she hung up the first. "Hey superstar, what's up?"

The conversation exploded on the other end of the connection. "Ohmygod, Iwantedtocatchyoubeforeyouleft, Igottamessage..." Madison spoke over the outburst on the other end, eventually stopping Randi McIntosh in the middle of her vernacular spasm. "Randi sweetheart, slow down a little so I can understand you, and breathe before you pass out."

Randi cackled nervously on the other end before she took the advice and reset. "OK. Some guy from Facebook friended me and sent me a message to call him. He said he was a photographer who had friends who worked for Maxim magazine. He gave me his number to call him. I was kind of creeped out at first, but I called him just to make sure because I didn't want to miss out if it was legit." No answer from Madison as she was taking the time out to cringe. "Madison?"

"Randi sweetheart, you have to watch yourself when guys contact you like that."

"What I did was risky, I know," Randi responded with an element of shame in her voice, then continued with the renewed enthusiasm of a girl who learned no lesson. "Anyway, I talked to him, and he and his friend from Maxim want to come in to talk to us on Friday!"

As Randi's enthusiasm caused her conversation to verge on the unintelligible again, the phone in Madison's hand beeped and she pulled it from her ear to check the incoming call.

INCOMING CALL: 911.

She replaced the phone to her ear to cut the conversation short with Randi, whose ramble was ongoing and continuing. "I have to go, sweetie. You have to be careful with guys like that. Take care of yourself."

She dropped the call on the tail end of Randi's unintelligible good bye and answered the other call. "Hey. Where do you want me to meet you?"

Madison turned into the back road behind the Wal-Mart parking lot and drove along the road running parallel with the parking lot, passing by the congested sea of every color in the prism of cars, just about every type of metal composing their wheel covers with their poorer, silver colored plastic equivalents making up the much of the mix, until the sea receded in intensity to the point that the far rear quadrant of the lot was practically empty, with the exception of a lone, red 1977 El Camino in the corner.

She turned into the parking lot and parked near the El Camino, each car pointed in different directions with a little more than a parking space separating them. She got out of her car, and Ronnie Stover got out of his. As she moved closer to meet him in between the cars, she could not hide the macabre amusement in the curves of her face as she saw Ronnie move toward her with a wince in his step.

"Karla was supposed to stay away from the kidneys. They still hurt. It's not funny. I'm lucky I'm not pissing blood."

"I'm not laughing."

"You're smiling," he said as he read her face. She was not overtly smiling, but he either must have been able to read her thoughts or she had work to do on her poker face.

"I'm just happy to see you, that's all."

As she got within an arm's length, Ronnie wrapped an arm around her waist and began to give her a kiss. Madison giggled and pulled back away from his advances. "Whoa. Easy does it, cowboy."

"Come on. Just a little," Ronnie coaxed defiantly with a halfhearted smile that did a less than stellar job of hiding his immediate disappointment. "I'm happy to see you, too."

She restored the arm's length between them and got a good look at the disappointment in his face. She swallowed the guilt and continued. "Sorry to keep you waiting. Kerry talked to us this morning after suspending us. Now he's unsuspending us because the protesters started giving him hell."

It was Ronnie's turn to show the facial creases of amusement. "Unsuspending. Is that a real word, college girl?"

"Give me a break," she declared as she mocked throwing a strike at his neck again. He threw his hand up and jerked away, causing a jolt of discomfort to strike in the area of his kidneys. She juggled bemoaning his pain with enjoying his quandary. "Relax and let yourself heal. And I will apologize on Karla's behalf for your pain. So, how are things going on your end?"

Apology on Karla's behalf...Bullshit. He knew bullshit when he heard it, but brushed it off with a smirk because getting back to the subject took a higher priority. "My lawyer had a talk with the corporate office of Lovelee's, and their lawyers were squirming the whole time while trying to act tough with me. By the time we left, there were talks on the table of a settlement."

Her excitement erupted at the news and she threw herself into his arms for a celebratory hug. She just knew the embrace would walk her into the receiving end of one of Ronnie's kisses. She didn't fight it but their frequencies clashed enough for Ronnie to take notice. After spending a few more moments engaged in a luxury of which he had been deprived for the past two years, he relented from his grip.

"Have I told you since I've been back how great it is to see you again?"

She smiled and rolled her eyes. "Every time you see me. Every time you come back."

He tried to keep the tone light, but her body language and waning smile were not willing to play along and he followed suit.

"What's wrong?"

"I haven't changed my mind. I still think we should keep it business this time around."

Ronnie could no longer try to mask his hurt when her smile all but disappeared in the conversation. "We didn't keep it to business a couple of weeks ago."

"That was a mist..." She cut herself too late; they both heard 'mistake' in her fricative and suppressed subtext. "That other night is not how it has always been in the past." She was still laboring to make it true in the absolute, but succeeded in impedance; Ronnie absorbed the dealt blow and dolefully retreated to his car feeling the undertow of regret: *stayed away too long, too many times?*

"You know, I'm not taking off anytime soon." He saw no change in her intentions. "I'd better go. We can't be seen in public like this. As long as we're careful, there shouldn't be any problem. I'll keep you posted."

Madison was saving herself this time around. If history was a factor and the opportunity expired here or presented itself there, Ronnie would be gone the way he came in. She tired of the feeling at the closing act even though she had performed the show numerous times. Part of her deep inside wanted to say she was sorry and avoid disappointing him, like a learned reflex. *Let's just finish the deal and see what happens in the future.* A deep breath later, she figured it would be best to keep their relations as much to business as possible this time around and not slip up like she did a couple of weeks ago.

Madison blew him a good bye kiss, which made Ronnie at least soften his frown. He opened his car door and reached in to start his car. "I'll give you a call if anything changes, and you can tell the girls. Tell Karla I said thanks for the kidney bruises." He cracked a little smile when Madison giggled. He got into his car and drove away.

Madison watched Ronnie's El Camino leave the Wal-Mart parking lot almost like a scene from three weeks ago played out in reverse, a scene where she kept a lookout from the front windows of Lovelee's as she was held captive standing in front of one of her tables.

PART TWO
THREE WEEKS AGO

5

"Well, can I start you with a round of hot wings while you decide what you're in the mood for?"

She knew what was coming next as she stood over the table of four occupied by two. She refused to sit down next to either of them. The one on the left had facial features of a baby on an adult's head, like a baby who instantaneously grew into a medium sized adult. His beard was probably as fully grown as he would be capable of, and reminded Madison of pubic hair glued onto an overgrown baby head. The one on the right had a fuller beard and a more oversized head which was disproportionate to the body on which it was perched. It reminded Madison of an attempt to make a human head out of a balloon that ended in a big, creepy failure.

"What we're in the mood for is not on the menu." The stale reply came from creepy balloon head on the right and they both snickered.

Madison flexed her hands into fists to crack her knuckles. *Where the hell is he?*

She had been balancing on needles since the day before when she received a call from Ronnie Stover, a bipolar cyclone of emotions building since as she waited for him to pull into the parking lot. When she first heard his voice she felt numb as the clouds circled inside. He was vague on the phone while she waited for answers to questions – why did he just leave and not tell her, no phone call, nothing? His call answered nothing but came with a tone different from the usual announcement of being back in town for some kind of scheme and it would be really nice if the two of them to spend some time together and last night was incredible and I'm sorry I have to leave so soon as he goes off to chase yet some other scheme. This phone call came with an opportunity he wanted to discuss with her in person. So Madison told him when she was working and he would meet her then, and as Baby Face and Creepy Balloon Failure consented to a plate of hot wings, Madison waited for Ronnie to show up.

Ronnie Stover and Madison Davis were a connection destined to happen since the first time they met, the jagged ends caused by their broken families fitting well enough to each other for comfort and symmetry. They first met seven years ago back when they were still in high school, Madison a junior and on the verge of dating Alex Kiser and cheering him on from the basketball court stands, Ronnie a senior at age twenty and on the verge of just walking away and concentrating on making money. And walk away from high school was what he did, but not before introducing himself to her soon after their eyes met while Alex Kiser was playing Four Corners offense with the possibility of taking her to the upcoming dance just before the Christmas break.

Ronnie returned to school on occasion to visit Madison, while Madison played hard to get with a frustrated Alex Kiser. In between those occasions, she and Leanna St. John talked over the courting competition Leanna made her suggestion while ribbing her friend and her homebody ways. *Ronnie wants to sweep you up and take you away from this place. Or maybe you and Alex can have a big family and plot yourselves here for life. I say you choose Ronnie.* For reasons not necessarily in alignment with her friend, Madison took her friend's advice, and she and Ronnie quickly meshed together a network of feelings friendly and sensual. By the time her junior year approached its ending and Alex Kiser moved on to another interest, Ronnie left town to chase an opportunity down in Georgia, and Madison Davis was left standing with empty arms. In the lifelong labyrinth of their partnership this visit to the valley of loneliness would not be her last.

After a summer stint in mall retail hell, she took a job her senior year at Tucker Country Bar-B-Q. She had just started and was on her fourth day when Ronnie came in on his first day back from having a two week vacation. They spotted each other immediately and Madison had that feeling their broken pieces would find a way to fit together again. She let him know she still had the same phone number. Ronnie naturally had a different phone number and brought her up to date. She knew she would hear from him again. When he nonchalantly arrived to the time clock to punch in twenty-five minutes late, the shift manager, a hothead terminally riddled with tension and sporting a flattop crew cut and thick horn-rimmed glasses – whenever Madison saw the movie Falling Down, it brought back memories - jerked his head up from his paperwork and yelled out to him.

"You can't make it in to work on time, Ronnie? You sure as hell can make it out of here for vacation, though."

Ronnie Stover flashed a cocky smile his way because he was just not ready to take in any stress on his first day back.

"Did I blow my chances to be the General Manager someday? Why do I get the feeling it won't be the biggest regret of my life?"

Ronnie was met with sporadic laughter from some of the rest of the crew. He did mention the manager's name, but Madison could not recall it anymore, that first time her eyes connecting with Ronnie's for the first time in months sticking more to her memory through the years. The later part of the shift was hectic and Ronnie was told by the same manager he could not take any breaks until the rush died down. Between the directive from the hashery despot and the not-so-welcome greeting, Ronnie cared little for the attitude or the environment, so he pinned his open tickets on the cork board beside the computer and clocked out permanently. No one knew he left, not even Madison, and especially the manager until his four tables complained about not receiving their dinners.

Their meetings would continue with Ronnie as a customer as well as meeting her after her work shifts. She shared the news with him that his tickets were discovered on the board about three weeks after the manager was forced to refund the dinners of three families and a high school couple on a date, and subsequently referred to as 'that son of a bitch.' He was delighted to know his mischief came at a cost for the company and that his legend would be cemented into Tucker Country Bar-B-Q folklore.

Madison and Ronnie reconnected again and their kindred worked closer to getting it right. Even his father seemed to be taken with her. He showed little enthusiasm for much surrounding Ronnie's life, but Madison took what she could get in the form of what would be the closest to a compliment to come from Ricky Stover's lips regarding her as she waited outside by his car.

"Don't fuck this up too, kid."

All the euphoria she felt in this new round of love made the new letdown just a little more painful for her when Ronnie found another scheme to chase down.

Madison mutually exchanged the disappointment at times that he tried in vain to get her to come with him; when she was in high school, it was simply out of the question; when she was in college in Charlotte, she did not want to postpone her studies; when she was out of college, she worried about leaving Lovelee's and finding steady employment, and the destination turned out to not be a decent marketing employment market.

The predictability in the pain acted as an anesthetic, but the pain was still unavoidable that night about two years ago when he just disappeared and she did not hear from him again.

Until last week with a phone call which took her by surprise. She was still waiting for the reason.

He told her that he would meet her at work and to be on the lookout for a red 1977 El Camino, which entered the parking lot as the hot wings entered the server's food station. She hastily transported the plate to the two creeps at her table and made no attempt to hear the requests they made to the back of her head as she continued to the side exit door.

She did not realize how cold she was from the dining room air until the humid midday air put her body at ease as she approached Ronnie's car wondering if he looked the same as he did when he left, and possessed a slight worry inside that he would.

He did. Ronnie looked nearly the same as he did two years ago through the filter of her eyes as he got out of the car; his shaggy dark brown hair; his medium framed shoulders; his lower face, slightly shadowed from a regimen of shaving every third day because he hated the irritation on his neck if he shaved any more frequently.

As he squared his stance with a smile on his face and opened his arms in preparation for her hug, Madison sealed herself around the edges in retaliation to the worry she felt rooted in her hormones. *Restraint;* It was the word she could imagine as an etching on the emotions she was feeling. She needed to make sure she did not follow familiar paths of pleasure because all it did was retell the familiar painful story of her past. *A little fun, maybe? Just don't get attached again.* As soon as the thought processed, it sounded like the same recipe for more heartbreak, like setting a barrier and finding out too late she trapped herself on the wrong side of it. Like she did every other time. She hoped this meeting would be kept strictly to business with the exception of discussing the past that left her ill at ease, wondering why he abandoned her, much like her father did so many years ago. And continuing the battle for chiseling through the stonewall. She was preparing for it all.

Madison put on pause the fallings out and on-again, off-again acts of their relationship saga temporarily as she hopped into his grip, grasping him in return in a hug. The reunion of the two drifted in a realm between surreal and bittersweet; the happiness of reunion was crossed in the current with the tension caused by his enigmatic disappearance. "It's good to see you again, Ronnie. It's been too long." She was convincing enough to keep the sourness from her voice. He knew it was lingering underneath and would have had reason to question it if he could have looked at her face in that moment of embrace.

"I know. I've been a stranger around here for too long." Like a sail shifting direction in the wind. "How has this hell hole been treating you?"

Madison chuckled with knowingness. "It's not that bad for most people around here. You just get tired of stuff way too easily and bail." Her banter had a blade.

That testament to his character was one on which Ronnie definitely could not argue with her. Everyone who knew him could attest that his presence was preceded by his reputation. Fortunately, many who had known him through the years had spread themselves throughout the Charlotte area or out of the area completely, which Ronnie figured would make this plan work without a hitch. That is what he was hoping for, anyway.

"I've got about another hour before I'm done with work today. And I got the other girls that you wanted me to pick out. They should be here soon. Do you need a drink?"

"I think I could put one or two down before we get started."

"Let's go inside and you can have a seat in my section."

"I'd better have a seat at the bar."

The bar. The alcohol. It brought back some of the first bad memories of her father before things really got out of control. "Okay, suit yourself. And when the others get here you can give us more details of this plan you've got."

6

The two partners entered Lovelee's and parted ways in the dining area, Ronnie to the bar and Madison to check up on her two creepy characters, but they were gone and replaced by her manager, Will Graham, who was standing by the table.

"Hey Madison, I took care of your table and cashed out these two guys. I'm shocked they didn't leave you a tip," he said sarcastically as he handed her the cash from the transaction.

She took the money and cleaned up the table. "Screw them, anyway," she muttered under her breath. She noticed Ronnie took a seat close to the center of the bar and sat sideways with his ear facing Madison and her manager and the empty table. She figured from the smile on his face that he heard their exchange.

Ronnie had already given her an overview of his idea: they stage a scene at the restaurant where she along with a couple of other girls would kick the crap out of him, after which he would sue the restaurant a beaten and humiliated man, and all involved would share in the money. He had been gone long enough for the place to have had a steady turnover of servers, staff, managers, and customers, so he was hoping he would practically be a stranger to most of the witnesses on the night they attempted to pull this plan off.

It was Madison's first responsibility to choose the other participants they would need. She conducted a mental roster scan and concluded that most of them were not a safe choice; most of the girls were either too soft to make the assault look realistic, did not possess the will to keep the plan a secret, lacked the emotional capacity to not crack under the possible pressure of the incident being questioned, or disqualified themselves from a combination thereof.

When she finished the assessment of her co-workers, most were out of the question, with a few left to toss the idea to. But one definite choice stood out among the rest.

Karla Nuñez was a single mother to a seven year old boy and the only other girl who had been at Lovelee's as long as Madison. She and her mother shared a house and a similar story of women left by a man to care for a child on their own, so Karla moved in so she and her mother could share the bills and the responsibility to make sure their little man is brought up to take a better path when he gets older. The family alliance of Karla with her mother and son was very close and not susceptible to urges of chasing dreams by shady means, no matter what price tag was attached in either direction, so when Madison was ready to approach her about the plan, she knew what factor would dominate the conversation.

"I'm sorry, Madison. I just can't risk losing my job here. I've got Tyler to worry about, you know that."

Madison saw it coming before she started speaking. Karla did not make any major decisions, or most minor decisions for that matter, without deciding how it would affect Tyler. "I know. Believe me; I wouldn't even think of trying to pull this off with Ronnie unless the money was worth it and I knew there was a really good chance of getting away with this."

Karla's demeanor shifted with the mention of the co-conspirator; Madison and Karla got along when it came to most subjects, with Ronnie being one of the few exceptions.

"Ronnie is showing his face around here again?" Karla asked in a way that clearly demonstrated she was not part of the welcoming committee.

Well, somebody still remembers him around here, Madison thought with a retained smile. "He's not that bad, is he?" She leans in closer to Karla and speaks in a more confidential tone. "If we pull this off right, Ronnie is going to get quite a bit of money from a lawsuit with this place. I'm not sure how much we're talking about, but a share of that is yours. Maybe it'll be enough for a nice college fund for Tyler."

Karla still hadn't stated either yea or nay yet, but Madison still had her attention. "Do you really think we're that likely to get away with it?" The hint of wonder tinted to doubt. "What chance is there to get caught?"

"We won't get caught, Karla, I promise. This is practically guaranteed to work." Madison was not as sure about this as she was leading on to believe, and she could tell by Karla's reaction that she could read it on Madison's face. Madison remained as confident as possible and stuck out her hand in partnership.

Her proposal worked, and she and Karla exchanged handshakes and smiles.

"We'll get together with Ronnie in a few days. Right now it's the three of us, but I've got a couple more people in mind. I'm going to get them to join in," Madison relayed to Karla, whose face no longer had the smile of conspiracy and opportunity, but that of an aspiring cringe. Madison pleaded with hopes the discord would not inflict an encumbrance. "Come on, Karla. Please don't be grumpy."

Karla broke eye contact and took their empty glasses to the sink behind the bar to get ready for her shift. "I can't believe you're talking to him again, Madison. Remember what happened the last time you guys got together. Did he even explain what happened?" She lost the edge in her voice upon Madison's stricken reaction of a response. "Are you sure this is a good idea?"

"Yes, this is a good idea, Karla. You just have to trust me on this. We're getting together for business and money and then he'll be gone, nothing more," Madison declared in a guarantee, for as far as a guarantee could be thrown. Karla knows about the plan, and is reluctantly on board. "Is he that unbearable?"

"Just let me know when to meet up, okay?"

Charlotte's club scene attracted a chamber pot of many types to a melting pot of lighting effects and rehashed beats to time: those nameless, faceless employees who endured forty hours each week of mundane corporate office purgatory or an ungodly amount of hours fetching food and drinks looking for something to live and thank God for each Friday; participants who played the game of finding a temporary mate and fulfilling carnal desires; self-absorbed parasites of attention showcasing celebrity where none exist; those attracted to the darkness of the environment to enjoy moments under the influence or make transactions in order to aid others in that quest.

Eve Kennedy was a character who, on any particular night, fit into a combination of those categories, and on rare occasions, all of them. She was a feisty petite woman who had a good head on her shoulders when she abstained from subjecting it to cocktails of grain alcohol and methamphetamines or nose candy and other occasional experiments. Her cell phone bill was taken care of by her dad, and her room and board alternated between her dad's home and Randi McIntosh's apartment, so whatever money she made at the restaurant went to the sole purpose of funding as many trips to as many downtown Charlotte clubs for as many days of the week as possible.

Some of Eve's nights of drunken bearing and outbursts approached the level of legendary status in the Charlotte club scene, a reputation she claimed without hesitation or regret. Those particular nights, with the spotlight devoted to her, defined Eve's life, which had been a recurring problem with her hormonal alliance with Randi McIntosh; very rarely did Randi accompany Eve on the scene, because most of Eve's wild displays of outburst almost always seemed to happen if Randi was present, much to Randi's chagrin.

Madison had a different dream team in mind, with Karla and she being joined by Ashley Starnes (fired the night Madison was supposed to discuss the plan after work) and Leanna St. John (the team would remain a sad dream forever). That left Tanya Beaver and Eve Kennedy, not ideal, but better than anyone else she could think of amongst her co-workers. Madison chose the particular day for a reason; Eve was working early, Tanya was working later, and Randi McIntosh would not be there, making it an ideal opportunity to get Eve on board while keeping Randi out of the mix and keeping her fingers crossed that Eve could keep the proposition a secret. She was also hoping Eve's alcohol binges and erratic behavior were frictional elements that would not hinder the plan.

"Hey Eve, can I talk to you a sec?" Madison asked over the table where Eve was rolling up silverware set as part of her closing side work. Eve and Madison were not particularly good friends – a bystander could take a close look and see it in their faces – but shared a cordiality to keep it conversational. Eve motioned toward the other side of the table with her latest silverware creation.

"Be my guest. It might keep me awake."

Madison sat and began talking while Eve kept an attentive ear on her proposal while she finished her sentence. "Listen, a guy I know wants to pull a scam here at work and wanted to know if I could help him out." As Madison continued, Eve finished her side work and was getting antsy, but still listening and hadn't cut her off. *So far, so good.* Madison's mouth could now relax and grow into the similarity of a smile for now. "If we can get this thing on the news, and it airs outside of Charlotte, think of what kind of exposure you could be looking at. There's money involved, but if we make it look good and make enough noise with this incident, your picture could show up in a lot of newspapers, a lot of magazines. Not like what we usually deal with around here with these stalkers with cameras who hang around all the time." Eve was not a model; she just had a penchant for attention. It was more tempting bait than money to get her involved.

"To hell with these guys around here," Eve said. "The worst ones don't even try to sit in my section anymore. So, which creeper's ass do we get to kick in this place?"

Just when the pieces felt like they were coming together, a hand descended to the table to deliver a root beer to Eve accompanied by a voice that sent a stabbing thunderbolt of frustration to Madison's temples when she realized it was coming from Randi McIntosh as she swooped in on the conversation out of nowhere and materialized next to Eve. "Oh my GOD, that sounds awesome. What are you guys up to?"

Madison sputtered obscenities in her head as Randi got cozy beside Eve. Before setting out to recruit her partners, when Madison placed the names in her mental database of disqualifying factors, Randi's name was placed either high enough to smell the top or owned the pinnacle point on all accounts.

Too soft to make the assault look realistic: In addition to being an aspiring model, Randi is an aspiring actress, and will probably aspire for the rest of her life.

Did not possess the will to keep the plan a secret: Randi was a very high honorable mention in this category.

Lacked the emotional capacity to resist cracking under the possible pressure of the incident being questioned: Randi can be prone to bouts of anxiety at her best, and an emotional train wreck at her worst; she placed at the top of this list, with a star drawn in on each side for special emphasis.

Needless to say Randi McIntosh was crowned Miss Liability in this pageant, and her enthusiasm to join Eve in this adventure posed a problem for Madison, who saw her hopes for Tanya as the fourth member vaporize against the abrasions of Randi's erratic arpeggios of bubbly wails.

"What are you doing in here?" Eve asked Randi before squeezing her close to her side and planting a kiss on the corner of her mouth. "Don't you have the day off today?"

"Yeah, but I keep forgetting to pick up my paycheck from this past Friday. I have to grab it so I can drop it in the bank."

Madison smoothed the lines out of her face and wondered if a pleasant rejection for Randi could be had, that she could disappear without overhearing too many details, but did not get it out in time before Eve answered. "It does sounds interesting," she said Madison's way. And then turned to Randi and asked "Do you want in on this, sweetie?"

"Of course I want in. This is going to be epic. What exactly are we doing?"

"Actually," Madison said in a jab aimed to interrupt the flow of passive mutiny, "I was planning on bring Tanya Beaver in on the group with me, along with Karla and Eve. I'm sorry, Randi. But I don't want to bring in too many people and get them involved. I hope you understand, sweetie."

Eve stepped in when Randi's face settled into her 'upbeat to mask the hurt on the inside' mold. "Hey, Randi can do this. This is like acting in a play or something. Randi can totally do this just as good as Karla or Tanya, even better than them. I say let's bring Randi in as our fourth."

"Oh Madison, pleeeease," Randi pleaded on the verge of jumping out of her being in an out-of-body experience. "It'll be like an acting job." She said it like bubbles. Bubbles with fingernails, against a chalkboard.

The lines of grievance on Madison's face reappeared. She swallowed her frustration and repeated the brief overview to both of them while already missing Tanya and noting to herself to suggest five girls to Ronnie, to bring another girl she can trust. "Remember guys, we can't tell anybody about what we have planned. If anybody else besides us knows about this, it could get blabbed to the wrong people. We'll meet up with Ronnie later and you guys can meet him, and we'll go over the plan in more detail." She repeated, with special emphasis toward the fifth wheel of the project. "We can't tell anybody what's going on with this. Don't. Tell. Anybody." Randi nodded, and Madison hoped to heaven that she was committed to following simple instructions.

Ronnie picked out a seat near the middle of the bar while Madison cleaned up her empty tables and made sure the last remaining occupied table was satisfied. She noticed where he sat and took notice it was close to the same seat he took the last time he showed back up into town and reunited with her. That memory flash that was the source of past happiness no longer brought the same happiness in the present, just dull aches of memories. Ronnie drank a Jim Beam and Coke while he waited, and she predicted he would probably have another while they both waited for the other girls to arrive.

She dropped off the two draft beers to the table and took her place beside Ronnie, who was just receiving his second Jim Beam and Coke. *Right on time*, she thought and sat down.

When the lunch shift bartender walked out of earshot, Ronnie started.

"So, you've got the other girls? And you gave them an idea o what we've got cooked up?"

"Yes and yes. I only gave them a brief rundown; I don't even know the details yet. And yes, they are on their way. They should be here any minute. How much money do you think we could get out of this?"

"I've read about lawsuits similar to this at corporate restaurants. They have been anywhere from a hundred thousand to half a million before the lawyers cut their share out of it. How many girls do you have coming?"

"Three. What would you think about brining on another girl, have a total of five?" Madison was thinking of Tanya; she would feel better brining on at least one more girl besides Karla she could feel was really on her side.

"The more heads we have, the bigger the chance that two of them are going to clash. Let's keep it to a minimum, four girls. Besides, more people involved is gonna mean a smaller share all around. Do you get along with all these girls?"

A vision of Eve flashed in her mind. "Yes." Not entirely an untruth spoken; Madison and Eve were not BFF's by any means, but were not constantly clawing at each other, either. Although there have been tense moments on busy nights when the two stressed servers nearly broke through the status quo. "There they are."

Ronnie looked in the same direction as Madison at Eve and Randi, who entered from the side door, followed by Karla. Ronnie tossed his debit card on top of the bar receipt. "Let's get started."

Madison made their introductions to Ronnie in the order of their arrival. Randi beat out Eve to be the first, marching forward and sticking out her hand in larger-than-life gesture. Before she could babble at high volume, he stopped her short. "Tone it down. Let's not make it a party for everyone to notice." "Right," Randi agreed, all serious business and in a voice barely above a whisper. Eve and Ronnie exchanged smirks and nods. And Karla was brief and bare minimum cordial. "We've met already. So what are we doing here, Ronnie?"

"I need a few good girls to beat some sense into me."

Karla showed the first remnants of a smile for the meeting. "You can count on me," she replied.

"Count me in, too," Eve contributed. By now the snicker chorus achieved mezzo-forte.

Ronnie could not help but relax his lips into a smile at the enthusiasm to get on board. "Yes ladies, that's my plan and that's where you girls come in."

Karla saw Samantha return with Ronnie's card and receipt and got her attention. "I'll be back there to relieve you in a few minutes." Samantha was satisfied and gotten rid of. "So what exactly do you need from us?"

Ronnie made a quick look to ensure Samantha was out of earshot before proceeding. "We will need to get together and practice this ass kicking. This will work as long as nobody knows the ass kickers and the ass kickee are staging the whole thing, but it has to look believable. If we work together, we can pull this off. We need to pick a night to rehearse. Let's try for a night with a rowdy crowd. We need to make sure a lot of versions of this get out on video. For safe measure, we need to make sure the security camera films it, too," Ronnie said as he shifted his thumb to the camera pointing back at them, then gestured his head toward a spot behind the girls. "So we need to start the scene there, by your server station at the end of the bar, where the security camera is pointed at."

The vision of a dreadful day in the near future flashed in Madison's head. "There's a MMA night in two weeks. We could do this on that night."

Ronnie tapped the bar with two fingers like he was playing Blackjack. "That would be a perfect night. This incident will fit right in on a night like that."

"Um, Ronnie," Randi sputtered, an arc of concern sparking in her face.

"I always work the bar on those nights, so I know I'll be on the schedule," Karla said.

Ronnie replied, "Nice, so we know you'll be close when this takes place. We'll just have to make sure everyone puts themselves in a position to see and know when it's going to happen. But we have plenty of time to work on that."

Randi slightly but quickly took on a clammy demeanor. "Ronnie?" she tried again. She reached over to tug at his shirt sleeve but he did not notice.

Eve interjected. "So how much money exactly are we talking about? How much are you trying to get in a lawsuit?"

"Enough," Ronnie replied with a smile. Everyone smiled, except Randi.

"Hey guys?" Everyone finally heard Randi and turned to her. "You said we're not supposed to be seen together?"

"It would be a good thing for us to play it safe in public," Ronnie answered.

Randi trepidly gestured to the security camera. "Maybe we shouldn't be sitting right here, in front of the camera." A blanket of tension and concern layered the middle of the bar. Ronnie stepped up to dispel it. "That would be a good idea, wouldn't it?" He addressed Randi and Eve. "You guys are pretty smart. I'm glad we got you on the team. Let's move this to the back." The security camera filmed the newly formed team as they migrated toward the back of the restaurant.

1

Ronnie was staying at an extended stay motel located at the edge of Charlotte, just a few miles outside of the county line leading to Cannon. The Paradise Plus Extended Stay. It was anything but, definitely not the flashiest establishment known to man by any means, but was typical of where he would be staying in town temporarily. Considering he was still unsure how long he was planning to hang around after this plan was pulled off – if or when they pull it off - a place like this with no lease, furnished with old, cheap furniture that would serve its purpose for the next few months was the easy choice for Ronnie to make.

He had only been in his unit for about a week and was invisible to most of the tenants, showing his face only by chance and accident, save for the short bump-ins and brief evening conversations with Larry Helms, a Decatur, Georgia man in town for construction work, and Ronnie's neighbor until the construction work dried up.

Larry had stopped and talked to Ronnie a few times, usually for a beer and quick conversation before a quick shower and six hours sleep before doing it all over again, but never with company until today. Larry found his door key as he stood by the front door to greet Ronnie and his female entourage. "What do you say, Ronnie?"

Ronnie returned the greeting with a handshake leading the way. "Same as always, guy. Livin' the dream and makin' shit happen any way I can." He conducted a roll call of the group, starting with, "Madison, this is Karla over here. And the two in the back are Eve and Randi." The girls each took their turns being affable to Larry, Eve and Karla a little less than Madison and Randi. While Randi's cordiality consisted of the typical babbling which could have gone on for an hour if she was not stopped, Madison interjected as casually as possible without hurting Randi's feelings. Madison extended her hand and shook Larry's. "It's nice to meet you." She took notice of his cartoonish ship tattoo on his forearm and just knew on a hunch Larry must have been in the Navy, probably his very first tattoo he had to rush out and get right after boot camp.

"Where did you get this tattoo, Larry? It looks like you've had it for a while." Larry pointed to his tattoo and proceeded to tell the girls he got it in the Navy in Great Lakes, Illinois right after boot camp. Madison nodded and smiled, at his story and at her own cleverness.

Ronnie pointed in reference to Larry's dirty shirt and extremities. "It looks like you took a beating out there today."

Larry could laugh now that the work beating was over, as much as his energy level would dictate. "You can put it that way. I'm as tired as a damn dog. I might have enough energy to get a shower in before bed, but that's all I got left tonight."

"Keep doing what you gotta do, man. We shouldn't be too long. We'll keep the noise down and not disturb you too much." Ronnie knew Larry leaves early in the morning and comes home late, sometimes as late as in the evening, so he tried to keep the noise level to a minimum whenever possible for him. He felt a wave of sympathy for the guy, accompanied by a chill when Larry's day long pilgrimages reminded him of his past attempts at making an honest living, and the measures he was willing to try in order to avoid them in the future.

In the years since Ronnie first left the Charlotte area, he pursued entrepreneurship in ways legal, illegal, and dancing on a fine line in between: breaking and entering while freelancing as a swimsuit model photographer for non-swimsuit models, forgery and uttering while trying to sell products through an Amway knockoff company, obtaining property by false pretenses while harassing everyone he met in an attempt to get them in a pyramid scheme that involved buying prepaid gift cards.

He looked back at his shady ventures and fondly recalled the time he and his two buddies up in Hampton, Virginia, who got their hands on a list of public schools around the country and talked a small percentage of the school secretaries into agreeing to buy school supplies from them, the catch being the prices were deceptively high; when the price for boxes of pens were two dollars each, they were invoices for two dollars per individual pen. They had to deal with return calls and returns of the supplies, but some paid the invoices fearing facing the embarrassment of their coworkers and hoping they did not get fired for the mistake, and Ronnie wondered how they could have fallen for it in the first place. But as long as there were unwitting suckers to fall for cons, then people like he and his bygone buddy Eric were able to make money to get by.

His business ventures usually failed not long after they started, and he eventually had a falling out with Eric, but he had a multistate misdemeanor criminal portfolio to show for it in the end.

At times, he had attempted an honest living when his record would not hinder his chances. Those pursuits usually secluded him in the rear of a restaurant in a dishwashing room in between manual labor construction jobs, and he could not continue being honest unless he was willing to continue getting his hands dirty and calloused or so clean and washed they were worn and withered after too many shifts. In times like those, when he would think of the direction in which his life was headed while he counted the calluses on his hands, he figured the direction he was headed reminded him of the corner of a room with many locked doors, regardless of the direction he took.

Very little introspection was necessary for him to come to the conclusion that it just made more sense to keep his hands clean in the pursuit of happiness.

The girls claimed seating plots in the living room facing Ronnie while he got his visual aids together by the kitchen counter, Eve on the left side of the couch, Madison on the right arm, and Karla in the significant amount of space between Madison and Eve, in the valley between the middle and right cushions. Three of the four declined offers for a beer – Randi accepted, to the surprise of Eve; Rand never drinks beer when the two are out drinking. Randi sat on the floor between Eve's feet and took a sip of beer, immediately laboring to squelch her sour face.

"Do you even like beer?" Eve whispered through a bemused smile.

"I was just being nice."

"Give me that." Eve would not let any drink go to waste.

Ronnie held in his hand a strike zone chart of the body he was able to find on the internet from a police department baton handbook high enough for the girls to examine clearly. It displayed a front and rear view of an anatomically inoffensive man with different areas of his body colored green, yellow, and red, and was sufficient enough to display the areas of his body he wanted the girls to avoid.

"I want to make sure I go over this with you girls, and make sure you know where not to kick me at when we do this." He held up the chart. "Do your best to keep your kicks in the green spots. Try your best to avoid any of these yellow areas, but we don't want it to look too faked or staged, so if you move away from the green areas, move to the yellow areas. Whatever you do, make sure you do not kick me in any of these red spots." As he dictated, he directed with his free hand along the chart. First, when discussing the desire for the kicks to remain in the green areas, he directed his hand along the arms and legs on the figure, minus the elbows and knees, which he included among the yellow areas along with the chest, collarbone, and abdominal area. He paid extra emphasis on the red areas: the head, solar plexus, spine, tailbone, and kidneys. He then directed the focal point back to the groin area on the chart in a plea to the girls as to where he did not want to be kicked when he is attacked that night. The girls reflexively giggled at his concern.

They moved the coffee table out of the living room to make space so that they could try practicing his concocted scenario. Ronnie laid on the floor in a state that was halfway to the fetal position, facing in the direction of where Madison was standing. "Madison, I'll position myself this way after you hit me. I figure the next one on the scene will be Karla, since she'll be behind the bar," he said as he motioned behind himself to his left. "Am I right?"

"That would be correct." Karla gave an underachieving performance pretended to fling herself over an imaginary bar and positioned herself behind him at the small of his back. Ronnie twisted his head to see where she ended up at and stiffened. "If you're gonna take that place, watch where you kick me. Don't kick me near my kidneys!"

"I won't," she said. Madison took one look at Karla and could tell she was not absolutely committed to making the effort in sparing Ronnie any pain. She met eyes with Karla and mouthed 'Don't' as they both held giggles hostage with pursed lips.

Eve stood beside Karla, taking the position that covered the rear side of his upper body, and Randi assumed the last remaining section, Ronnie's lower front. His eyes met Randi's worried face and matched it. "Please be careful, honey," he began as a preliminary plea. She did not possess an A-game face for him, and the best she could give him was a bite on her lower lip to suppress her uncertainty. "I'll do my best." He forged ahead like a worried champion. "As much as I would like you girls to completely fake it, you're going to have to kick me hard enough to make it believable."

They refrained from making any real contact that night, and just practiced going through the motions for about ten minutes before Ronnie called an end to the first practice night and got to his feet. "We can meet here and go over this several more times before we do this for real. We can work on making a little contact in the next practice. But that's basically it, except for Madison's first strike." He took her hand. The official, instructional manner in which he took her hand shifted to a hold of a more intimate demeanor, fluidly, although inexpediently. "You're going to hit me here with the palm of your hand, on my brachial plexus origin." He shaped her hand into an open palm position and moved it along the side of his neck, while she could feel her tall standing guard against the past become pliable to relapse. "You can stick around if you want and we could practice this one for a while."

Madison could practically feel the heat from Karla's eyes on her brachial plexus origin. "I could stay for a bit," she said with a tin shield of confidence and a wavering steadfast that the overtime was strictly for professional reasons. "This one's going to have to be the best looking shot of the night. I'd better make sure it looks good." She thought she sounded convincing enough. Still, she could feel the flush in her face and avoided immediate eye contact with anybody as she evaluated her heart.

Ronnie ushered the other three girls to the door. "Does everybody want to meet here the same time on Wednesday?" There was a consensus on the date, time, and location. Eve and Randi exited down the upper tier walkway, while Karla said good night to the remaining two in the room. "Don't study too hard. Be safe, Maddie," Karla bade with a slight mock in her tone at Ronnie's pet name before turning to leave. Madison understood her subtext, and it was not too complex for Ronnie to decipher as well. He closed the door with a stone faced farewell just as soon as she turned to leave.

"Don't call me that," Madison stated in a preemptive strike, a declaration that the pet name lie dead in the former.

"Sir, yes sir." The prickly heat he felt on his face matched the heat he envisaged coming from the condom in his pocket to his right hip. He took his mark in front of her and lined up her striking hand along the side of his neck. She recoiled and swung her hand back toward his neck. He blocked it and grabbed it, both hands paused in mid air as he gently touched hers before letting it go, and her pliability disappeared for a moment.

"We can't have the attack just happen out of nowhere. There's going to have to be some kind of argument or disagreement first."

His nonchalance fueled her pliability to recoil in force. "Terrific," she said. "How about we talk about why you ran out on me two years ago."

Ronnie matched her stance, and the two found themselves in that familiar standoff which always soon cultivated into an off-again status. "I didn't just run out on you."

"So you ran out on everyone again. How does that make everything better?"

Ronnie turned and walked away before his emotions showed. "Don't start this now. It's just going to get in the way of what we need to get done."

Madison followed him down the hallway and to the bathroom doorway, and watched him watch himself in the bathroom mirror. "When are you going to tell me, if you can't tell me now?"

"I'll explain afterward."

"Am I going to be standing alone while I'm waiting for 'afterward' again?"

The answer would not escape him, and Ronnie continued to lock his gaze into his own eyes.

"Tell me."

"My dad died." He cut his answer through the silence, not breaking his stare-down in the mirror, not getting himself worked up.

The news softened Madison's face and left her momentarily dumbstruck. "When did that happen?" she asked in a daze. She already had a hunch at the answer. "Two years ago. That's why you left." She returned to the couch and sat wondering how she couldn't have known or seen a mention of his death in the paper. It was possible there was no obituary, or one small enough to hide from eyes not seeking it. And who was she trying to kid? For years she had made an unconscious habit of avoiding the obituaries for fear of running into her father in print. Ronnie stopped by the refrigerator to pick up two beers on his way to a seat on the couch beside her. "I wish I would have seen something in the paper and known what had happened," she muttered as she took one of the beers and took the first sip. "You could have said something instead of running off."

"I know. We didn't get an obituary in the paper. I had to get out of town right after dealing with everything and get myself together." He lied. He wasn't ready to replay the moment.

Madison leaned her weight against his shoulder and didn't protest when his hand found hers to interlock fingers in the moment of support. She knew he did not get along with his father and could remember the times she went to or even near his house and witnessed the arguments and confrontations. Sometimes, the shouting castigations escalated into one or both bodies shoved against the wall in the darkest of times.

"I should have said something before I left but I was pretty messed up."

"Don't, Ronnie. We're bringing up stuff that we don't need to revisit. Let's just say they happened in the past. Mistakes have been made..." She tapered off, and Ronnie got the feeling to let it be just as it was, in the past and hopefully forgotten, if only temporarily.

He wrapped his arms around her as the memories of their times together poured in. It was elation similar to all the other times he had her in his life again, all the easy moments: the first time their eyes caught each other, the unions at their reunions, the look of happiness on her face when he would surprise her at

Lovelee's upon each of his returns, the times they laid in bed after lovemaking while he brushed back her hair and talked to her about their promising future.

It was not many moments later when his lips searched for hers. When his lips found and brushed across hers, she pushed him away, just enough to let him know there were just as many events of affliction in their history.

"You still have feelings for me, don't you?" asked Ronnie, clearly taken aback by her reaction. "I'm sorry for being gone for so long. I told you that."

Madison got up from the couch and Ronnie followed. She faced him again with a relaxed posture without giving up the barricade between them. "Of course I feel for you. I have some feelings for you, but things are different now. I can't just keep waiting for you between these money grabs, whenever you decide to show up again."

"So what's different now? Is there another man?" It was a query not usually asked by him on his journeys back into town.

Her eyes drifted from his awaiting gaze. "Not right now, but there have been. There will be when you're gone again." Her remark tumbled to a mutter, and she felt her heart cramp up.

His gaze loosened and he finished his beer. "Are you getting tired of me coming back around?"

Madison took his empty beer bottle and set it on the table next to her nearly full bottle. She stood next to him and let him wrap his arms around her. "I'm getting tired of you leaving." She reached around his body in a full circle.

"What if I do something about that?"

"Don't make propositions you won't be able to keep."

Ronnie gently unlocked his arms from the hug and created enough space between them to reach into his pocket and pull out his condom. "I could try." His answer did not surprise her; she was used to hearing every line in his standard playbook. He was prepared for hearing another segment of protest at his actions when she took the condom out of his hands.

"Can I trust that you haven't picked anything up in your travels?" she asked.

"I'm clean," he answered. He was not prepared when she tossed the condom to the end table.

She had business of her own, but was putting their business to the side and hoping it would not be another bout of regret in the end.

8

The girls made it through to the end of another work week. Madison, with Randi flanked to her left, scanned the recently posted schedule for the next week, the work week that mattered. There were times when the work schedule seemed to Madison to be a fateful lot in the servers' lives; position it one way or the other and it shows itself to be either a strange mystery or a cruel joke; when she and a clique of her favorites want to work together, some or most are off that night; when an eventful night of debauchery is seen past the horizon, some or most are on the schedule.

Frown marks materialized as Madison studied it more closely. *You've got to be kidding me!*

Karla, predictably, was scheduled to work the bar for the Saturday night showdown. But Madison, Randi, and Eve all had the night off. She swore to herself this place must have ears, some insider toad planted to ruin any plans. Or just dumb luck, she guessed.

The schedule took up the center of the bulletin board after spending close to three years of living left of center, making room for Leanna St. John's memorial, her picture framed on either side by newspaper articles narrating her disappearance, the ongoing search for her, and the trial of her alleged murderer. The memorial turned her stomach every day she had to see it before going to work and before going out to the parking lot when she was done. It was displayed until Madison took it down herself when no one was looking and put it to rest in the trunk under the bed with the rest of her keepsakes.

Madison returned to the present with Randi McIntosh flanked to her left. "We're not on the schedule," Randi muttered the obvious to her. "None of us, except Karla. We have to be on the schedule for Saturday night."

"I know that. Bob is working tonight. Let me talk to him and see what I can do." She said this with a tone which suggested she would rather have had the task of cleaning the toilets in the men's room.

Madison stood to the side of the manager's office to negotiate a change in the Saturday schedule lineup. She watched Bob Baucom as he cashed out the other servers from the lunch shift: slightly overweight in the midsection and slightly underweight on the scalp, misaligned, beady eyes, which he respectively balanced out with a large, loose fitting shirt and overgrown, combed-over hair and silver framed glasses. As his eyes occasionally diverted for speedy intervals off the paperwork to get a subtle glimpse of her hips, Madison mused and wretched inside at his open perversion and pondered if there were any pedophile alerts in the area that might match his description, but pushed it aside when he finished with the others' paperwork and looked up at her at a level that passed for eye level, but kept her breasts in his peripheral vision. It would have to suffice, because at least now she had his attention and an important agenda to push ahead with.

"I know you usually work MMA nights. We were just changing things up a little and want to put some of the new girls out there to see if they can handle it."

"So you take experienced servers off the schedule and throw newbies out there?"

Bob scowled and absentmindedly eyed the vicinity of her chest as he chided. "I figured you would be thrilled to have one of those nights off for a change."

"I need to work that night. Can you make it happen?" Madison could tell he was frustrated and wanted to deal with as little as possible, which led her to believe it was a 'business as usual' day for Bob. *He's such a wimp.*

Two girls showed up to be cashed out while they were talking, and Bob hated to do favors such as this in front of the other girls because he did not want to cause a floodgate to be opened of others wanting favors done as well. They quieted about the matter as he finished the other two cash-outs.

The phone interrupted Bob's train of thought with its ringing. He tried to ignore it but couldn't. Madison could see his temperament stirring and offered what she could to help the situation. "The phone's ringing, Bob."

He tried to concentrate on his sales figures. "That's what the sound means. Answer that while I do this."

Madison considered her opportunity at teamwork in the office that night as she gazed at Bob's reddish tinge of the back of his neck. "I'm not trained for office duties at Lovelee's."

Bob reached the pinnacle of frustration and looked at her. "You're not trained for the phone?"

The staring contest commenced. Bob lost; he answered the phone as the girls giggled behind him. He fidgeted his way through a phone call which amounted to a ridiculous request for minimal knowledge and the cashing out of the two servers before addressing her with the return of silent grievance to his face.

"I guess I can add you on the roster and give the new girls less tables. Just keep an eye on them and make sure they can handle it."

Madison remained in the office when Bob thought the meeting was supposed to end, and both took their time to be the one to break the awkward silence.

Bob capitulated and rolled his eyes. "What else do you need, Madison?"

"I need two other people to work also."

Bob became frustrated at the extended request, and Madison was entertained with his tantrum. His frustrated state consisted of holding in his temper while remaining quiet and stewing over what was perturbing him. His face mulling over the schedule appeared that his breathing was on the verge of stopping. *Just write a couple more names on the schedule, you damn sissy.* Madison stifled her laughter, muting it as to not have Bob lose his concentration as he eyed the schedule. His labored fit almost made Madison regret tormenting him, but surely not enough to keep her from giving this a shot. He gave up on the schedule and set the completed cash-out paperwork beside the computer. "I don't know what to tell you on that. You're just going to have to find two working girls to switch with."

One spot was easy to remedy; Madison saw that Oakley Moore was scheduled to work that night, and she absolutely hated MMA nights. Within minutes, three problems were reduced to one. All that was left was for Randi to find someone to work for that night. Madison believed in hope that week in a spasm of naïveté that a problem left to Randi to fix would be resolved.

Madison watched the early morning minutes transpire from a horizontal position on Ronnie's bed. She felt one of his arms under her pillow and the other arm draped over and around her waist, and smelled the faint remnants of the Polo Blue cologne he wore the night before, just enough to be detected and bring back memories of the habit f falling back into his arms which took place several hours ago. The scent of that cologne had been on Ronnie for as long as Madison had known him and accompanied many memories she had of him for better or for worse.

The early morning was Saturday, the Saturday where everything was set to happen. She wrapped her hand around the hand of his arm that was wrapped around her waist, feeling those feelings she used to feel before everything fell apart, and wondered if she would be better off suppressing them before she got in too deep emotionally once again, or just relaxing and enjoying the serenity of the moment, which was in danger of dissolving from the loose end which dangled in front of them.

"Everyone's on the schedule for tonight. Everyone except Randi, of course. She's had several days to get somebody to give her their shift. She's come up with excuses, but I think she's just scared to push any of the girls when she asked them. It's not nearly as difficult as asking someone to work for you, especially on a weekend night, not to mention one of these fight nights."

Madison would have asked Eve to help out, but Eve took a week off to visit family in New York, triggering a wave of anxiety throughout the group. She claimed a death in the family, a second cousin. They were already getting enough of that with Randi. She was probably just using it as an excuse to take a week off of work, and Eve assured everyone before she left that she would be there Saturday night. No one had heard from her yet, not even Randi.

Ronnie cracked a smile and fanned the flames. "I'm sure it's all Randi's fault and you couldn't try any harder to do it yourself."

She twisted toward him and bantered with words and jabbing playfully around his blocking attempts. "I was working lunch shifts all week. And I did ask a couple of the new girls. Jennifer is worried she won't get as many days next week if she takes off days when she's scheduled. I told her not to worry about that, but she still said no. And I asked Tanya, but she wants to work." The mention of Tanya was the dreadful remedy to her serenity that Saturday morning. *Tanya...If only I had asked Tanya before Randi jumped on board. Oh well, we work with what we've got.* She stopped sparring with him and tugged at his necklace. She always loved his favorite piece of jewelry, the yin yang pendant attached to his necklace. The only material worth was a push back from the pawn shop counter, but to Madison it held emotional value; it reminded her of the more jubilant times in their relationship. She tried more than once to obtain it, but Ronnie believed in the power of its good luck in his life, although there was not an abundance of it to show for the effort. He rebuked her repeated requests and knew another was coming at that moment.

"No," he answered her preemptively.

"I didn't even ask you yet."

Her fit of sulk did not deter him. "I already know what you wanted. I can't walk the world without it. You know I need my lucky weapon."

She exhaled a pout as she resumed her original position. He could foresee the smirk on her face from the back of her head and knew she would be determined to ask again in the future. When his arm held her by the waist, she returned her hand over his hand again and kept it within an inch from a tender moment for an instant. Her hand jerked away, almost as if his hand was a burner on a stove. She slipped it back under the pillow. "We've got another plan. Don't worry. We will all be working on Saturday."

The alternate plan for the night was to have Randi show up in uniform to work, thinking she was on the schedule that night and hoping the manager would let her stay on for the night. Randi was scatterbrained enough for this plan to be believable.

Ronnie grabbed a card from the dresser and handed it to her. "Here's a name and number to some feminist group in Charlotte. If you end up having any problems at work after we do this, give them a call. Any press we can get going our way will help out." She took the card and tossed it with her stuff on her side of the bed.

Madison acquiesced and wrapped her hand over the top of his hand as they lay in the spooning and waiting for the sun to make its daily grand entrance, and he reached over with his free hand and gently brushed through her hair at her temple. He knew this had always made her feel at ease. She hoped for a few hours of regeneration by dreaming of the past with the fragments of somberness blinded from the storyline.

She could not quite place the pinnacle moment when everything did begin to fall apart. It was mostly miniscule actions and mistakes and slight gut feelings that grated thin layers from the surface while she had always clung to the core. When Madison's mind wandered in the search once again, she knew once again the dream was doomed to slow ruin. She sighed and contoured her right side to the terrain of the pillow and mattress.

She stumbled into the past and again faced that one memory which stood out among the collection of ache inducing events in their past: the time she got pregnant. It had been close to three years ago from the time she lay on that bed once again letting the past gnaw at her mind one cell at a time.

He appeared yet again in town four months ago and was up to business as usual the night it happened. Ronnie was usually Boy Scout prepared when it came to having the rubber in the wallet when needed. This night turned out to be one of those exceptions, but both sides gave up part of their responsibility to Jim Beam and Anheuser-Busch. The mediocre performance on both sides would have made for a forgettable sexual experience and would have quickly faded from Madison's memory had it not been for the cramping and nausea that anchored the moment in the weeks ahead. She stayed positive and went on with life, until the twelfth of the month came and went without a period to show for it.

When she failed the test, she decided it was time to tell Ronnie what they did. She just told him, with no buildup to the climax. She was certain he would handle the news the same way no matter how it was delivered.

"I'm pregnant." The next few seconds of time stretched for an eternity as she waited for his response.

"Are you sure? Did you take the test?"

Are you freaking kidding me? Some things never change, I guess. "Yes, Ronnie. I took the test and it was positive."

It took a little effort for him to kick start his enthusiasm. "Well, wow! That's terrific, sweetie. I guess it is unless you're... Have you decided if you're keeping it?"

Once the words of her pregnancy left her lips, she studied Ronnie's face for his true reaction under his words. His uncertainty and worry pounded at his excitement from the inside. It was the exclamation point in her final decision. "I'm still in college and I need to finish. Then I'll be able to give a child a more stable environment. I can't have a baby right now." It seemed to be the best direction for her to proceed, amplified by the disconcerted look on Ronnie's face as he tried his best to oversee their future.

She told Karla what had happened and had her drive her to the clinic, while she told Ronnie to meet her there; her faith in Ronnie taking charge in this situation was lacking.

Karla drove Madison to the clinic and waited with her for Ronnie to show up. After an hour went by and he didn't, she stayed with Madison until she was released.

Ronnie's excuse of a family matter to attend to sounded shaky and lacked substance in his voice, and he and Madison struggled through another six months of a relationship until his abrupt disappearance two years ago.

She broke from her bitter reverie back to the present. "So, what do you have planned while you're home?"

"I'm going to drop in and see Mom. I tried her old number while I was in Florida, but it's disconnected."

"I hope she's OK. Tell her I said 'Hi.' Ronnie?"

"Yeah?"

"You're not worried I didn't have you wear a condom, are you?"

"No, it's fine." Doubt and uncertainty edged the tone of his voice. "You're on the pill, right?"

"Yes. I'm covered." She was not covered. She stopped taking her pill yesterday. She also had a plan in the works.

The girls working the Saturday night shift gathered in the back section with Will Graham, the assistant manager for the night. Madison sat down next to Karla. "Are you ready for tonight?"

Karla smiled back at her. "Not one hundred percent yet, but don't worry; I will be when the time comes."

They were joined by Randi and Eve a short time later. Eve took no time to rub it in to her partners in fraud. "I told you girls I was going to be here. You didn't have to worry about me. Hopefully they don't give Randi a problem about being here."

By the time the nightly rush began to swell, Will saw no problem with Randi being there because Janet turned out to be a no-show. Madison was not able to get a hold of her that week, and figured that was the opportunity for Randi to get on the schedule that night. It was not a big surprise to anyone that night; Janet forgot to show up for her first day of training, arrived an hour late to her third day, and forgot her notes at the restaurant the entirety of her training. It even labored Madison to remember her last name, and now it would not even matter. Janet was off the schedule, and Randi was on in her place.

The given factor in the plan was Karla being at the bar. When the servers got their assignments for the night, the rest of the plan's landscape fell into place: Madison got the row of round tops parallel with the bar, Randi was given one of the sections at the front, and Eve was given one of the sections in the side patio area, but her main section for the night would be in the back with Philip Martinez, as far as Madison could anticipate; She was sure that was where she would be for most of the night, instead of serving her customers.

Madison met with Eve at the food station by the bar. "Just make sure you're hanging out somewhere where you can see here in this area. That's where it's going to take place tonight." Eve ran to the back and found the section between the kitchen and the dishwasher station, by the sink where the cooks washed their hands. Eve peeked through the little opening that gave her a view of Madison at the food station and gave her an O.K. sign in her signature mockery. "Gotcha."

Eve saw Philip and broke her meeting with Madison. "Hey, baby. Remember what you need to do tonight." Philip maneuvered away from the fryers. "I got you, girl." They needed to make sure the incident got on video, and wanted especially to get it captured on the security camera, to ensure a clear version gets recorded. It was going to need to be moved depending on where Ronnie landed. Eve took charge and enlisted the services of Philip. The group was concerned if compensation from the lawsuit money was needed to pay Philip, but Eve had it covered. *I spent the night with him and made sure he was committed to help me out. Trust me, he got compensated with a whole lot more than money.*

Madison stood by the server food station by the bar. She saw Karla in front of her. She knew Eve was on the other side of the wall somewhere behind the bar. She turned to the front of the restaurant, to where Randi was stationed at. Randi saw her and smiled and gave a thumbs-up at her side in an attempt to make the gesture in secret, and Madison smiled back in amusement. The place was filling up fast, the fight was about to start, and all the participants were on their mark with the exception of one of the players, who was on his way and let her know with a text message from the small disposable prepaid cell phone he gave her last week. *It's time*, Madison thought to herself and tried to focus on what needed to be done. Her Cobb salad was ready and tossed in the window. She inspected it with a look of dissatisfaction, and pushed it back to Donny.

"I need more than this."

PART THREE
QUESTIONS

9

Even though it had been two months since the night of their assault performance, Madison still felt an intuitive pleasure when being spotted somewhere in town, like she did on that day while waiting in line at the CVS pharmacy to pick up a bottle of conditioner on her way to work. She suppressed her smirk and pretended not to notice, and would wait to see if the two girls would break from their intimate babble session and approach to say anything to her. They kept their distance by the time Madison paid for her conditioner and the standard few unplanned items which found their way into her arms, so she went on her way to make some money slinging food and alcohol, which has become the residual stream of income lately, considering the other sources that have arrived recently with the girls' spotlight of fame fifteen minutes wide.

Working at Lovelee's did come with the benefit of a sharpened sense of detecting players and their offerings of opportunities of illusory grandeur. When Trevor Presnell told Madison last month he was an associate with Maxim magazine, the girls, with the exception of Randi, instinctively thought that he was full of shit. He was the friend of Marcus Smith, the guy who sent a Facebook message to Randi. But they did some research with the card he gave them, and it turned out that he was legit. He wanted to get one of their photographers into town to do a photo shoot in time for next month's issue. The agreement was made that the girls would meet with Trevor and his photographer that upcoming Friday before work.

Eve and Randi were incredibly excited about the Maxim photo shoot, but the opportunity that intrigued Madison even more was the offer from Jerry Fox, an associate with Us Weekly, to feature the girls in a story for one of their upcoming issues, preferably next week's issue. Their story was already covered briefly when everything went down, but they wanted to return to have the girls give a more detailed account and to convey how their lives have been altered with the advent of the spotlight. He was coming into town to talk to the girls the day before the Maxim shoot. Madison thought it would be a good opportunity to throw in a mention of her marketing degree and desire for a career in that field. *Maybe a company in Charlotte will see it.*

Karla would just as soon forget about any of the magazine endeavors, and just get this scam finished and paid for, and forgotten about as soon as possible.

The girls all agreed on one thing: business at the restaurant since the infamous Lovelee's MMA fight night was much better, especially for the four of them, to the disappointment of the other servers, but to the satisfaction of Kerry Blanchard; he knew what he was doing in keeping them employed. The feminist groups disappeared once the girls got their jobs back, and everyone with a financial interest in the game enjoyed the extra business from the people who came in to meet the semi-famous. And the girls were relishing the extra attention they were getting as they waited out their turn in the limelight before getting their hands on their share of the money from Ronnie's settlement.

All four of them were working on that Friday night following their afternoon Maxim photo shoot. Madison received a phone call from Jerry Fox to thank her and the others for their time the day before for the Us Weekly article, and let her know he gave her phone number to a close friend of his, Amy Reynolds-King from People magazine, who wanted the same time and story they gave to Us

Weekly. Madison satisfied his hopes that they would not mind and would let the other girls know of their next exposure that night.

Karla was busy at the bar, as usual, too busy for all the sensational publicity and hullabaloo, although she did break for a moment every now and then to inhale the atmosphere and take it in. Randi was one step away from exploding into a fit of cartwheels from all the attention. Eve was excited, but not so much as to keep from hiding in the back as to avoid as much customer service as possible. And Madison waded the euphoric limbo from the extra attention and money that was to come more comfortably than the others, showing a majestic display of restraint on the outside; the others did not know about her furtive rendezvous with Ronnie.

Now if she could only get her regulars to cooperate. Her potential for restraint was being tested that night.

"Are you guys going to get anything to eat tonight or just make out with those glasses all night? I'm sure the beers left in those glasses are body temperature, you've been holding them for so long." She was served with a round of laughter from Jimmy Goforth, Kyle Smith, and Waylon Barbee, taking up a round-top table in her section on a busy night, as much a fixture at Lovelee's as the multicolored globe string lights which adorned the ceiling.

Jimmy imitated a swooning fan. "Ain't you that star from the YouTube? I saw you in Maxim magazine."

Madison laughed with the others, but hers was blended with feigned annoyance. "You didn't see me in any Maxim magazine yet. We just did the shoot today. Where are your life partners tonight?"

"Darrell has to work all night at the high rise," Waylon bellowed. "I told him he should be sick tonight and use his sick leave time. He can't take that with him if he leaves that place down the road." Waylon seemed to know a lot about administrative procedure at other peoples' jobs for someone who is chronically unemployed. "And Steven is just being a pussy. Says he's got bills to pay."

"You watch your filthy mouth," Madison teased. "Why don't you wash it clean with a fresh beer?"

Jimmy stepped up to the plate. "Yeah, it's about time for another one. I've got this next round, baby doll. Put them on mine." The others did some swooning of their own with a reaction of gratefulness.

Madison matched pitch of gratefulness with the chorus. "It's about time." She grinned and winked at Jimmy. "I will be right back."

She put the order in and waited for the drinks at the end of the bar. Karla was incredibly busy, clearing pitchers and glasses and filling pitchers and glasses and washing pitchers and glasses at a expeditious pace, but not so busy to take the time to blow a friendly kiss to her friend as she laid the drinks in front of Madison.

Life was good to her in this frame of her life. She had reached the point where she was comfortable with the excitement encompassing her life, not expecting that it would actually get better until it happened just moments later when she locked to a pair of green eyes coming through the front door.

Green eyes, good looking face, Joe Montana. Those were Madison's first thoughts in some sort of daydream-at-night trance. She snapped herself back from a mirage and into reason but the guy was real. He looked older than she, may or may not have made it to forty yet, and a perspective free of bias might determine he looked more like a palette mixed of Joe Montana with a little of Tom Brady, a delight for women from a handful of decades. Nevertheless, he looked enough like Joe to make her daydream of childhood, and of her and her dad's favorite player. And as she scanned him from the neck down, she continued to find nothing to complain about.

She spent much of her early childhood watching and crushing on Joe Montana, her father's favorite football player. She remembered the Notre Dame Fighting Irish and the Washington Redskins being his favorite teams, but he was such a fan of Joe Montana, in a matter of a few seasons Leon Tate's loyalty shifted from burgundy and gold to the scarlet and gold of the San Francisco Fourty-Niners, and so did Madison's just as quickly. Some of her fondest early memories happened on Sunday afternoons and Monday nights, snuggled with her dad on the couch against his worn jersey, enveloped by the static audio of cheering crowds and broadcast commentary.

She had a door sized poster of Joe Montana on the back of her door. Her mother was a bit perturbed by it for a number of years, because it reminded her of the lack of attention she got from Madison due to her love for her dad, and the lack of attention she received from Leon due to his football obsession, among other factors. After he left home, her mother became more and more agitated with that poster, until one night during a big argument she ripped the poster off of Madison's wall. Madison responded by finding a new door sized Joe Montana poster and lacquered it to the door.

The past nine months have been uncomfortable for Madison, the notice of a baby around her wherever she went feeding the void left in her and helping it spread like a cancer inside her womb. She had yet to have her career, but she was ready for the baby in her life before the plan was achieved. Ronnie's return to town gave her the chance to have the baby she could have had when she wasn't ready, one who might look like the two of them, with or without him, most likely the latter.

However, she could not pass up the opportunity that entered her life that night, the man she thought she would encounter only the dreams of her childhood as well as her adulthood, and the chance to get into his genes.

The dream she was scoping sat at a two top table in her section. *OK, get yourself ready.* Her former paranormal euphoria was replaced with the emotional enigma in the form of a fever running in the core of a chill enveloping her body. *What's with the jitters, girl? Nothing to be nervous about.* Her head rationalized with her heart as she approached; this was a weird feeling for her. *Do your job first, and fish for a pleasure opportunity before he leaves. He's a horny bastard like the rest of them.* The plan looked easy on her emotional drawing board.

As she walked closer to the table and their eyes locked to each other, she could see the differences in his appearance. *OK,* she thought, *he didn't look exactly like a dead ringer Joe Montana, but he looked damn close enough.* Enough to make her smile. By the time she made it to the table, the only part of him she could fixate on was his green eyes. Just like her dad's.

"Hey, new guy. How are you tonight?" She fished for a smile with one of her own, and made a catch. "What's a good guy like you doing in an overpriced dump like this?"

"Let me find out who's spreading those rumors about me."

She giggled. "Is this your first time at Lovelee's?"

His smile widened a bit. "So far, so good. And no it isn't, good looking. Just my first time at this one. They'd better not catch you around here with that 'overpriced dump' talk."

"Aw, they love me around here. They'll never get rid of me." Madison felt a little lightheaded. She slowed her breathing so she did not sound too eager to get to a climax. "What can I get you to drink, handsome?"

His smile twisted on one side into a playful smirk. "Not as much as I would like. I have to work tomorrow morning."

"We'll see about that," she matched in smile and demeanor. "As you can see by my name tag, my name is Madison, and I can't wait to find out your name and story and what you want to start out with. But not too much because you don't want to overdo it tonight, and I always do what I'm told."

She winked at him, and saw by the amused look on his face he caught it and understood. He reached over and held her hand to initiate a handshake. "I'm from Florida, but work brought me here for the next month or so, so right now I live in a hotel in Charlotte. My name is Matt O'Dell, and I would like a Guinness. Did I answer all your questions? We can talk some more when you get back."

Madison's other tables were neglected that night, and they were just going to have to get over it as far as she was concerned. Matt gave her a general overview of his back story over a half eaten plate of hot wings and nearly empty glass of Guinness: he was from Florida, just outside of Orlando; he was an insurance consultant in town to oversee a claim for a client; and he made it a point to ensure his business trips were for business and pleasure. He drank some more of his Guinness, his third one of the night, leaving him one more sip before completion. Madison studied his glass. "Are you ready for another one, Matt?"

"Maybe. Let me think about it." He gave the last waiting sip some thought, and then made it disappear moments later. "You know about my story. I knew about your story when I recognized where I saw your face."

Madison had been getting used to the activities of that infamous night two months ago becoming the topic lately with her guests, but she liked to act more serious about it than she needed to be just to have some fun with some of the guys who came into the place, present company included. "Oh, you do? Tell me about my story."

"Relax you shoulders, pretty girl. You're going to give yourself a headache. I read all about it on the internet. And I saw the video."

She laughed and held his empty glass. "You're fine. How could you not know our story? It has definitely been a ride. We've had people from as far as California come in here to meet us. Of course, the guys from California were also NASCAR fans, so they probably already made plans to come out here and check out the Speedway and Hall of Fame anyway. But they took the time to come in and meet us. It makes us feel like we're a little famous, even if it's not going to last forever."

"So, this guy you ladies had to deal with, was he a regular around here? Did you know him?"

Madison pushed two ways inside, against the force working to retract her smile and against the force pulling her eyesight away from his. Ronnie and the girls were in accord not to meet in public or tell anyone about their meetings to play it safe. Madison and Ronnie were sure to meet more than they should have, so they had to be especially careful because it could spell disaster if the wrong people found out about them. But she knew Ronnie too well; if he had not changed much, then their meetings were only going to last as long as it will take to collect the money. So she was going to be available for Matt and procure some more meetings while he was in town, if he was willing. *Maybe even tonight.* She had no plans after work. "He used to be a regular, but he left for a long time. We just started seeing him not too long before this all happened."

"Have you girls had to deal with him any since that night?"

Poker face. "No, we haven't had to deal with him. He's trying to sue this place, with a lawyer telling him not to talk with anybody connected to the restaurant directly, including us."

"How do you know what his lawyer said?" Matt drilled in a fake accusatory manner.

Shocked at how just a few words said to the wrong person could have the caliber to blow the whole game, Madison smiled to hide the ripple she felt up her spine to her face and swatted at his hand. "Shut up. That's how lawyers usually are. They don't want their clients talking with the other side without them present, so they can do all the talking. And that's pretty much what it sounded like when he was talking on the news right after it happened, saying the usual lawyer crap. I doubt he would come back around and stalk us or anything and end up risking his lawsuit. So I'm sure we're not going to have to deal with him again." She performed a cheap levitation trick with his empty glass in a show of salesmanship. "Are you ready for another one, or are you going to sober up on me?"

Matt chuckled and fondled some of the sugar packets on the table. "Maybe I should sober up a little before I have my fifth one."

"It'll only be your fourth one, Joe. Suit yourself." She hit her cue on an oft-reached conversation point with Matt, and they traded smiles.

"So I take it you're referring to Joe Montana?"

"So I take it you hear that a lot."

"Yes, I hear that quite a bit. I used to hear it all the time, but I don't hear it as much as I used to. It's a shame. I hope these kids remember what a great quarterback he was."

"Like me?" she teased. "He has always been my favorite growing up. He was my dad's favorite player, so he was mine also." She brought herself back up from her pool of sad memories and back to the present agenda of milking his hormones. "He has *always* been hot as far as I'm concerned."

The more she talked to him up close, the more she could pick characteristics of him that that kept him from being a clone for Joe. But he was close enough for her taste. She guessed he was on the near end of the forty year old mark and around six feet tall, maybe a little more.

"How old are you and how tall are you? Just curious."

She threw it out like a hot route pass. He flinched, but maintained his smile.

"I am thirty-nine, and I'm six feet even."

Damn, I'm good at this stuff.

She also noticed his medium build in the shoulders. It reminded her of Ronnie for a flash through her senses, breaking her trance.

That diversion was subsequently broken by a customer service request. "Excuse me, Ma'am. Could I get another beverage when you get a moment, please?"

The request came from Waylon from two tables over, over the empty table between them; the place was emptying out and closing time was getting closer. Madison amused that Waylon could ask so politely. *He is obviously being a smartass.*

"Go take care of them," Matt interjected. "I've taken enough of your time tonight."

Madison started to get up, taking his empty glass with her. "No you haven't. So Matt, are you staying around here with me and having another Guinness?" Matt began to check the time on his watch, and she covered it up. "No, no, no. There's no keeping up with time around here when we're having a good conversation."

"It's late," Matt said as he smoothly moved his hands away. He maintained his smile, but Madison noticed that his leisurely demeanor shifted to one accompanying a preoccupied mind.

She began to give him a pouting face, but shifted quickly to a smile as she called an audible at the line of scrimmage. "You can't leave until I bring the bill." She bolted to her table of regulars as it was Matt's turn to pout.

She grabbed their empty glasses. "Another round of the same? Who's picking these up?"

"How much time do we have left?" Waylon asked.

She smirked. "You know our hours better than I do. We close in twenty minutes, but knowing you guys, you probably won't be leaving for about an hour or two."

"Time for three more pitchers." Steven announced as everyone else at the table whooped in delight, except Madison. She rolled her eyes.

Waylon leaned in for a confidential exchange. "Hey girl, you tryin' to get laid over there?" He asked her, enticing more laughter from the others at the table.

"It's none of your business if I was, nosy," she snapped in jest. "Do you guys want to make it a pitcher this time? Miller Lite pitchers are on special."

"That works. I'll get this one," Waylon said, stepping up at the buzz word of *special*. "Hey Madison, make sure you wear you sponge tonight, or your IOU. Or whatever it is you girls use for rubbers."

The hilarity triggered by Waylon's comment made Madison stretch a smile across her flushed face. She should have known the conversation would not evolve too highly with these particular regulars, but she hoped Matt wasn't picking it all up from a few tables down. "I'll keep that in mind, freak," she said with a smile and a couple of raised eyebrows as she took away the empty glasses. In several moments, she returned with a pitcher and a round of fresh glasses, and a Guinness for her other remaining customer, on the house whether he was up for it or not. She deposited everything but the Guinness. "Here you go. Don't try to drink them too slow, guys."

She received a near consensus of thanks, everyone except Waylon, who felt the urge to rub it in some more. "Wear you sponge."

She mouthed 'Shut the fuck up,' and left her howling drunk regulars to sit back down with Matt, dropping the tray on the empty table on her way there. He checked his watch once again as soon as she placed the pint in front of him. "This one is on me. One more before we get out of here." She wore her best flirtatious grin for him. "I forgot to get your check again."

Matt's lips were caught in the middle of a struggle between his responsibilities and his desires. He wrapped his fingers around the cold beer as he struggled to raise his lips into a smile. "Actually, I have to get going. I have to get up early tomorrow. I didn't expect to stay this long."

"So do I. I have to be back here for a meeting in the morning. And you don't hear me complaining."

Well played, girl, the thought that passed his mind as his lips yielded and flexed to completion. His smile caused her lips to match in reflex.

"Are you sure you have to get going so soon?" she asked while she eyed him in a way that demanded only one correct way to answer.

As she locked her gaze into his green eyes, she tried her best not to seem too desperate and played in her mind the notion that she could leave it to chance that he will find his way back in there, but she knew the chance a man like this was going to make an entrance into this place and into her section and life only a little more often than Halley's Comet, or realistically a Carolina Panthers Super Bowl appearance. Ronnie was still in town, but they had once again reached that ephemeral state that, despite the few intimate nights they had shared together since he had been back in town, floated in the familiar vacuum somewhere between high hopes and future disappointments. The hopes which had a reputation of eluding her lost the feeling of her emotional grip with each spent second of time she stared into that pair of green eyes.

Matt appeared to fidget unsurely in his seat at the gaze of her manager, the gaze fixed squarely on their table. "I think he needs you over there."

She turned around and smiled at him in defiance. It was some new manager named Dave working his first shift by himself. "He'll live. I'll get my side work done in a minute." Then a shot to her regulars. "And your checks are coming whether you like them or not," she said to the sound of mumbled protests. She turned back around and asked him a question laden with innuendo. "How about you? Anything else I can do for you tonight?"

Matt hesitated at the crossroads, and was not sure that, if he did want to make that turn with Madison, it would be best to not make it tonight. He knew it could turn out to be the term that was in the back of his mind, but his restraint managed to keep it there: a stupid decision. It definitely had the potential to be a careless one, a fact known by experience, because he did not have the best history of making the right choice in this department. A woman in Tallahassee, Florida by the name of Ellie Freeman could attest to that.

"What's wrong? Are you thinking about your meeting in the morning tomorrow?"

He appeared to be submerged in deep thought as he played with the rim of his depleted beer glass, or a persona disguised as such that acted as avoidance of what lied ahead.

"I can make up the sleep another day."

Matt was given enough hints from her that, if he said yes, Madison was making no plans on sleeping much tonight either, if at all.

Matt emptied the rest of his glass and gently pushed it into Madison's hands.

"Does this mean you would like another Guinness, kind sir?"

He chuckled. "You're about to close."

"How about one more with your check while you wait for me?"

Matt nodded. For the next several hours, he nodded to everything. He finished his beer and she finished her closing side work. He nodded to her invitation to a conversation in the parking lot, where her eyes eventually invited his lips to taste hers, and he nodded to that as well. Before long, a two-car motorcade could be seen headed toward Charlotte, toward Matt's motel room.

Matt had left his air conditioner running full blast while he was out. He noticed the temperature change as he held the door for Madison. "It's not too cold for you is it? I can turn it down."

"It's not going to matter in a few minutes." She grinned in anticipation of the coming few minutes, and how the warmth of the two bodies together will negate any frigidity in the room.

He emptied the contents of his pants and placed it on the nightstand, doing his best to file away the existence of Ellie Freeman.

Madison pulled off her T-shirt and laid it on the dining table as she detoured her own barriers, putting thoughts of Ronnie Stover to the side that night. It had been nice to see Ronnie again these last couple of months as always, but as always the question marks and abrasive memories in time pay their visit whenever he did. And although it was safe to say Matt would not be staying for an extended period of time and might not come back any time soon, at least she knew what she had with him, and what she might want to have of him.

From the contents he designated to the nightstand, he retrieved the condom from his wallet, and stripped himself of his clothing, matching Madison's exposure to him. He handed his clothing to her.

"Would you please put these on the table behind you?"

"Anything you say," she said as she dropped them to the floor. "You're welcome."

Matt embraced her and pressed their bodies together. As Madison connected their lips and revved up her generator, she heard the crackling below as Matt worked the condom package open. "What are you playing with down there?" Madison poked her finger into the center of the ring of the exposed condom, and began tugging it toward her with a mischievous look in her eyes. Matt had been here before, and had the supported bastard child to prove it.

The pheromones had their way of polluting his mind with a toxicity that affected his better judgment; he released the condom to her care, and gave into dancing the number her way with the wishful optimism to make better decisions in the future. They whirled to their landing place of his bed. The condom's destiny was on the floor next to his crumpled up pair of jeans.

Madison walked away from the past wonderful three hours toward her Accord as Matt watched from his doorway. When she reached her driver side door with her keys in hand, she turned around and waved to him to let him know she made it to her car safely. He shifted to a smile just in time to wave back and watched over her getting into her car and back out of the parking space. When she was out of his line of sight and on her way home he relaxed his face back to his worrisome state, wondering if sleep would continue to elude him until tomorrow morning.

She passed by the sign on her way out of the parking lot. *The Westingbrook Hotel, such a fancy name for a dump*, she thought as she turned left. Not that the

Westingbrook was exactly a dump so much as just an overmatched hotel compared to the luxury high-rise towers in the uptown area. Of all the information Madison wanted to know besides the vague details given to her regarding Matt's company, she wondered why they did not want to spend the money to put him up in one of the big luxury hotels, and he explained that they changed the policy to giving him a per diem as opposed to letting him charge everything to a corporate credit card. The move saved them a ton of money, and put more money in the employee's pocket if they were thrifty and frugal enough. Matt was tempted to stay in a roach motel on Sugar Creek Boulevard, and Madison was grateful he decided against it.

She was in the mood for Motown, so she searched her iPod for the ride home soundtrack, reminiscing about the time she spent with Matt, the simple blanket rush of lust and need. It was a break from the convulsions she tolerated from the rare casual date that turned remotely serious, or the swirling of loving memories and past frustrations mixed with the experiences she usually endured with Ronnie during his temporary returns.

Meeting Matt tonight got Madison to thinking about Joe Montana, which subsequently got her to thinking about her dad, and her drive veered into a montage of childhood good and bad. Some of her most vivid memories from her childhood included her dad, the happier ones remaining as clear as crystal, nearly all of them including him or one of her few early childhood friends, like Leanna St. John, the girl who lived in the neighborhood who would become one of her best friends.

They spent many childhood days together during the school breaks in the summer walking two miles from their neighborhood to the nearby Stop 29 convenience store even though their parents did not allow them to do so; *It can't hurt them if they don't know about it*, Madison was fond of saying to her friend. They would sneak out on clear nights to Leanna's back yard, which gave them an open space at which to gaze at the stars. Leanna always talked of growing up somewhere much bigger than Cannon, or even Charlotte, somewhere like New York or Los Angeles, and dreamed of seeing the stars in these dream lands, seeing bigger and better things. Madison always countered with her contentment with her little town and its size. *I can see the stars in Cannon, so what's the point in leaving?* Madison recalled how irritated Leanna could get when she heard her say that or something along those lines. Even though either was hardly old enough to debate on the cities of the world, Leanna had her dreams, and this town was just fine with Madison.

They played every day after school, and every day possible during the summer, until Leanna St. John's family moved away. Madison stayed in a chronic state of tantrum for nearly a month when she got the news. *They all end up leaving eventually, after I get used to them being around.* Leanna got her wish in the seventh grade; her father was relocated to New York to work at his company's corporate office. Her family moved back two years later, and Leanna came back to a new house in one of the newer neighborhoods and brought with her old dreams of singing giving way to new dreams of modeling. She still had a really good singing voice, but being able to see the bustling runway scene in one of the hotbeds of the industry ignited her soul, and she wasn't going to let her petite five feet five inch frame stop her. But work once again pulled Leanna's family back to North Carolina and Leanna away from her Mecca. For now, until high school was over at least, she and Madison Davis were reunited back in Cannon, but the bond was changed; Leanna's drive to increase her class load in order to graduate high school early and to get herself ready for her permanent move to New York to pursue her modeling career did not mesh with Madison's cruise control Cannon life smoothly.

Both got their wishes; Leanna successfully finished high school an entire year early, convincing her parents she was ready to take on New York a few months shy of her eighteenth birthday, and Madison secured her place for a life position in town. Madison was still around – never left - to greet and console Leanna when she regretfully made her return to Cannon carrying the charred remains of her big city modeling dreams with her a little more than a year later. The two became close again quickly, although Madison could not get her to talk much at all about what went wrong – only in a general way regarding 'sleazy, creepy perverts' and 'getting taken advantage of' – and finally accepted Leanna's promise to tell her all the details in time when she was ready to relive it. That time would never come, and Leanna's ghost would linger to reinforce Madison's fear of the unknown of the big city.

Madison had just gotten the call letting her know she was hired at the new Lovelee's restaurant in Charlotte and got her friend to follow suit and apply, hoping she could join her as part of the first wave of servers at the place. By this time, Madison's dad had gone, but she got another part of her childhood back. But within four months grave change and misfortune would rear its ugly head once again in Madison's life, much more so in the St. John family.

Leanna left work one night about three months after the restaurant opened and never showed up again. Were it not for all her belongings still at her parents' house, where she was staying at the time, some would have believed she made a break for one of the big cities again. A search began and continued, and before the belief set in with many involved that she could have been murdered, a suspect was found and indicted while shouting his innocence but Leanna's body was not. Madison took the ordeal with a numb face, and the thought of the assumed fate which met her friend infiltrated the back of her mind every night she had to walk to her car at the end of a closing shift or stop at a gas station afterward, though she tried her best not to let the final memories of her good friend to linger at times she felt nostalgic. She had a way of blurring them and storing them in a way where they did the least amount of damage to her emotions, similar to the way she dealt with the memories of her dad that were not as cheerful and most of her early and current memories of tolerating her mother's good intentions. She chose instead to direct her emotional blinders to the fond memories of Sunday afternoons sitting with Daddy back in the good days watching Joe and the 49ers on TV. Joe Montana was traded to the Kansas City Chiefs in 1993; a move depressingly conjoined with Leon Tate's leaving his wife and daughter. Madison still watched him play with his new team for the final two years, but without her dad there, the moments on the couch in front of the TV lacked the same warmth and electricity.

Sometimes her blinders failed her and her mind drifted to unwelcome territory.

One night about nine months before Leon left his family turned out to be one of Madison's less than pleasant memories of her father that she has had trouble blurring with the rest. She awoke to muffled chatter that started to sound like an argument, followed by a series of bangs and a loud thud. When she opened her bedroom door, her dad met her in the hallway to let her know everything was all right. He picked her up and tucked her back into bed, and kissed her good night while the odor of the alcohol on his breath overtook the aroma of the potpourri on her dresser. She spent the next several days chalking up the occurrence as a dream as best she could, while trying her best to attribute the bruises on her mother's neck to some accident she must have had on another day. Sometimes she could conjure a vivid imagination when she needed to.

Madison had another strange and disturbing dream a couple of years after her dad left which refused to be obscured mentally. She woke up in the middle of the night to sounds in the living room. The bedroom door opened, and she quickly sat up in her bed to the sight of her dad. She thought it was her dad, anyway; it looked like him, but cheeks that were sunk in, and dark circles under his eyes. He came to the bed saying "Don't get up, baby. I can't stay. I just want you to know that I love you...always." Madison laid back down, and let him tuck her into bed. She noticed his twitching and jitters as he tucked her in and wondered if he was alright. It looked like he was really cold in the springtime, and it did not make sense to her.

"I love you too, Daddy."

He gave her a kiss on the cheek, and she could not help but notice the strange and slightly fetid smell emanating from him; he had never stunk like this before, not even on his worst day. He left her bedroom quietly and went back to the living room. She then heard footsteps coming from her mother's bedroom going out to the living room, scrambling in the living room, then the sound of her mother yelling in the front yard out to the street leading to the main road. Madison shut her eyes tightly and went back to sleep.

From the next morning on, she relegated the vision to another bizarre dream, although she could never discard the smell from her memory.

Madison felt the chill and ache in her stomach. She took herself back to Joe at the line of scrimmage under the static of a Sunday afternoon as she and her daddy watched, the scent of beer and Pepsi and the occasional glare from her mother in the air.

Another fifteen minutes of Motown and memories carried Madison to her home. She pulled into her parking space, declaring it time to shut off her emotions as she shut off the ignition, to discard the tribulations of the work night and her trip down Memory Lane. The only scene she kept as she laid down in her bed for a four hour power nap was her meeting a man named Matt O'Dell, and her guess as to how many times she would get to see him again before he was on his way to somewhere else. Like all the other men in her life.

10

The crossing of the plane from the mid-morning heat and brightness, whose light rays reflected off the white lines of the parking spaces into Madison's eyes, into the more tolerant brightness level of and air conditioned environment which awaited her inside the restaurant, was a refreshing welcome on her journey, but not refreshing enough to nullify the aggravation of having to attend a mandatory impromptu meeting at Lovelee's. *Like I don't see this place enough as it is.*

The other girls looked just as ragged and exhausted as Madison; the ones who did not work last night played just as hard until the early morning hours. She only bothered with the minimum of hygiene and hair setting, so as not to seriously offend those around her, but she had to get up a little early to at least wash a few body parts. She was so tired after work, and her meeting after work, that she went straight to bed. If she walked into the place in that state she would probably have been given directions to the nearest homeless shelter. With that visual settled into her mind she made a note to do a load of laundry later and to include her bed sheets because that was a task overdue, especially after this morning. She was not scheduled until five that afternoon, and thankfully did not have to close again that night. That would give her plenty of time to look presentable for that night to hustle tip money and have herself ready in case she scored another meeting with her new friend.

A majority of the crew noticed her entrance. The only greetings which made it through besides the waves were mostly grunts and groans. The only coherent response came from Kerry Blanchard. "Madison, lock the front door so nobody sneaks in before we're ready. We don't open for business for another twenty minutes. We're waiting for a couple more stragglers. We'll open the door for them when they get here."

"Then why don't we wait for the rest to show up before we lock the doors, so we're not locking and unlocking the door for another twenty minutes," she sighed. The giggles at her response showed the first signs of life from the audience.

Kerry was not in the mood to fight her common sense and acquiesced. She discovered someone made the effort to make some tea for the occasion and helped herself to a cup before locating a spot beside Karla.

Before she had a chance to sit down with the rest of the ladies, she heard the door open and felt the slight wave of heat invade their space. Most of the girls joined Madison in looking back at the door.

Matt O'Dell squinted from the light reflection which irritated Madison a mere couple of minutes earlier. Her heart began to beat faster, but then excelled to a thumping when she realized she had not even taken a shower this morning. *Shit! Of all the days I decide to slum it when I have to come into one of these meetings...*

She made her best attempt to covertly fix her hair and was hoping she did not smell too ripe, although it might be a little much to check in detail for odor as she approached the door. There was nothing she would be able to do about it now anyway, so she poised herself as met him in the doorway and remained optimistic he would understand.

"Hi! You're back early."

"Hey, Madison. Long time, no see," he said in a tone mostly cordial with a hint of croon.

"We don't open for another twenty minutes, but I guess you can hang out in the back until we get done with the meeting."

"It's all right. I'm not here for lunch. I'm part of the meeting. I'll talk to you when we're done." Matt carefully phrased his greeting considering this was a surprise she would have appreciated to hear last night, but not carefully enough to keep from altering her smile.

"Sure. I'll be in the back."

Matt knew from her tone that he had some damage control on his agenda after the meeting as they parted ways, Madison to the back of the grumpy bunch of other crew members, and Matt to the front to join Kerry Blanchard, who had been waving at him to come up ever since he walked inside with concern cramping the side of his face at the image of Matt having a private conversation with one of the girls so soon in his visit. Karla, in uniform because she was working the bar for lunch, possessed a newfound urgency when Madison returned to her seat next to her.

"How well do you know that guy?"

"I met him last night. His name's Matt."

"I know," Karla interrupted. "I saw you two together. How *well* did you get to know him?"

Madison should have sensed a reason to be concerned; she was tired as hell from lack of sleep. "Yes, he hung out with me while I was at work. Then we were together pretty much all night." She would usually tell a story like this with a dialect of sexual suggestion that blatantly suggested the obvious, but her confession was altered with a tint of confusion with Matt's unexpected appearance that morning as her brain connected the interlocking edges.

"What did you tell him? About us and Ronnie?"

"Nothing much at all. We mostly talked about other stuff. What's wrong?"

"I heard Kerry telling Bob that someone was coming in from Corporate to talk with us," Karla said as she motioned toward Matt. "That must be him."

Madison was too exhausted and merely worried about her hygiene in the presence of Matt to believe there could have possibly been a problem of the magnitude she was being slapped with at that moment. So it took her the entirety of Karla's response and a couple moments of delayed reaction for the dilemma to register. She continued to look Karla's way, definitely not at Matt, but in a zone, looking at herself sleeping with the guy who might pose a problem for all of them by investigating what they all want kept quiet. "Oh shit." The only strength in her voice lay in the desire to have turned back time, to have turned off the alarm by her bed and slept in for the day.

Kerry spoke over the girls' murmurs, until all the voices subsided except his.

"Let's go ahead and get this started, so those of you who aren't working today can get out of here. I have the feeling the stragglers we're waiting on are no-shows. As you all know, we had a fight about two months ago that gave us a bit of publicity. The corporate office wants to make sure everyone is doing well, and not feeling traumatized from this experience, or any experience such as the one that took place that night.

"The corporate office has someone hired in a position that is in charge of damage control and counseling for such experiences, as well as managing waste, fraud, and abuse. I would like you all to meet Mr. Matthew O'Dell. He will address all of you, and will let you know what he needs from you."

Madison's skin prickled when Kerry said the word *fraud*. And she could tell from Karla's face and posture that enjoyment was not felt her way either. She glanced in the direction of Eve and Randi, and felt surprise mixed with her worry that Eve was not one of the no-shows Kerry was referring to. She figured Randi and Eve spent the night together, and Randi's anxiety of being punished won out that morning over Eve's resistance to authority. Eve glared at Matt's face with a boxer's intensity. Madison felt sorry for Randi and the quiver she imagined happening inside her nerves at that moment.

Matt took Kerry's place in front of the group and some murmuring resumed among the group, mostly from the part of the group of the female persuasion. "Good morning, ladies...and guys," Matt said as he gestured to the kitchen crew and dishwashers, who were standing off to the side, with the exception of Philip Martinez, who was sitting next to Eve, which made Randi visibly irritated. "I am Matthew O'Dell, like Kerry just said. Just call me Matt. I usually don't answer to Matthew unless I'm the one being interviewed." This drew some chuckles from the group, with a specific handful of people noticeably absent of a response. Madison may have been a bit paranoid for thinking it, but she could swear he took notice of the ones who did not find it amusing, especially if those in question may have been hiding something. It was his job.

"The corporate office has given me a job to make sure everyone is happy and doing fine, especially when things don't run normally, and may have caused trauma to any of our employees. I am here to make sure everyone is taken care of, because Ms. Love and Ms. Lee, the two ladies who run things at the top, believe we are all one big family in this company, and we want to ensure no one feels neglected when issues come up that affect us.

"Most of you will not need to talk to me. I just need to talk to those of you who were working the night of August the second, the night of the MMA fight. We have printed the names of everyone I need to talk to, and we will post this on the bulletin board by the manager's office. I'll need to get in touch with you within the next week, but if you see me in here and I am not busy, please feel free to come to me. Thank you for your time."

Matthew O'Dell's smiling eyes and best friend smile served the listeners with the absolute assurance of his support in this time of friction in their figurative corporate family. But Madison Davis was not buying any of what he was selling. That's what she told herself anyway as she reasoned through her scorn.

It's always got to be something, Madison thought as the meeting broke. Everything seemed to be going fine, and then... *Maybe he's not here to try to find a fraud. Maybe he just wants to make sure we are doing well. And after last night...* Who was she trying to kid, anyway? His speech was typical corporate bullshit. *Maybe they were just waiting until the protests and extra business settled, and now they were getting the official paperwork ready to fire us. Or worse.* This caused Madison to give a quick glance to Karla, who was getting the bar ready. Her eyesight caught Matt coming toward her.

"I'm not hanging around this morning. I haven't taken a shower or anything, but I will be working tonight. You can interview me then."

Her irritability at Matt's perceived duplicity was noticeably visible, particularly when she said the word *interview*. Matt's voice assumed a more intimate tone as he sought to relieve the tension between them.

"It's OK. Go home and get some rest. Madison, I should have said something last night, and I'm sorry. We can talk some more tonight, and it doesn't have to be completely about that night."

"Sure. I'm getting out of here."

"Even though I knew you were going to be here, shower or no shower, it was nice seeing you again."

He gave her a warm smile. His comment took her a bit by surprise. Nice. Sincere.

Part of his routine?

"It was nice seeing you, too. I'll be back tonight."

Madison walked away with more questions than answers. *Is my interaction with him going to be a factor with this investigation? How about my continued interaction? Is there going to be any continued interaction? Did he know who I was before he sat down in my section? Is he going to use this interaction to his advantage somehow? Can I use it to my advantage?* She was definitely attracted to him. It was evident, after last night and through her eyes, that he was attracted to her. But, on the other hand, he was there to sniff around in the possibility any wrongdoing had occurred, which there has, a detail he did not need to be invited to discover. She brushed off the feelings that accompanied the fact that it was no surprise, just typical that she would put herself in a situation such as this as she made her exit.

Matt, walking away at the opposite end of the connection, had the wrong answers to questions he already knew. He had a job to do, and was hardly surprised and profoundly disappointed it did not take him long to cross the line. He had better take care to know why he was there, and what he needed to do, and not to get tangled up in a trap with one of the servers. He knew all of this was easier said than done as he saw Madison that morning, after what he did with her last night.

He was still a little shell shocked over the matter of his past. Ellie Freeman. She came into his life back in his days as an officer with the Tallahassee Police Department. She was a transfer from another district, and worked closely with him for a few weeks as she settled in to her new office. The shop talk in between overviews of district- and precinct-specific procedures bled over into lunch break conversation together, where talk of insane stories of the nights she had to work in the county jail to his calls to settle domestic disputes, some of which could be entertaining and interesting, to say the least, to hobbies after work and stories of past relationships. Before they knew it, they were continuing their talks over dinner a few nights a week, with their talks shifting each night in nature that was less and less vocational and much more personal. Matt waited to cross that sacred threshold with a composed shell which threatened to burst at the seams until Ellie granted him permission to release. He released twelve times; he remained confident she did all twelve times as well.

Business during those twelve nights of lovemaking transpired as usual, keeping everything business at the precinct and losing the uniforms off the clock. Until Ellie decided to have a private meal outside of town on one of her nights alone and found Matt having dinner with another woman. She left without confronting him, deciding to tell him at a later time.

He tried to tap into too much of a good thing from too many wells, the reagent he provided producing a psychotic reaction from one of them.

She did not answer his phone calls and waited for work hours for him to get too close to her and let his hands drift where they shouldn't have been when it appeared no one was looking. She erupted in shock and caused a scene, losing her composure and putting on an incredible, emotional performance.

Matt was left dumbfounded and spent the next six weeks under the radar of a sexual harassment investigation, the last three of which he decided to spend his vacation time on and get away. He was told not to attempt to contact Ellie Freeman in any way, but she contacted him first. She carefully worded her conversation and kept it short in the event he might have had a chance to record any of it. By the time she was finished, he knew what she saw, and not to worry too much about this investigation because she found a bigger reward waiting down the road.

He was greeted upon his return to the news she had dropped her claim in exchange for his apology in Captain Thomas's office in front of all the brass. The sergeants saw the production it for the farce that it was, and even one of the Lieutenants who was friendly with Matt was in on it as well. Still, he would have rather been fired instead of having to go through with this embarrassment. So, in a fit of righteous anger and to the astonishment of the chain of command, he showed up to Captain Thomas's office on the day of the event with a typed and handwritten notice of resignation.

His bullheaded stunt took the possibility of a smudge of ink on his record with the department dropping a sexual harassment matter on a basis of inconclusive findings and transformed it to a resignation in the midst of a sexual harassment investigation. The doors to some job prospects were closed on him, but was given a chance to enter the corporate office to sell his worth at one company who he thought would not have given him a chance in hell given the company's theme. He marched into the human resources department of Lovelee's and stated his case. He was put under the scrutiny of Robin Love and Jessie Lee and, after a moment in the middle of the hiring process where he felt that hiring was in danger of being derailed, was given the seal of approval and a second chance. He would later find that, off the record, the policy of crossing the threshold on assignments with Lovelee's was less intolerant than the Tallahassee Police Department.

After two months of anxious transition, he was rewarded with two months of serenity as he settled into his new beginnings as the Waste, Fraud, and Abuse Investigator for the Lovelee's corporate office with a bigger paycheck and less work-related bullshit to deal with. He was on the tail end of the exhale when he was updated on Ellie Freeman's life.

When Matt resigned in the middle of the sexual harassment investigation, the stage was set for Ellie to hire a lawyer and get a bonus check from the police department; they settled quickly. When she found out for sure she was pregnant with Matt's child, she debated whether or not she should stay on the department and risk anyone finding out a major inconsistency in her claim that his advances were not as unwanted as believed. She checked into his employment and how much he was making, and calculated how much she could get in child support; she resigned from the department.

Ellie waited for the birth of the baby boy and for the ink on the letters of resignation to dry in the file cabinets to break the news to Matt he was the father of an illegitimate child and start the process of receiving the child support payments from him. By the time he finished with the ordeal, he jadedly gave in to the system and waived all rights to see his son in exchange of the possibility of never having to see her face again.

The matter with Ellie Freeman started just as innocently as it had between him and Madison. Matt put his game face back on, and hoped he could get this job finished before walking into another inevitable relations disaster with a member of the opposite sex.

11

Karla returned to the bar with an armful of fruit she pulled out of the refrigerators in back. As she picked out a couple of each of the assortment of lemons, limes, and oranges, and storing the remainder in the lower cooler, she felt the irritation of a pair of eyes tracking her. That feeling was common in a place like Lovelee's, but considering she knew whose eyes were directed at her, the sting felt different, and she knew it would probably get worse before her lunch shift started. She concentrated less on getting rid of the feeling and more on shoving it under the surface.

Matt figured the interview with Karla would be short and sweet, and she was working the lunch shift that day, so he would start with her. He stalked his way toward her to get started, and by the time she stood up from the lower coolers and returned to the garnish trays and fruits to be prepared, they were standing face to face in the same coordinates as that night, Karla behind the bar by the server station, and Matt on the other side of it, where Madison and Ronnie were standing.

"Hi, Karla. Karla Nuñez, right?" They shook hands.

"That would be right, Mr. O'Dell."

"Sounds good, and..." He paused when she turned and walked away to the sink to wash her hands. He projected his voice to carry the length of the bar. "And please, call me Matt." Karla grabbed a couple of paper towels to dry her hands on her walk back to where Matt was standing. She noticed his warm smile and non-threatening, demure persona. He even gave her the favor of letting her call him by his first name, just like they were buddies. *Lessons he was taught on influencing people from corporate, no doubt.*

"Forgive me for walking away. You don't want me handling food with dirty hands, do you?" she jabbed. "Do you want to go ahead and get my interview over with?"

Matt worked against gravity to pull the corners of his mouth into a hint of a smile and continued through the force field Karla set between them. "I see you were working the bar that night. Please tell me what happened from your point of view."

She waited until the cutting board was placed in between them and her fruit to be cut to start the shift were in position before she began. "Well, as you already know, I was back here when it happened, so this all happened right in front of me," she said as she cut the limes into perfect wedges.

"The advance this guy made at her, it wasn't provoked in any way?"

Why do these assholes always think we're asking for it!? "No."

A shift in Matt's mien, noticed by Karla. "You didn't get hurt in any way, did you?" He knew how to turn the interviews to a more personal atmosphere when the tension level made things a little uncomfortable.

Karla thought he sounded sincere but maintained that the act was arranged by design. "I was fine, nothing I can't handle."

Karla cleaned off the cutting board with a damp towel, and a silent moment's ripple in the air elapsed where her confidence and casual defiance meshed with his respect for her resiliency. Then it reverted back to the business at hand just as quickly, with his interrogation and her slicing of oranges for the Blue Moon drafts. "This guy that was involved in the incident that night" – he looked at his paperwork – "Ronnie Stover...Did anyone here know him before this night?"

Karla kept a good poker face, but she was sure some emotion was exposing itself through her face and hands. She could feel and sense it, but the moment could have just been chalked up to paranoia playing its game with her. "Some of us knew him. A couple of us knew him. He used to live around here several years ago and left. He's only been back around for about a couple of months or so."

"Who remembers him from several years ago?"

"Me ... and Madison." She maintained her role with as cool a hand as possible while she paid particular attention to Matt jotting down some notes in his ledger book.

"Have you or Madison had any meaningful interaction with him since he's been back in town?"

"No. He just comes in here to eat every now and then, that's all."

"Were you friends with Ronnie Stover during this time?"

"No." Her response, and the force behind it, was just forceful enough to break Matt's domination of the interview temporarily.

"That was pretty definite. That about covers it. One more thing, quick question." He pointed to the security camera overlooking the bar. "The security camera behind me," Matt said while flicking a gesture to his rear and inserting a prolonged intermission before phrasing the second part of the question, too long of a pause to be coincidental in Karla's mind. The silence was just long enough for her to relive the meeting at the bar between Ronnie and the girls about two months ago that was captured by that very camera. "It was moved while the incident in question occurred. Would you happen to know who moved it that night, or at least, who was at the salad station in the kitchen that night? Some of those slices didn't turn out too great."

The final comment took her by surprise. She was about to retort by letting him know she had been working a bar for a while and knew a thing or two about garnishes, until she realized he was correct when her eyes caught the slices he was referring to, the slices that were way too thick than was needed to style a glass of beer, perfection from experience gone, the product of a drifting mind. She rebounded quickly. "I get tired of making these things. Drunken horny guys order these, and as soon as the beer gets set down in front of them, it gets dropped straight to the bar. I'd rather just give them an orange and a knife at the bar when they order these, and they can make these damn things themselves."

Matt made no altered posture to her opinion on garnishes. "I understand. So, do you know who might have moved that security camera?"

"I don't know who moved the camera that night. And I think it was Philip on the salads that night. Philip Martinez." She found the thickest slice of orange and made an attempt to slice it in half.

By the time she finished answering, Matt already had his papers organized because he already knew who was working salads that night. "Thank you, Karla. It was nice meeting you."

12

The lingering effects of the alcohol that spent the night filtering through Ronnie's bloodstream made the knocking on the front door a tortuous first event of the day, like a tiny mallet banging on his gong of an ear drum. When he finally conjured up the drive to suffer through the raising from his bed and stumbling to the front door, the momentum arrived a little too quickly; his equilibrium was off and his left shoulder met the left edge of the doorway, immediately stopping his progress. He indistinctly mumbled an obscenity and recharted his course to the source of his pain.

He felt the discharge of struggle when he finally reached the front door. When he opened it to the blinding rays of the daylight flashes his grind continued. The burning in his eyes dulled in comparison to the one in his ears that joined the conversation in progress with Randi, who started as soon as she saw his face. And as she babbled away with her emotions getting the best of her, Ronnie tried his best to keep a calm composure as he battled the dual task of adjusting his eyes to the blaze and keeping up with Randi's explanation of the turn of events.

"There's a man at work..."

Ronnie answered when he regained focus, not knowing for sure if it was in interruption.

"What kind of man at work?"

Randi was still babbling at the end of Ronnie's question – he figured she didn't even hear it - and he tried to keep up through his haze. "...He's there asking questions...knows we're lying..." Emotions welled to the brim on both sides as Randi's nearing the point of panic was stifled by Ronnie's roll of the eyes and motion of his hand to stop. "You tell him, Madison. I have to go pee."

When the combination of Randi's emotional boiling over and Ronnie's reaching the point of bewilderment through his brume of inebriation intersected, Madison took over while Randi searched for the bathroom. Madison stopped by Ronnie's place on her way to work to let him know about Matt's presence and interviews with them at work. When Randi stopped over at Madison's apartment on her way to work because she was scared as hell and needed someone to talk to – Eve's phone went straight to voice mail - Madison let Randi accompany her to Ronnie's in order for all respective parties to be informed about the situation, to keep from having a panic attack, and to feel more at ease.

"Have a seat, Ronnie. You look like hell," Madison offered with a smile on her face. He took the offer, making a stop first to the refrigerator for a bottle of beer. Madison could tell he was on his typical beer breakfast routine again, and from his greeting posture it appeared he was not finished with last night's dessert. The words kicked at her palette: *Don't you think you have enough alcohol in your system?* But all it would do would inject more conflict when there was too much to deal with. She kept it to herself this time around and continued. "We had a meeting this morning at work. There is some guy from the corporate office who is interviewing everyone who worked that night. He's already interviewed Karla, and she didn't get good vibes from him at all. We're all a little worried." Madison was sure she was successful in telling Ronnie about today without showing last night, although she had trouble reading Ronnie's reaction due to his impairment; his frequent drinking is one of his habits she wished he would overcome.

His snap of a response caught her a bit by surprise. "I'm going to come in today or tomorrow and check this out."

"After what happened, you could get in a lot of trouble if you're caught lurking around there. Imagine what will happen to all of us if we're caught hanging around together. This whole plan might fall apart."

"Relax. Everything will be fine. I'll keep myself low-key and just check out what we're up against. What was he saying, anyway? Did he say she was lying?"

Madison shook her head. "I don't think he did, not outright, anyway." Her look veered to his beer bottle.

He noticed. It tinted the blend of tension already between them. "Then everything is good so far. We don't have to worry about bad vibes. We need to worry about his interviews and his reports. You girls just need to make sure we don't crack under the pressure."

As the toilet flushed in the background, followed by the running of the water in the bathroom sink, Madison and Ronnie could read in each others' faces the same signals of distress; if anyone was going to crack under the pressure, Randi would be the likely candidate. They also wondered how long it would take for Matt to recognize that, if he was not aware of it already. Randi did not look that much more relieved when she came out of the bathroom.

"We have to go soon, Madison. We can't be late for work." She looked pathetically distraught.

Ronnie motioned her to come to him. "Hey, sweetie. Let's have a talk." He got up to meet her halfway and take care of her worries. He did not handle the work involved with getting up off the couch and walking to her any better than he did with the earlier of journeying to the front door. But considering his morning drinking on top of a night of drinking, Madison was running short on sympathy for his troubles. When they met a sight short of the midpoint, he held Randi by the shoulders so that they stood face to face.

"Listen, we all just have to stay calm and keep our story straight. Don't let this guy control the emotion in the interview. Randi, you're not going to be at the police station. If this guy starts to make you feel like you are going to freak out, think of a way to take a break from the interview. That way, you can regroup and get back on track."

Randi's breathing began to normalize. "That's good advice. Hopefully I can remember all that."

Ronnie rubbed and shook her shoulders lightly in an effort to psyche her up for the day, and she smiled and chuckled. He smiled a little also, but Madison could see signs in his face of losing motivation and giving up for the morning, and she stepped in to take up the slack. "Tell him you have to use the bathroom. He won't be able to follow you in there. It'll be a great place for you to hide from him for a few minutes and meditate."

"Don't let this guy come in there and shake you girls up," he said confidently as he made another trip to the refrigerator. "He doesn't have any kind of evidence of us planning this shit." He looked at Madison's eyes looking at the fresh bottle of beer he brought back from his trip.

Randi had more fears and concerns on her mind and aired them once again. "What about the security camera?"

"The security camera." Ronnie's answer came out more like a statement than a question, his armor of confidence exposed for the veneer it was.

"We were sitting in front of it that one day. Do you remember when I brought it up?"

"I remember, the first day we were all together. That was a couple of weeks before everything went down. How long do they actually keep those videos, anyway?" Neither Randi nor Madison knew the answer, and gave him a look as such. "I'm sure they don't keep them for long," Ronnie continued, "especially if they don't think there's anything interesting to look at. Don't let stuff like that worry you when this guy wants to talk to you."

Randi split her concentration between Ronnie, Madison, and the clock on Ronnie's microwave, constantly taking notice of the time and putting her trust into Ronnie keeping the correct time on his microwave. "OK, we really need to get on the road now." Madison let Randi pull her to the door this time.

"Alright, we're going now. Don't worry about us, Ronnie. We'll handle everything at Lovelee's."

Ronnie followed them to the door to see them off. "You don't have to rush off. They can get along without you if you're a little late," Ronnie said to Madison more personally as they headed toward the door.

Madison paused at the door. "We can't. We both drove together." Her concentration gravitated once again like a Neodymium magnet to the bottle of beer in his hand. "You should get some rest and take it easy. You look kinda rough today."

"Well, let's meet up after work. I could use someone to talk to."

"I have to drive Randi back to her car. It's at my apartment. Besides, we'd better not risk the chance of having too many meetings in public, at least until everything is taken care of on your end." As they moved away from the doorway she added, "I'll call you later."

They said their goodbyes as Madison and Randi headed to the car, leaving Ronnie to commence his thought race. *She's been distant with me the past couple of days. She could have come here without Randi, we could have spent a little time alone together. Maybe she'll come back after she drops Randi off after work.*

He chucked his empty beer bottle into the kitchen waste basket next to his wishful thinking and reflexively secured another cold beer from the refrigerator, the last one he had left from the case he picked up after his trek to the bar. The way things felt out of place since he had been back in town made him feel surprised he hadn't gotten pulled over and have his license checked. And the way things had been going made him feel Madison probably wouldn't come back tonight. *Could I blame her?* he thought, given his previous record whether it be leaving for brief bouts of jail time or taking off to visit a nearby partner to run down a scheme, his nature gravitating toward the nearest set of circumstances that would clash with the fragile bond holding them together.

When many of his partners started doing hard time he opted for to going it alone and keeping things small time on the misdemeanor level. He could now look back and laugh on the time down in Georgia. *What town was that? I was driving to Savannah but just kept going after passing the signs. Richmond Hill, I think.* He had a gun for protection and decided to pick up a few dollars from some unsuspecting woman walking down a side street one night. He found out quickly he held up a concealed carry permit holder with a revolver to show for it and heard what it could do while he ran like hell in the other direction. He also found out soon after that he was not cut out for holding people up.

Then there was What's Her Name, the girl who came into his life several years ago, right about the time he was setting out to conquer the West Coast with his newly erupting fever to once again find his niche as a filmmaker. She was an actress and gushed over the prospect of winning her big break. In no time they were passionate toward each others' signals and plans for bigger and better scenery. The buildup to the exit blurred the love of his anchor in Cannon. They were drifting in separate directions again and she needed to talk to him. He told her he would call her, neglecting to include the information about his bags and her bags packed and his gas tank full and the maps wedged in between the two front seats directing them to their journey.

He could remember the phone in his hand so many years before the next morning, his other hand instinctively fidgeting with the necklace pendant Madison had always been fixated with, on the verge of calling her. He could definitely remember with clarity the sex the night before, every kiss, the scent, every curve of her body, every moan she made in calling to him, etches of memory that forever laid claim to his mind. He could also remember the next morning, with phone in hand, in all his ignorance, convincing himself that he had not had sex, but made love, and the beauty sleeping beside him had captured a special place in his heart, enough so to not necessarily say goodbye to Madison, but to refrain from saying hello to her for now.

What's Her Name never made it big in Hollywood. Ronnie wasn't even sure if she made it to California or not; they had a big fight and parted ways somewhere in the middle of Oklahoma. *I can't even remember her name now*, Ronnie surmised about the past as he started the coffee maker after loading it with an overdose of ammunition; he was going to need it to kill the inebriation and self-inflicted misery.

His smile disseminated when he thought of the baby without a face. His natural instinct of running in the opposite direction when the stakes on the table were too high cost him dearly on that go-around. He could feel sobriety drowning under the fresh morning fermentation and pondered how old their child would have been right now as he passively watched the coffee bleed from the grounds.

He felt Madison moving on, just as his mother had moved on. *Quit torturing yourself...Stop it.* But he could not help it. It weighed down on him ever since the news hit him yesterday. He talked to his mother shortly after disappearing from Cannon two years ago, right after his dad died. He found a place to settle down into and get another phase of his life in order as his mother took care of affairs back in Cannon. He called her a few months later and was greeted with a notice that the number was no longer in service. He revisited that message just in case he made a mistake when he dialed, or whenever the thought of the message ate at him on drunken nights in Florida.

Among pulling off this scheme in Charlotte and seeing Madison again, he could not wait to come back to solve the mystery of his mother's disconnected number, feeling the chill to his nerves that his mind had already solved it.

He drove to his old neighborhood and took in the memories both happy and carefree and bad and flinch-worthy. The only thing that looked different was his old house, its new paint job on the siding, and the 'For Rent' sign from in the front yard from the local company known for buying up every available house in town stagnating on the market for the lowest possible price and turning it into another gear in its churning rental money machine. He called the rental company and asked about her whereabouts but got no answer he could use, so he returned to the neighborhood to ask around. Half the houses were occupied by the same people he grew up around, half of those were not home, and the rest could not help him any more than the rental company. His answer came from old Mr. Martin on the corner. When he caught Mr. Martin at home with his Silverado parked under his United States Marine Corps flag, he went for his last chance and got in the ballpark what he needed to know. *I think she went back up to Vermont to be with her folks.* His curt tone was still there. He must have still fondly remembered the handful of a punk kid the neighborhood adults always had to deal with, toilet paper on Halloween, school papers before the first week of summer break, broken beer bottles on the last week of summer break, snowballs on the rare snow days.

There was enough coffee in the pot to fill his cup. He did so with an occupied mind, hoping all this history did not pull a karma trick on him before Lovelee's agreed to the settlement. As his concentration drifted, he spilled coffee on his hand and he jerked it away from the line of fire. "God dammit!" he yelled out to no one, and began running his ailing fingers under a stream of cold faucet water.

He could almost feel his mother's hands over his trembling seven year old hands under the faucet back at the old house, could see the cramped back yard from the window by the sink, smell his mother's flowers and his father's nicotine stains on the walls, his mother running cold water on his hand after his father pressed it against a hot engine part in the garage, done as punishment when Ricky Stover drove into the driveway, home from work just in time to witness Ronnie dropping his torque wrench while playing with it. He had no trouble bringing the scene back up in his mind: the sound of the car hood being popped by his father, who came around to swing it open, 'You want to throw my tools all over the god damn place? You want to work on my engine?' The memory of the pop and rusty abrasion in the swing of the hood of the old Chevy still brought a slight wince to his facial muscles. Ronnie rationalized in later years that his father didn't mean to burn his hand, as he apologized within the hour after a period of cooling off. But the feeling never would wash away after the burn healed.

Andrea Stover meant well in caring for Ronnie after he was punished by his dad. It was some of her fondest memories as part of the family to know someone needed her, but was too docile to stand up to Ricky when he employed too much discipline on his son, and would usually make the normal excuses to explain why he acted the way he did, like stress at work and his struggle to quit smoking, or repair issues with the car and dealing with his ulcer. Ronnie could not recall many times his mother straying from her level of docility to push against her husband's stress mismanagement; it did not take too many times of being quickly corrected for her to return to emotional origin.

Through the years following his childhood, he could recall there might have been some substance to his mother's claims of the stress his father had to deal with. *Still, he should have dealt with it differently.* Ronnie also began to feel in recent years that he himself should have dealt with things differently as he grew bigger and capable of defending himself.

As Ronnie became older and more rebellious, he began to stand up to him and fight back. Those attempts often ended with adverse results for several years, like the time when fourteen-year-old Ronnie was playing his music too loud and, after a few words were exchanged, his father thought Ronnie was still young enough to be given the belt; Ronnie ended up getting the belt, but not before he was able to put a couple of bruises on his dad's face. Before long, Ricky's wave of antagonism receded in intensity, more often taking the form of verbal barrages, which Ronnie matched at every turn.

Equally vivid in Ronnie's memory was the day his father doubled over from not being able to breathe and his mother rushed him to the hospital. The test came back and told the story of Ricky Stover's emphysema. Ricky's tendency to chimney stack chain smoke made for a predictable end to that story. There was a brief period of mourning and truce but returned to contentious soon after, the difference being Ronnie was now in control and in charge of rewriting the script.

As Ricky got sicker, Ronnie won more of the standoffs. Instead of cultivating the gift of forgiveness at a time when it could have helped heal the family, Ronnie used his father's sickness to assume the alpha male role and live life as he wished, which did not include helping around the house and helping with the bills – that extra responsibility was hoisted on the shoulders of his mother. Instead of making life better for her in the time of his father's illness and using that opportunity to help achieve what their family was close to obtaining many years ago, Ronnie dealt with his pent up resentment toward her years of silence by splitting the time between responding with silence of his own and lashing out verbally at her, choosing to see the side of her that did not have the courage to stand up to her husband instead of seeing the side of his mother who tended to his wounded body parts and spirit when he was younger.

While Andrea Stover fulfilled her lifetime commitment by tending to her husband, in sickness as in health, during the span of the year that turned out to be Ricky's last, Ronnie escaped reality with a move to California. 'What's Her Name', the eager small town girl with big plans, burst at the seams to move across the country with him. It was the polar opposite reaction he imagined Madison giving to the same proposition; she would not have even approached considering it. The two had big hopes for the future as his car merged onto I-40 West, but only made it as far as Henryetta, Oklahoma, when he ran out of money and had to look for work to get him going again. That was when he lost her. He did not hear from any place right away, from places either not hiring or just not willing to hire him, so he searched for wages through the windows of nearby houses. He made the decision to go back home during an overnight stay in the Okmulgee county jail, leaving without regard to his future court appearance; he wasn't planning on visiting Oklahoma again. The road trip played out in reverse, this time on I-40 East and with a melancholy atmosphere as Ronnie drove back in the car alone. By the time he made it home, his father was in the hospital in the last stages of life.

He spent the next three months getting and saving money any way he could through a third shift job at Pick-Quick Mart convenience store, lasted long enough to act as an outlet for selling stolen merchandise out of his car during his working hours. He had no plans to be in town or anywhere near the hospital at this time as he scrambled to get into a mobile capability again. His mother called him and broke his wish.

Ronnie entered the Piedmont TriCare Medical Center through the emergency entrance and was directed to the intensive care unit. A pair of mechanical doors separated him from his dying father. In front of him were directives to not touch the door, to his left was the paging device to ask for entrance. He faced the barricade as his heart battled to escape his chest. He lost focus of the signs surrounding him.

I should have done things differently.

The cold water had been running on Ronnie's fingers for the past half an hour. He turned off the water and dried off his hands and sat on the couch. He could remember again his mother's hands on his again telling him everything would be all right, and like a dam giving way, felt the abrasive sensation of tears brewing behind his eyes as he looked out the window, thinking he had had enough of running away from life in the pursuit of life, having nothing shown and everything lost for all his trouble, thinking that it might be time to drop an anchor. Once he had the money, he was going to have to decide if the plan was still to move to Florida, or if there would be a change of plans.

One thing he knew for certain: Madison's answer would be the deciding factor.

13

Madison was not on her best game that night and everyone knew it, from the customers in her section to the other servers who were not getting her usual help in keeping the customer service machine running, to Matt entrenched in a table at the rear of the dining area with his files and a glass of water presented between him and those he intended to make feel warm and secure and conversational in the most subconsciously uncomfortable way that made him prime for the job.

She and Matt noticed each other and took turns at glances while staying fortified in their prudent zones.

Her group of regulars were absent, save Michael Seitz, her quiet loner. He had been acting weirder than normal; he was jitterier when approached, his eyelids were a little more constricted around his eyeballs, and Madison thought he appeared tenser. The other girls felt creeped out by him, and she could relate in what she saw in him that night, but he had always been nice to her in all his time coming in to Lovelee's, so she tuned out the feeling and approached the lonely two-top. "How are you doing over here?"

He twitched his head upward. "Good."

"Can I get you some more tea?"

"No."

The obnoxious round top was calling for her, again. She rolled her eyes. "Let me see what these guys want again." Michael didn't answer as she moved away.

Kyle and Waylon were in earlier for a time hovering directly in between lunch and dinner without the others in tow. In their place at her round top was a group of drunken boors. From their end of the liquor lens, they were the army of charmers setting the standard in the place. From Madison's end of the kaleidoscope, a table full of jackasses awaited. She heard the vulgarity as she approached, lurking amongst the profanity, a belch from deep down in the gut like a demon trying to escape the digesting processed meat. She wished Karla was working the bar for dinner instead of lunch. At least Tanya was working that night, and Randi, although Randi was a walking wreck due to Matt and his rear table setup and the fact she had yet to be interviewed by him for his investigation.

The couple who sat at her other two-top table who looked a little too dressed up for Lovelee's – they had plans and were in a hurry – were taken care of and had their check in hand. Madison was within earshot of the table giving her the most grief, who had unofficially reached two sheets to the wind about ten minutes prior. The stubby, bald guy who let his presence be known when she would get within an arm's length of him discovered a new joke and started letting any passing girl know about his new found wit about halfway through the group's stay at Lovelee's.

What's the difference between a penis and a bologna sandwich?

She answers 'I don't know.'

He gets up and pretends to start undoing his pants. *Would you like a bologna sandwich?*

The couple was ready to go and did not need change. She retrieved the checkbook and visited the zoo to see if they wanted to drown more brain cells. "Another pitcher for the table?"

Shorty wasted no time. "Hello, Dolly. I got something to ask you. Come over here."

Here we go. It was her turn for the second time of the night to be dazzled. "Does this mean the next pitcher in on your tab?"

"Come over here a sec."

"I already heard it."

"Just come over here. I've got something to ask you," he stammered while trying to keep his composure. It seemed Madison was the first girl giving him resistance in his joke telling.

This could be fun. "What's on your mind, stud? I need to get your order in." She moved closer and stopped just outside of arm's length.

"What's the difference between a penis and a bologna sandwich?"

"You tell me, big daddy."

He struggled to stay in a jovial mood for his buddies. "Come on. We want to know what you think. What's the difference between a penis and a bologna sandwich?"

"You tell us. You seem to be the expert on both. We're all dying to hear the answer."

His face showed he was not used to getting his way when it came to joke time, making the whole situation even funnier to his buddies. "Come on, Sammy. Let her get us some beer," one of his buddies shouted a little louder than was necessary.

Shorty Sammy gave up. "Yeah, put that next pitcher on my tab."

Madison's work shift mechanics of smiles, customer service, and suggestive selling materialized when she put her concentration into them, but mostly they took a back seat that night to the new person in her life at the back table, with the twister of memories and sensations that influenced her thinking shifting in the past twenty-four hours: an amazing encounter turns out to be a real pain in the ass for their plan. Still, she occasionally stole a glance when she could and pondered what a beautiful baby could be made in those green eyes, to hell with the danger it might pose to the whole picture. Sometimes she could be as hard-headed as Ronnie in her own way.

Ronnie's open invitation back to his place was on the backburner for the moment, but it was on her mind. She would like to spend more time with him if she knew he would be around for any extended length of time, but the predictability of being abandoned by him had definitely worn thin on her. She could set her seasons to it. But then again, Matt had no plans of staying around for long, either.

Maybe, she thought, she should find complacency in the trap that had become her relationship history.

She had not had any serious relationship in the two years since Ronnie left town, just the occasional guy she would meet outside of Lovelee's that could keep her company when she needed it. But the seed of wanting something more had been planted and had been sprouting for the past couple of months. *Why can't I just find a nice guy in the area in a stable environment?* Like the nice, quiet blonde guy at the round top full of employees from IntelQuest Communications who had come in for drinks and a little early dinner after work at the very beginning of her shift. She heard some of the others call him Stan, his bearing suggested to her that he was one of the newer guys at the company, and he had a really nice demeanor, or could fake it in public on the surface at least. She thought to herself he acted very unbecoming of the typical Lovelee's alpha male when she made a quick trip to the round top to drop off the beer pitcher.

It did not matter anyway, because the truth was she could find guys like Stan in this city; she just doesn't pick them. The nice guys, the ones her mother definitely would have liked, the ones her Daddy might have liked to see her spend her time with if he was still around.

And the thought was a sure fire trigger to transport to mind to that day that ended up being the last day she talked to him while she was fully awake. She received no answer when she asked him how long he was going to be gone for... *I can't tell you how long. I'll be gone for a while. But, I'll come back as soon as I can. You just never forget that I love you very much.* She believed it much more than her mother did, and her mother turned out to be right. If she had not achieved the level of a bad mood already, that truth did the trick of tipping her mood past the teetering point.

The nice guys.

She had come close through the years, but before she could make a sound decision Ronnie found his way back into her life, either on her doorstep or in her mind.

Or through the front door of Lovelee's. With practically no disguise whatsoever.

Ronnie's lackluster level of cautiousness explained the frown on Madison's face as he entered and sat at a secluded table in the obscure nook at the end of her section, with complete carelessness of being at the restaurant with a lack of an elaborate disguise.

"What the hell are you doing here?" she demanded to know, forgetting his stated intention from last night.

"This has been on my mind since you girls stopped by. I wanted to drop in and check out what's going on."

She motioned to a table near the back of the dining area. "That's what's going on today," she said as she made a discrete attempt to point toward the table in the back where Matt was set up. "We've had three food carrying accidents this evening. Two of them were Randi's. She's a mess tonight." She turned away from the circus of angst. "How is your mom doing?"

Ronnie's wavering core tread to the surface with the question and could be viewed in his eyes and the corners of his mouth with a trained eye. "I don't know."

"Something didn't happen to her, I hope."

"I don't know. The grunt on the corner told me he thinks she moved back up north."

Madison felt the blow of the news and imagined how hard it must have hit him, not with the time released deceptiveness as in the case with her father, but with an overwhelming final punch all the same. She reckoned that he likely took the time to compose himself before making a confident entrance through the front door, and gave his hand on the table a soothing grip as she swallowed back the questions and advice and criticism. *Did this have to do with you running out when your dad died? Would things have been different if you stayed? Will they be different if you learned from past mistakes? Will bringing this up even help or just cause a scene, and he just runs away again?* "I'm sorry." She took the safe route and left it to him to solve his issues for yet one more round in life. "You should try to look for her online. I looked for my dad."

He was amazed and distracted. "You found your dad?"

"Well, I'm going to. We should both look into it," she said in a backpedal.

Ronnie changed his position in their hand hold, turning his palm upward to lock their fingers together. "You might want to think about that before you check into it."

His comment brought out defensiveness in her. "What do you mean?"

"I mean, you haven't seen him in a while. Don't set yourself up for a letdown. It might be best to keep things the way they are, you know?"

They heard a commotion, quickly followed by a thud. Ronnie shot a look in the direction of the clamor and Madison whirled around in the same direction. One of the members of the round top nuisance, gangly with a horrid comb-over who tried in vain to keep up with the lager consortium, lost control and keeled over the center of his stool. His buddies tried the best they could with outstretched arms and yelps to stop the inevitable, but could not help themselves to laugh at their drinking buddy's misfortune. Shorty Sammy turned to Madison and retorted with the comedic timing of a moderately inebriated amateur. "Miss, I think we're ready for our check." This could possibly have been the funniest line uttered in the group's history given the reaction of those in the group not floundering on the floor.

Thank God. She looked over at Michael with an empty plate and glass. He still seemed on the edge of discontent, and he and Ronnie traded shifty glares. "Are you ready for your check too, Michael?" He nodded, and she turned back to Ronnie. She finally achieved a disposition resembling relief on her face. "So, are you having anything today or just keeping me company?"

Ronnie curled a smile across his face. "I think I could go for a beer and mozzarella sticks, and keep you company."

She darted her eyes to the back table. Matt had invited Philip to have a seat. "You can't stay long."

Matt O'Dell waited for Philip Martinez to sit down before he took his own seat. "You're on the clock, so I don't want to keep you long."

Philip cracked a smile. "That's alright, take your time." They both found that amusing in their own way.

"Give me just one moment while I get my papers in order. Feel free to get a drink while I get prepared."

"Nah, I'm good."

Matt finished preparing his paperwork, reserved in his expression so as not to reveal that he was noticing Philip's fidgety demeanor. After taking a few moments longer than he needed to, he got started.

"So, from what I've pieced together, the night this incident took place, you were working that night. Is that correct?"

"Yeah."

"You were working in the salad area in the kitchen?"

"Yeah."

"And you were the one who moved the security camera?"

"Nah, I didn't move it."

There was a short, tense silence. "Well, now there's a problem. That means someone's giving me a false statement." Matt made a note in his report, allowing Philip to mull things over; it is against policy to move the security camera, but more serious consequences follow giving false testimony in an investigation. Matt peeked from the edge of his vision at Philip's right hand from just outside the edge of the table. He was squeezing his hand slowly and repeatedly into a fist, like he was loosening it up for a fight. *A nervous habit?*

"You mean the camera by the salad station? Yeah, I moved the camera. I thought you meant..." He was adding too much. "Yeah, I moved it."

"Why did you have to move the camera? Don't you have a camera on your phone?"

A little more silence was the immediate answer. It was also against policy to use their cell phones while they are on the clock. Philip's fist worked at double time. "I don't have my cell phone when I'm back in the kitchen."

"Don't worry about your manager. I'm not going to tell him if you use your phone at work. I'm just looking for the answers I need." Matt's tone steered into a noticeable shift. He sounded like a confidant who could be trusted under the corporate curtain and relate to the bending of the policy rules. Philip stood his ground and kept silent, refusing to fall into any trap. When Matt got no further on that point, he proceeded forward. "So no one put you up to moving the camera?"

"Nah." Not the most convincing answer, and not delivered right away. And the notification that he received a text message shortly after he answered added a little more awkwardness to the moment, though Philip was not entirely sure if Matt heard it or not. "I figured I should move the camera so the restaurant could have it all on tape, for the reports," Philip added. The last statement was more than what was needed to be said, and not as authentic sounding as Philip would have liked for it to be. Philip had the feeling this did not go unnoticed by Matt.

"I think that covers it, as far as what I need from you." Matt faced the contact sheet toward Philip and pointed to his phone number. "This is what Lovelee's has as your phone number. Is this the best number to contact you, in case I need anything else from you?"

"That's right."

"Is that your cell?" Matt nodded his head toward Philip's lap, toward the source of the text message notification.

Another hesitation. "Yeah, that's my cell phone."

"Thanks, Philip. That's all I need, for now." Philip caught the tail end of Matt's goodbye – *for now*. Matt knew he caught it and intercepted Philip's gaze when he shifted his eyes in his direction. As Philip walked back toward the direction of his work, Matt traced his pen down the list of employee names - some untouched, some lined out. He found Philip Martinez's name, and drew an asterisk on both ends.

Lovelee's suffered its fourth merchandise accident of the night, the third of which that belonged to Randi McIntosh.

Randi was feeling uneasy all night at work, but it was not until Matt and Philip walked away from the table that her anxiety kicked in and the shrimp cocktail appetizer and two Long Island Ice Teas did not have a prayer or future.

Philip's done interviewing. Matt's probably going to start another one soon. I could be next. And I made another mess. Oh shit. She picked up the messy and dangerous portions of her catastrophe and stood up with the tray.

"Excuse me, Miss..."

"Oh shit!" Randi dropped the tray and spun toward the voice while jumping away from it. The voice belonged to a customer who was sitting in Tanya Beaver's section and was now equally as startled as Randi.

"Or could you just ask Tanya if I can get a refill on my sweet tea?"

Tanya veered toward the awkward meeting in a pause from the changed course to the drink station. "No problem, Terry. I'll be back in a sec," she chuckled as she comforted Randi with a hand on the shoulder in passing, "Don't give yourself a heart attack, sweetie."

Randi stared at her mess that she started from scratch. She froze for a moment in time to survey her life on the floor while she exhaled and released some of the angst from her body. "Thank you, Tanya."

A man's voice overlapped her sentence, and the angst returned to her neurological pathways once again.

"Thank you, Tanya. I was hoping Randi could help me out for a few minutes." It was Matt. "Do you think one of the dishwashers could take care of this mess? I was hoping to take care of our interview today."

And Randi felt like she was going to piss all over herself, complimented with a face which gave wonder as to whether or not it had happened as they stood facing each other. "Just a second. My tables..." She hurried to the server section by the bar to give her table's order a second try.

Matt waited at the edge of the drink station and watched Randi check on her tables haphazardly in a manner unlike the glide and saunter he had seen in the more seasoned servers. Her motions reminded him of a puppy being taunted at opposite ends by a couple of cruel kids. He veiled his amusement when she returned. "I'm set up back here. Feel free to get yourself a drink before we get started," he said as he gestured to the drink station.

Randi remembered what Madison told her about getting away from the table if things got too tense. "Um, I'll wait," she gasped.

A pause and a reaction that could not have been better had Randi thumped him on the tip of his nose. "Sure. Let's go."

Matt escorted Randi back to the table where Philip previously squirmed. Although he finished the previous interview just minutes ago, the papers still seemed to not be organized to his liking, and they spent several moments in tense silence as Matt organized his documents once again and jotted down a couple of notes.

Randi could still feel retained heat from Philip's time in the hot seat. The shuffling papers in front of her blurred as her thoughts darted in her head at an intense pace.

Weren't those in order when he was talking to Philip? Those WERE in order. I was watching when he did it in front of Philip. That son of a bitch is doing this on purpose, that son of a bitch! I feel sick. "You can never be too organized," she whined, the tone a product of her sour mental ramblings. It came out like a pathetic excuse for the break in the silence that it was. "You're really organized. Let me know when you're ready."

Matt looked up at her and grinned politely, and could imagine her having to snap to herself at that moment to shut up and stop sputtering nonsense. The grin twitched slightly into more of a smirk. She spotted Madison at the drink station, and they exchanged inconspicuous waves that Matt casually noticed.

"Actually, I'm really thirsty. I could use a drink. I should have gotten something to drink when I was over there, but I need one now." She was babbling again and his face was on fire.

Matt's smirk flared once again just for a flicker at her premature attempt to cause a distraction. "Feel free to get yourself a drink, and then we'll begin."

For all the times where Randi needed to be told repeatedly to do something, and in her scatterbrained haze could not find a way to make it stick when it mattered, this was not one of them; she hastily met Madison at the drink station. Madison handed her a cup. "Don't be nervous, sweetie. Just tell him where you were, what you heard, stuff like that."

By the time Randi finished her attempt at making a drink, ice was spilled around the station table, and the soda cup and remainder of the contents were relocated to the ice bin. Randi's nervous time bomb was ticking.

"OK. What did I hear again?"

"Are you kidding me?" Ronnie materialized at the other end of the drink machine. "You had better get some confidence when you go back and talk to this guy, because you look like hell right now, Randi. Or at least do a good job of faking it. Think of it as acting job."

As Randi nodded and pumped the universe for some confidence, Ronnie and Madison both resigned to the reality that Randi was not ready for this interview. Randi saw the looks on their faces and quickly joined them. Madison played mother and made another soda for Randi. "Don't worry about this, I'll clean it up. You just worry about the interview. Don't worry about it, I mean." Madison handed Randi a soda and straw. "You heard me call out 'You asshole,' you saw me and assisted me in defending myself. If he tries to throw any curveballs, tell him you can't recall and you'll have to get back to him. If you get too flustered, excuse yourself and go to the bathroom."

"Got it."

"You ready?"

Randi had no answer, only a look on her face that was every bit as bad as a 'no' answer. Her eventual audible answer lived in the vicinity of a groan and a whimper. "Uhhhaa..."

Madison sighed. "Honey, you're as ready as you'll ever be. Go get this over with." She nudged Randi as long as she could while being provided cover from the drink station and the wall behind it.

As Randi returned to the table, the other two could drop their pained expression of hope. "This isn't going to end good, is it?" Ronnie teased.

Madison preceded her answer with two parts serious declaration and one part flirtatious punch in the chest. "Get the hell out of here. And stop being negative."

"What I left on the table should take care of everything. Come by my place tonight after you get off work."

"Thanks," she said as she ushered him in the direction of the door, her mind hurrying the situation along. "I'll try. If I can't I will call you, but you'd better get going while he's in here."

With a push Madison made Ronnie disappear through the side door. Her section was in the midst of a mass exodus, with the zoo crowd and an agitated Michael Seitz soon to follow the hard-headed co-conspirator who should have stayed away from the scene in the first place. She got the checks ready and dropped them off with the added touch of charisma that Madison hoped would add at least another dollar or two to the pot, and left to clean up Ronnie's table while everyone settled their debts. Mozzarella sticks and a beer, a nine dollar ticket, ten dollars on the table. A ten percent tip: par for the course in Ronnie's world, so she was not surprised. She lifted the ten dollar bill and discovered the yin yang pendant necklace, the pendant she would consider lucky to even be able to hold it in the times he graced her with his presence in Cannon; he held it sacred to his chest. It was laid under the check and money too neatly for him to have dropped it by accident. She picked it up and felt its surface with her thumb and finger as her smile slowly overtook the end of the afternoon, combating the anxiousness she had to endure from the back of the Lovelee's dining area that stirred what would have otherwise been a fairly mundane work day.

She was distracted by a flash of red in the parking lot and looked ahead. Ronnie's El Camino rolled to the parking lot exit and stopped momentarily before disappearing on the road. Madison could see him look back at her through the rear view mirror and they connected glances. Madison lost herself in the moment, for just a second forgetting what was taking place in the back dining area amidst stacks of papers.

As Ronnie was disappearing through the side door with the aid of Madison's pushes, Randi took her seat across from Matt, who had his papers organized. He was not expecting Randi to take so long at the drink station, and began with a fringe of agitation. "Let's get started, shall we? I don't want to keep you from your tables for too long."

"Yes," she stammered nervously and immediately sipped her drink.

Matt looked up from his paper citadel with a bemused smile. "So yes, you do want me to keep you from your tables?"

"No, that's not what I meant. I meant yes, let's get started...Yes to the first part, no to the second part...I'm ready." She was not ready. She was tail spinning to the destined crash site.

"I'm ready, too," he replied with a grin. The early reaction was what he was hoping for; she already sounded like she was being interrogated. "So, you were working the night this incident in question took place, is that correct?"

"Yes. I was working in the front." She pointed to the front section of tables to her right. As she talked, she felt the momentum of a little more confidence in her blood. It rushed brutally to her face and by her ears before she knew it. She continued clumsily, answering questions she had yet to be asked. "I was working, and heard Madison call out 'You asshole.' I saw her defending herself and jumped in to help her."

"How do you know she was defending herself?"

The curveball felt like it was made of ice and hit Randi directly inside her heart, and she felt it through her whole bloodstream. *I was hoping that wouldn't come up. I can't tell him I don't recall. I just told him I recalled it. Don't let him see your fear.* "Because she was."

"That response wouldn't hold up in court, Randi. Are you sure she didn't instigate it?"

No answer from Randi. Matt wondered if she was thinking her answer through, or maybe she was not exactly sure what 'instigate' meant, or just merely scared; the look on her face suggested the realms of confusion, fright, and constipation. "Are you sure she didn't start it?"

"Of course not."

"But you don't know, do you? You said to me you did not look over until after it happened."

"Well, I'm pretty sure she didn't. I don't think she did."

Matt looked down at his papers and made notes during this exchange. He finished his notes and looked up at a rack of nerves.

"Do you know who moved the security camera?"

Why is it important if I know that Philip moved it? Is it important if I know that or not? Should I tell him? Television police shows popped into Randi's head. This was that moment when the suspect who later turns out to be guilty spouts out one of those clichéd lines in order to pretend they have no idea what is going on. 'I don't know what you're talking about,' or some kind of garbage like that. *Oh god, Randi. Don't say it, Randi. Don't say it...*

"I don't know what you're ... talking about ..."

She closed her eyes and felt like she was going to throw up. *I want to go to bed. I don't want to do this anymore. Remember what Madison said...* "I don't recall, and I'll have to get back to you on that one." That appeared to pacify Matt for the moment, although his eyes did not entirely suggest it. Randi felt it was safe to gingerly nudge ahead. "I'm just curious. Why does it matter if I would know who moved it?"

Matt perked up, similar to a dog noticing a stranger getting a little too close to his yard. Randi regretted her poke.

"I was also just a little curious, Randi, as to why someone who is always carrying a camera on his phone would have to capture it on a store camera that's not to be tampered with."

Shit, Randi thought, *He knows it was Philip. I shouldn't have said anything. What should I do now?* She glanced over to the drink station, but Madison was not in view. She already said she didn't know who moved it. *Then why did he ask in the first place!?*

"Randi?"

Randi could feel the break from her inner conversation throughout her whole body. She felt like she could cover the entire surface of the table with more than Matt's papers at the next interrogatory assault hurled her way.

"Do they even check those cameras up at Corporate?" she blurted out.

"We keep the camera footage on file for ninety days. Unless something out of the ordinary occurred that we felt should be kept in a separate archive and that would be stored for an indefinite amount of time. I provide the authorization for that to happen."

Ninety days, longer than two months. This is not good.

"We are looking at all the footage before and after, just to see if any clues pop up that would lead us to believe it was not a spontaneous incident."

Oh shit.

"By any chance, did you happen to know this guy, Ronnie Stover, before this incident took place?"

By the time Matt placed the question mark, Randi was on her way out of the chair like a rocket and to her feet. She did not quite make it squarely to her feet, left leg in front of the chair and the right leg tangled somewhere on the side of the chair on the right. She still tried to tear a path toward the bathroom and accidentally whipped the chair out from under her and to its side in a crash close enough to a nearby table to make its occupants jump as much as Matt and Randi, who witnessed a miracle that she was not at that moment face to the floor in an embarrassment of a performance. "I have to use the bathroom. I'll be right back," she whimpered and took off running as Matt trailed her with his startled eyes. He found her name on his list and ticked a unique mark next to it.

Madison got a break with her emptying section and less than stellar customer traffic and was one of the first to get cut for the night. After she finished her transactions with Michael Seitz and the zoo at the round top, she took care of cleaning the tables and worked on her closing side work, the drink station beside the server food window. Upon her return from the stockroom in the back with enough supplies to finish up her duties, it was her turn to be accosted by Will Graham, who was standing at the server window overlooking neglected plates and addressing an audience of indifferent girls with deaf ears.

"Can I get some help? Please? This is all going to Randi's section. Has anybody seen Randi?"

Madison dropped her supplies and grabbed the plates headed to the table closest to the back, where Matt shifted in his seat and looked impatiently at the corner by the rear drink station. She took care of the table with a smile on her face directed at elsewhere humor, then paid Matt a visit. "What is a handsome man like you doing sitting all alone in a place like this?" she asked drolly.

"Oh, Lovelee's of Charlotte, home of the gifted comediennes. I'm supposed to be interviewing your friend Randi McIntosh. Where did she go?"

"I'll find her. Where did she say she was going?"

"She told me she needed to go to the bathroom. She told me that about forty-five minutes ago. If she's still in there, tell her to pinch it off and get back out here."

Madison grabbed his nearly empty water glass. "I will not, and that is gross." She made a mock show of being nauseated by his comment but her inner chuckle beamed through her face too much to pull it off. "You'll have to forgive her. She's a nervous wreck in interviews. You should have seen her when she interviewed at this place."

"I can imagine."

Their line of gaze was distracted by a notification from her phone that she received a text message. "But you never use your phone at work, right?" Matt quipped.

She glanced at the screen to read Ronnie's message. *Hey girl. Wanted to make sure you got it. My place after work?* She knew what "it" meant; she could feel the yin-yang pendant which meant so much to him forging a new foundation to her chest. "Let me get you some more water, and I will check the restroom for Randi."

"Please do."

Madison was certain she found Randi in the middle toilet; it was the only locked door in the bathroom, and its occupant's feet and legs were hiked up out of sight. She knocked gently on the door. A timid voice answered.

"Is that you, Madison?"

"Yes, it's me. Mr. O'Dell is still waiting for you out there."

The latch disengaged, and the door slowly opened. Randi dropped her feet to the ground and reentered life outside the bathroom stall but delayed the exhale from her lungs or release of tension from her body.

"I ran your food, and everything is OK, except the guy at table 408 needs another vodka and tonic."

"I don't know if I can do this anymore."

"Yes you can. Just put on your game face for a few more days, and we'll all get through this."

Madison was not sure if this would all be done within the next few days or not, but it sounded good enough to brighten Randi's spirit enough to want to leave the bathroom and continue working the rest of the night. Madison reached out and squeezed Randi's hand, and Randi mustered a smile that halfheartedly masked the helplessness and overbearing anxiety as she squeezed back.

"I'll get rid of him. Just stay in here and get some cold water on your face until I can see what I can do."

She returned with a full glass of water to the table, where Matt had already packed up his files in anticipation of an interview cut short. "She's still in the bathroom and won't be able to continue. She's in bad shape." It was no absolute lie she told him. "I'm sorry."

Matt exhaled and sipped some water. "I figured as much. I guess that means I call it a day, unless you want me to go ahead and get your interview over with tonight."

She could get that over with and off her mind. But she also needed to get him out of there and restore Randi's composure. "Why don't we have our interview later?" she asked with a hint of flirt in her voice. She had to tread carefully down that avenue from that point on, but a little flirting couldn't hurt.

"It would be best to interview you sitting up at a table." He played along with a tinge of tension in his face.

"Same place, right? You can bring your files with you."

Matt forced a smile on his face. "Behave yourself, woman."

Madison noticed the extra effort to remain blithe. She couldn't shake the worry that he saw Ronnie in her section or at the drink machine talking to her and Randi. "Is everything OK?"

He entered this trench with the caution of post-traumatic experience. "Everything's fine, Madison. It's just a battle with my conscience, being in the position of authority I'm in and all. Maybe I should respect that position while we sort everything out."

She flexed against the corners of her mouth to keep them from shifting with her thoughts. *That didn't stop you from crossing that line before I knew who you were, did it?* "You don't have to worry. I know you're not staying in town."

"I just don't want a situation that spirals out of control. I've been there before," Matt said as he glanced down in a direct shot toward her belly, a clear prenatal reference.

It triggered a slight jolt to her nerves – *He's more perceptive than I thought.* "You have nothing to worry about. I'm not looking to trap anybody."

"I'm just saying, I need to use some caution."

"Whatever happens, it's my business. I don't know where you live, right?" Her response came out with intertwining signals of jest and diplomacy. It worked well enough to make Matt relax enough not to have the meeting end on a dramatic note.

"You could find that out easy enough with the internet," he teased.

"I could, if I wanted to." Her smile was infectious, and it put both of them at ease. "I have to finish up my side work."

"And I have to get out of here for tonight." There was a hesitation before he grabbed her cell phone and typed in his motel room number. "If you are going to make it out tonight, give me a call before you head out to make sure I'm in. I don't want you driving all that way for nothing. Tell Randi it's been a pleasure."

As Matt headed toward the door, Madison dropped his cup off at the drink station and stopped by the bathroom door. When he was close enough to the exit she knocked. "He's gone, girl. You can start breathing again." When the door opened and she saw Randi's face, she stroked her hair and gave her a kiss on the cheek; it was the moment Madison truly regretted bringing Randi on board.

14

Forty-two bucks.

That was how much was left after her cash-out with the manager, after the customary tip-outs to the busboys and bartender. *I sure hope this plan works.*

Madison threw the bag containing her uniform and apron pouch in the back seat and ignited the Accord. *It just doesn't seem worth it some nights. I could make more than that at a nine-to-five, and I wouldn't have to work on the weekend.* Not to mention, if she got molested at a nine-to-five marketing job, she could file a complaint and not have it blown off by the creeper manager as fun and games and practically part of the off-the-record job description.

Madison turned on the radio in the car so she would not have to handle the iPod while she left the parking lot and headed toward the interstate. She caught the radio station just in time for the wrap-up of a generic pop song and a DJ leading into a commercial break. *Just my luck.* She opted instead for setting the iPod to shuffle play her library and let it make the decisions for her ears as she merged onto the interstate from the onramp.

The shuffle resolved with Taylor Swift's 'Our Song.' Madison marveled at the quasimythical thought of her iPod somehow knowing she was thinking of Ronnie and what he left for her on the table, or perhaps something bigger in the world was in play, or just plain, old-fashioned coincidence. That song came into her life shortly after Ronnie and he let her make it their song in those early days before he disappeared to chase schemes. She had time on the journey for a couple more songs and decided to backtrack and find her album to play when she noticed she was running low on gas. She also was distracted by the headlights belonging to the car exiting with her at the exit taking her to the gas station. She brushed both of them off with the gift of the green light and staked out the station with the cheapest gas. *It's only going to be one cent cheaper.* But after her forty-two dollar night she needed all the help she could get.

She found the gas station she was looking for and pulled in to a pump in the nearer row to the station. She got out of the car to a set of headlights at the pump behind her. They looked like the headlights behind her on the interstate. The headlight's owner got out of his car.

Michael Seitz's appearance at Lovelee's paled in comparison to his shivering disposition in front of Madison at the gas station. Something was on his mind and it showed in his contorted facial muscles.

"Madison."

It took an act of weathering a brainstorm to process that Michael was there at the gas station in front of her an hour after he left her at work. "Hey, Michael. I'm bumping into you everywhere tonight," she remarked tongue-in-cheek as she started the pump transaction. When she noticed he was in no hurry to pump gas in his car she asked "Do you need something?"

His hands fidgeted noticeably under his tightly crossed arms. "I just needed to talk to you."

"OK, sure." She occupied mind caused a slight struggle to release the nozzle from the dispenser. She inserted the nozzle and hoped for a defiance of physics, for the gas to flow and fill her tank in an instant so she could be on her way; she had seen him in a state of nervousness before, but never like this, and never outside of Lovelee's.

"You were so damn busy with that table full of assholes and with that guy who came in to see you."

Madison rolled her eyes at the flashback of the repeated bologna sandwich joke, although it was a surprisingly welcome temporary distraction. "I know. Those guys were really annoying. I'm so sorry." She stopped short and saw his eyes as they twitched, as he appeared to wait to hear about the other guy she was rather friendly with and whose table she spent considerable time at. She did not want to bring him up, not even mention Ronnie's name. *She should never have dropped by.* "How did you know I was going to be here?"

Michael's preoccupation of stewing was broken by surprise. His eyes widened in her direction. "What?"

"How did you know where to find me?"

His answer was delayed in surfacing as his eyes convulsed near her breast level while hid mind raced for the most correct answer. "I didn't get a chance to stop you in the parking lot. And you were busy at your other tables. With those who matter, I guess." He had a more difficult time swallowing his agitation.

Madison's heart reached for her mouth. "Did you wait in the parking lot all this time for me? For an hour?" He didn't answer. *For an hour. My phone's still in the car. Shit.* Her mind flashed a snapshot of her dear late friend Leanna as she casually opened her door to get her phone. *This gas station has to have cameras. I should be fine.* It seemed even her mind was stuttering as she thought of a reassurance to herself. She pushed back her urge to bring to his attention how creepy it was to follow her where she went. "What's troubling you, Mike?" she asked as she retrieved her phone for insurance.

The desperation and agitation that had been clawing its way to the surface from the time she called him out on staking her out in the parking lot and following her to the gas station found its opening when she offered the platform to grieve, and it bled more freely, and she longed for the rush of gas through the nozzle to match the rush of blood through her heart and temples. It was the longest filling of a gas tank in her life.

"I just don't get paid attention to when I come in. I'm a nice guy, I tip really well, I bake cookies and bring them in. I'm just tired."

The final rush and thumping stop of the gas nozzle she had been waiting for had arrived, its thudding sound more to her like a well wish for a speedy getaway. She took the nozzle out and replaced it into the dispenser as best she could considering her emotional circumstances.

"I'm just tired of being ignored."

Madison's heart stopped in time when she felt Michael's hand gripped around her elbow, and in that instant captured in time she could see the ominousness hiding unsuccessfully behind the creepy corneas and spread through the rest of his facial features, the face the other girls saw and commented on as he came into Lovelee's nearly every day. In that instant, just she and Michael locked in a box from the rest of the world, until another set of hands entered the moment behind

Michael, one prying his grip from Madison's elbow and the other clasping around his windpipe.

Ronnie kept Michael positioned so he could not see his face. "What the hell do you think you're doing?" Michael was still too startled to answer. "Answer up, you prick!"

With the two side by side in comparison, Michael was smaller than perceived in that moment of terror. He began to brew a pathetic helpless discomposure. "Madison?"

His uneasiness was nothing compared to Ronnie's. "Forget it, you son of a bitch! I'd better not catch you creeping around Madison or any of the other girls at Lovelee's again. You hear me?" Ronnie opened Michael's car door with his non-choking hand and hurled the broken spirit back into his car. "Get in your car and get the fuck out of here. We don't want to see you in there ever again."

Michael's body slammed hard into the console between his front seats and the door slammed hard into the other side of his body. He reflexively looked up at his assailant, the guy who was spending time with Madison tonight, the guy who looked familiar from somewhere else. "Where do I know you?" he breathed with enough force through the open driver's side door with enough force to take Ronnie by surprise and to startle Madison into a defensive frenzy.

She marched to his door. "You heard him." She threw the heel of her palm toward his face, and he ducked as he brought up his window. She struck his window repeatedly as it closed up to protect him. "Don't you ever come around again, you stalker son of a bitch! Get out of here. Do you hear me, asshole!?" The rattling of the window receded when it finished closing, but Madison continued to hit it. "If you ever come around Lovelee's again, I'll get a goddamned restraining order!"

Michael backed up and peeled out of the gas station parking lot hastily, seeming to Madison without regard for anyone who might have been behind or near him. As he raced away in the other direction, she could feel the tension release its hold on her nerves and they began to cause chilling quivers in her extremities. Ronnie reached for her shoulders from behind to console her and was surprised by her abrupt and adverse reaction. "What in the hell are you doing?"

"Excuse me? I'm saving you from a psychopath. I guess that's what I'm doing," he countered. His agitation caused him to debate trying to console her again.

"Michael wasn't going to do anything. He's always been fine." She wrapped her arms around herself and could still feel Michael's grip around her elbow; she didn't completely believe it this time, either. "He saw you. He saw us together! Do you realize how bad that can mess things up for us?"

"He's not going to come back around after what happened tonight. Trust me."

A few deep breaths slowed her heartbeat so she could think, and she tended to the burning in her pocket and pulled out the pendant. "You left something at Lovelee's," she said to Ronnie, who had come over to her upon seeing it and wrapped his arms around her.

"That's not mine. Not anymore."

She smiled as she put up a mild protest. "You've had this just about your whole life. Why do you want to give it up now?"

"If you have it and I still have you, then I haven't lost it, have I?"

She relaxed and exhaled to give his arms room to squeeze her tighter. "How is everything going with the settlement?"

"I really don't want to talk about that right now."

"Why not? Is there a problem?"

"No, no problem. Everything looks like it's going the way it should. My lawyer's confident and their lawyers are ready to put it behind them." He could feel the thrill she felt from his words through his grip. "I would rather just get out of here, and talk about us." He took the pendant from her hand and unclasped her necklace. He advanced as he refastened the necklace with the pendant attached. "We're getting close to the point where I run, don't we?" Madison did not answer; he would have known her answer if he was facing her. "I've been that predictable for years. I find a new connection in another city and a chance to get some money, and I take off running. I also end up running when I get in a situation where I have to show a little too much emotion and commit to something.

"One of those times I ran into Leon County and got myself into some trouble, and had to stay in jail for a little while. I got a chance to check out some of the books they had in there that I was allowed to read. Some of them were spiritual, and they really got to me, the ones that talked about finding compassion in people for things done in the past, about finding forgiveness in people..."

"I hope it makes you feel better to know that I forgive you for the times you had to leave me. It's been hard for me as well, but I know you had your reasons."

"And I forgive you for decisions you had to make because I wasn't around, or got scared and couldn't be a man when I had to." Madison felt a chilling crosscurrent when the talk steered toward that avenue, and there was silence as they both took in the rare breeze in the humid late summer air. "Joe Montana."

"What?" That always seemed to get her attention.

"I figured you would have agreed on that, about our child if things turned out differently: Joe if it was a boy, Montana if it was a girl. If things had turned out differently and I didn't take the easy way out of responsibility. If I would've told you the truth about how I felt about having a child with you."

Madison remembered it all and how it all felt, and she stood within a wall of resistance from his phone call letting her know of the plan and his return home. With his declaration, she stepped outside. "I hope you did the right thing by picking Charlotte to pull this off. I constantly have this fear that it's going to go wrong, that someone is going to put the pieces together about you being from this area. Or that this investigator Matt is going to pick it all apart."

"Don't worry about him or anyone else in this city. Just worry about the two of us. I was actually going back down south when this was all over. I had some plans down there when I got back. I could make it my last run down the interstate."

Madison could feel that familiar feeling of a sinking heart and the sour taste aim for her tonsils in that temporary cloud of silence.

"Do you want to come with me?"

Madison took in what he asked and the deliberation in her head kept her from being overtaken right away from the swelling emotion. She was momentarily speechless as she assessed the story of her life. She had never lived outside county with the exception being her college experience, when she lived in Charlotte for two years. A proposition such as this has always been branded Dead On Arrival, but Madison Davis was reacting to the taste differently this time, hoping on everything she could believe in that this was anything but a normal conversational letdown and life as usual between the two of them. It happened long enough without an answer to worry him.

"Well, you don't have to answer tonight. Sleep on it tonight and we can talk about it tomorrow."

Madison realized the time of their conversation hiatus and snapped back from her pondering and into the moment. "No. I mean no that sounds great!" Her smile contradicted the struggle within her to show her excitement and push down the trepidation.

And Ronnie saw it. "You're scared. I can see it. And I understand. You don't have to tell me one way or the other tonight. You tell me when the time is right.

His words were her relief. "I like what I just heard, but I've never lived outside of North Carolina. I've never lived fifty miles away from Cannon. I'm going to think about it. What kind of plans are we talking about here?"

"Maybe I shouldn't get your hopes up. How about I wait until you give it some thought and I find out if everything is set on my end?"

She smiled over the undertones of his backpedaling to a self-imposed barrier in grand plans for his future, that all-too-familiar stutter caught in his throat just as she gets her hopes up for an alternate ending, and resumed her focus on the possibility of joy and her basking in it. "That sounds good. Who knows? I might be the one who surprises you and finds out I'm the one ready to go running someplace else for a change."

Their embrace released thoughts and pheromones that carried the conversation for the next thirty seconds of silence to the background track of passing cars and the tones of a debit card transaction at one of the pumps.

"Do you have to work tomorrow?"

"I have tomorrow off."

He smiled. "So do I."

She smiled. "You don't work."

"Let's go back to my place."

"My place is more of a home. Let's stay there tonight." Madison let him know with her invitation that her answer to the zenith invitation was more of a 'yes' than a 'maybe,' and with a pressing of their lips as a send off until they continued satisfying physical wants, they parted toward her apartment on the other side of Cannon.

She continued her drive up the interstate. *Can I really leave this place? He sounds sincere. I think he really means it this time. Lately I never seem to be happy no matter what. But then again, I'm complacent here. It's what I know. But it just feels complacency isn't enough anymore, the same city and the same people, year after year. I'm scared, too. Of going somewhere new. Always have been. But I might actually be happier someplace else. I could relocate to another Lovelee's if there's one nearby. To hell with that, I'll work somewhere else...a marketing job! It's about time I put my degree to use. I may actually be ready to get out of this place. But I'm going to give it a couple more days to think about it. I need to give it a couple more days just to be on the safe side. Please don't let this be another disappointment.*

Ronnie drove the same route, following right behind her. *I think I'm ready to do this. I should have done this a long time ago, if I had any sense. But I shouldn't have said anything to her about leaving until I know it's alright to bring her along. I'd hate to disappoint her. Again. Maybe I should just say 'To hell with the plans' and stay here with her. I feel happy now. I feel happier now than I have in a long time just saying what I said to her tonight. Maybe I should have stayed here two years ago. I could stay now. It wouldn't make everything from the past alright, but it would be a good start. We could both use a good start. You'd better be ready to follow through, buddy. Look how things have changed in the last two years. You've almost lost her. You just can't keep running forever.*

They arrived at her apartment, her home, and continued their conversation in her bedroom, spoken in diction of lovemaking that felt different than it ever did in the past. This night's coming together of their bodies and souls felt more than the history of kissing and touching and sensations which satisfied carnal appetites and always held the same selectively loving memories and lofty hopes and promises that were destined to be unfulfilled, ignoring the lingering blanket of letdowns quilted through the years that covered them. They came together anew and stripped the blanket to the ground, and the caresses forgave the past and the sensations each felt held tight to the new optimistic possibilities the future held for them. They became one and Madison still had her confidence in the two bonded together and their future, and could feel it in Ronnie's breath on her neck. Still, she would wait a few days and see if this desire to leave her town and the embedded roots behind would remain as firmly in her heart as they were at that moment.

Enough energy remained to keep sleep from following, so they found their way back to the couch to spend the rest of the night watching television, while Madison's head rested on Ronnie's lap, while Ronnie brushed Madison's head back with his fingers. Both minds raced parallel while they gazed at Fargo on AMC. Madison thought of the concept of many nights like this from here on out with no lapses of loneliness in between and could imagine nothing more enjoyable, even without factoring in the money that would be coming their way. *Please let everything work out the way it should, just this once.*

In a bed thirty miles from where Madison and Ronnie travelled to a dynamic sensual juncture, Randi lay stressed and weary on Eve's bed, struggling to relax and enjoy quality time as Eve stroked her hair with one hand while the other rubbed her back. It was one of the places Randi could hide and not feel so confused and scared of the world's impediments. She was not able to achieve that serenity with her comforter after the day's travesty of a work shift.

"I was so nervous when I was talking to him tonight. Has he talked to you yet?"

"No," Eve answered. "Not yet. I have to work tomorrow night, so I'm sure I will run into him. What kind of questions did he ask you?"

"He asked me how I would know Madison was defending herself, and he asked me about the security camera. He asked me who moved it, but I'm sure he already knew who moved it. I don't know, but I think he was playing games with me." Randi had that tweak in her voice that usually preceded tears.

Eve hugged her tighter. "He was playing games with you, because Philip told him he moved it before he talked to you. That's good info for me to know for tomorrow. What do you have planned before we go to work tomorrow night?"

Randi was still antsy but occupied emotionally with what she just heard. *Eve's talking to Philip again.* "Nothing. Why?"

Eve picked up her phone and typed with the hand not holding Randi.

My place tomorrow ASAP before work. Call me.

She sent the text to Madison and Karla and dropped the phone on her nightstand. She appreciated Randi's face before pressing their lips together. "I'll see what I can do," she said as she returned her arms to their original position.

15

Madison had a rare day off and imagined spending it with Ronnie. Her daydream was short lived with the arrival of Eve's text the night before. Now she had a meeting at Eve's place before she and Randi had to go to work. Madison had to pencil in that meeting between their dinner shift and her current trip to Piedmont to visit her mother, whose invitation to visit was seasoned with urgency and Madison had not made the twenty minute trip in close to two months, so now, on a day off, was a better time than any to check in and hope the chastising would be minimal.

She pulled up into her mother's neighborhood, a series of houses that all looked mostly similar, all in the same style – her realtor referred to it as 'transitional' – the only major difference was in the exteriors of each, and the shade of bland color each possessed. Her destination was reached, her mother's two-story transitional house a paler shade of beige than the one to the right and a darker shade of white than the one to the left. And a 'For Sale' sign in the finely manicured front lawn.

"You're selling the house?" was Madison's greeting to her mother, who took the time to sigh and hug her daughter before she answered.

"Yes, I'm selling the house. You might want to have a seat and brace yourself for the unabridged answer."

The answer unnerved her in the same manner when her mother announced she was selling the old house, the house of her childhood. She had only had this house for several years, but Madison still did not take kindly to news of change within her close circle of life. She took a seat without making herself a drink and awaited the rest of the news.

Sarah Davis continued promptly as to not keep her daughter in suspense for any longer than needed. "Yes, I'm selling the house. And I've been discussing a transfer at work, to the Raleigh office." She said it slow enough for Madison to take it in one section at a time and to take it all in as best she could.

Madison took it in with a progressively despondent look on her face. She already absorbed the bit on the house being sold, but the part of her mother moving to Raleigh, far enough away to be out of physical reach, left her chill and numb and regretting the times she had a chance to reach and touch her mother and chose not to. "What does Chuck think about this?"

Chuck – her mother's boyfriend for the past ten months. "I guess we haven't been keeping each other updated. Chuck and I haven't been together for about a month now."

"When is this all happening?" Madison asked without the ability to mask the embarrassment from lack of information about her mother's life.

"Well, the transfer is not definite, and it mostly depends on the house selling. But if I was set on Raleigh, Aunt Suzie has said I am welcome to stay with her if I decide to transfer before the house sells. Suzie asked how you would feel about giving Raleigh a chance." Sarah's face of hopefulness quickly dissolved at Madison's reaction to the latter of the comment. She reconsidered her thirst and retrieved a bottle of Vitamin Water from the refrigerator.

"I could always transfer also and work at the Lovelee's in Raleigh." She wasn't serious, just knew this would get a rise out of her mother.

"Madison, after everything that has happened, aren't you tired of that place? Don't you want to move on?"

Madison released caution and the breath she was holding onto and decided to let her mother in on what they had planned. She told her everything, that the incident was all planned, including what had transpired between her and Ronnie Stover, but conveniently left out the part about Matt O'Dell and the investigation at work. "So I am moving on, Mom, once Ronnie gets the money and we get our share. And things are looking like they are finally going to work between me and him." She got it all out without looking her mother in the face. By the time she finished, she noticed her mother's hand of sympathy stroking her forearm. Madison stood up and away from the patronizing gesture. "I'm serious, mother. Things are optimistic. You never liked Ronnie."

Sarah tired of the confrontation and of talk of Ronnie. *But at least we're having dialogue for a change.* "When I first saw the footage, I thought that was him. And I was glad to see the beating he got. But Madison, I'm disappointed to hear you guys are up to this scheme. What if someone finds out what you girls are doing? These are serious charges you're playing with."

"No one is going to find out, Mom," Madison stammered defensively with whatever composure she could muster from appearing calm while also hammering down the image of Matt and his investigations and her insistence that her mother need not know about it.

Sarah got up to refill her coffee cup. She barely made it to the pot before she had to release what was on her mind. "I can't believe this. Didn't he just leave two years ago and not say anything to you at all?"

And there it is. Madison knew the inevitable chastisement was on its way, but it gave her a headache just the same. "Yes, we're thinking of getting back together. Actually, there's a good chance we are, and it's going to work out." She needed to stand and return oxygen to her bloodstream. She walked around the room to the computer and sat down. "You would think differently about him if you heard what I heard from him last night." She moved the mouse to break out of the screen saver and saw herself at ten years old. Her mom's wallpaper was a photo which brought back a warm memory of a cloudy day at the park. Young Madison was playing with the camera, with the lens pointed toward her. She was about to press the button and shoot herself into posterity when her mother hugged her from behind. Her face softened as she forgot about the sun blazing outside.

"I have heard it, Maddie," Sarah said, pulling Madison out of her time capsule. "I heard it just as many times as you have. I heard it in so many terms from your father countless times, so I know from experience. Ronnie reminds me so much of your father."

Madison snapped the mouse like a gavel. "That's enough! Don't start talking about Daddy like that again, or Ronnie. I don't want to hear it." She faced the computer again and filled it with her mother's home page, and clicked the cursor into the search bar. She wanted to find her dad right then, in front of her mother.

Stop being afraid. She was working on tuning out her mother's reaction when she realized her mother wasn't saying anything in response, just standing behind her, and placed a reassuring hand on her shoulder. Madison typed Leon Tate in the search engine and found her stopping point, barricaded by trepidation of what she might find, of what had flashed across her eyesight in the brief synopses of results which had shown up on the screen in the past.

Sarah got up and walked away to some destination behind Madison's back. "His middle name is Henry. Leon Henry Tate."

Madison moved the cursor back up to the bar in between the first and last name and added Henry to the search. She lowered the weight of her finger onto the enter key and began to focus on the computer screen when Sarah dropped a stack of papers to her left side. Madison was torn between looking through the papers her mother had just dropped and peering at the end of the search.

"I was sure you wanted to go searching for him sooner or later, and I knew what you would find, so I got the report you would have wanted to get your hands on. Go ahead and get a report for yourself if you don't believe the one I just gave you. Prepare yourself before you start looking."

Madison let go of the mouse and moved her fingers around the edges of the report. It was from one of the background check companies which popped up near the top of the search results page. She finally moved the pages apart while her mother returned to her side and caressed her shoulder. Madison's eyes scanned the address history: many addresses, almost all of them in North and South Carolina, some in southern Georgia and northern Florida, apartments and personal mail boxes and post office boxes. Her fingers marked one of the middle pages, the same links on the brief, unresolved internet searches her eyes were drawn to before she closed the window. The arrest history.

"There's a lot to look at in the arrest section, I'm afraid," her mother said in a soothing tone, the one she always used when trying to reach out to her daughter. It was the one Madison hated the most, because it put her in a familiar state of vulnerability. "It only goes back seven years. Some of the arrests I can recall from a long time ago are gone now, but he managed to keep replenishing them. Do you remember the summer back when you were eight, when you and Leanna went to that summer camp up in Virginia? We came up with that as a surprise at the last moment. That was the first time your father had to do jail time. You guys left right before he was to appear in court. I was hoping it would have been the last time. I was wrong."

The memories of summer camp that year came back to her. She and Leanna were so excited when her dad surprised them with the news and packed way more than they would have needed. They spent ten weeks together in another state, the longest span of time she had been away from her home and North Carolina, and became officially homesick in the third week, but swallowed it for fear of being teased about it. *Leanna and her stars again.* They watched them on most nights from our bunks in the warm, still air when they were supposed to be asleep. Now Madison knew while they dreamed of the future her dad was doing time in the county jail. And yet, some place in her mind and heart already knew, from the two weeks after she returned from summer camp and her dad was gone on some mysterious trip, and perhaps from the information she caught from the edges of her eyesight on the computer screen and beyond its casing through the years. The closure to the mystery helped little with the hurt she felt in her chest, and she struggled through the dull ache to move her fingers away from the report's pages and scoop them up into a neat and complete entity. "I'll read it later." She had been sweeping and scanning the whole time, but reading in detail might break the wall and bring the tears; the reading will be put off until she is alone sometime in the future when she can continue without fear of the wall's collapse. The struggle was intensified with the presence of her mother's reassuring hands on her shoulders. "I have to go, Mom. I need to meet up with the girls before they have to work tonight."

"You have to meet up with your girlfriends?" Sarah asked and saw an answer in the look on Madison's face. "Oh, the girls." The look on her own face folded back into the creases of disappointment. She wanted to ask if she was also meeting Ronnie but held back. "Be careful, sweetheart."

16

The rugged southbound slab of the interstate and the Charlotte streets leading to Eve's were paved with the grains of change and unresolved issues and conflict and Madison disliked the feeling that came along with it. The ache in her temples associated with the stress was exacerbated by the constant compulsion to reach for the report on her passenger seat and read the Cliff Notes version of her father's feckless and irresponsible life.

Eve lived in a ten unit condo-style apartment complex in the Starmount Forest subdivision in Charlotte. It was a little pricier than Madison figured a server at Lovelee's could afford and wondered how she managed to pull it off, but with the cramp in her temples decided at this point the last thing she needed was to spend her concentration on trying to figure out someone else's business. But without the headache and tension, the urge was tempting.

By the time Madison found the parking lot and entered it, she saw Karla's headlights approaching from the other direction. Considering the flustered mood she was in, Madison thought it best to wait for her as opposed to suffering through the wait alone with Eve for a few fleeting but painful moments. She waited at the staircase that led to Eve's apartment until Karla met up with her. Madison wished she was meeting at Tanya's place, with Tanya in place of Eve. *I should have waited and asked Tanya first.* Tanya and someone else; there would not have been Eve; hence there would not have been Randi.

Karla was just as thrilled to be making a special trip to Charlotte. "I wonder what this is all about," she said as she approached. They began ascending the stairs.

"Beats me. I'm really not in the mood for dealing with this today. It's my day off."

By the time they closed in on her unit, Eve opened the door and waited for them. As they came closer, Madison could feel the increasing heat of the tension in the atmosphere between her and Eve. "I saw you guys pull up. Randi's running late. She's on her way." Madison had a seat on the couch, while Karla stood at the end of the couch. Eve had a seat on a stool by the dining area nook.

"Have either of you guys talked to this asshole from Corporate yet?"

"Yeah," Madison said with her face pointed toward Eve's, but without making direct eye contact with her. Then Karla answered her. "I have."

"Randi has as well. It seems I'm the only one who hasn't interviewed with this guy, but I'm working tonight, so I'm pretty sure he's going to interview me tonight. Should we be worried about this guy sniffing around?"

Karla showed the confidence in the circle, more assuring than she showed to Madison outside. "I don't like this guy. He interviewed me the same day he talked to us. It seems to me he has a shady side to him. We shouldn't let this guy rattle us."

"That's what Randi told me, too. He was asking her about the security camera."

"He asked me about the security camera, too."

"Did you tell him who moved it?"

"No. Did Randi tell him?"

"No. He asked her, but it turns out he already knew. Philip told him he moved it. That's how he found out. It turns out he was just fucking with her. What kind of questions did he ask you, Madison?"

"I haven't interviewed with him yet."

Eve stared at Madison with an inquisitive look and a scornful eye, and it occurred to Madison that Eve's curious look began with the last question. "Didn't you say you talked to him?"

Madison felt the flush hit her face. She was already feeling nervous sitting in the room while this subject played out, but now she had the spotlight. "I did. I just haven't interviewed with him yet." She did not want the other girls to know she had had a couple of informal conversations with him, both in and out of his motel room. The idea of her having sex with the guy that could blow their plan to bits clearly would not win over this audience, so she prayed it would not become a subject of conversation. But she had the feeling Eve knew something.

"I saw you and this guy at one of your tables having a nice conversation the night before all this started. Well, what the hell have you guys been talking about? What have you been doing?"

"Don't get your panties in a wad. I didn't know who he was the first night, and since then I've just been getting a better sense of who we were dealing with."

"Listen goddamnit, you were the one who got me and Randi into this, so ..."

"Nobody forced you, either of you!" Madison vented through visions of her alternate lineup.

"I want to make sure all of this doesn't end up being thrown back in our face."

"Both of you cut it out! Settle down." Karla stepped in as the mother figure as Randi stepped into the apartment. "It can't be such a big deal if he knows Philip moved the camera, as long as Philip doesn't tell him anything about the plan."

"Philip doesn't know about the plan. I just had him move the camera in exchange for other favors. He got his, so he didn't ask any questions. So there's nothing to worry about on that end, at least." Eve noticed that Randi had entered the room, and that what was said had visibly disturbed her, because Randi knew nothing about her girlfriend's arrangement with Philip. Randi retreated through the front door. "Randi!"

"It's time to get on the road. I'll be outside," she quivered.

"Randi, come back in. We're talking about ..."

"I don't want to talk about this anymore! I just want this to be over with." Randi left the apartment with the threat of crying in front of all her partners.

Eve had something on her mind, a spark that had been flickering since the night before, but she also had a headache and crisis of conscience she did not want to have to chase out her front door and deal with. "Look, let's get rid of this guy without letting him find anything out, so we can get this money. I have an idea about how we can do that. But I have to tend to Randi right now. She is about to have a nervous breakdown."

"We don't need any more ideas." Madison should have kept her mouth shut. She instigated anyway; Eve was on the receiving end, and the projection dulled the regret in thinking she picked another wrong coconspirator. "You didn't make Randi's day by fucking another guy. Another one of your bright ideas?"

Eve snapped her head in Madison's direction and stood up, reaching her boiling point. "Everybody get the fuck out of my house! I'm going to take a ride with Randi and make her forget for a while. Then I have to go to work. I'll probably have to deal with your fucking lover."

Madison's scowl still scarred her face as she and Karla watched Eve and Randi drive out of the parking lot in Eve's car. Karla regained her sense of worry, not gone unnoticed by Madison. "You're worried about this, aren't you?"

"Yes. I'm already riding uphill, being a single mother and having to rely on my mom to help me with Tyler when I work. I worry about what will happen to Tyler if I got into trouble. Do you think we'll be in a lot of trouble if this doesn't work out?"

"Listen, this is going to work out. If by any chance it doesn't, it's not like we'd go to jail or anything. Ronnie might go to jail, because as far as Lovelee's is concerned, Ronnie is the one trying to get money from them. We might get in trouble, but we wouldn't go to jail. We would be the victims." Madison was not certain what would be the result if this plan did not work; she anticipated what Karla wanted to hear and followed the hunch. She had to stop herself when she was about to tell her that if this plan didn't work, they might be fired. And despite the pitch of her spiel, she knew she could not rule out just yet that they might be in trouble with the law as well.

No money, no job, a mark on her criminal record. Karla would snap.

"You'll be fine, Karla, and Tyler will be fine. We're all going to get through this if we just play it smart until Matt leaves." Madison was relieved when Karla looked out to some distant point, maybe the future or the past and not at her face, because Karla was insightful enough to have read it and called her bluff.

It took Karla a moment to respond. It was a long, uncomfortable moment for both. "I've seen you talking to this Matt guy when he's in the restaurant. Is there something going on with you two? You're not getting close to this guy, are you?"

Not any more. "No, don't be silly. This guy will be done with us and heading back to Corporate soon. Besides, Ronnie told me things are looking good with the settlement on his end." Madison wondered if telling Karla about her and Ronnie would cause further friction within a group stuck in a foundation of it, and proceeded believing Karla was the only loyal partner she had within the alliance of girls by a comfortable margin.

But Karla was smart enough to know the pure truth was being filtered and held back as Madison spoke. Madison saw it in her face. "Nothing is going on any more." Karla's eyes widened but her face did not alter much to the news, the only surprise being Madison's willingness to let the pure truth escape her teeth. "He came in the night before and I didn't know he was in charge of finding out we're doing what we're doing."

"Did you tell him anything?"

"No."

"Did you have sex with him?"

No answer.

"Have you had sex with him after you found out who he is?"

"No, not after the first night. Please don't bring up anything in front of Ronnie. We've had a talk and it looks like it's going to work out with us. I've got a good feeling about it this time around."

Karla looked back to that place along the horizon where she could form her words instead of letting them spill and have the product of her pessimism dampen Madison's hopes for the future. "Just be careful, Madison. If my opinion matters in this situation, I think you need to not have any more relations while this is going on. There's enough time after all this is done to worry about that stuff. Be careful, okay?"

Madison reached for Karla's hand, found it and gave it a reassuring squeeze. "I need to get home and get some rest. You should do the same. Don't worry about any of this."

They walked to the driver side of their respective cars, Karla not feeling any less worried, and Madison feeling as much regret for bringing Karla on board as she did for brining Randi into this mess. And when the headache was brought on from the memories of battling Eve and her accompanying bitchiness, she figured she should have made a completely different choice of roster. Madison Davis was going home to the retreat of her bed and remain under the covers longer than she normally would have on a normal day off and escape this mess for a little while. She would recharge and revisit all of this sometime tomorrow when she would see Matt and see where they all stood, even though her gut and her heart were squeezing and kicking each other, and telling her that a bad idea was just around the corner.

17

The interstate defied the laws of physics and stretched to infinity. The spirit of Edward Murphy, Jr. also overdosed on acrimony and placed in Madison's path nearly everyone in the state of North Carolina who received a complimentary no-holds-barred driver's license sponsored by Cracker Jack. The whole day was spiraling into a burlesque tragedy to the beat of car horns and the throbbing of her temples. So it was just kismet at its finest that Ronnie would be waiting outside her apartment when she pulled up.

The car's engine was killed, the eyes were rolled, the door was swung open, the steam was flared from the nostrils, the doors were locked. As soon as she stood up outside the car she threw her keys at Ronnie with Major League intensity and pointed toward her apartment door. If she would have given a verbal order with the gesture, it might have made a Marine drill instructor flinch. Ronnie followed the order without debate.

Madison's first few words could not wait and spilled out before her door was closed. "What are you doing camping out by my apartment when nobody is supposed to know about us being together in this?"

"I just wanted to see you." Trivialness peppered his intonation as he headed straight for the refrigerator.

"What if one of my neighbors was watching right now?"

"They would know how much I love you. That I love you too, because you also love me?" He threw humor at her ire apparatus which appeared to be running out of steam. He smelled success when she closed her eyes and began to breathe again.

She realized the outside world was closed out on the other side of the front door and they were protected, and her shoulders relaxed. "Things are volatile enough as it is. We can't take chances like that. Wait until you know I'm home, okay?"

He wrapped his arms around her. "Anything you say," he replied with a sympathetic, understanding grin, and their lips pressed together in a kiss he had been waiting to share with her all morning. "Volatile, huh? How did things go with the fireball?"

The flashbacks of that morning's battle resurface. She rolled her eyes in reflex. "How do you think it went? Everyone is freaked out about this investigator, Eve acted like a bitch, Randi started crying. Things fell apart before we really had a chance to talk. She threw us out of the house. Don't laugh." She punched Ronnie in the chest and it made him laugh even more. She followed and drew herself back into his arms and chest. "So, too much didn't get talked about. She and Randi left, and they're probably going to see Matt tonight. Maybe I should just show up tonight and talk to him at work so we can just get him out of here quicker."

"Relax, baby," he said as he was doing the opposite, moving his hands to her shoulders. "No harsh moves, no panicking, let the process happen. If you guys freak out and he sees it, then he can use that to his advantage. You always have to be careful that he can find something to use against you guys. Just keep your distance and don't tell him more than is necessary."

"You're right. You know what to do." The rubbing of his hands on her shoulders brought her to the first state of relaxation all day, the final blow coming from the musky cologne that always had a knack for pulling her under the blanket of vulnerability. She exhaled and expelled the remaining pockets of space and resistance between them and gave in completely to his chest. "I just want this all to be done."

"Don't expect the best, baby. Always expect the worst." He hugged her tighter at her moan of discontent. "There's always going to be something that comes up if you're completely hopeful and messes up a perfect thing." She didn't answer, and he couldn't feel her thoughts through her movements. "What's wrong, baby? Talk to me."

She lifted away from his chest and found her normal breathing cycle before she was able to meet his eyes. "Do you have to leave town again, when this is all over?"

"It's happening again, isn't it?" He saw that familiar look in her eyes again, the one that starts the rupture of the fusion and the separation to different geographic and emotional locations, the distance stretching from her home to no home, wherever he ended up. He fought the familiar taste. "I take it you've given some thought to running off with me. I have a feeling I'm not going to get the answer I was hoping for."

"We've been here before, Ronnie. You know me. As soon as I get any idea I might want to leave the city limits, I feel the anchor tug back at me. You know this has always been my home. I don't like it when things change on me, and now Mom is talking about leaving, and Matt is asking questions at work, and you're wanting me to make someplace else my home," she forced through the impending salty taste in her mouth and sinuses and the developing hurricane in her chest.

We have been through this before, he thought during the familiar phase they collide into. He fought back the predictable script because the teeth of the gears between his usual dialogue and what he felt in his heart didn't align like they always have in the past; it all felt different this time around. He held her and put his face in her hair at the top of her head. He struggled to talk as much as she did.

"I know what your answer is. Are you ready for me to be the one who comes back?"

"You are back," she harmonized with her bittersweet giggle.

"For good, I mean. Do you want me to come back to you, for good this time?"

The first good news of the day brought her up for the breath of fresh, restorative air. She could hardly believe what she just heard. She attempted cheerfulness without skepticism but was not able to swallow it down. "Really? Is that on the table this time?"

"Is that what you want?" he asked, knowing the answer.

She had been saving her answer for a very long time and waiting for the day she could use it. "That is what I've always wanted." She stopped trying to dam the flow of joyous tears and gave in to the flow and urges to kiss him again like she did last night, this time with new hopes and promises with no lurking feelings of letdown. "I wanted to get some rest. I think my plans are falling through," she beamed.

Her plans did fall through, at least for the next hour or so. Then they fell asleep on her bed. She forgot to set her alarm clock to get up in time to make it to Lovelee's and get her interview with Matt out of the way and get him out of their lives. But she enjoyed the silence and relaxation. It reminded her of an eye of a storm, and prayed the rest of the storm stayed away.

The light in the sky disappeared while their eyes were closed, the only light left from her phone reminding her about the latest text message, the total of three messages sent to her that she brushed off to enjoy her pocket of serenity a little while longer. With the latest alert she decided it was time to check her phone.

She had three texts, and they were all from Eve.

Call me. We need to talk.

Hello?!? Did you get my last text? We need to talk ASAP!

CALL ME GODDAMNIT!!! KARLA'S AT MY PLACE, RANDI'S ON HER WAY! WE NEED TO DO SOMETHING ABOUT THIS SON OF A BITCH!!!

18

Where are you at, asshole?

As soon as the rush of conditioned air hit her face and began to cool it from the hot, humid air of the world, Eve looked around for Matt. The restaurant was not yet busy at the start of the evening shift, before the dinner rush, so she saw him out of the corner of her eye almost immediately as she entered Lovelee's. Matt was leaning against the last table customers pass before reaching the restrooms, talking to Bob Baucom. Eve led while Randi followed, both having to pass him in order to go into the restroom to change into their uniforms.

Eve was not going to give him the satisfaction of avoiding him where she worked at, in her domain and habitat. She stopped in front of him, while Randi scurried past him into the restroom.

"Do you need to interview me?"

"And you are...?"

They both answered her first name, almost in cadence. "Eve. My name is Eve Kennedy. You have my name on the bulletin board."

Bob Baucom laughed that nauseating laugh of his, partly in pity for the headache which laid claim to Matt's future. "I'll leave you two alone. You know where I'll be at if you need me."

I sure do, you creepy prick, she thought as she could imagine him watching internet fetish videos on the computer in the manager's office. She remembered the time she caught him, only saw the screen for a split second but swore she distinctly saw the mouth gag strapped around the screaming girl's mouth. Bob walked on eggshells for the next three months and gave Eve prime sections as insurance to keep a secret just in case she knew of one.

Matt was taken aback by the one-woman ambush. "If your name is on the bulletin board, then yes, I need to interview you. I take it you're working tonight?"

"Yes, I'm working tonight, which means I don't need you pulling me off my tables when I'm trying to make my money so that you can ask me some questions."

"Are you in need of money that bad?" he inquired, punctuated with a smirk. He was seasoned enough to target an opening and exploit it at a moment's notice, fully qualified to shake up a target. Or in Eve's case, to merely piss her off.

Eve restrained emotionally the urge to lash out at Matt already starting his game. "Is that one of my questions? Has the interview started?"

Matt, a little surprised that he had his work cut out for him with this one, chuckled a noise that passed for a groan. "Let me get my paperwork, and we'll get started."

Matt did not get the chance to leave for his files before Eve retrieved some paper towels from the end of the bar, took out one of her pens, and placed them at one end of the table Matt had been leaning on.

"You can transfer your notes to the paperwork later."

Some of the flavor of amusement had left Matt's face. "It will only take me a few moments to get my paperwork."

"And I have to get to work in eight minutes, and I still have to change. So we have four minutes for your interview. Otherwise, I'll get to work and you can mark me down as refusing to interview with you."

Matt felt flares of shock and anger fighting against his face and the back of his neck, and his wall of patience. But he was intrigued to find out what she was thinking and what she was hiding, so he declared a temporary cease fire by sitting at the table on the side where his double-ply correspondence was ready to assist him, and Eve followed suit by taking the seat across from him.

"'No' is the answer to your first question. No, I'm not that desperate for money. I'm doing just fine at my jobs."

"Jobs? Where else do you work?"

"That is none of your business, as far as you and Lovelee's and this interview is concerned."

Jesus, she's a real bitch, he mentally muttered in Morse through fits of teeth grinds. "Just trying my best to keep it from being all business. What is your story on the night in question?"

"I was working, I heard Madison yell 'You asshole!', and I ran over to help her out."

"How did you know she was defending herself?"

"It appeared, from my point of view, she was acting in self-defense." Her answer sounded to Matt like a prepared statement to a question she was studying for.

"The restaurant has had an issue, stemming from that night, where the security camera was moved in order to film the footage. Would you happen to know who moved it?"

"You already know who moved it, don't you? And you know he had his phone on him also. So why ask me, too?"

Matt was surprised only for a second. She was no mastermind in any realm - *besides her own mind. She was forewarned by her friend, the one she entered with, the anxiety princess. She must know that Philip kid as well.*

Eve relished the urge to suddenly, albeit temporarily, turn the tables and interview him with the spotlight burning in his direction. She threw a jab and Matt did not see it coming. "Did you ask Madison those questions?"

"I haven't interviewed Madison Davis yet."

"I know that. You haven't interviewed her but you guys have talked. What have you guys needed to talk about before your interview? I take it the meeting wasn't official business."

It only took Matt until his next question before he was able to knock Eve off balance and shift momentum back the way he wanted it, but the brief scene leading up to it ignited the catalyst of worry and tension in Matt's psyche as he wondered how much Eve knew of their meeting, and tried to read it in Eve's face without bringing too much attention to the act.

"So, answers are 'Yes' to both questions. Where was your assigned section that night?"

She tried to recall her assigned section that night, having more confusion doing so than any of the others who were questioned. "Shit, I can't remember all of my past sections. I forget them as soon as I get done with them."

"It wasn't a regular night. I'd figure it would stand out in your mind." Matt's poker face stared down Eve.

"I don't know what to tell you." Eve's poker face stared down Matt.

"Well, where were you standing when the incident took place?"

Eve pointed back to the junction that connected the kitchen to the dishwasher station, a small portion of which was visible from where they sat. "Back there. That's where I was at when it all happened."

Matt felt a clue waiting to be explored in his brain. He stood up to investigate, and Eve stood up as well. The game of chess flickered in his mind when he got into this mindset. It helped him to think and focus when a lead felt hot. His rook moved into position, his opponent's king pinned between rows occupied by his rook and queen, isolated to where he wanted, little room for movement while he awaited the checkmate moment.

"So where exactly are we talking about?"

Matt walked to the sink and surveyed the area in question, scanning the perimeter, wondering if something would stick out and present itself to propel his agenda and satisfy the hunch he felt. He turned to Eve and saw her back as she walked in the direction of the restroom.

"Right there, on the sink at the server hand washing station. I have to get ready for work now, so we're done here."

"Just show me for one second where you were at exactly. Could you do that for me, please?"

Eve impatiently stopped to explain. "On the sink, at the server hand washing station. There's a sink, and a sign above it that says 'Wash your hands.' That's where I'm talking about. I gave you seven minutes, and now I only have sixty seconds to get ready for work."

As she resumed her journey, she said to the guy now staring at the back of her head as it shrunk from his view and disappeared into the forbidden portal of the ladies restroom, "Good luck with everything. It was nice meeting you."

Matt walked to the server hand washing station and scanned the restaurant from the point of view of the sink once more as he handled his paper towel notes. He stopped at a point and thought, and calculated, and smiled.

Eve arrived at the night shift muster late, but Bob cut her some slack on account of her being tied up in her interview with Matt, although it did not help extinguish her aggravation; she was present, a little late, and drew a shitty section. Now it was time to wash her hands and get ready for work.

The way her day has transpired so far, she just knew Matt would be standing at the server hand washing station when she arrived. She washed her hands while he stared at the small window which allowed him a limited view of the server station at the end of the bar from where he was standing, where he could barely make out the action on the other side of the wall.

"You know, the guys who work here like to stand here pretending to wait to wash their hands, so they can get a better look at our cleavage," she remarked to him without looking up from her act of sanitation, taking a jab of a sexual nature in his direction, in the event the probe would trigger a defensiveness in him to not appear creepy in any way toward her, in order to distract him from noticing her concern over his snooping around anymore than she wanted.

"I could only imagine. I bet they try to do that all the time." His response took on that cringe-worthy tone of old friends bonding. He gestured to the opening. "That's a pretty small opening to see what's going on in the dining area from inside here. I can't make out most of what's going on out there. Can you?"

Eve looked out with him. "You're absolutely right, Mr. O'Dell. I can't see much of anything, but I can see the area where the sexual assault on my friend took place. It was to the right of the beer taps, wasn't it?"

Their exchange of equable, conversational tone, possessed the ambience of the bitch and the misogynist in combat to the trained eye.

"You tell me. You were the one who was here, right? I guess you could see it happen, if you were expecting it. But if it was a surprise, I don't know."

"Check your paper towels. I didn't see it, I heard it, remember?"

Matt watched her leave his side, then continued his evaluation of the area from the hand washing station. The sound of the machines behind him joggled his concentration, and he turned around to the dishwasher station where the guy on duty maneuvered the stainless steel beasts to action, the machines hissing and roaring as they brought the dishes and silverware to a state of cleanliness.

Matt turned back around and listened, to the dishwashing, to the cooks, to the dining area, thinking about chess again, his rook and his queen still positioned where he left them, strategizing against their enemy. *The rook or the queen?*

Matt turned to the sink to sanitize his own hands. The smile returned to his lips.

"Little shawty knows what I like," the disgusting fat ass with the fake gold chain and smell of cheap cologne over unwashed skin sang off key through a screen of inebriation, and Eve knew his right hand would once again find her left ass cheek. When the parts made inevitable contact she imagined – once again – breaking the empty beer bottle she just picked up and cutting his hand off. Just one of five tables in her section, all seated and all pissing her off. Even the middle aged couple at the two-top was pissing her off; they were nice, but they were *too* nice, chirping about love and her cool job and his 401k as they nursed their beers all night. At least the packs of molesters and other assortment of pigs were doing their part in cycling the beer inventory. Not that Eve in her certainty would see anything significant in the form of a tip.

And it was only nine-thirty. Eve had had enough of this calamity of a day.

Philip Martinez dried off his freshly washed hands as Eve met him at the hand washing station, a favorite place for Eve to escape and temporarily forget her current tables. Her shapely frame was small enough for her to sit on the side of the sink without risk of a safety incident.

"That fucker at table 724 has been putting his hands all over me tonight. Did you take care of his jalapeño poppers for me?"

"You know it," Philip said with that wicked grin which let Eve know that what he did was good, really good, and when they were outside of Lovelee's he would tell her about it.

"Fuck this day. I'm done. First I had to deal with Madison and Karla, and Randi had an attack so I had to help her relax. Then I come in and have to talk to this douche bag from Corporate. Why did you tell him you moved the camera?"

"Don't worry about that dickhead, lady. Fuck this place altogether. I'm ready to move on."

There was a moment of unresolved pressure in the air.

"So, can I count on you?" she asked.

He quickly knew the subject she was referring to and lost eye contact. "Too risky. I didn't want to get that involved with this."

"You don't have to get involved. Just give it to me. It's not like you bought it at Wal-Mart with your credit card."

Philip did not answer and dried his hands longer than was necessary. Eve was in Philip's way to the trash can to throw away his paper towel. She took it from his hand and threw it away for him. "You wanna chill with me tonight and we can talk about it?"

"I can't," he said as his eyes scanned and found Randi. Randi was in Eve's section, delivering a jalapeño popper appetizer to the guy with the right hand. Fat ass gave Randi the same treatment Eve received all night as one of the other guys gave her a plate to take back to the dishwashers.

Eve noticed Randi was on her way back to the dish room as well. "What do you have going on tonight that you can't hang out?"

"Nothing. I was just thinking, if Randi's being all emotional, you might want to spend time with her and we cool it for a while."

"We don't need to talk about this again, do we?" Eve expelled a pout and applied some lip balm. "I told you, I've talked to her about it. We're pretty open about this thing. She doesn't mind."

Randi arrived at the meeting point and saw Eve and Philip together. She attempted to pass by them while bypassing conversation, but Eve stopped her.

"How are you feeling?"

"Good." Randi eased into a glance at Philip, but quickly shifted her eyes away once contact was made. "I dropped off those poppers at 724."

"Thank you, baby. I'll take that for you." Eve took the plate from Randi, who travelled back to her own section.

Philip waited until Randi left before he said anything. "I think she does. I'm just saying she's a good thing in your life. Don't take it for granted and end up losing her."

Eve flaunted her seductive smile at him. "She's not going anywhere. She loves me as much as you do."

Oakley Moore appeared from the dining area with a look of concern on her face, although Eve thought in hindsight that a layer of Oakley's expression hinted at enjoyment of viewing and declaring someone else's unfortunate business.

"That Matt guy from corporate who was talking to you earlier, is he one of your new stalkers now?"

"Why?"

"He's out there, wanting to see you. He's, uh, calling out for you." One of those statements that came out sounding like a question that made Eve fight wrinkling a scowl and balling a fist.

A cook stepped to the side of the kitchen toward them. "Philip, get your ass back in here. Eve, some crazy dude's calling for you out here."

As Eve paced out to the dining area she could now detect a hint of a voice, now that it was brought to her attention. She saw Matt by the other end of the bar, very close to where Madison was standing that night, at approximately the spot where she stood over Ronnie. Matt turned to Eve when she came into view.

"Hi Eve, I forgot to tell you earlier, it was nice meeting you. You have quite an attitude, little lady."

Eve stood dumbfounded and nervous. "That's it?"

A random drunk guy swaying back and forth at a round top in front of the bar sputtered, "Yeah, fuckin'," as a belch rumbled deep inside as he worked to mold his sentence together, "you were screamin' like a crazy guy. You'd think somebody stole her fuckin' car, god damn."

His buddies at the table laughed at Matt, and Matt laughed as well, at the guy who had no idea what was going on, at himself, at Eve. Eve was not laughing.

Checkmate. Possibly a checkmate. The type where the potential victor follows the move with silent gloating in the direction of their opponent, who concludes the moment with acknowledgement of defeat or an overturning of the board, sending the remaining negligible pieces airborne.

"I wasn't that crazy," Matt testified to the guy whom most of the witnesses in the restaurant prayed was not the guy driving the group home. "I guess she just didn't hear me with everything going on. Don't mind me. I'm sorry I disturbed everyone." He typed on his phone as he addressed Eve. "If I need anything else from you, I'll let you know. Have a good night."

As he turned to leave, he turned in the direction where he faced the kitchen. Philip looked at his phone because he received a text.

Just wondering why you guys didn't hear me tonight, but you heard Madison that night. I'm still trying to figure it out. When I do, I'll talk to you later.

Philip looked up at Matt, as Matt flicked him a quick draw of his finger gun in a good bye wave and a wink as he walked to the door to leave, the only hesitation being to lock eyes briefly with Megan DeWitt, barely eighteen and out of uniform, hanging around after her work shift for something to do. She already discussed it, and now she was waiting for him to leave so she could follow, but not too quickly. The charade was pointless; a handful of the other servers already started the gossip offensive before the door closed after Megan's exit.

Eve marched to the manager's office in a hot mess of malevolence, where Bob Baucom was about to eat a veggie burger. Eve paused as she wondered when in the hell a place like Lovelee's started serving veggie burgers with the shock similar to walking into a catholic church and witnessing a baby sacrifice. Bob read her mind. "I brought it from home. You think I eat the crap here? What do you need?"

"I need to go home."

"We're not cutting people until ten-thirty."

"I need to go home now."

"Can't you wait forty-five minutes?" Bob asked, exasperated.

"I'm on my period today, and I feel like I'm going to have my period again any minute now, and I'm trying to save the dish crew a cleanup!" She waited until Bob had a mouthful of veggie burger for added effectiveness, and from the look on Bob's face, the move paid off.

"Can I go home now?"

"Jesus fucking Christ," he labored in mealy-mouthed blubber around his mouthful of veggie burger. "Tell Oakley and Sarah to split your tables until we figure it out."

She stopped by Philip on her way to Oakley and Sarah. He showed her his text message from Matt.

"Can I count on you now?"

19

Madison failed in her attempt to get out of bed while not stirring Ronnie awake. He rolled over in a groggy haze and slurred what Madison translated into what was going on and where she was going. "I have to go out and deal with something in Charlotte. Don't leave on me. I'll be back soon."

The sanctum of calm and felicity was invaded by Eve and her urgent meeting at her place in Charlotte. She decided to keep Eve waiting as she detoured toward uptown to pay a visit to Matt O'Dell at his motel. If any of the girls were to talk to him and get a feel for how serious these interviews were and if anyone was in any real danger with the company, she was the one. That was her hope, at least: to bring some good news to the girls when she showed up for the meeting, which was sizing up to being a late arrival.

Ten-fifteen was the time on her dashboard clock when the Westingbrook Hotel materialized across the road's horizon, just a few moments and a couple of cars behind Matt's black Escalade rental. *Must be coming back from Lovelee's. Must be what Eve wanted to talk about so badly.* A chill spark ignited her nerves as she wondered what exactly she would say to him, how to phrase it. She was on friendlier terms with him than any of the other girls – *Well, the only one of us on friendly terms, I guess* – but she debated if she could be too comfortable with what was on her mind and risk incrimination. The scenarios not so favorable played with her head and nearly caused her to deviate to the side streets and detour to Eve's, but continued and followed the Escalade to the Westingbrook.

Matt lagged in his exit from his car, and he and Madison both exited at the same time, about five seconds after another mystery car that pulled in to the parking lot at the same time, one of the cars that was between Madison and Matt on the way to the hotel. The driver was Megan DeWitt. Little Megan DeWitt. *She's only eighteen.* And has only been working at Lovelee's for a little more than two months. In fact, her first night was the night of the incident. Madison remembered hearing that she came in on her eighteenth birthday and filled out an application and was immediately hired. She must have been one of the girls Matt interviewed tonight since she was there that night. *And now Matt's going to wrap it up by giving her a late eighteenth birthday present. Pig. Keep smiling, Madison.*

"Hey," Madison called out to him with a short accompaniment wave. Matt had prepared himself to face Madison from the time he saw her car behind his as he entered the parking lot, and pitched a hurried greeting in her direction as he darted to Megan, who was not prepared to see Madison and was standing at the far rear corner of her car. He and Megan had a brief, silent exchange before he handed her the key. They exchanged slight smiles and low-key waves of greeting as Megan passed by Madison looking friendly but just as uncomfortable of the situation, neither of whom were as uncomfortable as Matt. He attempted an attitude of dominance as he met Madison.

"Jesus, Madison. You can't just show up here like this."

A few days ago, before Ronnie's renewal of promises for the future, this opening would have triggered an emotional scene. But now, his statement could not end before her laughter and shaking of the head started, breaking off a piece of the tension.

"I can't believe you. Did you check her birthday in your files? Are you sure you're not committing a crime here?"

Matt laughed her comment off with an unstable guttural chuckle. "I'm sorry," he said and let a bulk of his tension escape his pores. "So, what are you doing here tonight?"

Her words hit a quick mental checkpoint. What would be his reaction to tell him about Eve's texts and meeting tonight? Even telling him about the other girls being upset could imply guilt. Would he understand their worry? *Or would he use it to his advantage?* As the words came closer to escaping, Madison felt more and more like this visit might have been a bad idea. "If I talk to you tonight, am I talking to the investigator? Or am I talking to my friend?"

It was not incriminating, but it was a bold gamble. She read its success in his relaxed posture and smile which followed.

"I'm a dick. It's my job. Please don't get too worked up about it."

His composure was catching; she could breathe involuntarily again. "Randi is getting worked up. But Randi gets worked up when she gets double-sat also, so that doesn't tell you much."

Matt chuckled at his recollection of his time with the whimpering Randi. He put his hands on Madison's shoulders. "I have to go in there and make some noise. What is Corporate going to do to me if they catch word that I'm coming in here and being a nice, happy sissy with all of you girls?"

"That makes sense, but," she started. *Mention names, or don't mention names?* She began to feel safe under the watch of his green eyes. "Randi felt like it was too much when you talked to her last night. And I take it you talked to Eve because she's left me some text messages." *But don't mention anything about going over there tonight.* "I'm assuming you were just as hard on her."

"Nobody has anything to hide, do they?" His melody was in the key of joviality, but Madison heard the words and not the beat, and shuddered. "I'm kidding."

"I know." She didn't. "It's just that we've been through a lot with all this mess, just want it to go away."

He gave her a hug but kept it short; Megan was still watching from the second floor railing. "You're the last one on the list, and then I am done. Are you going to be at work tomorrow?"

"Yes. I work the lunch shift tomorrow."

"Then go home and get some sleep, and don't worry about the way I'm acting. Nobody's being targeted. I'm a fraud investigator for Corporate, but I've been sent here to find out if this guy that's involved in this incident is trying to defraud the company. But they also told me to check out everybody and leave no stone unturned. I will create my report and fax it to Corporate when I'm finished, and then I will go back home with the original after another several days off. I hope that puts your mind at ease."

"You're taking several days off on the job?"

"Why not? I might as well make a vacation out of it. As far as Corporate is concerned, I'm finishing with a few more generalities with the general manager, and since my title is actually the Waste, Fraud, and Abuse Investigator, I'm sticking around to monitor employee behavior in detail at one of the restaurants, in order to ensure integrity and efficiency."

"Damn, I wish I had a job like yours."

Only remnants of the tension remained, but enough had dissipated to make both of them feel at ease, but Matt still had a lingering issue he was going to have to deal with sooner or later, the issue that always seemed to get him in trouble, and how he planned to handle it if her reaction was negative. He knew it would be a mistake to become too close to another server at a restaurant where he was conducting an investigation, but that had never stopped him from exercising bad judgment in that respect before. And now here he was caught with a second one. A second one that she knew of. He remembered the crash of his condom to the floor, and now he was the one who felt a shudder.

"How have you been, since the last time you were here?"

"I've been alright," she said, answering the question assuming its intent was for simple well being. But after looking into his face more intently in the seconds that followed, she felt he was digging for a hint of any symptoms that might develop into another child support payment. Truth be told, she was feeling a slight nausea and a change in her body's chemistry, her inner engine not cycling in normal alignment. She wouldn't know for some time before it couldn't be attributed to the stress and paranoia, or just a bout of psychological wishes and a possible false alarm. But this feeling she had is very similar to the way she felt a long time ago, the other time she became pregnant. She debated once again what she should tell and how much she should tell of it. "I've just been feeling a bit out of sorts." She motioned with her head toward his guest for the night. "Someone's still waiting for you. I'm out of here. I work tomorrow until four. You can get my interview done any time before then."

"Sure thing," he said as he backed away toward the stairs. "I will try to make it there early. When your interview is done, I'm unofficially done. Then my vacation starts," he said with a grin. "I'll see you tomorrow."

"I'll see you then," said Madison. Her grin was not nearly as wide and was mostly for show. He seemed alright, and what they had was just a casual encounter, but he was still on his way up to his room with a girl who was young enough to be his daughter. She actually hoped in amusement for a group of Lovelee's servers ending up pregnant with products of Matt's DNA. *Another national story?*

They said their goodbyes and parted feeling at least a little more comfortable than when the confrontation began. Matt felt more comfortable she would not show up again at his doorstep, either here at the motel or back home bearing burdensome news and causing him trouble in the future. Madison walked back to her car feeling she could deliver good news to the girls, and put an end to extracurricular intimacies, holding out with optimism that this ending with Ronnie is the happy alternative she had been waiting for. Her smile blossomed with the idea.

The first thing in her car that caught her eye was the illuminated screen of her phone. She left it in there when she was talking to Matt, and believed she heard it go off a couple of times, and knew she had at least two text messages, and knew who they were from. It was time to finally drive to Eve's place.

20

There was no route from where she was at to get to Eve's place as quickly as the others would have liked, which was twenty minutes ago, so she took whatever side streets felt like the quickest path and rolled the car from there. The closer she got to Eve's, the more doubt she felt that the sincerity of Matt's intentions was not merely a trench coat hiding vulgar intentions, a piece of wardrobe for his farce. But the hope that it wasn't was all Madison had to go on to keep herself at ease and to keep the group from declaring a panic.

She was so entranced with her worries through the trek of darkness and asphalt that she almost missed the turn into the parking lot at Eve's place. She was too busy observing Randi by the front door, looking like a frightened puppy locked out of the house, to look for a place to park, but an open space found her. When Randi spotted her, she opened the front door and called inside, likely announcing Madison's arrival.

"Randi," Madison said as she reached the top of the stairs to the upper floor. "Eve has been lighting up my phone. What the hell is going on?"

"Matt stopped by Lovelee's tonight to prove her story was bull, and now she's pissed," Randi answered in her classic whimpering dialect.

That must've been where Matt was coming back from. Confusion mixed with the rehashed anxiety, intoxicating Madison's being, as she got close enough to Randi to notice the redness of her overworked, sorrowful eyes.

Eve overtook the doorway and faced her new guest. Madison could tell by the look on her face that one of those nights had arrived where the ibuprofen in her kitchen cabinet would have been better suited in her purse. She could feel the ripples of discomfort infiltrate her cranium's comfort zone.

"It's nice you can finally come join us. Were you waiting for red carpet?"

Eve's sarcasm rubbed against Madison's skull like sandpaper. Randi heard Eve's quip and let out a nervous giggle at the reference to celebrity worship, and quickly shut up and lowered her eyes at Madison's reflexive hawkeyed stare.

Madison immediately felt a shroud of remorse smother her. "I was in bed. And I made a stop to try to sort this shit out."

Eve rolled her eyes in the first sentence and Madison knew she stopped listening by the end of the second sentence. "You mean you couldn't text me back? Get in here. We need to talk."

The faces told Madison the morale hit a low point some time before she entered, and there was no time for hesitation. "Listen, guys, we need to stop this worrying. I stopped by Matt's hotel on the way here and had a talk with him. He has to put up this kind of game for Corporate, but he's not going after us." It was clear by the time she finished with her say in the matter that the daggers of distress in the tension-filled living room were aimed at her. She even saw it in Karla's face. Randi was still too trapped in her own solicitous world for Madison to know the verdict from that juror, although the change in her expression hinted from initial surprise to eventual disappointment. But no such mystery occurred from Eve's direction. She was consumed in regret for the words she spilled which could not be returned.

Eve's words struggled to escape passed her teeth. "So, you were talking to Matt tonight. What else were you two talking about? Feel free to share everything with us." Madison knew the comment was not intended for an answer, and would have been met with the accompaniment sounds of resentment had there been an answer. It was meant to linger like a blaze of combustion in the air around her head, sucking up the oxygen and giving her the feeling of suffocation in front of the others.

"Madison," Karla said, speaking for the first time since Madison arrived, "I told them about what you told me earlier today, about you and Matt."

Eve cut back in to the conversation. "About how you can't keep your vagina in your pants, and the guy you pick could end up ruining this whole thing for us."

"I didn't know who the hell this guy was when I met him!"

"Well, it's too bad you can't take a day or two to get to know someone before the clothes come off."

Fuck that bitch. She has some damn nerve. But she's right. Madison's anger was drowning in her embarrassment but it fought for life. "Wow. Make way for the Virgin Mary over here with her stone throwing."

"Listen, bitch," Eve gnashed, and a bitter exchange of hatred followed that shot between the two of them while Karla's patience and Randi's emotional threshold hit their limits.

"Settle down!" Karla yelled in exasperation. She was finally showing her irritation about having this late meeting. Her mother had to work late, and will have to get up early for a morning doctor's appointment before heading to work tomorrow, which made for a very inopportune night for Karla to have to rely on her mother to watch Tyler. In an effort to keep this meeting from melting into a screaming match, she smothered her anger and took a shot at the role of mediator and was going to try to escape as soon as she could. The look of discontent on her mother's face still ate at her as she talked to the others.

"Listen, ladies," Karla said, "it was a mistake for Madison to get involved with this guy. But it's not going to be constructive for us to spend all our time in this meeting tonight attacking her."

Eve utilized the time Karla had the floor to grab a bottle of beer from the refrigerator. "What do you suggest we do, Karla, let her keep fucking up so we can all get in trouble?"

"Matt told me he's not going after us..." Madison started, her confidence noticeably deflated.

Eve took command of Madison's unfinished sentence. "...he's going after Ronnie. And you believe him? Even if that's true, I can't believe I have to remind you if Ronnie gets in trouble we all get in trouble."

"Do you think we're going to get in trouble?" It was a quieter version of that tone in Randi's voice that they all learned to fear, the fragile and wavering voice that would inevitably become an eruption of emotions. Eve tightened her cheekbones, visibly frustrated to withhold her own emotions while she performed her duties, and escorted Randi to the door. "I'm going to take Randi outside for some air before she has a panic attack. Karla, talk to her," motioning to Madison as the pair went outside.

Madison never wanted to be far away from Charlotte more in her life than in that painful, embarrassing trial before the six-eyed jury. At least for the time being it was just her and Karla in the room, the silence a few precious moments of luxury where she could close the door in her mind on anything but Ronnie and their happiness – the hope of it going right this time, the money that awaited them, the possibility she could put the Lovelee's lifestyle behind her. The inner world of possibility and hopefulness lasted briefly through Karla's dialogue infiltrating the hazy surface adjacent to the outside world, and Madison didn't make out what was spoken to her. "What?"

Karla tried again. "I was saying, do you know where Matt was before you met him at his hotel and talked to him? He was at Lovelee's playing games with Eve and Philip. At least, that's what Eve was telling us before you showed up. You might not want to be careless enough to take everything this guy says at face value. That's just a little friendly advice coming from me. We just can't trust this guy, you know?"

"I have to interview with him tomorrow during the day shift." She lost enough of her confidence in Matt's benign intentions toward them to lose the positive inflection in her voice. "Listen, I know Ronnie. He wouldn't bring us down with him if this went bad. What do you think?"

"I don't want to think about Ronnie. You can ask him when he gets here. He must have gotten confused with Eve's directions. He should have been here by now."

"He's coming here?" Madison gasped.

"I think he's coming. Eve has been pounding her phone texting him just as much as she was texting you. I'm surprised her phone isn't broken."

"His phone must have been turned off. I could have brought him here with me. We were at my place tonight." Her thoughts were shocked back to the talk of her night of gratification with Matt being disclosed, and she was glad she did not bring him along with her. "Please don't bring up anything about me and Matt in front of him." Madison could see the shift in concern on Karla's face as she endured talk of Madison's ordeal and the multiple men in her life. Madison caught herself in the catch of a slippery slope. "Karla, I think things are working out for us this time. I've got a good feeling about this," she completed in resistance to the undertow of Karla's guttural groan and closed eyes.

When Karla regained herself and faced Madison again, the look was priceless and worthy of a thousand chides, almost as judgmental on the level of Madison's mother. "You're a mess. You know that? I'm not going to say anything, but maybe you need to get your priorities lined up. And by priorities I mean this group and on getting out of this problem we're in."

Her shock gave way to relief in spite of the lecture hitting her in the ears. But if Ronnie shows up anytime soon, he'll be greeted by Eve in the doorway, and she wondered if he'll hear the news when he arrives. Her worrisome insight put the background soundtrack together, the car door slamming shut, the footsteps, the voices conversing on the other side of the door.

The door opened. Ronnie followed Eve and Randi's return to the living room, and as Ronnie found Madison she could tell from the look on his face that he heard the news she did not want broadcast. And she could tell Eve enjoyed giving him the news from the glint in her eyes and smirk in her lips that showed just enough to flaunt the deed, and the insidiousness which emanated from her in general.

"I'm late, but I'm here. I guess I just don't know my way around this place anymore." His face and remark smacked of perplexedness and frustration. And Madison added her guilt to make for an awkward embrace and kiss. "So fill me in. What is all the texting about?"

"This guy from Corporate is really getting under our skin," Karla said against the urge to remain silent in Ronnie's presence. "I don't know what this guy is going to try to pull. Just tell us if everything on your end is going just as we planned."

"I don't know what this guy's angle is, but everything sounds like it's going the way it should when I talk to my lawyers. As a matter of fact, he wants to meet me on Monday. I may have some good news for you ladies after I get done talking to him." His words brought a little much needed relief to the room. "I say the best route is to not make a bunch of waves and let this guy do his business. Don't tell the guy too much and let me take care of business on my end."

The brief feeling of celebration was a nice change of atmosphere for everyone, but especially for Madison, who enjoyed the break from getting verbally pounded. She had Ronnie's attention as he continued talking to the group of ladies, but that reminded her of the remaining strand of conflict for the night. "Was this all I was brought here for?"

"Pretty much, yeah," Eve said with a trademark apathetic gaze. She handed him a bottle of beer from the fridge. "Here's one for your troubles."

"Terrific," Ronnie murmured. "Time to find a bar and get a couple more of these after this one, I guess."

Karla quickly found her cue to make an exit. "I have to get back to Tyler so my mom can get some rest. I don't want to throw all the responsibility on her. And I have to work tomorrow for lunch on top of that, so I'm out."

"Not so fast, Momma," Eve interrupted. "We have girl talk to tend to."

Karla had no bandage for the bleeding agitation. "What girl talk?"

"Girl. Talk." Eve's eyes quickly flashed toward Ronnie and recoiled to Karla.

Ronnie took the hint. "I have a penis, so I'm finding myself a bar." He used his now half filled beer bottle for a halfhearted goodbye wave with a frown telling of the frustration he still felt from the night's news. His departure did not even wait for the chorus of goodbye from three of the girls while Madison followed him to the doorway.

"Where are you going?" Eve asked to the girl leaving the room.

"I'll be back in a minute," Madison answered in a matching tone of objurgation. "Keep yourself entertained."

Ronnie slowed down on the way to his car because he knew she was behind him and wanted to talk, and he knew what she wanted to talk about.

"I'm sorry," she said, getting to the point and hoping against an argument.

"When did it happen?"

"What day?"

"When? Did he tell you who he was? Was it before or after I told you I wanted all this to change between us? When?"

Madison rid of the space between their two bodies even though Ronnie wasn't completely ready for it. "It was before I knew who he was and what he was doing here, and it was before things changed between us. And there is nothing that happened after. I'm ready for him to be gone." She buried her face into his chest and cloaked his neck with her arms. "I'm so sorry."

He softened at the emotion in her voice and reciprocated her embrace. "It's OK, angel. Tell me nothing's going on and I'll trust you."

"It was just that one time. It's over now."

He held her and relished the moment for a while longer. "I have to go. Go on inside and have your girl talk. I'll call you tomorrow."

"Do you have to go out drinking tonight?"

He had heard this question and concern before from her through the years, when his drinking exceeded to a level which poisoned his bloodstream. When his poisoned bloodstream rivaled that of his father's. In the past, he used to react with the shoulder chip, a rare event of spitting imagery of his father. The past gave him a shuddersome feeling, and he planted a kiss on her forehead, a kiss he hoped his mother got a chance to experience from his father in private after some of his dark days. "If I do go out for a drink, I won't overdo it. I promise." He felt her exhale and could picture a smile pressing against his chest. He lifted her face toward his and kissed her. "Go inside. You've kept them waiting long enough. I know Eve is getting impatient because she is standing guard at the window."

Madison followed his gaze and they both saw Eve at the window, looking through the front curtain, and Eve's patience emptied when they chuckled. Eve motioned for her to speed it up and get inside before throwing the curtain back in place.

"I have learned to hate her," she said through a smile.

"It's almost over," Ronnie assured her and planted one more kiss on her lips before continuing to his car. "Get in there and finish up. I'll call you tomorrow."

"I love you."

Her send-off stopped him from opening the car door. He found himself in thought to the point that finding the right key to ignite his car engine and the whole world for the two of them was put on hold. He felt it from the moment he opened his heart to her, even before that, from the time he heard her voice again on the phone before coming back to this town he has been so apt to discard when the first opportunity would arrive. But the words would always circulate his soul and never want to escape his lips. She was waiting for an answer.

"I love you too, angel."

Her eyes widened and relaxed, and the world resumed turning again. "That'd better be your answer," she teasingly shot back. No one else mattered in the moment; Madison waited for Ronnie to drive away before returning to the dark interrogation room of Eve's condo.

Even Randi had joined the ranks of Eve and Karla in disquietude and impatience by the time Madison returned inside. Eve had already used and disposed of every sharp-tongued retort for her eventual return after taking her time, first to actually get there, then to say goodbye to the pig who has left her standing in the dust so many times she should have been much more efficient at sending him off by now. There was nothing left in the way of witticism when Madison walked in and sat down next to Karla, only seething agitation pushed to the back so they could get down to business.

"OK, we're all here," Eve began, looking at the floor. "Let's have a show of hands. How many of us cannot even remotely trust this guy Matt from Corporate?" With the advantage of establishing and knowing the question, Eve raised her hand to the air immediately, and was followed by Randi and Karla. All eyes hovered to Madison, for a moment the apparent lone dissenter. Her hand jerked up but did not rise completely to the level of the others.

"I know anything I say is going to come under fire because I crossed that line. There's no more conflict of interest with me. He's officially interviewing me tomorrow and then he's out of here. I don't think we have anything to worry about."

There was a moment of quiet contemplation which lasted a mere rush of wind in time outside while the oven of the living room began to simmer inside.

Eve's turn. "OK. How many of us are not able to believe what Madison told us about her other man, and that we do have something to worry about?"

The hands raised in a vote once again. The result was three to one, and the lone objection scanned the room. Madison knew Eve's eyes would be driven straight into her skull and Randi's would be diverted to a spot on a faraway wall. She looked to Karla in a grasp for what appeared to be an only ally. "This guy has already done his work. If there was a problem, wouldn't we have already heard from someone else? The police?" Madison could see Karla was just as convinced as Eve and Randi, and even she herself lost conviction in her statement as she spoke it. "Fine, you guys think we have something to worry about. What can we do except wait it out and see what happens?"

The temper resurfaced, and Eve took control again. "Waiting it out and seeing what happens can get us thrown into prison. Not jail from two months ago, prison." Randi moved to get out of her seat and flee, and Eve grasped her shoulder to stop her. "No going anywhere, sweetie. We've already had enough of that tonight. Let's get this out and over with, at least for tonight."

Madison now joined the group, in agitation and subconsciously inching toward consensus on dealing with the potential thorn in their plan. "So this guy can't be trusted and we have to do something about it. Again, what is there to do about it?" she asked to the room, to no one in particular, then noticed the other two were facing Eve. She put together mentally that, while she and Ronnie were either outside saying goodbyes or even before they arrived at the condo, the solution was already being discussed.

"Ever since last night, when we found out our partner was jumping into bed with our detective, I started thinking about the story Big Chuck always brings up with his buddies. You know Big Chuck, don't you? That big fat guy who's one of my regulars? He always brings up this story about his wife, like he forgets he's told it every time he comes in and gets drunk. He also forgets I don't like my ass grabbed by a big, fat loser, but he still does it every time right before he tips me.

Anyway, he likes to tell how he would do away with his wife if he ever came home and caught her cheating. I've seen a picture of her. He has nothing to worry about. He would gloat that he would get his hunting rifle and tell the guy to stay on top of her. He would shoot him in the back, but aim it low enough to kill her off as well. I think it's one of the bullshit stories I've had to sit through and listen to at Lovelee's that we can use."

Karla and Randi kept their eyes to the floor and did not react; they have apparently had this conversation already and had time to let it absorb. Madison was overwhelmed at the silence, assuming the others felt the idea of murder was a justifiable solution. She, however, was hearing it for the first time and felt otherwise. "Are you serious?" she asked, still trying to let the idea settle in and make sense of the insanity of it. "This is a line we can't cross. It's one thing when all we're taking is some money. If things go bad, at least with no money taken, we can try to make a plea. We can try for a lighter sentence, but we're probably not going to even have to worry about that. What you're talking about is something we won't be able to bargain with. We can't take this back!"

"If it's done right, we don't have to worry about taking it back. Since you've already jumped into bed with him, you and I are the main players. You get back into bed with him. I don't know about your mating habits, so for the sake of clarification, you let him be on top." Eve's razor tongue stoked Madison's anger and made a horrible combination with the nausea in her stomach.

"When I show up with Philip's Glock, your night of sex becomes a rape in progress, and I jump in to protect my friend and co-worker."

The concepts hit her quickly, but they felt slow and creeping just the same, felt it stinging in her chest. Being used for sex. Murdering a man on top of her. *Murdering Matt on top of me.* Madison's throat cramped and made it hard to breathe and concentrate on a debate. "I can't believe this."

"Believe it," Eve responded.

"Do we have a choice?" The question came from Karla and caught Madison off guard. She was at a loss for words to answer her.

Eve continued. "You're the lone member not on board yet, but you're the most important player, so you need to be on board. You're the one who knows where his motel is, and you can get into his room and get him on top of you. So, are you in?" The cloud around them thickened in the silence. Eve closed in with armored up vocals and paralleled her gaze more firmly in front of Madison. "Are you in?!"

Karla intercepted the controls before tempers could escalate. "Everybody settle down, and no yelling. Madison, we need you. This is not a situation that we can just wait around on." She hooked her arm over Madison's shoulder and took on a more confiding posture. "You assured me I had nothing to worry about when I stepped into this plan. Now it's my turn to assure you. We need you to be in on this with us. It's going to work. We need it to work."

Madison desperately wanted to feel more at ease in the blanket of Karla's comforting, but it was out of reach for her to grasp it. "How do I explain Eve coming out of nowhere to save the day?"

"We already have everything figured out." It was Eve and her razor tongue; what little existed of the comforting serenity of assurance was short lived. "The guy used this situation to cook up some imaginary scheme to extort money from Lovelee's. He has been coming in and harassing you and making you come up to his hotel room, and if you didn't do what he told you to do, he would tell the corporate office we were involved in this scheme."

"The imaginary scheme is our real scheme. Get it?" Randi said gingerly. She sounded as if it took her the longest to get it.

Eve continued. "The real plan to fraud the restaurant is just as good as any to claim was the made-up plan in Matt's scheme to trump up on you if you didn't give him the sex he wanted, if it came down to it." She chuckled. "The way we sound, we could run for office after this mess."

"It makes sense," Karla said in agreement. "He harasses you, you confide in us what he's doing, he wants you to come up to his room again, and we save you in what ends up being his last time he does this to anybody else. I've seen him around all these other girls at the restaurant. I guarantee you he does this at every Lovelee's he goes to. But you're the only one out of the four of us he has taken up to his room. So we need you to be the one who can open up the door. You get him to open up the door and we'll take care of the other part of it."

Madison heard what was needed of her and knew how she would get him to open up the door. It was too soon to tell, but she bought the test already and had it waiting on her bathroom sink. The queasiness and imbalance she felt each passing day felt more and more like the state she found herself in when Ronnie started a life in her, the site of a memory marked by a scar deep in her soul. She wondered if it would work or if he would refuse to open the door, just pack up and disappear. *Disappearing would be good.* "I have to go home. I work lunch tomorrow, and Matt is going to interview me and wrap up his work. So I'll be talking to him then." Murder infiltrated her mind and she became cold. "I'll have to give this some thought."

Karla looked up and saw the apprehension in Randi and the exasperation in Eve. "I work lunch also," she said. "We don't have much time left to think about this. We'll talk tomorrow."

"We both work tomorrow night," Eve said, referring to herself and Randi. "I'm going to get out of there early. I don't care if I have to shove my fingers in my throat and puke all over one of my tables. And I will be getting the Glock from Philip tomorrow before work." She turned to Madison. "I guess that means you've got twenty-four hours to do some thinking and make a decision for us."

21

Madison's shift was quickly coming to a close, getting nearer to shift change, and still no sign of Matt. Will Graham called him several times but his calls went straight to voice mail.

"I don't know where he is," Will told her. "That round top with your fan club seated at it will be your last one today and then you're done."

Madison was darting her eyes toward the parking lot as she spoke to him, and also catching a glance at Waylon Barbee waving his hands in the air toward her like he was an amateur air traffic controller. "I can give them to someone else. I'm sure they can survive one day without me. He should be showing up, and I'll be busy doing my interview with him."

"It's only going to be one more table, Madison." He spoke to her like a grade school teacher chastising a student not living up to their potential to a simple assignment.

"Then you put on a pair of shorts and wait on them. Remember to suggestive sell the appetizers." Just as she placed the period on her sentence, Matt's Escalade pulled into the parking lot at breakneck speed. "He's here. Who do you want to cover the table?"

Will wheezed out an exhale that reminded Madison of a Chihuahua with asthma. "I don't care."

"Nice decision making, General. I'll take care of it."

The round top was filled with her regulars and a couple of not-so-familiar additions. She approached the table to greet and give them the news. All the regulars were present: Waylon Barbee in a retro Ronald Reagan T-shirt, Steven Jenkins in his Reid Auto uniform, Jimmy Goforth in his Coleman Freight garb, Kyle Smith in his getup he wears on electrician duty, Darrell Sloop appearing to be the only one out of uniform.

"Hey, boys," she announced as she eyed the two new guys in the circle. "I have business to attend to, so someone else will be taking care of you today."

The group expressed their sorrow at the lineup change with pitiful grunts and deflated groans. "So, who are we going to get today?" Waylon asked.

"I don't know. Maybe Tanya."

"She's mean," Waylon replied to Madison.

"She doesn't take his crap," Darrell replied to Waylon, and everyone had a round of laughs, and he continued. "Obviously, I'm off today. I brought a couple of co-workers with me. This is Wesley Marx on my right and Patrick Bledsoe on my left."

Wesley Marx was new to Madison's eyes, but the other was one she had seen before. The man in front of her had a somewhat toned physique, decent complexion – clear, a shade or two darker, more evenly balanced – more poised and confident mannerism, not what she remembered. But the Patrick Bledsoe from five years ago was gaunt and emaciated, sallow and unhealthy looking, an edgy and uneasy wreck who borderlined somewhere between sociopath and psychopath, and memories of those days summoned a queasiness in her. He used to come in every day back in the early days of Lovelee's and latched himself in obsession to her friend Leanna St John. He apparently had nothing to do with her disappearance, but back then all the girls, herself included, were sure he did. He looked improved but still had those werewolf eyes with the green streaks in their hazel irises. She didn't have cause for feeling the way toward him at that table on that day, but the memories of the old days conjured the five year old bile to her throat.

Patrick Bledsoe. Michael Seitz. The masses of pigs and weirdoes that have come and gone and pinched and groped and obsessed. All the memories. *Something needs to change.* She filed her feelings away and returned to duty. "Hello, boys. I'm Madison, and I was going to be your server today, but I have something to take care of, so I'm going to find someone else to handle this zoo. I can get your drink orders though, if you know what you want." They called off their drink orders. The regulars were predictable, same opening round all the time. Wesley was indecisive and was going to have to take a few moments longer to decide. Patrick was the last to order. As he made his request, each other knew of the past and could not help but to have it show in their faces and the air in between, despite its masking and without confessing history.

She walked to the end of the bar opposite the food station, where Matt was talking to Philip. Both sets of eyes caught Madison in her path. Matt was all business. Philip was anything but happy. She quickly recoiled from the distraction and momentarily forgot about the other end of that bar, and that night, and all the interviews and games.

And talk of fraud and jail.

And murder.

She continued to her destination, where Karla was talking to Tanya as she made a drink.

"Hey, Tanya. I'm getting cut for the day. Do you want my round top over there? Before you answer, the guy next to Darrell in the black shirt...Patrick Bledsoe."

Tanya registered in a instant and gasped. "I thought he looked familiar."

"Oh, God. I remember him," Karla muttered.

Madison smiled. "Do you still want the table?"

Tanya pretended to think it over. "Um...fuck no! Who else do we have?"

Madison hurriedly scoped the dining floor for a victim. "Let's hurry. I don't want to keep the others waiting."

Amilynn Martin unwittingly saved the day as she headed back toward the dish room in a rush to drop off some dirty, discarded plates. Madison and Tanya chorused before she could get away. "Amilynn! Table 112 is yours."

The letdown stopped Amilynn in transit. "Seriously?"

"Yes," Madison answered. "I've been cut. I got their drink orders for you."

Amilynn sighed. "Sure. Leave their orders at the end of the bar and I'll pick them up when I get back."

Matt had finished with Philip and taken a table up front, a different table and atmosphere from the back table interview Randi had to endure two nights earlier. He did not have his official business ensemble of portfolio and briefcase, or even paper or pen, merely his presence at the table waiting for her arrival. She made herself two sodas and walked to the table and sat down.

"I hope you don't mind root beer," she said with enough cordiality but with a tone that implied he had no choice. "Are you ready to start? You don't have any of your stuff to make you look important today."

He mimicked the smart-alecky smile on her face and took a sip of his root beer. "This will have to do until I can get myself something stronger tonight. Are your friends still mad at me and think I'm a prick?"

Her smile maintained only as a mask as she strategized – *Should I tell him we talked last night?* "Yes, they're still mad. What do you expect, with the way you treated them?"

"We talked about that last night, remember? I have to put on a good show around here. Did you tell them that?"

"Yes, I did. They're not convinced."

He took another sip of his root beer in the pause. "Are you convinced?"

"Don't you need your papers if we're going to get started?" was her non-answer to his question. She took a sip of her Sprite as Matt waited to see if a real answer was forthcoming. When it wasn't, he began.

"This is going to be short and sweet for you, so we can put this to rest." There was a break in the tension for both sides, and he continued. "It appears your story has already been pieced together for me from everyone else's account beginning with you yelling at the man in question. What is the story before that event?"

"He hit on me, I told him to go to hell, he put his hands on me, and I hit him."

Matt cracked a smile and briefly broke from the monotonous show. "That was one hell of a hit. I saw the video."

"I think everyone has seen it by now," she said, almost in a braggingly tone.

"The problem I've brought up that has everyone worked up is that everyone has been telling me different or conflicting stories. I was just telling Philip when you came in that one of his Facebook friends is someone I know from back home. She has an ungodly amount of friends; she has four thousand friends on Facebook she doesn't know. So I had her become friends with him so we could check out his page. Sure enough, he had a cell phone video shot from the kitchen posted on his page the morning after this incident occurred. He told me he didn't have his phone that night, and that's why he moved the security camera. It seems he's not as intelligent as he builds himself up to be. Why would he lie to me about that?"

"I don't know. Did you ask him?"

"Yes I did. He's not giving me much of an answer." A mist of tension blew in both directions; Madison thinking about Matt's friend he associated with at home, just as he associated with her for a night – *I wonder how many associates he has back home. I wonder if I should get a checkup* – and Matt getting the feeling Madison was reluctant in answering questions and putting up a guard like the rest. "Then I have Eve telling me she heard what happened that night from the hand washing station, when you can't hear much of anything going on in the dining room with all the noise from those dish machines in the back. Why would she lie to me also?"

"I don't know as well. She'll have to explain it to you if she wants."

Matt could tell the interview was agitating her again and pulled back, choosing to end their meeting. "I don't need to put you through this. I have everything I need for the report. I'm going to wrap it up in a few days. So I take it I can summarize from your account you were acting in self defense, you don't know why everyone has discrepancies in their stories, and you guys aren't working some other angles in this."

"That would be correct," she answered.

"And you're not lying to me?"

"No."

"Is that how you want me to type everything up when I get back to my portfolio?"

"That sounds fine to me."

"Then I guess that means I'm done with my investigation."

Madison felt a sense of security with that statement, felt it for as long as it took for a vaguely familiar man to approach the table. He knew and recognized both of them. To him, "Matt, how are 'ya?" To her, "Hey Madison. It's Madison, right?"

Madison masked her puzzlement with a grin as she tried to place him. "Hi. Yes, that's me."

"Hey, Larry. Madison done for the day. I was just wrapping things up with her. I'll come over and talk to you when I'm done."

"No problem. It was nice seeing you again, Madison."

Still riddled. Still smiling. "Thanks, you too."

"Something tells me you ran into someone you don't remember," Matt joked confidentially as the guy walked away.

She tossed sarcasm onto the table with her widened eyes of feigned sarcasm. "What makes you say that?" she asked with her head cocked a little to the right. The laugh they shared diluted the bitter-sweetness of the moment, the air taking on the quality that made it feel like their last.

Matt pushed his root beer closer to her toward the middle of the table. "I will be finished in a few days and out of everybody's hair. I guess it's better if we don't make this last any longer. It might not have seemed like it at times, but it was really nice meeting you, Madison." The denseness of the air and moment increased between the two. Matt said a farewell but was far from running from the table. Perhaps he was feeling the same feelings on his side of the table, memories of pheromones past.

Madison drowned out the sounds of the world with the tone of his voice. He was sounding like a man who did not deserve to die. A cramp seized her throat when she started thinking about the plan again. "It can last longer. If you want it to."

He raised his eyebrows at the unexpected surprise. "What?"

"It doesn't have to end, at least not right now." She felt the ping of trepidation as she reached over to his half of the table and placed her hands over his. "Are you doing anything tonight?" *Don't get nervous, stay focused.*

He did not make eye contact, and instead focus his sight on smoothly slipping his hands away from under her envelopment. "I'll be leaving soon, and I have so much to wrap up."

"When do you leave? Maybe we can get together before you leave."

"In a couple of days." A pause. "Your friends already think I'm a prick. Hopefully I don't make you join them. I just feel making it last longer is just going to make it that much harder when I leave."

If you only knew Ronnie... She had to put in the effort to suppress the curling of her lips at her consideration of how trained she was for moments like these. "I'll be fine. And I'm sure you'll manage as well."

The stonewalling in Matt was evident while placing his hands on the mark, track spikes dug into the blocks ready for the gun shot. He chuckled and focused on the half-empty glass of root beer. "I think we'll both survive." The ending towered above them like a bell in a tower overlooking the city block before its inevitable signifying of the time. "It was nice meeting you," he repeated, and stood up and walked away from the table.

Madison watched him walk away as she took in the ending. She remembered their first meeting that one night merely days ago, barely a week, although with everything that had happened, between the two of them and the girls, and with Ronnie, it was difficult at that moment for her to believe the calendar was not in a conspiracy to play tricks on her mind. The blend of emotions she felt, the warmth of some moments blended with the angst and frustration of quite a few others, created a weird combination within, none of which meshed well with the shock she felt when she revisited the snapshot in her mind of the mystery man who visited her table, the cartoonish navy ship tattoo on the forearm on the guy named Larry, and remembered where she met him.

She walked toward the bar while looking at the table where Matt was making an appearance and talking to Larry. They both stole a quick glance at her as she passed.

"Do you know who the hell that guy is that Matt is talking to?" Karla asked her when Madison barely made it to the edge of the bar.

Madison didn't answer, just stood there and matched ghost faces with Karla. She didn't have to, because they both knew the answer. It was Larry Helms, Ronnie's neighbor at the extended stay hotel near Cannon on the edge of Charlotte, the man who saw the group of girls together with Ronnie, the man who was now talking to the man who did not need to know this precious bit of information, if he did not know it already.

The cognitive register of his name made Madison as sick to her stomach as it did Karla. Karla turned around to her thinned out pack of three bar patrons. "Is everyone good here for now?" She was answered by a muddled consensus of groans. The two girls walked to the back of the restaurant without saying a word.

Matt bolted from the side exit door with a to-go box of food and a wrapped up fraud case. He hopped into his Escalade and peeled out of the parking lot, in enough of a hurry to get on the interstate and beat traffic that he missed the red El Camino at the end of the parking lot, Ronnie Stover behind the wheel with his right hand resting in the passenger seat on top of a green burlap bag. Ronnie broke from his trance when he saw Matt's big black behemoth of a car pass across his eyes, and his hand clutched the green bag in reflex before resuscitating the engine and following Matt O'Dell into Charlotte.

22

It was the time of day when the lunch and dinner shifts met and transferred their duties; most of the lunch crew had thrown their responsibilities to whom it might concern and bolted to their cars, and most of the dinner crew had sluggishly trudged to the dining area, dreading the weekend crowd to come, another MMA night of all nights.

The lowest spirits in the place lay back in the employee break area, where Madison and Karla sat on one side of the room, tired from the work shift and weary from the episode of meeting old acquaintances. Eve and Randi sat on the other side and listened dishearteningly as they were told what happened. Randi was purely dismal and was not so much as listening to anyone anymore as she was being stabbed by the words and beaten by the shouts of anxiety in her head. Eve, meanwhile, took the news like a kindle.

"Goddamn, what a great work night already. What the fuck is Ronnie's neighbor doing in here talking to Matt like they're best friends?" Eve asked Madison but got an answer from nobody. "Hey, Madison. It looks like Matt's making more friends in town. This one has a dick, though. Do you think we should still trust him?"

Madison's reservoir of patience with Eve was purged but little could be done in the way of dominion by that hour; she could not have budged her voice to a level of authority to save her life. Her eyes met her feet. "It's not going to help us to be negative right now."

"This here," Eve said, referring to the four moping girls in the break room, "is not helping us. What is going to help us now?"

"Quit yelling," Madison shot back.

"Listen, everybody." Randi spoke up for the first time, able to finally churn the gears in her vocal chords through the storm in her life, the front of the real life situation, and the consequences associated with them, pushing their way from the outside in an equal and opposite direction against the front of drama in her inner world's stage. "We need to stop yelling at each other and think of a way to not end up in trouble." As she spoke her piece to the other girls and sought to restore order among the chaos, the other girls witnessed Randi's predictable spiraling to her state of helpless emotional invalidness. "We need to figure out a way to have anybody find out anything and people we don't want to see showing up around here." The words didn't get the best delivery, but the others got it and listened sympathetically. Her words quickly deteriorated into twisted, barely coherent syllables pushed out from her tear streaked lips. She collapsed into a big vegetative mess in Eve's arms.

Eve brushed her hair and kissed the top of her head. "You'd better get to the bathroom and freshen up, sweetheart. Jimmy and Bob will have a fit if you don't get out to your section pretty soon."

Randi enjoyed the soothing strokes to the back of her neck. She looked up at Eve when she regained the power of clear speech. "Aren't you coming, too?"

"Fuck them. I'm going home," Eve spat. She focused back on Randi, who was gazing back at her in wonderment, and wondered herself if she should explain and add even more drama which would further rattle her nerves. "It has to do with what we all talked about last night. You don't worry about it, just go out and get to work. I'll handle it." Eve kissed Randi's temple and held onto her hand until she found the strength to leave the break room, anxious about the unresolved.

"You're leaving early?" Karla asked Eve as everyone noticed a movement at the entrance.

Philip Martinez was relieved and clocked out. He stopped by the break room before heading out to the parking lot. "Hey, baby. You ready?" he asked Eve.

Eve got up and met him at the doorway. "Yeah, I'm ready. Let's go." She turned to Madison and Karla. "I'm going out to get our happy ending. If you guys are with me, then follow me."

Eve left with Philip without waiting. Madison and Karla sat just long enough to agree without meeting eyes. Madison was the last to leave. She stopped by the manager's office in the rear of a traffic jam.

"I'll meet you out there," Eve said to Philip, and waved the others to keep moving. When everyone had moved on toward the parking lot, she marched to the office and stood in the doorway.

Jimmy Thompson, the incoming manager for the dinner shift, sat in front of the computer to type up the next week's schedule. If one could imagine Helen Keller with two fingers, one for each hand, then one could imagine the computer illiteracy of Jimmy Thompson. He only knew of Eve's presence when he felt the sting of her stare on the back of his neck. Jimmy could take it no longer and looked up from the keyboard to face the distraction. "What?"

"I have to go home."

He rolled his eyes; this was not the first time a server had tried to escape on one of these nights; she was not even the first to try to escape that night. "Are you serious? It's MMA night tonight. You know how busy this place is going to get."

"Then give the other girls more tables, and they make more money. Or call Oakley in to work." Oakley hates MMA night, and Lovelee's accommodated her with little or no resistance, and Eve figured, *That bitch can do her share of MMA nights like everyone else*, because it did not live up to the fairness preached about in their corporate family meetings they were forced to attend.

Bob Baucom looked into the office from over Eve's shoulder. 'What's going on?"

"Eve wants to go home. Can you do this schedule for me?"

Eve turned to Bob with a teasing flare in her eyes. "We've talked about this last night."

Bob looked at his packed dinner, another veggie burger hidden behind its walls. "Let her go. We'll work it out. Trust me on this, Jimmy."

Madison and Karla tapered off their parking lot march and let Philip go to his car alone. Karla stared off into her own world as Madison fixed her gaze on Tanya Beaver walking toward her. She was a little late for work but not fazed, knowing none of the managers were going to get far by laying any wrath on her. Eve passed them and crossed paths with Tanya as she joined everyone outside and sang out to her. "Hey, Tanya. Jimmy's on tonight and he's wondering where you are."

"I'll forgive him," Tanya responded, not missing a beat. Eve continued toward Philip while Tanya stopped by Madison to give her a hug. "Please tell me you're working tonight."

"No, I worked today. I'm sorry, hon."

"Well, work a double so I have someone to talk to."

Madison laughed to offset the sadness. "It should have been you," she muttered.

"What?"

"I'll tell you some other time and it'll make more sense. I have to deal with something out here. I'll talk to you later."

"OK. Let me get in here so Jimmy doesn't piss himself. Text me if you need me."

Tanya left Madison to go inside and Madison left what might have been, while Philip left Eve as he pulled out of the lot in his car. Eve returned with Philip's gun in her hand.

Karla broke from her mind preoccupation when she saw Eve walking toward them, gun in hand, in full view of the public, with her finger on the trigger. "You think you want to, one, get your finger off the trigger, and two, hide that weapon while we're out in public, before you cause a scene out here?"

Eve stopped and soaked in the words with a bitchy scowl on her face. "Relax, Mama Bear. Anything you say," she bellowed smarmily and spent an extra seven defiant, showboating seconds on her way to her car before tossing the loaded Glock onto the front passenger seat.

The tension between the three began to build to a crescendo the closer Eve returned to the group. Madison fought to speak through her returning anxiety. "So you've got Philip's gun. Do you think you can just go out and shoot someone? Kill them for no reason? Jesus Christ, what do you think is going to happen if you shoot the guy who has been investigating this shit? You need to think about that before you do something you can't take back."

"What is this 'killing for no reason' shit? I can shoot and kill him if he's raping my friend. Do we have to go over all this again?"

All hearts hearing the proposition again, this time one step forward to the happening, seemed to take turns skipping a beat, even Eve's, who when imagining the act felt as engaged as a moviegoer, but the words of the act expelling from her lips producing a different rush altogether.

"Once again, you know where Matt's hotel is, you have already been up there to fuck him. Does anybody else know that besides us?"

The shame from Eve's statement stung Madison's face. "No. We didn't make that much of a scene." She sounded defensive in her response. She no longer wanted to hear the rest, but she no longer had a choice in the matter. "I just asked him if he wanted to meet again, but it sounded like he just wants to get out of town."

"Well, that's just tough shit. He doesn't get a say in this."

"This won't work," Madison muttered, more to herself and not strong enough to take control of the conversation from Eve, whose tone shifted to the side of mockery.

"You might as well finish, get one more in with him. Before I protect my friend from a rapist from the corporate office of Lovelee's who has been abusing his authority with a co-worker. It's time to get our defense memorized."

"Can't we tell him what we're up to, about the money, and offer him a cut?"

Unlike Karla, whose face showed consideration, Eve's state remained grating and unmoved. "And admit our guilt? Brilliant, Madison. Do you think your other boyfriend would even consider it for a second?"

Karla sensed a reeruption of the magma between the two and stepped in, placing a hand on each. "Everybody take a breath," she said in her motherly tone in hopes to diffuse the tension. "Before this goes too far, let's get out of here and see if there's a way we can get out of this without taking away anything other than money."

Eve shifted her arm away from Karla's hand and faced Karla untouched as her own woman on a mission. "You don't need to worry, Karla. Madison will do her thing and I will do mine. Randi will be here working tonight, and you won't have to be involved."

"I'll be there," Karla cut in. "I'll follow you there, Madison. What I'm saying is, is this the right thing to do?" She restrained her voice in an attempt to keep from enflaming an out-of-control situation.

Eve's agitation could no longer be contained. "We haven't been doing the right thing from the start! Let's all do the right thing, so Matt can have us all thrown in jail, and you can get separated from your goddamned kid! Come on everybody. I'm going to give Philip his gun back, and we can all go do the right thing!"

"Shut the hell up," Madison lashed out in a suppressed bark, "Keep your voice down."

They silenced when they noticed a couple of customers leaving through the side door. The guys heard them, and from their smirks and snickers most likely chalked it up to a typical catfight between two competing girls. The two gawkers were greeted by Eve's middle finger, their evident cue to continue the journey to their cars.

"We go there tonight, and you find a way to get the door open," Eve finally said to Madison. "Let's get out of here for now. We meet up here at ten." Eve's choice words silenced Karla for longer before and after. Eve reunited with Philip's gun and tore out of the parking lot, with Karla following suit without a word.

Madison gazed at the tail of Eve's car as she pulled out of the parking lot. *Matt doesn't need to lose his life over this*, Madison's first instinct to surface as she processed what was about to happen if Eve was to get her way. But in the moments that followed, she remembered the actions that contradicted his assurances that everything would be fine. And it's not like she would have to pull the trigger herself; Eve was ready to take care of that task. *What the hell am I doing? Am I actually rationalizing this?* She had to, though. As much as she would have liked to find another way out, a peaceful way out, the path paved was looking like the only option of getting away. Besides, as much as she would hate to see this happen, she would feel far worse if Karla lost Tyler, Randi had a nervous breakdown, and she lost Ronnie. She came to the conclusion that if Matt was their key to failure, then his unfortunate death may be the key to the door that leads to the only way out of this mess of a plan.

She pulled out her secret prepaid phone and called Ronnie. The exhaust from Eve's car still stained her nostrils, and the haunting of visions which most likely would greet her that night captivated her attention until she realized she ended up with Ronnie's voice mail. "Hey, it's me. I'm not going to be able to meet you tonight. I'm meeting the girls later tonight, and we're going to deal with this. I'll explain everything tomorrow." She stopped and thought of telling him about what they had planned for that night, and decided against it, and said "Good night. I love you," before hanging up.

PART FOUR
ANSWERS

23

His engine sounded off a few pings from under the hood as it just started to cool, as he fixed his stare at room seventeen on the upper floor of the Westingbrook Hotel. Ronnie took a deep breath and looked over at the green burlap bag, and felt the surge of finality and motivation. He grabbed the bag and got out of the car.

Inside the room of interest, the television flared with a meteorologist turned toward the graphics imposed on the screen behind her and motioning her hands in the direction of the mass of storm clouds that were moving in on the lower southeastern Untied States, not enough to cause any serious damage, but possibly enough to make for a trying journey back to Florida. "As you can see, these two fronts are coming together and pushing this storm east, southeast just in time for rush hour tomorrow morning for the Tampa and Orlando areas."

Matt watched the television with his attention split between the swirls on the map and the weather girl's bust. He pressed his jaws tighter and resumed his task of throwing all of his shirts on the bed next to his suitcase. "Give me some good news, you fucking cunt," he muttered to himself. "I need a good drive home." He picked out a burgundy hoodie sweater and a heavy black long sleeved sweatshirt. He put on the black shirt, tossed the burgundy one on the desk, and transferred the rest into the suitcase.

As he placed the suitcase back in the little area designated for storing the wardrobe, he glanced at the reflection of the front window in the back mirror leading to the bathroom. His paranoia of swearing he saw a flash of a shadow was confirmed with a knock at the door.

"Who is it?" he asked the other end of the door as he approached it.

The voice on the other side answered back. "Who else were you expecting, dickhead?"

"Publisher's Clearinghouse, jackass." Matt opened the door and let Ronnie inside. "Do you bring good news with you?" Matt asked in the time it took Ronnie to sit on the bed and set the green canvas backpack down to his side.

"As a matter of fact, I do."

"Is that the good news beside you?"

Ronnie flashed a grin. "Better yet, this is your half of the good news." He opened the backpack to reveal the promissory contents: Bank-wrapped packs of cash, a few stacks of hundreds, mostly twenties, totaling $125,000. Matt channeled his excitement in a fist bump, on which Ronnie connected.

Matt's smirk showed at the side of his mouth. "I interviewed her today. She was the last one. What I didn't expect was that your neighbor Larry showed up today while I was talking to her. I got him away from the table before he could say too much and let her know that we knew each other to the point that she would find out what we were up to." He laughed. "I think it scared the piss out of them. So when we finished I talked to Larry and told him not to say anything to the girls about me knowing you. Have you packed yet?" Matt asked Ronnie while he emptied the desk of his belongings. He didn't hear a response and turned around to see Ronnie lost in the weather pattern on the television. "Ronnie?"

Ronnie snapped back into the conversation. "Yeah?"

"Are we good, about Madison?"

"Sure," he said, but did not show absolute surety on the outside, giving Matt a source for his caution. "You didn't know."

Matt resumed his packing so he would be ready for their departure whenever Ronnie was packed and ready himself. The dialogue was a spillover from their late night discussion the night before in this motel room, causing Matt to cut short his own meeting with Megan DeWitt, after Ronnie discovered Matt and Madison had an encounter outside of his official report, before Matt knew having an encounter with Madison would place an unwanted barrier of friction between the two partners.

"No, I'm not packed yet. I'm waiting until tomorrow morning." The changed chemistry still swirled in the air between them like the weather map on the screen, but he brought it up anyway. "Listen, how would you feel about Madison coming along?"

Matt stopped and turned toward Ronnie with a book in one hand, an MP3 player in the other, and a forced look of perplexity on his face. "Do you think that'll be a good idea, considering what happened?" Matt placed the contents of his hands into his duffel bag in order to use free hands to give the money in the backpack a closer inspection. "I thought we had this all set. You come up here and get the girls on board, I distract them while you get the money, we go back to Florida before they know what happened. Those plans don't include bringing any of the girls back with us. Even her."

"Then there might be a change of plans."

Matt's facial features smacked of frustration in the short pause as he took the backpack and set it under the desk. "Are you serious? If that's what you want, you can give her half of your half. But you don't have to worry about me screwing you over like that again."

"What I meant was I might not be going back to Florida with you."

Matt stopped in mid-zip from closing up his duffel bag. He sat down beside Ronnie. "Don't get sidetracked on me. This plan worked just like we planned it at the Eire Times back home. We got the money, and now we go back home and open our own pub. We have the name decided and everything."

"The Gaelic Horse Ale House." Ronnie's smile represented reflection on good memories, when the window of memories weren't so complicated.

"Exactly. We're that close to making it happen," Matt said while patting the backpack. "Let's not lose sight of that after we've made it this far. Are we still on?"

Ronnie still thought about it. He didn't hear the question. He was thinking about the memories, the good memories from two years ago which greeted his life in the midst of all his pain.

24

The dispiriting mixture of lingering decay of life slipping away and the institutional pursuit of cleanliness   overtook Ronnie Stover in the hallway outside the Intensive Care Unit at the Piedmont TriCare Medical Center. He stood and stared at the sliding door separating light and dark, the only visitor entrance to the Intensive Care Unit where his father was lying in bed number seven facing death. Andrea Stover had been sitting beside the bed which looked day by day to be her husband's last, and put aside the nightmares of the past to allow Ricky Stover a final few days of peace. She was hoping her son would do the same.

Ronnie made it as far as the black paging box to call a nurse to let him in to fulfill his parents' wish before the emotional whirlwind overtook him, and he turned and ran from the hospital, from the pain and the bad memories and nightmares, and from Cannon and North Carolina yet one more time.

Ronnie packed all of the essentials he owned and drove through a myriad of emotions down Interstate 85 on his way to Florida. He swerved left and right and passed the slower South Carolina drivers as he shifted from anger to sadness to bitterness and back to anger. The echo of his father ranting at him as a child rung in his ear. *I don't get to go out and live my life because I have to clean up after your god damn messes.* And his mother watched it all and let it happen. And Madison made the decision on their child, and he felt the sadness and bitterness at the baseballs not thrown that will never be caught, and the stories about life that will never be spoken to deaf ears. *Who am I kidding? I'd start running, go out and live my life, like my father wanted to do.* He winced at the backdraft of anger, this time on himself, for backing away from the courageous decisions through the years when he should have stood his ground and faced them. That period of solitude on the road was what he needed to exhaust his emotional tank through South Carolina and Georgia, and by the time he crossed the state line into Florida he grasped at the optimistic fervor he needed for new opportunities that lied ahead.

He wanted to go – he *had* to go – someplace new. Time had infused the urge into his DNA. He brainstormed alcohol-hazed bar conversations about faraway lands where he could make a fresh start. He recollected talks at Lovelee's from visitors from the corporate office who lived in or near its location of Lakeland, Florida, and had no complaints. Ronnie declared his destination.

And he made it just in time; by the time he reached Florida, his wallet was as empty as his soul. He had the good fortune to come across a dark used car lot in southern Georgia in the middle of the night, so he could steal a tank full of gas in order to get across the state line. He drifted into Florida and settled his machine somewhere between Interstate Four and Route thirty-three, passing a temporary labor staffing office. He set himself up in a nearby motel and paid a visit to LaborNow, swallowing his pride temporarily to assume some cash to get by. He worked double shifts; he worked a shovel by day, digging trenches on the side of a nearby highway construction site, and worked a crowbar by night, breaking into drink machines along the same highway. Within days of arrival his euphoria for the future settled back below the surface and regained its hiding place under his resentment of the past. He scoped his new surroundings, both for an ideal permanent residence and for bars in the area. He found the Eire Times Ale Pub and enjoyed the atmosphere, but his first night at what was sizing up to be his new watering hole was ruined by a panel of flashing blue strobe lights that periodically found a way to make it back into his life, these particular lights belonging to a Polk County Sherriff's deputy who greeted him just blocks away from the pub, directly in front of the Lakeside Estate Apartments complex. The name was a crock, because it was nowhere near the lake, but it had cheap studio apartments available and it was walking distance to the Eire Times. He would have to check it out the next day when he got out of jail; that move would save him a bunch of money in the long run, when that handful of money could be found.

After spending the night at the county hotel and rescuing his Civic from the impound lot, he spent the next few nights touring nearby suburban neighborhoods and vacated houses for sale, and a few day trips to pawn shops and metal salvage yards. When he amassed enough for a security deposit and a month's rent, he secured his new home at the Lakeside Estate Apartments, then gathered his belongings at the hotel and slipped away in the middle of the night.

The studio apartment consisted of a twelve feet by twelve feet living area, and a separate kitchen and bathroom, and paper thin walls. The limited space with a monthly rent of $450 suited Ronnie just fine. While he listened to the apartment manager discuss the details of the amenities, he counted how many steps it would take him to walk to the Eire Times and how many steps to stagger back.

He spent the next couple of weeks becoming familiar with his surroundings, looking for a job while he took a few assignments at LaborNow to tide him over, and meeting regulars at the pub. Some faces came and went, while some looked more familiar each day he bellied up.

Then one evening he found someone he could be friends with.

Ronnie didn't like the look of the overcast and darkened sky, much darker than usual for five o'clock, and he didn't have an umbrella, so he made his walk to the bar early. By the time the impression of four draft beers marked his bar tab, he looked three seats to the left and noticed a curvy, fair skinned blonde whose hazel eyes focused on nothing and no one in particular. Ronnie got up the nerve to shift to the seat next to her, and her sense of defensiveness was activated. She did not appear as pretty anymore with a mild scowl on her face, but Ronnie persevered in his attempt to meet someone new.

"Hey. Are you waiting for someone?" She said nothing. If he were someplace familiar, he would have had a more confident opening. But he wasn't, so he didn't. He squared himself at the plate for another swing. "My name's Ronnie Stover. I'm new to the area and still trying to make friends with the locals. What's your name?" He extended a hand to her which returned empty, not even a name for the effort. He was about to give it one last try when she turned toward him and their eyes locked for a stretched out second that absorbed the surrounding idle bar chatter. "How about I buy your next one whenever you're ready?"

Her first signs of life toward him had the edges of suppressed hostility. She inhaled sharply and rolled her eyes. "Let me stop you right there. I'm not interested. And I won't be interested after another drink, so buying me a drink will not be necessary."

He tried to hide the hurt and make some more conversation. "No problem, suit yourself."

"I'm just waiting for a couple of my sorority sisters, and then we are going out."

"What have you got planned?"

"It's none of your business. It will be somewhere where you will not be sitting at."

Ronnie was taken aback, and would have been angrier if he had been in familiar territory, but on that night in that bar he momentarily felt the vast pitfall of a sinking spirit, until he heard a guy's brash voice break through a booth full of chortles from behind them.

"Well, somebody engrave us a plaque to commemorate the occasion. We have a sorority sister at the Eire Times Ale Pub."

Naomi Simpson, the regular bartender on the busy nights, spoke in a loud tone resembling authority, although by the shape of her lips Ronnie suspected she was amused by what was about to transpire. "Give it a rest, Joe Montana. Finish up your medication. I'm sure it's getting warm," she said in competition to the swelling chuckles of his friends nearby.

"Get us a plaque," he continued in an arrogant, drunken air. "We'll all take a picture together. Oh, like my fucking god, are you in a sorority?" he mocked lyrically.

The annoyed and embarrassed girl tried to maintain her edge. "Like it's any of your business, but yes I am. I'm Phi Kappa..."

"I don't give a damn if you're Lambda Lambda Lambda," he spat as the congregation of his supporting drunkards in the booth lost control of what little composure they had.

"I'm also Pre-Med, and I'll be making, like, six figures while you..."

"You, my dear woman, are a pussy with a mouth attached to it. And in a few years after your precious degree, you will be an expired pussy with a mouth attached to it. And you will not cut it in the health care field because I just have this hunch they employ people who have some worth. And the only way you will get near six figures is if you whore yourself in the affluent part of town. Here, let me get you ready."

The girl did her best to impede the unraveling as the man of medium build and wavy reddish blonde hair approached her at the bar. "You think you're some kind of hot shot, don't you?"

Not looking for this interaction to be a conversation, he continued. "No woman, I don't. I'm an ordinary guy who knows a whore when he sees one. There's no dresser in here, so the bar will have to do. This ought to cover it," he said as he laid two twenty dollar bills on the bar next to her.

The slap of the hand and the money on the bar was enough for the girl to lose what little composure was left. "You asshole!" She tossed her drink in the guy's face and began storming off.

Naomi called out to her before she could reach the door. "Hey! I still have your card back here. I need to run your tab."

She remained stationary, debating whether or not to declare the card a lost cause and report it lost, or just come back in the morning. The mystery jerk said to Naomi "I've got this. Put it on my tab and give her the card back so she can get out of here."

The girl started regaining her nerve and advanced to the bar. "I can pay for my own drinks. It's the least I can do because this will be my last time coming in here!"

"Good for you," the source of her torment sneered with decisiveness. "That's great news for everybody, because we don't need a next time from you. Take your card and shake your fat ass out of here. We don't need any more stuck up bitches coming around here taking up seats. Leave those seats open for the real trashy women we like to hang out with. In the meantime, we'll make up for the lost business." He picked up the two twenty dollar bills from the bar and dropped them into the tip jar. Naomi's smile hovered over the sorority girl as she scribbled her name on the receipt. She grabbed her card and hastily exited nearing tears.

Ronnie smiled for the first time since moving to Florida. He knew that night he had made the right decision in making this his favorite watering hole, and that the future might actually treat him in friendly terms. He was still taking in scene as the impromptu entertainer cleaned himself off with a stack of napkins.

He turned and addressed Ronnie as he worked on the mess around his neck. "It's not always this exciting around here, just when we get live ones like her. I prefer it when they're drinking beer, because I don't like getting these fruity drinks thrown in my face." Naomi heard him, and tossed a clean damp towel his way. "Thanks, Naomi. What's your name, new guy?"

"Ronnie Stover." They shook hands.

"Welcome to the freak show. My name's Matt O'Dell."

Ronnie had never been used to being part of a group, and hardly ever tried to be the leader unless there was money to be made. Luckily Matt had no issues in assuming that position.

Ronnie passed Matt a newly poured Guinness. "Here's compensation for all your pain and suffering."

Matt smiled and received. "Thanks, Ronnie. I haven't seen you in here before. How new are you to these parts?"

"I've been around for a couple of weeks now."

"That's why we haven't seen each other. I've been on assignment for about a month. I just got back last night."

"I'm still looking for work. What do you do?"

That was when Matt explained to Ronnie his job as the Waste, Fraud and Abuse Investigator for the Lovelee's corporate office. Ronnie briefly referenced his visits to the Charlotte Lovelee's while omitting the portion of his memories and the stigma and dull pains attached to them that came from all directions inside and out; he was not fond of them and not ready.

Even though Matt disclosed he was getting tired of the confines of the corporate compound, he seemed to enjoy some of the benefits not directly included in the employment package. "You've seen the hot pieces of ass that work there in Charlotte. They look that hot in all of them. And every time I have an assignment at one of the restaurants, there's always at least one girl who sees me strut into the place with my official ID card and gets wet for some guy in a position of authority."

Ronnie finished the beer he had been nursing for an hour, with a renewed appetite for getting wasted and feeling at home in Lakeland. "It sounds like you skirt as many twenty-something servers as I do responsibilities. I'm getting another one."

Matt stopped him before he could get up. "No. *I'm* getting you another one this time, my friend. Sit tight and I'll be right back."

Ronnie finally felt a home. In the succeeding months, he bonded with Matt and the other regulars Matt introduced him to. He noticed the polarized gender makeup of the place; the male patronage of the pub stayed mostly the same, while there was a steady turnover of women, with about half of them always looking new to the place. Matt and his buddies at the bar had a knack of cycling the flow of women in and out of the pub using their brand of misogynistic humor. Naomi Simpson had no problem with the atmosphere or she would have been gone long ago. She could handle them with her own brand of toughness, which she displayed on some interesting and entertaining nights, which is why she had job security as the bartender at the place.

Ronnie found this out one night in the middle of April. He had been in town a little over a year and was familiar with the regulars by this time, and decided to become verbally over-familiar with Naomi on this particular night with embarrassing results.

"This next one is on you, right?" Ronnie asked in an inebriated state to Naomi when he knew he was reaching the end of his nightly beer allotment.

"You can pay for your own, and I'll serve them for a fee. How does that sound?"

"Come on. This one is on you, sexy."

"How about this one is your last one tonight," she stated as she laid it down in front of him. She said it more than she asked it; she was getting that tone in her voice which the regulars detected was their cue to back off, but Ronnie was too drunk to know better.

"You can pick that one up, good lookin'. Then when you get off work you can come home with me and I can make it up to you."

Ronnie was kidding, but he was also drunk enough to not notice the stirring up and giggling of the regulars as Naomi, who did not pick up on the kidding around, squared up to him from the other side of the bar.

"Look, boy. If you try to take me home after work tonight and put me in your bed, in the morning when you regain consciousness, you'd have wished you just paid for your goddamn drink." She continued a little while longer, but the remainder was inaudible to Ronnie from under the uproar of laughter from the audience. She attempted to repeat the lost portion of the conversation, but her words were overruled by Billy Singleton, the owner of the pub, who was sitting in one of the back booths.

"Don't give up, Ronnie. I believe in you, buddy. Let's make a YouTube moment."

The embarrassment swelled his brain and pushed against the laughter and chatter from outside his head. Naomi was talking to him, most likely friendly banter acting as an apology for the outburst that shot him down, indicated by the wink and being referred to as 'honey,' but it all blurred in the background and lost precedence to the seed that began to grow in Ronnie's head.

The seed grew overnight in a gradual progression: How would Naomi kick his ass? Would she bring in backup? There were no other girls who worked there to join in. The video of that on YouTube would be embarrassing as hell. Would he be able to sue the pub if that happened? The pub let it happen, and he was humiliated. How much could he get? But Billy didn't deserve that.

But what about Lovelee's? Was Matt's loyalty loose enough to jump on board with him? It was worth a banter to feel out the possibility.

The next day, Ronnie quizzed Matt about his job duties: How did he go about investigating an incident at one of the restaurants? How did the corporate office decide on cases? How much freedom and authority did he have when investigating?

"Why do you want to know what I do at my job? Are you wanting to take over when I tell them to shove it?" he joked.

"No, nothing like that. My resume would just get laughed at. I got an idea I've been thinking about since last night." Ronnie continued, hoping Matt was serious about looking for greener pastures soon and not become apprehensive about committing fraud on a company that had placed their trust in him to combat that very fraud. As he laid out what had been conjured thus far of the potential plan, Ronnie liked what he read in Matt's face. Matt did not need more convincing before he replied by adding details to the voids.

"If you instigated getting attacked by a group of girls at one of the restaurants, they would really have to lay into you if there's any chance of a judge ruling in your favor, and that would have to be the case for Corporate to consider a settlement. After all, it's going to have to start with you giving her a reason to attack you."

"Something like, me putting my hands on her. A slap on her ass."

"Exactly, unless there was evidence of fraud. But that's where I come in and investigate, and they trust me to be the final word in that department." Matt took a sip of his beer and sunk deeper in thought. "Charlotte... I wonder if that would be the best place to try this. They still know you there, right? Maybe it would be best to try this in another city."

"It's been a year and a half, almost two years. There has to have been a lot of turnover since then."

"Are the girls in Charlotte tough enough to pull this off for us? That's what I'm wondering. We have to make sure we pick the right place the first time around. We don't have the luxury of shopping around."

"I'm sure they can if we practice it enough with them. Charlotte's as good as any place to make this happen."

The plan moved forward, now with a membership which included more than two people, and Matt's brow furrowed at the thought. "Is that wise? We'll need the girls to make this happen. But there's bound to be problems if we bring too many people into this. Plus, we'll have to split the money into more portions. Do we really need to bring them on board with us?"

"But we can't leave it to chance that the girls will attack me how we want so I can sue. And there'll have to be more than just the one I put my hands on. Having just one girl attack me might not look realistic. She'll have to have other girls in on this with us."

Matt finished off his Guinness and stared deep in thought at the insides of the empty glass. "I don't like the feeling I get when we're talking about bringing more people in on this. But you're right. If we have to bring them in, it'll have to be a minimum of girls. Keep it to three, four max. And whoever attacks you is going to have to know to take it over the top. If she doesn't and only slaps you, this won't work. Who knows, she might like it and then we're really screwed."

Ronnie laughed until he noticed two empty glasses, and stood up. "I've got the next one." Ronnie left Matt with a face which suggested he was wrestling with an inner irk. By the time he returned to the table, Matt appeared to have defeated the demon.

"Hey Ronnie, I have an idea to run by you."

"Go for it."

"What if the girls know about the plan and we let them in on it, but they don't get any of the money?"

Talk took precedence over beer for the first time of the night; Ronnie didn't attempt a first sip while he absorbed what Matt proposed. "How does that work? If we bring them in but run out on them when we get the money, they turn us in."

"True, if *we* bring them in." Matt waited a couple of beats for Ronnie to echo understanding. When he didn't see it in his face, he continued. "They don't know about me."

The missing piece of the puzzle flowed like a glue that filled in the loose ends: Ronnie arrives in Charlotte alone and recruits the girls with the end product of the settlement money split among them. The staged attack takes place and gains publicity and the lawsuit is on the table. As everyone awaits news of the settlement, Matt is sent up to Charlotte to investigate the incident. As Matt distracts the girls with mind games and clouds of uncertainty, he would complete his investigation reports early; the corporate office would be informed by their WFA Investigator no signs of fraud have been detected and the claim appears to be legitimate. While the façade continues, as the girls try to twist their way toward an exit with their best game faces on, Ronnie collects the money, and he and Matt disappear from the stage and return to Florida.

Ronnie made sure all tabs were paid at the Eire Times, pawned what wouldn't fit in the car, and slipped out of what used to be his apartment in the middle of the night, leaving behind the untouched paper trail of overdue rent demands and notice of eviction in the doorway – closing his obligations in signature fashion – and parted ways with Matt to return to Charlotte and recruit the girls. Plus, he could figure out the mystery of his mother's disconnected phone number and make amends for his sudden disappearance. *She would understand, just typical Ronnie. She always does.* He wondered how many of the girls from two years ago would still be there. Should he make the proposition to any of them or attempt this plan with new girls who don't have any history with him?

And who was he kidding? Not himself, but he wasn't going to tell Matt he had no plan to try this scheme anywhere but Charlotte. *Would Madison still be there?* With the fruition of the plan on his mind, so were his return to Charlotte and the memories of Madison, and he was starting to feel the void again. Knowing her, he was certain she still lived there and had the same number. But did she still work at Lovelee's? And would it be a good idea to bring her into this? The terms from which they left each other were not the best. In fact, there were no terms, which made the situation worse. Would the potential reunion play out like it always did or was he in for a rude awakening? And if the blood was bad, would it be wise to bring her on board, or even to not bring her on board, find out about the plan and feel scorned? If the blood was forgiven, could he use her and not have it follow his conscience back to Florida?

He spent two hours and a hundred miles mulling over the pros and cons of acting with his heart. When he woke up from his farce and realized he was deluding himself he picked up the phone and dialed her number.

It'll only be temporary. Get the money and go. Don't get attached.

The connection on the phone was made. Again.

"Hello?"

His ear took in Madison's voice, only sound waves in a phone but better than what he had, for the first time in two years.

He also heard another man's voice. "Hey." And he heard another phone. It was Matt's voice, and his present-day phone letting him know he had a voice message, and his flashback dissolved as he sat in a present-day run down Charlotte motel room.

25

Matt waited as patiently as he could for Ronnie to return from his mental journey. He tried again. "Ronnie!"

"What?"

"You had me worried, man. I was going to try calling you if I didn't hear anything soon." Ronnie exposed a hint of a smile and gave Matt a hint of relief. "Are we still on with our plans?"

"Sorry. I had stuff on my mind. Yeah."

Stuff was still on Ronnie's mind, and Matt could see it. "You're still deciding, aren't you? I can see it in your face. I'll tell you what, checkout time is ten o'clock, and that's when I leave. If you haven't met me by then, I'll call you, and you can tell me your decision. Sound like a plan?"

Ronnie stood up from the bed. "Sounds good."

They locked hands in agreement, not a definite and binding agreement as of yet, but Matt was relieved to have salvaged what he could of the partnership. The moment the three saw each other at Lovelee's the day he was interviewing Randi, and Matt saw Ronnie and Madison standing so close to each other as they coached the worrying mess by the drink station, he made the discovery that the girl Ronnie had been close to in this city was the same girl he had chosen to be close to for his brief stint in town. He should have said something the next moment he was able but chose not to, and he regretted it the moment Ronnie showed up to his room the night before knowing the truth. The argument was tense but not bond breaking, enough for Megan DeWitt to shuffle away smartly before talk of Madison and the plan surfaced. An hour later at a nearby bar the issue was deescalated enough to proceed.

Ronnie left Matt to pack the rest of his things. The voice mail on his phone from Madison that was waiting to be heard was burning in his mind, and he waited until he was on the outside walkway on his way to the stairs to listen to it. When he finished listening he turned back and knocked on the door and waited for an open doorway. "Hey Matt, I would watch out tonight and not go out to Lovelee's anymore."

"I wasn't planning on it. Why?"

"I'm not sure. I got a voice mail from Madison. It sounded like she was going to try to contact you tonight. It might be a good idea to not go anywhere."

Matt read Ronnie's face and wondered if the carrying undertone was concern or jealousy. "Gotcha. Don't worry, everything's going to be fine. Thanks for the heads up. I will see you tomorrow, buddy."

Ronnie left Matt to finish packing his belongings, glaring at the news on the television, feeling the green burlap bag itch the back of his brain, and wondering whether or not he would be returning to Florida alone tomorrow.

26

Death was on Madison's mind as she attempted her nap. Murder was more like it, invading her bubble in Cannon again. Only this time she had a hand in causing it, or stopping it. The nap was supposed to relieve the stress before heading out to the task, but the stinging pinpricks on her cheeks returned just as soon as she woke up around eight-thirty. She shut her eyes again and tried, but the thoughts kept swirling in her brain, of death and her long lost friend and the uncertainty of life. Leanna St. John survived New York City but not Cannon. *Nowhere is completely safe, I suppose.* After less than an hour she gave up and got out of bed to face the night.

She used the shower as a sanctuary since the bed betrayed her, taking longer than she usually would have, just trying her best to zone out and let the water enfold her as she wished her standing still and stalling in that shower could somehow prolong time itself. The events waiting for her beat down on her in tempo with the water, and she gave up and turned the water off.

She spent some time after her shower looking at her reflection in the mirror. The extra moisture on her skin electrified the chill she felt as she decided if she was ready for what lied ahead. She didn't have much of a choice at this point. One can psych themselves to the heavens to prepare, but only when the time comes and the act presents itself will one know if their soul is ready to follow through with an act with consequences such as these.

Her ringing phone made her jump out of her trance. She knew Ronnie was calling because she was tracing the sound of her secret prepaid phone. "I'm sorry. I heard you call earlier but I was trying to sleep."

"Hello to you, too. I was wondering if you changed your mind before you made up your mind." Ronnie picked up on the weight under her chuckle on the other end of the connection. "Are you okay, Madison? What's wrong?"

She was not up for answering questions but a voice not arguing with or chastising her gave her a moment's relief. "Things are getting out of hand. Karla and I are meeting Eve later tonight."

"I'm guessing this is why the two of us aren't meeting later tonight. I was hoping things wouldn't change tonight."

Madison closed her eyes and tilted her head toward the sky, feeling the stress and wishing she could find the lack of commitment to ditch tonight's plan with the girls and spend the night with Ronnie. Another indication she was finally ready to leave this place? "I know, I know. But this is something we have to take care of tonight. I'll make it up to you." She welcomed the blanket of temporary serenity. With each split second of tense silence the blanket slipped away from her.

"Madison, you said things were getting out of hand," he finally said on the other end. "What's going on? Is everything all right?"

"Eve's got a way for us to fix all this. We're handling it tonight."

"How is it getting out of hand?" Ronnie asked. *And what does she mean by 'handling it?'* he thought. Madison didn't answer. "Let me come with you girls."

She did not want Ronnie to come along; she figured the less of them involved in this act the better, not to mention how Ronnie would take to watching her engaged in sex with Matt, even though it would only be an act this time around. "We can't be seen together for now. You know that. Let's not be too careless and get caught." She couldn't believe what she was saying as she said it. "You'd better not come, just in case someone would see us. We'll take care of this tonight."

"Let me take care of it."

Madison stroked the line of responsibility and was close to taking Ronnie up on the offer, calling up the other girls and telling them to stay away, but worried any plan Ronnie had of taking care of Matt would lack the details Eve's plan had. "It's better if we keep this to as few people as possible. I even wish Karla wasn't coming with us. You'll know what happened soon enough. I'll talk to you tomorrow."

"Wait, are you guys on your way there now?"

"Soon. I'll call you tomorrow. Good night, Ronnie."

"Good night, Madison. Call me if you need me."

The connection broke and Madison took in Ronnie's goodbye. Her eyes barricaded the outside world from her tears. She spent a couple of deep breaths on her way back to the mirror.

"You're ready." She was still working to convince herself.

"Good night, Madison. Call me if you need me." The connection broke. "Damn," Ronnie muttered into his phone as he dialed Matt's number and listened to the ringing. He only reached Matt's voice mail and only knew it when the prompt pierced his ear and broke him away from reliving his conversation with Madison and trying to stir up a mental game plan. He shook off his business when he heard it. "Hey, give me a call when you get this. It's important."

He squeezed his phone in one hand and reflexively grabbed his car keys in the other. The will to act pushed him forward, but he stopped short of the doorway, stuck in a diminutive contemplation squeezing his keys, the framework for his game plan collapsed before it had a chance to stabilize. He dropped both keys and phone on the end table, sat on the bed and stared at the door while rubbing each side of his face with his free hands thinking about what he should do.

Matt heard his phone go off, breaking his pause from life while he showered. He had already heard from Corporate and had his balls busted about an early meeting he had to attend on Monday. He was hoping to go the rest of the weekend without another call. He suppressed a man-sized pout and continued washing. "Leave me alone, you fucking people. I'm doing something." He let the call go to voice mail. "I'll get back to you later," he sang out while he cleaned up and looked longingly to the fast approaching day he could walk away from that office for good.

Madison could not ignore her alarm clock on the end table as she talked to Ronnie to save her life. The time stabbed at her every second it became a victim of her peripheral vision. 9:31 when he asked her what was wrong. 9:32 when he was worried about her message. 9:33 when she got off the phone. It was time to get on the road with no more time in her apartment for motivational revving of her engine; that would have to take place in the car on the way to Karla's house.

The drive felt to Madison like the destination was ultimately a nervous wreck impossible to be avoided, but worth the try and had to be done. Gripping the steering wheel tightly kept her hands from trembling, and navigating an iPod in her current state was next to impossible. She managed to set the play to shuffle for the trip, which was beside the point anyway, considering the song now playing was losing the battle between the tempo of its playlist and the beat of Madison's accelerated heartbeat which reverberated throughout her body. She could even feel the pulsating through her eyeballs, each thump through her heart gyrating them and affecting her eyesight. She could still keep her car within the lines but debated the benefits of a car wreck that would cause her to miss the job.

She had to get into the right state of mind, because she knew they only had one shot to get this right. She spent the rest of the drive to Karla's house shouting a cadence of commands to herself, sometimes thought, and sometimes shouted to herself. *Relax...Stop being a nervous wreck. We have to get this right.* She took the exit off the interstate that took her to Karla's neighborhood. *Concentrate...You're not any good to the group if you don't focus. There's no more time for this.* She pulled into Karla's driveway. "Relax!" In the midst of all the banter with herself, she almost forgot to breathe. She took in a few deep breaths of fresh air as she waited.

Karla exited the house soon after Madison pulled into the driveway. She walked up to Madison's driver side door. "You look nervous. I could see it as soon as I walked out of the house."

Karla was nervous as well, Madison could see now see at close range. But she was doing a better job of handling it. "I'm actually much better now than when I started." Madison searched for the silver lining in the hands gripping the steering wheel and tried channeling Karla's nerve.

"We'll all be much better when this is done, I hope. I'll follow you."

Madison led the way on the road as the uncertainty bit at the back of her neck – what could go wrong, and what to do if it does? *What if I can't get Matt to let me inside the room to talk to him? Then we are back to square one... One less day to decide on another plan. What if he fought back? Then we've got the possibility the murder* – she paused to collect herself at the word's crossing in her mind – *that the killing* – wasn't much better – *might not appear to be in self-defense, or worse, we don't succeed in killing him and he gets away. Or...*

Madison was so preoccupied in thought she did not realize she was driving in both lanes and corrected herself before she really did get her wish. Karla made Madison's phone light up and chime at her. She answered "I'm fine," and hung up.

Eve sat in her car in the Lovelee's parking lot as she waited for the others, breathing sour commentary about guys who trickled out of the restaurant. "Jack off . Smacks his lips when the girls walks by and tips five percent, and he wonders why the service sucks." She reflexively looked at the clock and fumed. Another Elvis left the building. "Stalker Pete. See you again in about ten hours." She looked at the clock again, a mere ten seconds since she last looked. "Where the fuck are those whores at?" she stung in the air with a more peppered, bitter tone. Three clock glances later Madison and Karla pulled up past the parking lot entrance, with Madison signaling with a flash of her brights and sitting in idle just past the driveway so Eve could fall in line behind them, Madison leading the way to the destination and an ending to the mess they were in. Eve turned the key in the ignition, roaring the engine to a temperature matching her face, and fell into line with the others.

The Westingbrook Hotel's outer walls have witnessed the rising and modernization of the city's center through the past several decades, its inner walls the witness to petty drug deals the size larger than a handful and half-hour long episodes of cheap sexual gratification. It had even been the site of two murders, both in the seventies, both crimes of passion. As the girls neared the landmark, Madison Davis could feel inside her the tremor of the inevitable, the building's witness to another episode in its seedy history.

As soon as the drive down the interstate began, Madison doubted in her ability to make it to this macabre action's end. All the alternate scenarios that could possibly trip them up popped up and would not leave her alone as she moved the air conditioning vents to be hit in the face with the cold air. She still felt hot. She made progress as the drive progressed, found the confidence within her and returned to a normal world of breathing and a highly held chin, her eyes narrowing with determination and cold calculation. Then she saw the Westingbrook Hotel on the horizon and felt a relapse. By the time she reached the crackling structure, the confidence she collected felt to have vaporized and steamed away. The aged white walls, fading dark green of the shutters, and hard life of the beige curtains that once held a quaint, vintage quality in Madison's eyes now just looked grimy.

Eve parked her car behind the hotel on the far end of the empty lot to the hotel's rear, while Karla parked on the opposite side of the main road looking away from the aspiring metropolis of uptown Charlotte, positioned to get out of the city as fast as possible when this was all over. Madison parked her car on the edge of the parking lot with her car facing the hotel. By the time Eve met her at the side of her car with Philip's Glock in tow, Madison felt as if her nervous system had flashbacks of 9:30 in the harsh light of her alarm clock.

"I hope you're ready to do this," Eve declared while shifting her eyes to either side, clearly agitated at having to wait for Madison to finally build up the momentum to get out of the car. "Nice of you to join us. We have to get this started while Matt is still in the room. We can't risk doing anything out in public view. Do you know if Matt is up there right now?"

Madison overlooked Eve's umbrage in her solace that Eve was also enduring this event with her own share of nervous tension, hiding under the skin but visible to the attuned eye. She located his car in the lot and saw the illumination through the curtains in room seventeen. "Yes, he's up there."

The girls walked toward the staircase in position, Madison in front, Eve behind her, Karla still monitoring from her car on the street. The closer Madison got to the upper floor, the more nervous she felt, but the feeling paled in comparison to the feeling in her that intensified as she neared the door, the product of her heartbeats moving up to choke her in a frantic rhythm. As far as her hand was concerned, the door of room seventeen was a barricade of molten hellfire capable of melting it on contact; it refused and ignored the messages from the brain to do what needed to be done. Madison's hand constricted crippled in a fist and aimed hesitantly for the door. Each knock on the door sent a chilling vibration up her arm to her shoulder. She willed a breath into her lungs and squared herself face-to-face with the frightful door.

The other side of the door was a different paradigm of nervous excitement. The pace was slower than earlier as Matt O'Dell was now almost entirely packed for the trip out of town, with the exception of the few items he was planning to utilize that night and the following morning. Some of which were clothes for tomorrow and tonight but none were being utilized at the moment as he lay naked in bed as he air-dried post-shower while watching the television. He separated papers from a stack that were needed and shoved them into a small tote bag then sprang from the bed with the others and dropped them into the wastebasket by the desk. He braked his momentum back to the bed when he heard the knocking on the door. Matt reacted to the knocks on the door as if no one in the world was supposed to be bothering him for the rest of his stay. He was in the process of hastily donning a pair of jeans when his phone came to life. "Sure would like some peace on my last night," Matt mumbled to all concerned as he tried to operate the phone while simultaneously finishing his task with the jeans. "Who is it?" He began with the phone, but the question was loud enough for Madison to think it was directed toward her.

"It's Madison." Matt didn't hear her.

The voice in the phone answered. "It's Ronnie. We're not looking at our displays now?"

"Give me a break. I'm juggling a few things right now. What's up?"

"Listen, do me a favor, buddy."

Madison knocked on the door again. Matt pulled his face from the phone. "Hold on out there."

"Matt! It's Madison. Open up."

Matt heard her loud and clear this time. "What?"

So did Ronnie. "Madison?"

Matt hung up the phone.

"Matt. Matt! Fuck." Ronnie fumbled his fingers across the keypad and dialed Matt's number again. This time the call went straight to his voice mail. His brain wondered what the girls were up to as his ear heard Matt's voice greeting. He hung up the phone without speaking after the beep and snapped into action, grabbing the keys to his car and running out of the barren apartment.

"What are you doing here?" Matt called out to the other side of the locked door.

Madison choked on the frustration at starting their conversation across the barrier with the tarnished brass numbers staring her in the face and not Matt himself. She braced herself and tried her best to keep from letting it resonate in her voice. "I really need to see you tonight. There's something I need to discuss with you."

"Tonight's not a good night," he shot back with the intention of sounding cold and defiant. His intention failed and was defeated by his swelling arousal. On his way to the door to play with the chain lock he had unbuttoned his pants to vent out the arousal, but that wasn't working for him, either.

"Matt, this can't wait. I really need to see you." Her fright almost made it sound like she was on the verge of crying.

He could envision her beyond the door, what she looked like, could almost take in her scent through the door in his mind, and he could feel himself stumbling on that familiar road that had led him in the past to an intersection with trouble. His hand playing with the chain clenched into a fist and he righted his veer. "Does this really have to happen tonight? Not a good time in here. Come back tomorrow night. We can talk then." The only stab at the silence in the air was the ambiance of traffic on the street in the background and Madison's breath against the door.

He wasn't making any overt indication he wanted her on the other side. Suddenly, a thought entered his mind and he followed it. "You're not pregnant, are you?"

She didn't answer directly. She answered with a pause and another question. "Can I talk to you?"

She stood what seemed minutes ago impossibly still while she anticipated hearing a smartass shot back toward her through the door – *we are talking, aren't we* – but instead heard a brush as his weight against the door disappeared, followed by the sound of the chain lock coming undone. The door was opening up in front of her. He was opening up to her. "Get in here," he said guardedly through the gap in the opening door.

Madison entered a surprisingly sterile room that seemed almost empty and unused. That concept disappeared from her consciousness when she turned around and faced off with a relocked door and completely naked Matt O'Dell.

"Are you kidding me?" he asked. The tone of his voice danced in a middle ground of sensual joking and irritable skepticism. Madison had trouble deciding which was the subtext dominating his lips; she was too busy splitting her attention to being drawn to his nakedness and diverting her eyes from it. "How long has it been? You know you're pregnant already?"

"It's only been a week. Too soon to tell," she stammered as she calculated. "But I have been feeling different. Not sick, but..."

"I'm sure it's nothing. Just give it a few days and see how you're feeling. You have my number, so whatever happens, you call me and we'll work it out." He planned on keeping his current number as much as he planned on being around tomorrow night to meet her again.

The spark within her reignited, what she was preoccupied with earlier: the cleanliness of the room, the emptiness, the condition which suggested one might not be there any longer really soon. She spotted his packed bags. "You're leaving?" No answer. "Before tomorrow night?" Her dialect began to match his. "So, how are we supposed to meet tomorrow night?"

"Why are you back here?" he finally replied, a question with a question, the same enigmatic darkness in his voice.

"Don't you want to see me again?" she volleyed back. By now, she felt like a veritable prostitute. She could virtually feel Eve's impatience on the other side of the door, and she lowered her guard. "Listen, you don't need to worry if I end up being right. I'm not going to come after you for child support or to be in her life."

He cracked a smile. "So you know it's a girl already, too?"

She had reached the point of exasperation and chuckled, almost deliriously. "Or a boy… Come on, don't be like this. Don't you want to see me again?" Her voice steadied to a tone highlighted with seductiveness, changing into her sex eyes and throwing the dice. She looked across to her target and saw snake eyes.

"We are seeing each other, right now," he said.

Snake eyes.

Matt had been at this junction before many times. Darlene Miller caused quite a scene in Columbia, complete with property damage. Patricia Crump was devastated, and quit the Knoxville Lovelee's less than a month later. Diana Stapleton in Atlanta, Gina Rodriguez in Tampa, Faye Stein in Raleigh, and scores of others struggled through this tragic scene. His face, at first braced for receiving that answer that would finish the night, punctuated by her barreling out the door and down the walkway with tears streaking her face, for his own good more than hers, was now transformed into the face of a man who still had not learned his lesson, each moving frame of life's camera exposing more of his bluff and impending mistake. The talk of a woman's altered chemistry stirred an upsetting inside him. He wondered about the talk of pregnancy, and if all of this ended in a new life, would it be another judicial nightmare of monthly payment and dragging through the mud like the last time, regardless of her insistence now to go it alone. Matt closed his eyes and wrestled with the reflux brought on by the irritation and the lust, and could feel the fever of his arousal clashing with the chill from the sinking feeling in his spirit because he knew, like an addict reasoning with himself, he was going to act against his better judgment in the name of pleasure. *Don't need her tonight. Don't be fucking stupid.* His stab at fooling himself at the last minute was a helpless joke.

"Do you still need help losing those clothes?"

His eyes rose to meet hers. Her eyes rose to his face, looked through his face to the fastened lock on the door, an action she was going to have to reverse in order for them to proceed; she was unsure of Eve's strength to kick the locked door in, and she did not want to chance it, although Madison was sure at this point Eve was agitated enough to pull the feat. When each others' inhibitions and trepidations and doubts no longer had the strength to keep them from their objectives, they raced to each other.

Matt made it to the waistband of Madison's pants before she could make it to the lock on the door. Her panic turned into motivation, and she forced herself into Matt and drove into the foreplay with an aggressiveness which took Matt by surprise. He pulled his face away and smiled. "Show me what you've got, She-Ra." Madison laughed at his remark to mask her disappointment in coming up short of the lock. She lost her advantage in the distance and felt it slip away as he guided her onto the bed. As her body dropped to a restful position on the bed, her left ear was consumed by the drone of the roaring air conditioner. She turned to the window unit, giving it her full attention, and picked up on the burning clue.

"That A/C is freezing," she blurted with a rush, then added a dash of playful leading in her voice. "Could you turn it off and open the window? It's such a nice night out."

He stopped in mid-fondle and looked at her in a dance between stupefaction and disaccord. "Really? It's hotter than fuck outside."

"It's colder than fuck in here," she said mockingly. "I hate the smell of the air in those things. It's cooling me off too much, you know what I mean?" She bit her lower lip and hoped it was enough.

Matt hesitated only momentarily before giving in to the subtext and pushing himself in a bound up off the bed and to the air conditioning unit. He executed it to a standstill with a twist of a dial, and with an impatient swing of his hand opened the window next to the door. "Does that work?"

"It feels much better already." Madison matched his fake smile to hide her estimate of Eve's arm length shortcomings. "Much better." But it would have to do. She would have to give Matt a great performance to keep him distracted while she let Eve work out the rest of what needed to be done behind his back. He gravitated back to the bed and stripped off her clothing until she matched him in his nakedness. The tension invaded her body once again as she tried to take her mind off the appearance from Eve that was soon to interrupt them.

The night air blew inside and felt refreshing against her perspiration. Madison was praying, more than a frivolous call to God during sex, but a burning desire for Eve's timing to work out the way Madison wanted. *Please...* "Oh, God..." *Please...* At first she wanted one more complete experience, but now wanted it to just be over, for Eve to barrel in and interrupt the deed which was now making her feel like a real professional and to get on with the deed to free the girls and Ronnie from their ordeal.

Her lucky day must have been hiding behind a horizon for some other time; Matt had the seconds needed to finish. When he did, punctuated by a sustained grunt, he leaned into her, and Madison went limp and relaxed, enjoying the capsule of time that rested between the climaxes. She just hoped and prayed to one kingdom or the other the next step to this operation would be conducted with cool heads.

27

The momentary shell of silence encompassing the hotel room broke with the force of a size seven shoe against the door, which swung open and hit the adjacent wall announcing Eve Kennedy's arrival. Matt shuttered back into reality, jerking his head toward the door.

Madison shifted back into her role. "Stop! Get off of me!"

Matt jumped at Madison's sudden about face. He began to leap off of her to grant her wish.

Eve raised the Glock toward Matt. "Stay where you are, motherfucker!" Matt assessed the two commands, and given Eve's object of persuasion, he opted to granting Eve her wish, and stayed put on top of Madison.

"Madison, what the hell is going on?"

The show went on, and she was still in character, pointing her voice toward the open window.

"Please stop. Get off of me. STOP!"

Eve's turn. "Get the fuck off of her, asshole!"

Matt winced at the pain of contradiction. *She just said a few seconds ago... Fuck.* He started wondering if staying where he was at would get him killed, and started to get up, but Madison's grip on his elbows impeded his release. He could not think so clearly through a cloud of contradictions and threats, not to mention the consequences attached to making the wrong decision, so Matt stayed where he was and attempted to calm down and clear his mind.

Madison could feel him tremble through the grip on his elbows and the contact of their lower bodies. She looked up at the ceiling and made a wish that this would all be over as soon as possible. She was almost as scared as he was. "Madison? Madison, look at me," she heard him plead. There was a crack in his voice to which she gave no acknowledgement. She just steeled her eyes and continued to fixate her eyesight to a spot on the ceiling and not try to speak until this was finished. Very nearly the longest six seconds of Madison Davis's life travelled the axis that was the small world the three of them lived and played out their terrible tragedy.

When the six seconds unraveled and Matt was still alive, Madison felt like she woke up from her dream and into a nightmare. "Eve? Eve!" Madison leaned her head to the side and discovered she and Matt were not the only ones in the room that were trembling. Eve fought to maintain her steady hand and menacing presence and was failing; it was dawning on Madison that Eve was not as tough as advertised when it really mattered.

Karla entered the room. "What's wrong? We can't waste time like this. Pull the trigger."

Eve's frustration was broadcast through her bark and her agitation. "Get off my case, goddamnit! Give me a second." The short outburst did not help move business forward, and the mistake Eve made in taking the liberty of appointing herself to the wrong position was becoming obvious.

Karla was the only confident person in the room. She walked into that hotel room to support the others, but had a gut feeling before she left her house she would have to take a more paramount role in this show, and came into that room equipped for the role if needed. "What now? Did you think about what to do if this happened, if you didn't have what it would take to pull the trigger? How about trying to explain how you just happened to be carrying around Philip's gun with a scratched out serial number?"

Matt heard the conversation and peeked toward Eve. He could see she was scared, and would most likely not use any of the rounds living in and waiting to be emancipated from her weapon. He started to slowly make his way off Madison and the bed. Karla shifted in his direction and withdrew from her purse a Taurus .357 revolver and pointed it at him with a much steadier hand than Eve's. Matt took quick notice of the gun, a compact gun that could easily fit in her purse, but definitely had the potential to do the needed damage.

"Get back where you were at."

Matt could see in Karla's eyes she had no problem taking it to the necessary level if need be, and did as he was told. Madison felt his tremors of terror again when he returned on top of her.

Eve lowered Philip's gun and placed it in her waistband. "I didn't think you were coming up here," she said to Karla, not intending to sound so defeated.

"I want to make sure this happens how we need it to happen. I'm not losing Tyler." Madison had heard Karla reach her boiling point with drunken customers and bitchy servers on occasion, but only the threat to her family and her way of life with them could bring her to the transformation in her character Madison was witnessing.

Matt's manhood eroded before their eyes. "Listen, you guys are not going to get into trouble. This is all fake. We're just faking you girls. Just let me go. Please listen to me."

Matt's eruption of babbling was abruptly stymied by Karla. "Oh, that's bullshit. Shut your mouth!" Matt's surprise and astonishment at Karla's potential for authority created a capsule of silence. Karla continued as a fog of tension seeped into the room and made everything pertaining to living a struggle. "We can't take that chance," Karla declared as she drew back the hammer. "Eve, get out of here before this happens." Eve left the room without goodbyes or eye contact.

Resignation to the inevitable set in for everyone. Madison brought her eyes straight ahead to meet Matt's for what would most likely be his final minute on this earth. Unless some angel was ready to intervene and spare his life, but Madison doubted it, and Madison felt like the one in need of an angel, and her thoughts drifted to Leanna, wishing she was there to help but mainly to numb her mind to what was about to happen. She saw the hurt in his eyes and anguish in his face, felt the tension grip everything in the room, and tread in the realization of the loss and damage she was having everyone close to her suffer. Even in this traumatizing moment, she gravitated back into her own inner world and wondered to herself if, given the opportunity to go back to the beginning of this mess and do it all differently, would she do it. An epiphany captivated her attention: True, this man made the decisions which led to his whimpering his final moments away, but her decisions contributed to it, and at that painful junction in their lives her soul hungered to exchange her apology for his forgiveness.

The tableau raced through her imagination, steadying her nerves for one brief moment with a sweet ring that was abruptly interrupted with a piercing, intruding ring she knew could only be the shot everyone was waiting for. Then the warmth of the blood hit her face, and Matt slumped in his final position before death, gasping in vain for a breath of life. Madison's head echoed with the lingering gunshot in her ear and the regret that her actions could not be taken back, and everyone's life had been changed, and worse, as a result. Matt, in all his flawed presence in their lives, did give her a tiny moment of pleasure in this adventure, and this was his reward, and the least she could have done was met his eyes and told him in the end that she was sorry, truly sorry for the actions upon which this had to end. She lost her opportunity, and felt the emotion attached to the regret reach her chest.

She fought to see through the mist in her eyes and breathe past the knot in her throat and through the smell of blood as she pushed Matt's lifeless body to the side and freed herself enough to get out from under the carcass and out of the bed, and was greeted at the foot of the bed by Karla with a sheet from the other bed.

Madison let Karla wrap the sheet around her. She grabbed the top edge of the sheet and attempted in vain to scrub away the effect from her face. When it was no use and she tore the sheet from her eyes, she noticed Ronnie at the doorway. He entered around the time of the gunshot, either just moments before or moments after, and the two both stood frozen into each others' eyesight until she felt the product of her agony from the ordeal she just endured, and jogged to the sink next to the bathroom, feeling she might be sick.

There was no product of sickness as she hovered over the sink, although she thought she would have felt better if there was. A turn of the valve started the hot waterfall cascade in the sink, its sound filling her ears and trying to help her drown out the ghostlike echoes of the gunshot that refused to go away. Ronnie's presence could be felt behind her while she wet a washcloth to wipe off as much blood as she could find around her face and arms. It was nearly impossible to get it all off without a bath and therapy, and her nerves refused to let her do a better job. The blood, stress, and trauma were enough for her to deal with, but the whole picture was becoming intolerable with the added paranoia brought on by Ronnie hovering in the immediate background, so she had no choice but to postpone the cleansing and confront Ronnie.

"Are you okay?" he asked over her shoulder.

She peered up at his reflection in the mirror, her glance hardening into a pointed stare as she wrung the riddle out of the turmoil around her.

"How did you know to come here?" Her senses were still shell shocked; she was only able to intake clouds and blurs around her. She heard the running water and the trace of the gunshot that now haunted her memory, creating a disturbing melody with the accompaniment of the city's heartbeat in the background and her thumping heartbeat in the foreground. She even heard the faint sound of sirens in the distance and wondered if they were headed their way. She heard anything imaginable except an answer from Ronnie to her question. Her rising anger dug fine edges into the clouds and blurs in the room. "You knew where Matt was staying at? I didn't tell you that on the phone. How did you know to come here?"

"How did you?" It was all he could muster from his lips.

Madison grew resentful of the reflection and turned to face him. "You know Matt."

He did know Matt, now in the past tense and memories he would carry like chains behind him for years. Ronnie could feel the last of his fortitude get sucked away. "We both know Matt," he commented, a few last words swatted desperately at her face before giving up the fight.

She had no response except for the look of stupefying incredulousness on her face glaring back at him. If she had not been through so much that night, she might have been able to devise an answer with which to try and bamboozle him, but tonight she had no clever answer for him because they were both right. Matt was now out of the picture, which could allow them to move on with life as he planned and she eventually hoped. But the problem that lingered was not going away: they both were not supposed to know Matt to this extent in the first place, and with the trust dissolved, they were exposed as frauds to each other. The ending they daydreamed about through the turbulence dissolved, and there was nothing left to say. There was nothing at all. The only gift they could give each other at that point was the thing that would hurt the most.

Ronnie turned to make his exit. The air in his path made sure to let him know that, if he kept walking away from Madison again this time, it would be the last time. Madison saw his pace slow halfway to the door and her heartbeat picked up her own pace. He slowed to an area in the room he scanned when he first walked in and picked up the green burlap backpack and wrapped it around his right shoulder, wondering if either of the girls would take a particular interest in an old, beat up backpack. He turned back around to take one last look at her before continuing his walk out of the hotel room and out of her life.

"Ronnie, wait," Madison called out, stopping him before he made it to the doorway. He turned around. The tension in the room was still smothering and the smell of the gunshot still tainted most of the air around them, but he gave her as much of his attention that he could, most of it already out of the doorway and on its way to Florida. She continued and brought him back to Charlotte. "What's in the bag?"

His voice caught in his throat and waited for his willingness to respond. He almost forgot Karla was in the room until she reentered the conversation. "So, are you going to tell us what's in the bag?"

"What?" His response sounded as pathetic as he thought it did. He picked up from the corner of his eye the shift in Karla's grip on the .357 in her hand, possibly his paranoid interpretation of simply shifting the weight to other muscles in her hand that were not cramped, but enough to not call any bluffs for money that night as the cramp that overtook him held tight in the center of his throat. He did not need to make eye contact with Karla to know the suspicious, incredulous look he would see in her face.

He walked back to the bed and opened the bag. "Your half, ladies." He sounded defeated as he grabbed the bag at its midsection and dumped half of its contents onto the bed. The smell of the money as it hit the mattress was a more inviting smell than the lingering blanket lead and iron, even if he was losing half of Matt's half. He didn't bother to count; he left before the sirens on the street could get any louder.

He was gone from her sight and the sirens reached their pinnacle as the strobes of blue lights from the parking lot reflected from the window and the face of the door. Madison and Karla neared the bundles on the mattress. Karla thought of the blue flashes and took the hardly used lining from the waste basket by the desk and one of Matt's long sleeved shirts, and used both to make the money disappear.

Madison clutched the edge of the bed sheet and drowned in memories and thought of everyone who was dragged in and altered because of her own selfishness. It was Ronnie's selfishness, and apparently Matt's selfishness as well, but Matt was dead and Ronnie was gone, and she was left by herself to cry her anguish out while Karla was saving everybody again. Karla finished her job and saw Madison on the verge of emotion, and wrapped her arms around her from behind. Her whispered words of comfort only took her over the edge faster. The dull, piercing ache of the emotions she felt rocked Madison enough to make sure she was in perfect character for the police.

28

The head-on collision between celebrity and reality the girls experienced for the next several months continued in another long played out chapter as the media narrated the drama the way Madison and Karla explained it to the police: Matthew O'Dell took an interest in Madison while he was interviewing them regarding what he played up as a fraud case, and told her he would falsify documents in order to trump up charges against the girls involved unless she would have sex with him against her will.

The police on the scene the night of the murder questioned Madison and Karla. Madison was emotional and could not give coherent answers on the scene.

He's been making me come here. He said he would make us pay. I can't do this right now.

She was taken to a hospital for a checkup to make sure she had no injuries and was kept overnight for observation. It was enough time to make sure the answers she gave were the right ones with a lawyer by her side, her answers in harmony with the ones Karla already had recorded.

He was brining her here and I wanted to protect my friend. I heard what was going on behind the door and stopped my friend from being raped. He reached for something by the night stand and I feared for my life. What did you want me to do, call the police and pray they show up on time and not have this be a rape and double murder scene? Or do I take care of the call for you?

She set the plot line for the authorities and took charge of supervising the well being of her friend and left the rest of the crime scene to the police, minus the money, which made its way with the help of Karla into a few empty trash can liners and out the bathroom window into the rear alleyway of the motel to hopefully be picked up later by the girls and not a complete stranger.

The interrogation extended to Eve and Randi, who stood firm on their contribution to the cause - Matt acted predatory to all four of them but ended up going too far with Madison, who confided in the others of Matt's intentions and resisted their pleas to notify the authorities on account of fear for their safety.

With no sign of Ronnie Stover and no rebuttal testimony available from Matthew O'Dell, the girls' accounts of what happened seemed consistent and sufficient to the police and for a shuddering corporate office. The situation was so dire that none other than Robin Love and Jessie Lee themselves arrived to provide a personal touch of counseling to those involved. The circumstances were laid out in such a manner that no charges were pursued against Karla, with self-defense cited as the cause of the murder, and the corporate office responded to the news by providing an offering of a $500,000 settlement in addition to sincere apologies and extensive counseling.

The circus ride appeared to be winding down to a close before Evan Honeycutt graced the presence of all concerned from his law office in Virginia Beach, Virginia. He was a trial lawyer who was licensed to practice throughout the Mid-Atlantic States, and worked sparingly in the local area on petty cases to keep his litigative blood flowing. But whenever a nationwide newsworthy story broke, the short, stout fireball with the slicked back cover of thinning ginger hair made sure his face was painted in the landscape, either as the representation for the side with the most money to gain or domineering the never-ending analysis on the network and cable news channels.

He was particularly interested in this case because he missed out on the preceding case Lovelee's was tangled in. The wife absolutely had to cruise to St. Croix in that season and take him along with her, so he made sure his entrance in this case was made before Madison Davis signed for and accepted the settlement Lovelee's offered.

The settlement that was offered was considered ample by the corporate office's legal team, but meager by anyone else who was to believe the circumstances. Madison would have liked to have more, but fear of the status of the settlement being as unknown as the whereabouts of Ronnie Stover propelled Madison to view the offering with acceptance. It was the point of calm in the stage of a storm's life; it was the moment Mr. Honeycutt, attorney at law, intervened. Years later, Madison would still be able to clearly recollect his fake look of pity as she told her story, after which he would shake his head and hold her hand and sing

'You can do so much better' in a melancholy tone. He brought his sympathy of imaginary proportions with her plight to the table and built her confidence to not settle for less, and by lunchtime armed her with a waiver to make certain her litigious needs were taken care of.

By the time the ink dried on the paperwork, the media circus began.

For the next four months, television news crews camped out in front of houses, Evan Honeycutt preached to the masses via the twenty-four hour cable news networks, and the girls were once again televised across the nation, their video from the scheming era just a few short months back being replayed at intervals with new videos and still photo shots of each trying to live their daily lives in the rape and murder trial era, old and new videos cycled in an endless loop. Karla was the most notably irritated member of the group as the cameras frequently caught her in the familiar pose of clutching Tyler's hand and covering him protectively from the line of fire. Eve enjoyed the attention only if she was in the mood and created entertaining moments which disrupted the flow of the endless excuse for news coverage. Madison just endured the stares from the cameras and dreamed of the ending to the drama. Evan Honeycutt and Randi McIntosh were the steadfast exceptions who ate up the scrutiny at every opportunity.

One name and face made Madison fret for the entirety of the court drama: Michael Seitz. She had not seen him since that horrible night at the gas station, not so much for his return to her, but for his return to the courtroom with his standing witness to her and Ronnie together when they were not supposed to be. One night during a visit to Lovelee's while on her leave of absence, she ran into some of her regulars. Later during the night Waylon Barbee pulled her aside to get off her chest what had been scratching to get out, and she told him about Michael Seitz and her fears for his return. And consequently, she had to piece it all together for him as to why she feared his return, including Ronnie and the original plan. She knew she could trust Waylon, who swore his secrecy and listened to her angst, and told her he would do what he could if given the chance.

Meanwhile, back in the courtroom, the defense council for Lovelee's was given the godlike task of making a case with no evidence, while Mr. Honeycutt tugged on heartstrings with mighty reins. The defense tried to play on the coincidence that this same group of girls was involved with both high profile cases, to no avail. Since the security camera footage of the girls with Ronnie at the bar during the planning stage was purged when Matt signed off on the fraud report, the potentially incriminating footage no longer existed in the archives at Corporate and was not available to help the defense. The prosecuting team was already benefiting from momentum in the case when the clear markings of a plus sign on Madison's pregnancy test added another headline to the story. This piece of breaking news provided a new chapter to the cable news saga and gave its viewers new material to gawk at for the next several months. Mr. Honeycutt would take advantage of every available window of opportunity to proclaim Madison Davis is welcoming the responsibility and choosing to keep her 'rape baby' and hoisted her to a level that, if tilted a certain way to the cameras, made her appear on the verge of sainthood. The defense lost their footing and was about to cave.

And then two witnesses appeared with testimony that gave the defense one last fighting chance.

Alex Bowlin was a semi-regular at the Charlotte Lovelee's who witnessed Madison and Matt at the table together at what turned out to be the night they met. Alex forgot about witnessing the encounter until he saw Matt's picture on television early one morning after a night of drinks. His testimony of their encounter was displayed by the defense to show that she instigated their future meetings. The defense rested and handed the witness over to Mr. Honeycutt, who quickly struck him down as one who was making assumptions based on hearing an incomplete conversation after Ron was forced to admit he did not hear everything spoken by the two that night, and upon further drilling was not absolutely certain of what day the encounter took place. Mr. Honeycutt, attorney at law and master manipulator, even ended with a court stenographer engraving for the record of Mr. Bowlin admitting that the possibility existed the man

Madison was seen with that night might not have been Matt to begin with. A befuddled Alex Bowlin was dismissed after having been sliced up by the prosecutorial showman.

Joseph Carrington from Macon, Georgia, was staying at the Westingbrook Hotel on the night of the shooting, and appeared to be the only other hotel patron not out on that Saturday night. He gave his account to the police that night, and the defense brought him back to North Carolina to give his account of what he saw. Upon hearing the gunshot, he ran out of his lower level room in time to witness Eve Kennedy as she descend the last few steps of the staircase and escape to the back. It was too quickly after the gunshot for her to be in the room at the time of the shooting, and the question was hung out to the judge as to why she was at the scene as well, and insinuated this was not a run to the defense of Madison Davis, but might have possibly been an orchestrated effort of get rid of Matthew O'Dell, although with Matt's documents stating there was no fraud committed in the first incident that started this ride in the first place. But then Mr. Honeycutt took the stage and had his opportunity with the witness. He began with a stripping in the reliability of his eyesight, which was average at best in the well lit courtroom and would very well be poorer in the dim lighting of the hotel parking lot, demonstrated with a pop quiz of general signs and objects in the area in question taken at the same time and shade of darkness as the night in question. Joe failed the quiz, and just in case that was not sufficient enough to strike down the witness, Evan Honeycutt put Eve's appearance in question with an alibi. Randi McIntosh, who treated every appearance in court or on television as an audition reel segment, lit up with energy and thespian fervor as she testified that Eve was with her when the shooting occurred. The testimony stood with no discrediting since, luckily, Randi was allowed to go home early that night.

Larry Helms never showed, an absence which brought relief to Madison and gang. And neither did Michael Seitz. There was always the possibility that he learned his lesson from the parking lot and didn't want the hassle of the spotlight, or maybe he really didn't get a good look at Ronnie Stover that night. Or maybe

Waylon Barbee had something to do about it. She still didn't know what he did for work. And she hadn't seen Waylon or Michael since.

The defense accepted their fate and rested, leaving it up to the judge to decide the company's responsibility in Madison's traumatic ordeal. The revelation of Matt's documented reputation with the Tallahassee Police Department and testified reputation with Lovelee's in the past did not sit well with Judge Gina Theisman, and let it be known to all present the day she awarded the prosecutors an award of 2.3 million dollars.

There were the respective cheers and moody, silent exits from inside the courtroom, and some of the worst of the narrators dictated the epilogue with a glum undertone as '$2.3 million' and 'Over 2 million dollars' panned across cable news tickers all over the television landscape. By the time Evan Honeycutt, attorney at law, collected all fees overt and covert, Madison Davis was awarded an end result of about $1.3 million.

It seemed like it took forever for the certified funds to reach Madison's hands. Many days separated Madison from the money, many days that provided the opportunity for her mind to race like a flame across her moral fiber with a million copies of the temptation of staring at her future bank account balance and changing all the ways to get in touch with her. The more the thought crossed her mind, the more she thought about how the same penchant for greed brought them all in this mess in the first place. Once the money was received and separated, Madison greeted the girls on the phone the next day to arrange the meeting everyone was waiting for.

Madison Davis got out of her car and grabbed the shopping bags from the back seat. She felt uneasy about meeting at the Hooters in Charlotte, just down the road from a Lovelee's restaurant in preparations to close its doors after the loss of a lawsuit and gain of notoriety the CEOs had finally had enough of. They were still open, although merely a shell of what it was a few months ago, with half the servers, half the cooks, and half the customers, the other half of which had decided to haste in moving on. It all made for a very conspicuous place for the handoff, and it just would not feel right as far as Madison was concerned. She could practically feel the fog of gloom from down the road by the time she made it to the Hooters front door.

The place was more lively and crowded than she was prepared for, with the addition of the wave of guys making the transition of changing their watering hole and former Lovelee's servers making their own transition. Megan DeWitt was one of them, who sat at one of the side tables with her pen close to the center of her application for employment. Madison passed her on her way to a back table, where she was being signaled by a pair of familiar waving hands and the stares of the other two members of the group in what could be their final meeting. Megan flashed a quick, apprehensive smile to Madison before continuing to fill out her application, taking a moment longer to scan her eyes across the second trimester baby bump and three heavy shopping bags in Madison's hands.

"Did you see Megan up front filling out her application?" Eve asked Madison as soon as she reached the table, the closest Madison had ever been to getting a hello. "She was there when we came in. She said 'hey,' but she was so defensive, probably because she thinks we're here to fill out applications, too." She looked down toward the baggage and cracked a hint of a smile. "I see you went shopping."

"Yes, I did," Madison replied with a grinning return of joviality. "I picked up a little something for everybody." No one else in the crowded dining area took the time to notice as Madison rounded the edge of the table, placing bags at the feet of those concerned as she went; a Victoria's Secret bag by Eve; an f.y.e. bag by Randi; a Bed, Bath & Beyond bag by Karla. Before she had a chance to sit down, their server was back with the drinks. Karla left it as a surprise for Madison that Oakley Moore was going to be their server that afternoon. "Oakley!" Madison waited for her to drop off the drinks to give her a hug. "I'm so glad you got hired on here. Who else was able to get a job here?"

"So far just me and Jenn, but they're going to try to hire a few more. Hopefully not too many more, or we'll be fighting for shifts." The two exchanged smiles, but Oakley's seemed to Madison to be a bit forced. Oakley looked down at her belly. "How much longer do you have?"

Oakley's question and Madison's answer were both interrupted by Eve. "Um, we're going to get some mozzarella sticks to start off over here," Eve said, referring to the side of the tabled where she and Randi sat. Oakley's feigned smile was more clearly translated.

"What can I get you to drink?"

Madison blanketed her with a warm wave of sympathy. "A sweet tea, please. And I think I'll have a mozzarella sticks myself." Oakley wasn't always one of her favorites, but Madison was glad to see any of the Lovelee's servers get a break after the restaurant closed. They would all have jobs if it wasn't for the girls sitting at this back table at Hooter's, and Ronnie and Matt. It was the first time since the end of the court proceedings that she thought of Matt, and she felt the burn of guilt spread across her face. She always thought of Ronnie, now with clashing waves of mixed feeling which made her wonder how much of her lunch she was going to be able to eat. The money in her bank account gave her a blanket of security she was glad to have, but the cost of the jobs of those she worked with for so long hung over her head, and no amount of sugar in the sweet tea she would soon put to her lips was going to mask that bitter taste. From time to time, she felt like finding all the girls and handing off shares of the money, but then she would see the baby bump in the mirror and decide against it. She had a seat at the remaining vacant spot at the table.

"I'm going to warn you right now. By the time that lawyer was through there was just a little over a mil left, a quarter each." Madison followed with a look at Eve; she knew the first response would be from her.

"Are you fucking serious?" Eve spat. "How much did that scumbag take?"

Madison rolled her eyes. "1.3 million, divided four ways..." She stopped and smiled as Oakley returned to the table. "Thank you." Madison waited until Oakley left the circle of earshot. "Somewhere around three hundred grand each. Count when you get home and do the math. He had a good payday."

Eve released a pocket of excess carbon dioxide through her nostrils. "You need to get all the paperwork and find out how he managed to pull that off. We should get a lawyer and sue him. He's a bigger crook than..." She did not need to finish that line for Madison to know the ending. *Ronnie, Matt, us.* There were no grounds, and there would be no lawsuit.

Madison turned to Randi in the hopes for more positive dialogue. "I can guess what your next move is. Hollywood, right?"

"It's time to take my chance." When Madison saw Randi flash an anxious smile, she could now sense the tension between her and Eve.

Karla saw it as well and spoke up to change everyone's attention. "I'm hoping I can put most of this in a safe place that will make enough interest so Tyler won't have to worry about paying for college."

Before Madison could say something, she was interrupted by Eve. "The way tuition keeps going up, you might need some more by the time he gets there. We may need to rob a bank." The last part was hushed, as well as the chuckles which followed. Eve Karla had to join in the tension tamer.

"You're a smart girl," Randi replied. "I'm sure you'll make it work."

"Yeah." Eve's response was the equivalent to one of her compliments, with an added flinch from the trigger she was not able to pull.

"I'm sure there's going to be enough there," Madison said, thankful for the change in spirit at the table. *Leave it to Karla to come to the rescue again.* "I don't want to talk about robbing banks or schemes anymore. Hopefully that's all behind us and we won't need to do anything like that again. I'm just glad we all got out of this okay."

Eve glanced down momentarily at the pool of presidential portraits in the bag by her feet. "Well, maybe one more time, or two. If I need any help, I'll let you ladies know." The chorus of chuckles even included Karla as she rolled her eyes. Eve turned her attention to Madison and smiled before taking another sip from her lunchtime Bacardi and coke, and Madison traded unspoken flatteries with her.

Their network of camaraderie was temporarily disrupted by a man who looked vaguely familiar. His dialogue let them know right away he was a former regular at Lovelee's, and their faces took the veneer of cordial welcoming while hiding the fact they didn't recognize him.

"Look at this table full of lovely ladies." The table full of ladies' facial veneers hardened. "You ladies getting jobs up here, too?"

Karla spoke up before anyone else had a chance. "I filled out an application yesterday." Madison turned to her with a shift of surprise on her face. "Just in case. It couldn't hurt to keep some money coming in for right now."

"We're retiring from the profession," Eve said, referring to both her and Randi. Randi stared straight ahead at the man's face, through his face, and kept focusing west in a three thousand mile stare.

Madison displayed her yet to be born passenger. "I'm not working anywhere for another few months. Then, we'll see what happens." She kept it to herself that, in the meantime, she was polishing her resume and updating her profiles on the job search websites. She was getting closer to saying goodbye, but not there just yet.

"Well, you girls should get hired over here, and me and my boys can keep you company while you work."

Eve's face was naturally the first to show signs of cracking. "My drink is about to be empty. We're in the middle of a celebration. I'm sure we could use a round of drinks over here, big daddy." When she called him 'big daddy' it came on a little bit too strong, and it cause a quiver of giggles at the table. "Madison, you're not in a condition to drink so I'll have yours. But Karla, you can afford just one."

Karla was the last holdout at the table. "I have to pick up Tyler soon," she snickered. "Or else I would have a Long Island ice tea."

"Come on, he's buying," Eve said and turned to the guy. "So I'll have a Bacardi and coke and so will Randi. Since Madison and Karla aren't having one, you can make it two Bacardi and cokes and a Long Island ice tea for me and one Bacardi and coke for Randi, and a Long Island ice tea and a side of gum just in case Karla changes her mind."

The giggles gradually swelled to the strength of causing a flush to the man's face. "I'm going to get back to my buddies. I hope to see more of you ladies in the future. You can find me on Facebook."

The volume of the laughter inched a notch. "Are we getting drinks out of this?" Randi asked Eve, and the laughter reached the point to where they hardly noticed the man's exit.

Eve pursed her lips and leaned her head closer to the middle of the table. "Is he gone yet? Take a look."

There was no need to look back to know he was gone, so the laughter at the table continued and reached hysterical proportions. It was the closest they got to being a cohesive group, right at the end. It was the snapshot Madison engraved into her memory, the way she wanted to remember it, not thinking of Matt, not thinking of Ronnie, not thinking of the confrontation or suffering in the middle. She placed a hand on her belly and maintained her smile, and hoped for the best for everyone at the table.

PART FIVE
ONE YEAR LATER

29

The latest favorite-of-the-month club in the area, Edge, closed for good last weekend, so it was time to move on again. Another new club with dim lighting, expensive drinks, and an unoriginal name was ready to make its debut, and she promised some people she would show up, but Eve Kennedy was still deciding if and where she was going tonight. Either way, she had enough vodka and cocaine at her disposal to make for a cozy night in if the walls of her bedroom did not turn on her and suffocate her like they usually did after her fifth or sixth line on the mirror.

Most of her days recently have been endured with a light haze fueled by narcotic and liquor as Eve tried to forget the past eighteen months, or recall it as best she could when it ate at her too much. Despite the pleasant tone which trailed the group's final meeting she is not, nor will ever be convinced, that Madison split the money evenly. *That bitch has always been shady. She wouldn't even call us right away. It took her a while to call, didn't it? Why did she take so long to call?* Eve caught on to Madison and Matt's immediate friendliness from the beginning and had always harbored feelings of distrust toward Madison. *Makes me wish I had pictures of them fucking so I could hold them over her head, just in case things didn't work out like they did.* Eve always harbored one of those vindictive streaks that burned for a fight with those she decided to hate; she was actually disappointed Madison did not attempt a holdout, because it would have been yet another reason to have a confrontation with her; she needed the confrontation almost as much as the vodka and blow.

Eve inhaled, and another line was gone, as quickly as Philip was gone and as suddenly as Randi left. She could have cared less about Philip's departure. Her discovery of the woman he was having sex with on the side was the perfect excuse for kicking him to the curb because he was just a toy to begin with. The void left by Randi's leaving was a different story altogether. When Randi collected her share of the money, it was inevitable she was headed to Hollywood to chase down her dreams. Still, Eve didn't want her to leave right away, and the more Eve infiltrated Randi's closing crack of wavering, the more Randi broke from her docility with Eve until the private talks became downright confrontational. The talks reached a boiling point until Randi shifted gears and offered the invitation for Eve to join her out west. The more Eve showed her hesitation toward leaving Charlotte, the more the talks disintegrated and the clouds of inevitability which hung over their heads reached the dissipating stage. When the cash in the shopping bag was set by Randi's side the deal was sealed. Still, although everyone was certain of that foreshadow in the spotlight, they met her quick and unhesitant departure after the cash drop-off with surprise. In as much time as it took for Randi's feet to weigh down against a Hollywood Boulevard sidewalk, Eve received a phone call from her homesick and frightened girl wondering if she made the right choice. Two more emotional phone calls followed in that first month. She had not heard from Randi since.

Eve laid her paraphernalia on the end table and hoisted herself from the bed – the decision was made to make an appearance at the new club. She swallowed a mouthful of Smirnoff, a ritual she had been performing with bottles of Chopin and Crystal Head for the past year, but had since scaled back as the majority of her share of the money had escaped through her nasal cavity. Eve began working her appearance art to try to keep people she had not seen for months from shock and gossip about the drastic change in her looks, the noticeable weight loss, the frail hair, the circles under her eyes, the tenderness and irritation of her nostrils. *Some of those bitches would crave it behind my back.*

Ever since that night, whenever she felt anger and the urge to rekindle her tough girl side, she had flashbacks of that same feeling she felt when she held the gun in the direction of the back of Matt O'Dell's head. She was fine when she entered, full of fire as she barked orders, and her hand supported the Glock with a strong and steady grip. There was some anxiety travelling her circuits, which was to be expected in a situation such as this, but for the most part she was fine. And then the feeling hit her. The vibration felt like a jolt in the shoulder of her shooting hand. It remained just in her shoulder for the first few moments, then spread across her arm and down through her body with a blunt force. Soon she felt the vibration and its accompanying chill practically everywhere on her body, and it felt she was watching her own life take place from the background, unable to act, and she could no longer concentrate or hold her gun with authority. Visions of the woods across an old green house she'd never seen in her life pasted her sight during this metamorphosis. *What the fuck was THAT all about?* She had trouble figuring out or explaining how she lost her nerve and had had a hard time recuperating it since.

Her interest in meeting the public quickly waned within the time spent in front of the mirror, like a movie screen playing and replaying a growing unwatchable scene, playing it with more frequency as the months blended into a montage of time, and she retreated to the bed with her bottle of Smirnoff remembering brighter days as if they happened just last week, her apartment and her face matching equally in brightness and fullness of life, her life always running at a pace as upbeat as the house music at her downtown domain on Saturday nights. Every time Randi showed up at her front door, petrified with the uncertainty of life and in need of that comfort zone within her arms, Eve dutifully applied the brakes to her life and did her part to prevent the periodic breakdown of her friend and partner, brushing off the feelings of annoyance in the process.

She picked up her serving tray and resumed the task of making the lines disappear, wishing she had heard from Randi on the phone lately, proclaiming inside her head what she wouldn't give to have to deal with comforting Randi at her front door again.

"Mama, my pants are ready!"

"Okay hon, I'll be there in a sec!" Karla called out from the kitchen as she finished up Tyler's lunch. The washer and dryer are the stackable type, and Tyler is not able to reach the dryer yet, so that task belongs to Karla for another year or two. He could reach it if he climbed onto a box, but Karla forbade it. After his lunch was finished, she folded the paper bag tightly and proceeded to the laundry room. "Is your book bag ready? The bus will be here any minute."

"I need my pants before I can get on the bus."

She could hear him descend into giggles in the middle of his comment from beyond the door and leaned in through the doorway, welcoming him with a half smile on her face and his freshly dried pants. She tossed him his pants. "Here you go, smart guy. I've got your lunch ready in the kitchen."

Karla kept a look out through the living room window as she folded the last of the clothes from the dryer. When the bus they were waiting for turned the corner and approached the stop she called out to her son. "Bus is here, Tyler. Time to get moving!" Fortunately, the stop is a mere three houses from her mother's house. Tyler gave his mom a kiss as he organized his handfuls of belongings. She watched him off as he ran and caught the school bus, and after the precautionary pause while he found a seat the bus took him away for another day of school.

Karla would have all day to get the house clean while her mother was at work, and would have enough time to tend to Tyler before she had to be at work at Shorty Jim's Burger Joint, a family owned diner fashioned to pay homage to the 1950's. She did hear back from Hooter's shortly after applying but Shorty Jim's was only four miles away from their house, making it the perfect place at which to get a job once Lovelee's closed its doors. She was ready to get back to work. Until the process of the police investigation was finished, Lovelee's put the group on leave. The authorities with the restaurant and police cleared her of any wrongdoing, citing it as an act of defense against a rape, and after a brief period of counseling she was allowed to return. And she planned on returning, but Lovelee's closed six days before her expected return date. She had a hard time getting over the regret of all the girls losing their jobs, and prayed they all settled into something they enjoyed after all the trouble endured.

The amount of money received brought along with it the temptation to indulge, and in her own way she did; she reinvested her share of the settlement money back into her family. When she told her mother of the money, she gave a portion of it to her, to get ahead in the mortgage and to update some of the appliances. Her mother provided some resistance at first, but once she knew Karla was planning to put a portion away for Tyler, she relented and gratefully took the money. The other portion of money from the settlement, minus her own little comfort fund, she set aside for half of Tyler's college fund.

The other half showed up on her doorstep one day a little over a year ago, during the early stretch of the courtroom drama era. Karla heard the knock on the door and opened it, letting the breeze hit her eyesight for a few moments to let the scene sink in.

"Where did you run off to?"

"I started back to Florida," said Ronnie Stover, clutching at a green burlap backpack, "but then I turned back around. I had to stop and do a lot of thinking. I'm headed in another direction."

Karla's stiffened posture and narrowing eyes acted as a wall of defense in front of the open doorway.

"What does all that have to do with you being here?"

"Giving you this." Ronnie extended the backpack to her. She took it and opened it to the cash contents, which looked to be the entire amount of the money that remained in the backpack the night he left the motel, maybe and maybe not a few thousand lighter. "For Tyler."

Karla met the gift offering with surprise, but she remained defensive and was not about to let down her guard. She still harbored resentment at his abandonment of her and their unborn child and his pretending to not be associated with either of them at periodic reappearances, until the day he tried to come back into their lives and she redirected him to the outside of their circle, letting him know his presence was not welcome in her family.

She closed the flap on the backpack. "We're doing just fine," she said with her eyes fixated on her grip on the bag.

She began to hand it back to him, but Ronnie made no gestures to receive it. "Please, take it. It's for all the time I haven't been there. I'm leaving now. I promise you I'll never be back here again."

"Hey Mom, can I have a peanut butter sandwich?"

Tyler heard his mom talking to someone in the doorway and was curious, so he conveniently became hungry and materialized in the doorway.

Karla shot a glance to Ronnie for a quick second before answering. "Yes, sweetheart. I'll be back there in a second."

Tyler stood in the doorway and stared at Ronnie as Karla tried to usher him back inside. "Hey," he said to Ronnie after a brief moment of analyzing his face.

Ronnie grinned, appreciating what he saw. "Hey, buddy."

"Come on, sweetheart. Go to the kitchen and get everything out. I'll meet you in there."

"Okay." Tyler disappeared from the doorway after one more look at the man standing in it.

"That's a beautiful kid," Ronnie said to Karla, and partly aloud in deep recollection of past choices. "I missed out on a lot."

There was no answer for Karla to give him. He had the answer already: it was time for him to go. "That is Tyler's," he said, referring to the backpack filled with cash. "Keep it for him. I'm getting out of here now. Take care of yourself, and him."

"I will. You take care of yourself, too."

Her voice attempted at cordial while suppressing the resentment that he, of all people, suggests she take care of her son. *What the hell do you think I've been doing his entire life?* The feel of the burlap in her hands softened her posture and voice. "Thank you."

Karla met up with her son in the kitchen while Ronnie disappeared down the driveway. As she helped her son make a sandwich, she knew in her heart she would never see Ronnie again. Of all the girls, Madison was the only one she would talk to on the phone from time to time, but talk would never visit that path. During the making of that sandwich and laughing with her son, Karla decided to forget it all completely, no more talk of the plan or money or killing. Every time since then, when memories of the past would bubble up to the surface, Karla remembered that evening making the peanut butter sandwich with Tyler, and the rest dissolved away. She smiled at the memory of that night as she watched the school bus drive away.

The bitterly cold canyon winds ripped through California's San Fernando Valley, pushing against of the back of the mental and emotional winds of Hurricane Randi. The wind barreled its way almost parallel with highway 134 from North Hollywood through Burbank and beyond, and in between they whipped across Randi McIntosh's rental house just outside Toluca Lake into Burbank, but she hardly felt it that day as she ran outside to check the mailbox. She thought of Eve. *I need to call her.* None of the magazine articles or episodes of Entertainment Tonight, none of the travel websites or books she read on making it in the acting business did not prepare her for the bitter late fall and winter evenings. But even the threat of a ten degree drop in the night's low temperature was not enough to dampen her mood as she got ready for the meeting at her house that night.

The only items waiting in her mailbox were junk. She ran back into the house and grabbed her phone on the way to disposing of the contents in her other hand. She felt a quivering as she navigated to Eve's number in her contact list, albeit a different feeling from that which overtook her a year ago when she made that first call to Eve, crying and wondering if she made the right choice, if she should have at least waited another year or two to make her move. This feeling was exhilarating and slightly frightening at the same time. It was happening as the ringing vibrated her eardrum. It was happening. She met Eve's voice mail message.

"Eve baby, it's Randi. I haven't talked to you in forever. I've been meaning to call you earlier, but nothing has really been happening for me until now. I can't wait to tell you all about it. I was spending so much money the last time I talked to you, but I started acting better with my money since I talked to you. It has been so hard for me the past nine months and I didn't want to call you again to cry and talk about my problems. Nothing was happening for me. But I've missed you, and I can't wait to talk to you again. Call me as soon as you get this. Good bye, love."

Talking about the past caused her mind to go racing backward in time, back to when her mind headed west on Interstate 40 as soon as she counted the bills in the bag of money Madison Davis laid at her feet a year ago. And in the three days leading up to the big day when her body followed her mind to Hollywood, the fire spread between her and Eve, and the smoldering ash of those memories ate at her once again. She wanted to call Eve again, and chose instead to clean up a little before they showed up.

Her mind relived the road leading her to her destiny. It was a long five day drive, but it gave her time to think and make her plan. *Keep the car for now. The beater is reliable. I'll get a better one when the time is right. Remember what you read about headshots. Find a good, simple photographer. Don't get too many prints to start. Shop around. Find an inexpensive place to rent while you get familiar with the area. And don't fall for scams. And watch out for predators.*

Her plan began unraveling the first day in Hollywood when she set up temporary residence in none other than the Roosevelt Hotel, first in the most cramped room at $200 a night, and upgrading to the bigger and more expensive poolside cabana when she became further stricken with homesickness. *Twice as expensive, but I can afford it. I need to start watching my money. The desk clerk is so pretty. I wonder if she's an actress, too. I wonder how long she's been out here.* She made her first call to Eve that afternoon.

Randi picked up her phone and called Eve again.

"Hey, it's me again. I can't wait. I've got to tell you what's happening. To catch you up on what's happened to me this past year, I spent way too much money. I know what you said – 'Watch your spending, that money's gotta last you.' But you know how I am. I met a guy in a bar and he turned out to be a Jaguar salesman in West Hollywood. So of course I buy a brand new one. I ended up moving out of the Roosevelt about nine months ago and into a house in Burbank. There was no way I was moving into an apartment. The noise would drive me crazy. I'm not going to tell you how much I've been paying in rent, but it's a LOT. And the new wardrobe took a whole lot more of my money, and the headshots, but I..."

A loud beep interrupted her; she babbled her way to the cutoff point to Eve's voice mail service. She was going to have to bookmark her brain to where she stopped her narrative. As she chased the cruising car on the street through the front window to see if it was her guests, her mind stewed on the money she spent on her wardrobe, then on her expanded wardrobe when she was worried the first wave of clothes had become obsolete, and the headshots in between. *Oh my god, the headshots.* Her stomach turned at the thought of choosing the first ad she saw in Back Stage West. *'The Best in The Biz.' Eve would have kicked my ass. And why did I have to buy two thousand of them?* The car in the street was not the one she was waiting for so she dialed Eve again.

"Hey. I didn't get enough time. Shit hasn't been happening for a year and I've been really scared. All I have to show for the past year is extra roles and non-union theater rejections. But last week I got a call from Lisa McKnight. She's the casting director for Liaison of Kismet! You know that's my favorite show. They had me come in and read for the part of a robbery victim. I was so nervous, and when I read for the part in their office I blew it. I couldn't get myself in control. I missed my cues and they probably thought I was crazy or something by the looks on their faces. I was about to fucking die on the way out of the building. That's when I got stopped by two guys who heard me read, and they thought I was brilliant. I played along and didn't tell them those were my real emotions they heard. These guys are filmmakers and we…"

The beep rang in her ear again. "Damn." She looked out the window again for the guy's car, a Dodge Spirit with some age to it, a little beat up but not a hunk of junk. *Maybe they'll be driving something better when all this is done.* Her emotions revisited last week like an intro to a weekly serial drama. *'Last week on the trials of the next big thing, Randi McIntosh,'*: The sinking feeling as she left that casting office, the guy from the casting office across the hall who caught her as she left, the shift from dejection to elation as he introduced himself and proposed their partnership. She dialed Eve again.

"Hey. I should be able to finish this time. This guy stopped me on my way out. He's a production assistant trying to make his way into filmmaking. His name is Brent Parker, and his partner is William Roberts. They wrote a screenplay and have been shopping it around, but they want to make it themselves, and they think I would be perfect as the neurotic leading lady! I've still got some of the money, but I'm down to about thirty thousand. They said that should be enough to get started. If we need more money after that, they have a little bit saved up, and if I have to, I can sell the Jag. When this film takes off I'll get another one. They're coming over tonight so we can get everything going and start up the production company between the three of us. If you want to come in on this, I can ask them when they get here. When we're done here, I'm going to come back for a bit and visit. I really want to see you again. Give me a call later tonight. Oh, I see a car. I think that's them. Give me a call. I love you."

It was nearly noontime. He was headed to the bar again, and he was running late. The others were expecting him and he hated to keep them waiting. Ronnie grabbed his cell and dialed. "Hey, Brad. I'm running a little late. I should be there in about another ten minutes." Brad didn't mind, but still, Ronnie was trying to keep from disappointing people in this new chapter of his life.

He recently acquainted himself with the twenty-first century with the purchase of an iPod and almost had all the songs positioned where he wanted them. He stopped the scroll on a playlist titled 'Love and Pain' and dared to torture himself with the past. The playlist consisted of only three songs: 'Our Song' from Taylor Swift, 'Yesterdays' from Guns 'N Roses, and 'I Don't Know Why You Love Me' from Cotton, Lloyd, and Christian. He started at the middle and let the memories play.

As the lyrics of his personal song of growin' old, movin' along on the streets and all alone played on, he remembered that night walking out of the musty makeshift grave at the Westingbrook Hotel like a man, hard headed and hiding his emotions. Every time he felt the lurch in his stomach and numbness come over his face, he pushed it down, determined to keep the moment from reminding him of the abhorrent impression of his exit from the hospital as his father lay dying. *No trust, no love... I'm done.*

He dropped off the key to his temporary home early the next morning and took only the bare essentials with him, abandoning the rest. No matter how much he threw away, the memories would not loosen their grip as easily. The previous night layered on top of the day he knew for certain his mother was gone colliding with the two year old stigma of the night in the hospital and his dying father. His emptiness sank further to a new bottom, and his fighting to keep down the emotions resembled a drunk fighting like hell to keep from throwing up. He got in his car and headed south to Florida without either partner, wiping away his existence from Cannon for good. The CD slid into the radio and Guns N' Roses did his thinking for him. He pressed the repeat button when he got to 'Yesterdays' and looked for the state line. When the sign glided toward him welcoming him to South Carolina, he relaxed in the knowledge that the Tar Heel State would not break him into a hat trick of tears.

He passed the state line and the giant peach overhanging Gaffney, and soon found himself tiring of G 'n R. He explored the span of the tuner and was inundated with nuisances: commercials, crap, more commercials. He switched to AM and came across an oldies station playing "hits from the 60's and 70's," hits not in the literal according to the Billboard charts, but hits in regards to what the disk jockey had access to on a regular basis. The quality of the audio reminded Ronnie of the tape recordings his father used to make of his old vinyl records to play in the car on weekend trips to garage sales and flea markets. He set his nostalgia on cruise control and continued leaving the mid-Atlantic pasture of his past behind.

Soon into the reminiscence the DJ crooned "And here is a flash back with Cotton, Lloyd, and Christian." The song played, and Ronnie was taken back. He was taken aback, and brought back to the present. His father had the album, and it was one of his well worn audio tapes, so Ronnie knew the sound right away. He had almost forgotten the song, but the lyrics might as well be his anthem to knowing the wrong decisions and making them anyway, just like his father before him. And he wondered if Madison ever cared if he never gave back all the love given his way. And he wondered if his mother cared the same with his father or with him for that matter. The lyrics made Ronnie's face ache to the point any attempt to stop the flow of tears was impossible. He had to pull the car over and let emotions take their course. He yanked and punched the steering wheel as he cried and wished he could love the same as her all those times he left her so far behind.

After a time out to look over documents he collected from his internet investigation at a Rock Hill Waffle House, he continued on the interstate, this time in the opposite direction. The atmosphere in the background had a different aura to it, a darker complexion in contrast to the lightening he felt from his change of heart. He drove on hoping the clouds over the northern horizon cleared for him and gave him bluer skies, or at least less storms.

The first stop was to Karla's house to make things as right as he could with the son he was never around for. The pain of confronting Karla was nothing compared to seeing their baby grown to a little man and knowing he could not stay and talk to him, so he left the money with Karla, what he initially set out to do, and continued to Dogwood Fields Cemetery.

The eerie ambience he felt surrounding him at the hospital that served as his father's resting place in his final days were finding their way back to him as he stood in front of the tombstone of Ricky Darnell Stover, and the warm winds of autumn that remained in the changing of the seasons fell against his face as a welcome ballast to the chilling sensations pushing against his face from the inside. He was surprised that standing in front of this slab of marble brought more intimidation and dauntingness than standing in front of the man himself back in Ronnie's younger days. He tried to just stand there and think out a conversation but his thoughts just raced and collided and became a garbled blur of conflicts, desires, and unfinished business fighting for closure. He could already feel the emotional fault line shifting as he cleared his throat.

"Does it even matter where I start? There's nothing we can do about the past." His eyes focused on the contours of the tombstones edge, the equivalent to not being able to look his father straight in the eyes – more memories of their tumultuous past recalled. "You're dead; you don't have to do anything now. You could have been better when you were around, to me and Mom." Righteously venting while closing off his mind made him feel better, but it was the easy way out to get by without healing. He stopped and gathered his thoughts. "I remember getting into trouble back in the day, back when I was in school. You had to get up on a work day and pick me up at the police station at three in the morning. I hated the drive back home. You wouldn't stop yelling at me, telling me how I was fucking up and how I needed to smarten up. I hated you so much. I didn't think you cared at all about me. Now I can remember you yelling at me before all this, telling me how I was going to end up in jail and you would just leave me there for as long as you could. When the time came, you got up right away and got me out. You didn't keep your word. I could have been a better son growing up, too." The emotions caught up while he wasn't looking and he could no longer compose them by the time the tears overfilled his eyelids and rolled down his face. Suddenly, he could see through the years and all the time his father proved him wrong, but he was just too blind with anger and independence to notice. "All I can do now is say to your tombstone what I should have said to you when you were dying. I'm sorry," he said as he choked on the sadness and swiped at the tears. "And there's not much more I can do to make things right, but I'll try." It was the first time he ever apologized to his father. He did it in another typical scenario of Ronnie Stover overcoming obstacles when it's too late to make a difference, but this moment was all he had left with his father. He completed the final moment in stride by stooping down and kissing the nearest corner of the tombstone. "I love you, Dad." When he found the strength to lift himself, he left his father behind one last time and drove on, continuing north.

That destination he chose to drive for was Hartford, Vermont, on the edge of White River Junction. The place where the information from his internet research told him his mother lived at, where her parents lived at for decades, and where he now lived at as well. He remembered last year's stinging fear like it was still last week as he neared the house, that aching numbness as the front door stared back at him and he negotiated putting of the awkward reunion until he was settled in, if he was going to settle in…

He was pulled out of the past momentarily by 'Our Song' playing from his iPod. Within moments the melody tapping his eardrum began to thump at his chest and he thought of Madison again. He reached his exit from Interstate 91 and headed into town.

He spent the past year becoming acquainted with the new area while watching the rest of the adventure play out on television, the irritation of the past haunting him continuously as the details played out ad nauseam on every cable news channel, the pain he felt at the news of Madison's pregnancy, the relief when the judgment was announced, and the hope the rest of the girls got a share, especially Karla. He used what remained of the money, plus the money from the loan given to him from the only bank in Vermont willing to take a chance on him, to open the pub.

With the announcement of the settlement Ronnie longed for the guilt of the past to be subdued and left behind, a privilege never to happen; the guilt he felt over Matthew O'Dell would never leave his side. Not a day passes where the night does not replay in his head. He made it to the room in time. He might have had a chance to say something to the girls, make his case to quit whatever plan they had cooked up, and they all could have come clean and find a way to make peace and split the money evenly among everybody, the way it should have been to begin with. But then he hears Eve again as she was comforting Randi outside her condo house, the night he met the girls before everything went down...

What's going on? Everything's going on. Madison and Karla are inside. Things haven't been working out with this shit. This guy Matt is doing whatever he can to make sure this doesn't work out for us. And Madison already has a notch on her bedpost with this guy. It looks like she went up to his hotel room the night she met him. I don't know if we can trust her in this or not. What do you think?

Ronnie tried to mask his doubt when he crossed the doorway that night. He had been trying to mask his doubt since the day Matt was interviewing Randi at Lovelee's when the three saw each other: the way Madison looked at Matt, the way Matt looked at him. Ronnie felt the tense, transparent cloud of guilt that encircled all three of them, and should have suspected the two's connection of the love triangle. He shifted emotional gears thinking Madison could not be trusted, but he was not thinking beyond his heart, and he let it affect his plans with Matt. He stopped in the walkway, and was close enough to see Matt at gunpoint. He could have made it into the room that night but his emotions let Matt be taken out of the equation.

I could have stopped it. It was the worst mistake Ronnie made in his life. It was the mistake that turned everything around.

He turned into the pub's parking lot and met Brad halfway to the door. "Sorry I'm late. That's what happens when I try to squeeze too much into my schedule."

"Don't worry about it," Brad said. "Andrea kept me company. Now I know more about you than I care to know."

Ronnie laughed with him. "That's becoming a recurring theme around here." He quickly scanned through Brad's invoice and signed. "Thanks again." He took a few steps back and faced the outside sign Brad just installed, and took in the sign and the pub's name like a work of art. *The Second Chance.* He smiled at the future, but wished either Matt or Madison was here to share it with him, or both of them somehow, if he would have made the right choice in doorway seventeen at the Westingbrook Hotel.

Andrea stepped outside and met Ronnie at the edge of the sidewalk in front of The Second Chance. "Ronnie, somebody called while you were out here with the sign guy. He left his number."

He took the note. "Thanks, Mom. This is the guy that's coming in to install the beer taps." He looked up at their name. "How does the sign look?"

She looked up in the same direction and grinned. "I love it. I went to the coffee shop this morning. I saw Tiffany there and we talked for a while. She wanted me to tell you it was really nice meeting you the other day. You should go over there again soon."

He cracked a smile. "I'll be back there soon." She was trying to get him out there and meeting people again, but he was holding back while getting the pub off the ground. He still had Madison's phone number stored in his cell phone, and some days he liked to take it out and look at it, daring himself to give her a call and reconnect, like that night and all the drama never happened. Maybe it was for the best because every reunion ended the same: affliction to one or the other and two people who were never meant to travel in the same direction. But her number was still there inside his phone, and in time he might try to make contact with her and maybe right past wrongs. *Isn't that the game plan that fails every time I try it?* Regardless, he still had the uncertainty in his heart to move forward to the point he had not made his best effort to get to know the local women on a personal level while making his best effort to resist the insistence and prodding of his mother toward Tiffany and a couple of daughters of her close friends. In the meantime, he would concentrate all his effort on making the pub work.

Ronnie wondered where his life would be had he not moved around and refused to settle anywhere long enough for moss to attach to his shoes. Would there be a family? Would he have a tight network of close friends? From time to time he caught himself reflecting on all the roads that lead to schemes to make a quick note or two, almost all of which fell apart, believing most of them were meant to be regrets burned in his memory. Had it not been for his nature, he could have had a family. And be mired in a job with a retirement plan, and a watch to look forward to as a reward for a service well done. And, knowing himself, probably realizing twenty years down the road of life he should have steered in the other direction at a turning point prior, when he realized that was not who he was. His footprints would linger in a mortgaged house with an abandoned wife and broken family. If he never left Charlotte, he never would have had the idea of opening a pub with Matt, but Matt would not be dead had he not reunited with Madison. And he never would had made his way to Vermont after this mess and found the character to make the jagged pieces fit somehow and make his life work for him for once instead of against him had it not been for finding his mother and correcting errors. He chose to continue with life and assume a force higher than himself knew what it was doing, and that the journey somehow made sense in the end. He was, and it was.

Ronnie put his arm around his mother and stared at the sign, feeling grateful for the moment and the second chance.

Madison couldn't believe the wedding invitation she was holding in her hand, cordially inviting her to the union of Amilynn Martin and Patrick Bledsoe in matrimony. *Marriage? With him? Really?!?* She recalled the day she became the inadvertent matchmaker, giving Amilynn his group's table because she did not want to be near him. She cracked a smile briefly at the thought that things turned out well romantically for at least one of them. *Good for her.* Her eyes still stung at the recent news to hit the local area and tried to make it go away with the texture of the wedding invitation she rubbed across her fingertips. She exhaled and put the invitation down on a corner of the table, treating it in a manner which implied she would be keeping the invitation and the date, revealing the letter underneath it. She already read it twice, but wanted to read it again.

Maddie,

I was so happy to get your letter. I didn't know how you felt about me or if you wanted me to try to find you. I'm glad you chose to find me. I was able to transfer up here to the minimum camp on the edge of Raleigh and am doing much better. I was coming across a lot of guys from my past and was already getting into bad patterns of thinking. They were all making plans when they got out and wanted me to come along with them, but I've had a lot of time to think about my life and where I want to be headed when I get out (204 days). I went through the substance abuse program when I was at the Furr camp down in Piedmont and struggled on a lot of nights if I should try to write to you, in case you wanted to visit me while I was close enough for you to drive. Since I transferred to Wake, I started working in the maintenance department and getting my hands used to working with tools again. I am now in the work release program doing carpentry work again. I've also starting taking some college courses that the community college down the road offers us, some of the basic stuff, English and math, stuff like that. I enclosed three forms to request visitation privileges. I was so happy to hear you wanted to see me. I know I haven't been there for you like I should have in the past. That crap I used to smoke robbed me of more than I've ever thought about robbing from anyone else, but I really can't blame anyone but myself for that. I put the extra forms in there in case Sarah wants to see me. I'll understand if she doesn't. You'll also need to fill one out for Montana if you're going to bring my granddaughter. I also got a real kick out of hearing about that. I'm sure you had it down to Montana if it was a girl, Joe if it was a boy. I feel like I'm missing out on the world being locked up in here. 204 days. Christ, I'm tearing up while I'm writing this. I hope to hear from you soon and it will be great to see you in person again. I'd better get myself ready to see my little girl all grown up into an adult. Take care of yourself and I will see you real soon, angel.

Love,
Daddy

She smiled and swelled with a joy which washed over the chaos around her. She placed the letter just as gingerly on top of the wedding invitation and sat down to the computer, and after a brief reflection retrieved a notepad and pen.

Daddy,

I just got your letter yesterday. It's only been about ten days since I first wrote to you, but things have been CRAZY since then. Do you get to watch T.V. much where you're at? The local news has been all over the murder in Hollywood of the girl from Cannon. That was Randi, the one I told you about who went out there to be an actress after all the drama we went through last year. I hate to say it but it was the first time I thought of her in several months. It turned my stomach watching the news people talk about the details. The police found video footage in the house. The video cameras were INSIDE THE WALLS! It turns out the landlord renting her the house was videotaping her the whole time. And to top it off, there was no good footage at all of the two guys involved. The cameras were all at breast level. I guess her landlord wasn't interested in her face. The police don't know anything at all about the guys who did this. I really hope they find out something. Randi couldn't get a break in Hollywood alive or dead.

It was hard enough moving out of my favorite little apartment I had for years. I bought a house in Piedmont and had been doing O.K. on money but always felt that anxiety that it wouldn't last forever, so I started looking around for a marketing job after Montana was born. Mom has been a real help in that department. There have been times where it just felt like she was meddling any chance she could get, but as soon as she found out I was pregnant she was on top of everything I needed. Honestly, I don't know if I could have done all of this without her. If she comes with me to visit, don't tell her I told you that. One night during all of this court drama I sat her down and told her everything (EVERYTHING – I can't talk about it in this letter. I'll have to tell you some other time :) She was slightly annoyed. She understood. She gave me a big hug and assured me we would all get through this. She was a mother. I hope I can get her to come with me.

I looked for a job all around Charlotte and had no luck. Most were not hiring and some were only intrigued to have 'the victim of this tragedy who is trying to pick up the pieces of her life,' this girl who would be 'a big asset to us in the public's eye.' The more I thought of the interviews, the more it made me sick. I never called them back, but I did hear back from Gina Stevens, one of the girls who worked at Grant Southern. Gina met me for lunch and told me she was ready to get away from Grant Southern and wanted to branch out on her own. She was impressed with me and wanted to know if I wanted to come along with her. She had more contacts in the Raleigh area and was looking to move back there to set up shop.

I said yes. I'm moving to Raleigh! I was going to wait to tell you all about it when I visited, but I couldn't keep the news inside any longer. Mom is on board and we put both our house up for sale. Hers has already sold and mine is under contract. I've been boxing up my stuff all day. We decided to get a house together so Montana could be closer to both of us, and it frees up more money for the new marketing business. Gina and I still have to come up with a cool name. Maybe you can help us out with that. Since I'll be in Raleigh, I can visit you more often.

I was always afraid of moving out to the unknown. I remember how frightened I was when I went to college in Charlotte. And I always clung to my best friend Leanna's hard times she faced in New York. But I also clung to her death to reinforce my fears, even though she was murdered in Cannon. It's not like she was in Hollywood, like Randi. I guess no city is immune, so it's a new city and a new business and a new life for better or for worse. I have a good feeling about my new partner Gina.

Montana is calling me (crying), so I'd better finish up and see what she wants, and then finish packing. I can't wait to see you! Take care, Daddy.

Love,
Maddie

She laid the letter on top of her other correspondence in the upper left corner of the desk, her eyes scanning across the post-it note her mother stuck above the desk, the scribbling sticking in her head as she headed to what for the next several days would be Montana's room. Mark 8:36. Her mind stayed busy as she tended to her baby with Mark 8:36 and the profit that was made while her soul hung in the balance, Ronnie Stover and his exit from the motel room, Matt O'Dell and the chance to tell him she was sorry but just laid there while the gunshot ended everything.

The more she soothed her green-eyed baby the less Montana cried, until the crying completely subsided, and the rumblings in her mind vanished to that place where the past lay to return some other time. She still had Ronnie's number in her phone but had no idea how long it would stay. If her sensible side controlled the situation she would erase the number as quickly as possible and forget it altogether.

Madison brought Montana out to what was left of the living area in front of the desk, in front of the small stack of papers with her father's letter at the top. The letter still brought a smile to her face, and she forgot about Ronnie Stover, Matt O'Dell, and the motel room for one more day. "Are you ready to meet your granddaddy?" Madison asked. She placed a kiss on the top of Montana's head and put her in front of one of the last moving boxes standing, and proceeded to fill it.